THE ARKAN PATH

THE
ARKAN
PATH

L. L. MAN

ISBN: 978-981-11-5278-8

To God
Thank you very much.

TRELISEUM

4

Chapter One

COUNCIL OF THE RIGHTEOUS

Treliseum, a world situated above the highest stars in the galaxies, is a green planet with beauty and abundance like no other. Treliseum is the home world of the Arkan, a race of winged beings and master wielders of the power of flame. Both male and female Arkans were brave warriors. Once they reach the age of adulthood, they are blessed with the gift of eternal youth and the ability to summon the *Serdeus* or the Sword of Life. The Serdeus is the main weapon of the Arkan and each Serdeus is unique in shape depending on the purity of the wielder's soul.

Avetus, the great city of the Arkans is ruled by *King Satorex*, a righteous king whose powers are far greater than all the others. He is known as the sole wielder of the Fire of Justice, a power that can destroy a thousand souls at his will. This forbidden power can only be obtained once an Arkan from a noble bloodline becomes corrupted and impure. Only the mighty king of the Arkan can wield this terrifying power with righteousness. King Satorex is one of the founding pillars of the Council of the Righteous, together with his late wife *Queen Vasilia*, the Light of Life; his brother *Athanax*, the Light of Justice, and his best friend *Varkelos*, the Light of Faith.

Long before the formation of the Council, the Arkans were constantly warring with their neighboring stars who challenged their power and threatened the peace throughout the Arkan domain. Under the great leadership of the brave and wise King Satorex, the Arkans have always remained triumphant in conquering their enemies.

To ensure lasting peace in the domain, the Council was formed to constitute the Commandments, which became the law for everyone within the realm to abide by. To enforce the Commandments, the Council entrusted the "Warriors of the Light", consisting of the seventeen strongest Arkan warriors namely, *Aran,* the son of Varkelos and captain of the warriors, *Endemur, Kantar, Banian, Knar, Varas, Bairn, Arvo, Geod, Elhir, Adiminor, Darmeus, Erjurak, Bronax, Morsus, Geonoz* and *Ghalatix* to carry out this task. After the Council instated the Commandments, the Arkans lived in obedience and die if defiance to the law was ever committed. The Commandments assures the survival of the Arkan and secured a thousand years of peace throughout the kingdom.

King Satorex have two daughters, the eldest is *Sorah*, the Light of Strength, and *Althea,* the Light of Healing. As the king's bloodline, Sorah and Althea's powers are stronger compared to the common Arkan. Sorah inherited her father's strength and wisdom, whilst Althea partly inherited her mother's power of life. Queen Vasilia was known to be the last keeper of this power after her passing. To replace the vacated pillar, Sorah was appointed as member of the council in her mother's stead.

To guard the border of the Arkan domain against those who dare to invade, King Satorex commanded to build two monumental structures. The Great Gate of Treliseum and below the gate will be the second city of the Arkan, which will house the soldiers that will be guarding the gate. Athanax, the ambitious brother of the king, presented himself to the Council to lead the stewardship of the Gate and of the new city. But being the younger brother, Athanax was deemed unbefitting of the role by King Satorex. He knew that his brother was ambitious, naïve, impulsive and young. After all, Athanax was only seven years older than Sorah.

King Satorex decided to hand over the stewardship of the second city to his most trusted friend Varkelos, who had been with him in all the battles that the city faced and fought for him with bravery and loyalty. The king appointed Aran, Bronax, Morsus, Geonoz and Ghalatix to protect the second city and placed them under the direct command of Varkelos. Athanax was dissatisfied with the decision and his heart began to harbor hatred towards his brother.

Varkelos oversaw the construction of the gate and the second city from start to completion. He instructed his workers to build a secret passage within the gate that would lead back to Avetus. Varkelos thought of using the passage as an escape route for the Arkan should the gate and the second city fall.

After many years, the Gate of Treliseum was built and the second city was completed. King Satorex commissioned one-fourth of the Arkan Army and their families to move to the new city, which he named "*Fostrum, the Gate City of Treliseum.*" King Satorex proclaimed Varkelos, the title of *Altrus* or the Custodian of Fostrum. His son was then appointed General of the Fostrum Army.

There was a big celebration held at Fostrum to commemorate the proclamation of Altrus Varkelos and Aran's promotion. Sorah, Althea, all the Warriors of the Light and many noble guests attended the ceremony to congratulate and celebrate with them on that joyful occasion.

Aran's promotion to general status raised dismay among his fellow warriors specifically Bronax and Morsus, who silently accused Aran of being favored by the king due to his father's influence, and believed that they were more suitable to command the Fostrum army than he could. Athanax was also displeased with Varkelos' proclamation and found a common sentiment with Bronax and Morsus. The three began to ally themselves, schemed and conceived hatred towards the king, Varkelos and Aran.

Chapter Two

THE SIN OF LOVE

ooking back in time, Sorah, Althea and Aran had always been together since their early years. They were like siblings that spent all their times together as their parents were always away and busy winning campaigns. Sorah held so much love for her sister. They were still very young when their mother passed away, and with Sorah being the eldest, promised Althea that she will be there to protect her for as long as she lives. Althea the youngest of the three, was closest to Aran. She looked up to him as a brother when they were children, and now as they reached adulthood, Althea developed a feeling toward Aran that was beyond sibling love. But Aran sees Althea as a younger sister – nothing more and nothing less. Aran's love has always been for Sorah. He was captivated by her strength, her skills, her resolves and her beauty.

Sorah on the other hand, saw Aran as a rival for Althea's affection. She steadily challenged him in every training match and tournaments. During those times, the three of them were aiming to pass the trial of the warrior in order to earn their title of the light and to join their warrior brothers and sisters with pride. All passed the arduous warrior test and earned their respective titles. Sorah became the Light of

Strength, Aran earned the title of the Light of Courage, while Althea, after failing the test twice, later earned the title as the Light of Healing.

Althea always knew that Aran loves her sister, but she continued loving him in secret and hoped that someday, he would turn to her and see her not as a young child, but a woman that will earn his love. As the three became adults and fully pledged warriors, each one took a different path. Sorah, Aran and Althea were assigned to different campaigns to help secure and expand the Arkan kingdom. Stories of Aran's bravery in battles have spread across the kingdom, which caught the attention of Sorah who now begins to admire him. Sorah seek Althea's advice on why she's starting to feel differently towards Aran. Uneasy about her sister's feelings, Althea tries to discourage her about Aran. But the more she discourages her, the more Sorah's emotions grew and ended up falling in love with him. Althea couldn't stop her sister anymore, for Sorah has finally realize her true feelings for Aran.

Aran's bravery in battle earned him the right to become part of the Warrior of the Light, claiming the title as one of the strongest warriors of Treliseum. At the same time, Sorah also gained the people's attention and admirations for being the beautiful maiden, commanding and winning battles for the Arkan. Both of them were winning fame due to the glory they were bringing to the kingdom. As Sorah and Aran continues to bring countless victories, the Council decided to appoint Aran as Captain of the Warriors of the Light after proving that he is the bravest and strongest of them all. And for Sorah, being a brilliant battle strategist, was appointed to take the highest responsibility in the kingdom, by becoming one of the pillars of the Council of the Righteous, a position vacated by her deceased mother. Peace reigned in the Arkan kingdom for thousands of years and King Satorex was grateful to both Sorah and Aran for their devotion in helping the Council.

At the present time, during the celebration of Altrus Varkelos and Aran's appointment at Fostrum, Aran slowly approached King Satorex.

"My king with your permission, I would like to ask for Sorah's hand in marriage," Aran's body trembled as he faced the king.

Everyone especially King Satorex, Sorah and Althea, were surprised at the announcement Aran made. The king had no objection to Aran as he knew him very well and believed that he is the man suitable for his daughter. King Satorex then turned to Sorah and asked,

"Well my child, what say you?"

Sorah stood stunned and speechless by Aran's sudden proposal. Althea's heart raced and find it difficult to breathe. She wonders about what her sister would say, but in her mind, she already knew the answer. Everyone was looking at Sorah and Aran began to feel more anxious as sweat slid down his cheek. Sorah slowly lift her head to face Aran and said,

"Yes Father, I accept."

Everyone in Fostrum cheered as Sorah agreed to marry Aran. King Satorex and Altrus Varkelos shook hands, while Althea congratulated both her sister and Aran. But deep within her, she was hurt and couldn't hold her pain in front of Sorah anymore. She quickly ran out of the room and went straight to the balcony to pour out her tears. Sorah felt something was wrong with Althea and followed her. She saw Althea in tears.

"Althea what's wrong?" Sorah wondered.

"Nothing sister, it's just that I'm very happy for you," she answered and quickly wiped the tears off her eyes.

Sorah approached and embraced her.

"If something is bothering you, don't ever hesitate to talk to me. I'm your sister and sisters help each other. I'll always be here for you Althea, because I love you," said Sorah with a consoling tone.

As Sorah uttered those words to her, she couldn't stop crying. She knew that she could not tell Sorah the real reason for her tears. All she could do was to accept it and endure the pain.

Months had passed since Aran proposed and the wedding was on the way. Aran and Sorah took leave from their duties in preparation for their coming wedding. Both were very much in love. Sorah decided to stay in Fostrum after the wedding, a decision that made Aran very happy. He gave her a present — it was a pendant. As Aran was putting it around Sorah's neck, she noticed that the ornament glistened and glowed as if it were alive.

"What is it?" Sorah's eyes filled with amazement as she gazed at the pendant.

"It is my life-force — a part of me, which I'm giving to you," said Aran with a smile.

Aran took Sorah tightly in his arms.

"I love you Sorah and I'll always be here for you to protect you," Aran promised.

Althea watched them from afar. As she glared intently at Sorah filled with happiness, she felt hatred creeping its way into her heart. Suddenly, she was awoken by her emotions, surprised that she could hold hatred towards Sorah. She left the two alone. She was panting and holding her chest, scared of what she had just felt towards her sister.

Tears streamed down her cheeks as she asked her mother for strength and guidance to never let hate take over her heart.

Two years has passed since after the wedding, Sorah had given birth to a beautiful baby girl whom they named *Sarah*. King Satorex and Altrus Varkelos have never been so happy to finally meet their granddaughter. Even Althea was filled with joy to see her niece, the daughter of her sister and the man she loves. She held Sarah with all her love and didn't seem to want to share her with the two grandfathers. Althea was still holding Sarah when Aran approached her.

"I would be honored, if you would help us guide our daughter Sarah to become a fine Arkan like you and your sister," said Aran while caressing Sarah's face.

Althea was so happy upon hearing those words from him and gave her word to Aran that she will do everything she can to fulfill that duty. Aran smiled and Althea's cheeks flushed like the color of scarlet. Aran and Althea were still talking when Sorah pulled Aran away for a moment.

"Aran, I need to go to Avetus with my father today. The Council wanted to discuss some matters and it might take long," she informed him.

"I think it would be better for you to spend the night in Avetus and come back in the morning," Aran suggested.

"Maybe you're right. Will you be alright with Sarah alone tonight?" Sorah asked with a concerned tone.

"I think I can manage. Besides, *Prea* will be here. I can ask her for help if I need it."

Althea overheard their conversation and started to worry upon learning that the baby will be left with Aran alone. Sorah bid Aran and Sarah farewell and returned to Avetus with Althea and the Council. As they reached Avetus, Althea still couldn't help but to worry about Sarah being left alone with Aran. She decided to head back to Fostrum, but didn't want to trouble her sister. So she told Sorah and her father that she needed to go to town to meet with somebody.

"Is this somebody the one that stole your heart?" Sorah teased with a smirk.

"Don't be absurd, I'm just going to meet some old friends. Don't wait for me. I'll be out late!" Althea replied coolly.

Althea left in a hurry, Sorah was looking at Althea's back and felt uneasy in her heart as she watched her sister get farther and farther away. The King called on to Sorah and told her that the Council is about to convene. Sorah turned her gaze and proceeded to the Council room.

Althea flew back to Fostrum and by nightfall she reached Sorah's house. She quietly went inside Sarah's room and found the baby sleeping soundly. She caressed her face, gave her a kiss and felt assured that Sarah was fine. She was about to return back to Avetus when suddenly, she was struck with the thought that Aran was also alone that night. She wanted to see Aran before she leaves. She searched for Aran and found him seemingly depressed in the balcony quietly looking at the stars. By watching Aran she knew that he missed her sister so much.

Althea wanted to talk to him and accompany him through his loneliness, but she felt more than that. She's getting weaker resisting her desires toward Aran. She wanted to hold him in her arms and touch him, but she knew that it was impossible. She was in tears watching

Aran from a distance. Then, she remembered the time when Sorah was filled with happiness together with Aran. Remembering those moments brought back the hatred she once felt towards Sorah. Her desires and hatred combined was so strong that she was completely out of her senses anymore. As she continued to watch Aran, she took Sorah's appearance and essence and slowly approached him. Aran was startled to see Sorah walking towards him, but before he could say anything she held him and kissed him passionately. Aran was completely unaware that she is not his wife but Althea in Sorah's appearance.

"I thought you won't be back until tomorrow? What happened?" Aran was evidently startled with her presence.

Filled with desire, Althea answered:

"I love you Aran! I've always loved you."

Moaning softly as she kissed him passionately. Aran was caught off guard and left confused. He tried to calm her down,

"I love you too. Did anything happen with the Council?" Aran asked.

"Nothing happened. I just missed you so much." Althea uttered.

And in the heat of the moment, she told Aran:

"Make love to me tonight."

Aran, thinking that it was Sorah asking him, couldn't resist her and in the end succumbed to Althea's passion. He carried her to their room and the two committed an act that would change the fate of the Arkan Kingdom.

Chapter Three

THE FIRE OF JUSTICE

At the break of dawn, Aran found himself alone in the bedroom. He searched for Sorah but couldn't find her. He went to Sarah's room and saw her awake and lively. He noticed that the baby had already been bathed, clad in fresh clothing and surrounded by pillows. Knowing that somebody has already been there and cared for her, Aran asked Prea, the head chambermaid, if she or anyone attended to Sarah. He was told that no one had yet entered the baby's room. Aran went back to his daughter, picked her up and sat on the chair.

"I love you my little precious. Did your mother bathe you?" Aran gently whispered to Sarah's ear.

Sarah smiled upon looking at him. A cold breeze of wind passed by Aran that made him suddenly feel uneasy. He sensed something was different with Sorah last night. Indeed, he saw his wife and knew that it was her essence but her passion that night was something he had never felt before. He faced the sunrise with anxiety and uncertainties in his heart. He held Sarah, kissed her in the cheek and hoped that everything was just a figment of his imagination.

Back at Avetus, Sorah was preparing for her journey back to Fostrum. She was in the courtyard with the king bidding her farewell when Althea walked in. Sorah called on to her, but Althea ignored her and hastily walked inside the palace to her room. Sorah and the king grew baffled by her behavior. Sorah excused herself and went inside to talk to Althea. She went up to her room and knocked, but Althea didn't answer, and again Sorah knocked.

"Althea…is everything alright?" she asked with a concerned tone in her voice.

Althea was crying. She felt so ashamed to face her sister for what she had done. Sorah began to worry.

"Althea, could you please open the door? Are you alright?" Sorah repeated.

Althea thought that her sister might force to open the door.

"I'm fine sister. I'm just tired." Althea replied in a relatively indifferent tone.

Sorah was insisting on opening the door while Althea tries hard to hold her tears back and asked Sorah to let her rest a bit as she was not feeling well. Sorah did not want to strain Althea and yielded to her plea.

"Althea, if you need me, I'll be here for you. You are my sister, remember? I love you." said Sorah before leaving.

Althea couldn't stop crying. She thought that after all the love Sorah gave her she willfully defiled the sanctity of her marriage. She was ashamed of herself, confused and scared. Sorah had always been her strength, her confidant and best friend. Now she had no one to turn to. She felt daunted from the thought of the sin she committed against Sorah.

Sorah arrived at Fostrum and was welcomed by Aran carrying Sarah. Sorah missed her daughter so much and immediately took Sarah in her arms.

"Where have you been this morning? I was looking all over for you." Aran asked.

Sorah was puzzled at Aran's question,

"I was in Avetus with the Council and spent the night there... I did speak to you of this yesterday remember?" Sorah answered.

Aran froze in disbelief and once again asked.

"You didn't come back last night?"

Sorah's eyebrows furrowed and stared at Aran.

"Aran, I just came back — just now. Are you alright? Why would you ask a thoughtless question like that?" she answered firmly.

Aran felt that Sorah was serious with her answer and likewise puzzled him about last night. He did not ask Sorah anymore.

"Forgive me. Maybe I was just dreaming of you last night." Aran responded in a weary voice.

"Did you miss me that much? Worry no more my love. I'll make up for your loneliness now."

Sorah approached him and kissed him.

"I'll wait for you in the bedroom after I'm done with Sarah." she looked at him with a flirtatious smile.

Aran paced around, thinking about last night. Fear grew in his heart as he tried to make sense of his uncertainty.

Four months had since passed. In those time, Althea secluded herself from everyone. King Satorex and Sorah were very concerned about Althea's condition. They tried to talk to her many times but could not reach out to her. The king reminded her that he and Sorah were there to help her with her burden, but Althea begged her father to leave her be for a while, saying that she will deal with it herself and did not wish to involve him and Sorah with her troubles. The king understood and respected her decision, but he worry for Althea as he had never seen her like that before. All the king could do is hope that Althea could resolve her problems on her own. Sorah wanted to help her sister but the king advised her to give Althea some time and let her speak if she's ready to do so.

Althea was looking outside her window, quiet and motionless. She was tormented by the extent of her guilt, as her mistake bear yet another mistake. She was pregnant with Aran's child. Althea could not carry the guilt anymore, fearful about the future of the life she is carrying. She didn't know what to do anymore. She was losing her sanity. She then thought of telling someone and Aran was the first person that came to her mind. It would be difficult but she decided that she needs help. Althea secretly left the palace and travelled to Fostrum while the Council convened.

Althea arrived at Fostrum and immediately went to the palace to meet Aran. Aran was in the middle of a discussion with Bronax, Geonoz, Ghalatix and Morsus when she came in. Althea was visibly apprehensive while approaching Aran in the presence of the warriors.

"Althea, I was not expecting you to come here today. Are you looking for Sorah?" Aran wondered.

"Can I speak to you in private?" asked Althea in an anxious tone.

16

Aran felt flustered after hearing Althea's request. He excused himself to the four warriors and escorted Althea to the garden to talk. Seeing Althea's behavior and Aran's reaction raised Bronax's and Morsus' curiosity and desired to find out the reason. They then followed the two secretly.

Aran noticed that Althea was uneasy and trembling, and as he was about to ask her, Althea suddenly burst into tears.

"Forgive me Aran for I have done a grave sin to you and my sister." Althea sniffled.

Aran was shaken by Althea's outburst and wanted to know the reason behind her words. Althea, trying to hold her composure, confessed everything to Aran, her love for him, the pain she feels just by seeing him with Sorah, and the deception she committed. Aran's eyes bulged and his mouth gaped open upon hearing Althea's revelation. He began to realize that the fear of uncertainty that he once felt was coming into clarity. He never thought that Althea would commit such an act. He was confused and as he tries to compose himself, Althea then revealed to him that she was pregnant with his child. Aran felt a wave of fear rushed through him. He walked towards Althea and grabbed her by both arms.

"How could you do this to me? How could you do this to your sister?" Aran exclaimed.

Althea's heart was struck with anguish seeing Aran furious for the first time.

"Forgive me Aran" were the only words she repeatedly said to Aran that moment.

Bronax and Morsus heard everything and knew that if this information reaches the Council, they will surely be punished. The crime of infidelity is strictly forbidden in the Arkan commandments. The two silently left Aran and Althea and hurried back to Avetus to convey the information they've uncovered to Athanax. Ghalatix saw Bronax and Morsus leaving the same place were Aran and Althea was and find it peculiar that the two were leaving Fostrum in such a hurry while the meeting of the warriors has not even been adjourned yet.

There was a moment of silence between the two. Aran turned his back on Althea.

"You should return to Avetus Althea. Please give me some time to clear my thoughts." Aran pleaded.

Althea, reluctant to leave Aran's side, realized that she has no choice but to give Aran the time he needs as she brought him an atrocious burden. She left Aran still in a state of shock and returned to Avetus with a heavy heart.

Bewildered, Aran went back to the palace and abruptly ended the warriors' meeting. Geonoz and Ghalatix noticed something was wrong and asked him if everything was alright. Aran ignored them and proceeded to his room to collect his thoughts. As a warrior entrusted to enforce the commandments, he knows that the punishment for Althea's crime of deception is banishment or death. If the Council deems to banish her, she will be stripped of her Arkan honor and die as a mortal. But Aran was worried for Sorah the most. He knows that Sorah loves her sister so much even as much as she loves him. It would be difficult for him to face Sorah in this state, knowing that all of this will immensely hurt Sorah. He thought he needs to tell her the truth before everything goes from bad to worse.

Bronax and Morsus arrived in Avetus and immediately met Athanax. They told him everything they heard about Aran and Althea's situation and saw an opportunity to exploit their predicament. Athanax has been scheming for a long time to rebel against his brother and end his reign. He convinced the army under him, Bronax, Morsus and a significant number of followers to support his cause. He promised them of power through expanding the kingdom by conquest throughout the galaxy under his reign. After years of patience, he finally saw his plan coming to fruition.

That night, Sorah arrived back and saw Aran sitting at the balcony. She became aware that Aran was quietly looking afar, contemplating. She called on to Aran, but didn't respond to her, she took hold of Aran by the shoulder which startled him.

"Are you alright Aran? You look troubled." asked Sorah.

Aran hesitated for a moment before answering Sorah. He wanted to tell her everything but he was still weighing if he should or not. He decided to tell Sorah about him and Althea, he gathered his courage and turned to faced her.

"Sorah, I have something to tell you." Aran uttered.

He was about to speak when Sarah suddenly cried. Sorah immediately rush to the bedroom to see Sarah. She held her and came back out to Aran. Sorah then asked about the thing Aran wanted to tell her about, but after seeing his daughter cry, he waived and thought that it was not a good time to tell her.

"Maybe some other time," said Aran in a soft voice.

He embraced both Sorah and Sarah.

"Whatever happens tomorrow, remember that I love you and will always love you." Sorah was happy hearing Aran say those words, but it also made her heart feel restless.

19

Weeks passed. It was an ordinary yet beautiful day. People in the capital were doing their typical tasks and the Council was in session as usual. As the Council was about to adjourn, Athanax requested the members of the Council to indulge him on a case he wanted to present. The king inquired about the urgency of the case, which would then require the Council's time. Athanax stated that it is with great importance that they attend to the matter for it involves the fate of the entire Arkan kingdom. The Council was confounded at what Athanax was trying to arrive at, but granted him audience. Before Athanax began, he requested the presence of the Warriors of the Light to witness the event. The king granted his plea and the warriors were assembled inside the great hall.

The three Council members were wondering why Aran was not present with them. The king asked for Aran and demanded that as the captain of the warriors, he needs to be present. Athanax informed the Council that Aran will be called on later. The members were left doubtful about what Athanax was trying to lead them on, but as a Council, they knew that it is their responsibility to hear the plea of a member, a point of discussion that would involve importance regarding the kingdom. Athanax exposed to the Council that someone violated the commandment and committed a grave sin. The king asked Athanax the reason why this case needs to be discussed by the Council since enforcing the commandments is the duty of the Warriors of the Light.

"My King, this case requires your direct judgment, as this involves not by an ordinary Arkan, but a member of the royal family." Athanax sneered.

Everyone was jolted to hear Athanax's claim and the king reminded him to be mindful of his words. King Satorex demanded Athanax to present the evidence and the accused to face the Council.

Athanax then orders to bring forth the accused. As the door of the great hall opened, Aran and Althea were escorted in by soldiers with their hands bound together. Everyone was shocked and couldn't believe they were witnessing the event that was unfolding. A haze of fear surrounded Sorah as she saw Aran and Althea. The same emotions were felt by Altrus Varkelos. The king was furious and demanded:

"What is the meaning of this Athanax? Why is my daughter and Aran tied like criminals?"

"My king, we have learned that Althea committed a forbidden act of love towards Aran. She deceived him and willfully betrayed her sister, the commandments and the kingdom." Athanax responded.

Everyone was taken aback by Athanax revelation.

"Silence!" the king's rage echoed inside the hall.

Sorah stood up and approached Althea.

"Althea, tell me this is not true. Please!" pleaded Sorah.

"Forgive me Sorah..." said Althea while she cried and shifted her gaze away from Sorah.

Sorah was hurt at what Althea committed. She wanted to hold Althea but Athanax stopped her and was told that she may not touch the accused as the trial has not yet finished. Sorah was in disbelief, confused and lost. She looked at Aran and saw his eyes asking her to forgive him. Varkelos and the king were deeply held back with their thoughts.

"It is with great pain in my heart to see the truth unravel, but we as Arkans, were taught to obey and follow the commandments forged

21

by this very council. If anyone violates it, then no one should be exempted when passing judgment." Athanax stated.

Bronax and Morsus sounded their firm concurrence in the background. The king was terribly hurt to learn Althea's crime. As the king sat quietly in his throne, with his head down, Athanax demanded the king's judgment. Everyone in the hall was quiet and Sorah looked up to her father. The king raised his head and with a heavy heart passed his judgment.

"For the crime of willfully violating the sacred commandments, I judged you Althea to be put to death for your sin." King Satorex spoke as his voice trembles in emotion.

Sorah's eyes were wide open after hearing her father's judgment and pleaded her father for leniency.

"Sorah, as a Council member we should be the ones upholding the laws of our land without distortion." Athanax countered with a smirk on his face.

Sorah knelt down before the Council, pleading mercy for her sister. Aran felt a piercing pain in his heart seeing Sorah's tears and her desperation for the first time. In his heart and mind, he wanted to save both Sorah and Althea from these miseries. He took a deep breath and ran in front of the king and kneeled.

"My king, please have mercy, she did not deceive me. I was fully aware of everything." Aran claimed.

Everyone was again bewildered with the new revelation. Sorah looked at Aran. Althea begged him to stop and to not say anything more.

"My king, Althea didn't deceive me as what the Council member Athanax has implied." Aran pleaded.

Aran paused for a moment, closed his eyes and an image of Sorah's happiness was in his mind.

"Stop it Aran. Sorah and your daughter needs you. I beg you, please! Don't say another word!" Althea pleaded desperately.

Sorah was confused in the exchange of words but Aran stared at the king and his father.

"My king, it is I who has done wrong to the kingdom. I violated the commandments — not Althea" Aran stated.

He once again paused and seemed to have difficulty saying his next words. Althea was begging him to say no more, while deep inside Sorah's heart she too wishes Aran to stop. Athanax, Bronax and Morsus were astonished at what Aran said. They knew that he was trying to protect Althea from being put to death, but either way, it would still benefit their plans.

Aran then took a deep breath and mustered all his courage.

"My king, I knew for a long time that Althea was in love with me and as I learned about it, I took advantage of her emotions, her weaknesses and her purity. I beg of you to please spare her life and punish me instead.," asked Aran.

"No father. It is I who deceived him. Aran, please stop with these lies." Althea refuted.

Everyone in the council hall was disgusted with Aran while Sorah has lost herself amidst the pain she suffered from Althea and Aran's betrayal. Aran finally revealed to the Council that Althea is carrying his child and begged the king's mercy for Althea in exchange for his life. Althea denied it and turned to her sister Sorah.

"Sister, please forgive me. It is I who deceived Aran. He loves you so much. Please believe me." she begged Sorah.

But Sorah slowly stood up and faced her.

"Believe you? How could you possibly make me believe you now?" Sorah spat back at her.

Althea and Aran were shocked to hear those words from Sorah. She was in great pain; her sanity was hanging by a thread and only tears of anger and pain streamed down her face. As Aran and Althea continued to contradict each other, the king furiously raised his voice.

"Silence!"

Everyone was terrified to see the king's anger. Altrus Varkelos glanced at his friend and felt apprehensive about his judgment.

"Althea, you will address me as your king in the presence of the Council. From this day forward, I disown you as my daughter because of the shame you brought to our family and to the kingdom; for being weak from your desires I sentence you to be banished from Treliseum, you will be stripped of your Arkan honor, and die as a mortal." the king decreed.

Altrus Varkelos somehow felt relieved that the king showed leniency for Althea and was hopeful to give the same leniency to Aran's judgment. Althea was not afraid of the judgment passed down to her. Instead, she was more worried for Sorah. The king then turned towards Aran with a fierce gaze.

"Aran, I loved you as my own son and I trusted you with my daughter Sorah, yet you found discontent and even selfishly took advantage of Althea's emotions." the king spoke in a harsh tone.

Sorah and Altrus Varkelos were overcome by dread upon hearing the king. They both feared for Aran's life. The king then passed his judgment:

"Aran, son of Altrus Varkelos, for the sin you willfully committed against the Arkan kingdom, I find no forgiveness for you and therefore sentence you to die in the fire of justice," the king exclaimed.

Altrus Varkelos gawked and was left in shock. He tried to plead for Aran's life. Athanax knew that the king might give Aran a reprieve.

"Council member Varkelos, please be mindful that we, as a member of the Council, creator of the commandments, and Aran as the enforcer, should know better the consequences of violating them. We hold the important tasks of ensuring order in the kingdom, how would the people follow us if we are not complying ourselves?" Athanax quickly countered.

Altrus Varkelos was struck by Athanax's words and uttered no more. Aran looked up to the king.

"My king, I willingly accept your fair judgment, without enmity. The only regret I have is for my wife Sorah."

He turns his gaze to Sorah.

"I may not be worthy of your forgiveness, but I always meant what I've told you in the balcony", tears flowed as he spoke.

Sorah remembered Aran's promise that he will always be there for her and Sarah and that he always loves them. She looked at Aran and

25

wanted to hold him. Aran looked back and smiled. Althea was still pleading her father for mercy and giving piercing cries expressing that it is not Aran's fault but hers. Althea turned to her sister begging her to stop their father, but Sorah could not seem to perceive her words anymore because of the pain that has subsumed her heart -- pain for being betrayed by her beloved sister and the pain of losing a husband. Althea was devastated knowing that she was already dead in Sorah's heart.

King Satorex then lifted his hand as flames slowly came out and summoned the fire of justice. Sorah was tearful as she looked at Aran for the last time. Altrus Varkelos wanted to stop his friend, the king, but was bound by the law of the commandments. Althea still tried to beg her father, but no one could ever hear her voice. King Satorex unleashed his power and the flame began to consume him. Aran's face was twisted in a grimace of pain as he slowly dying in the flame. Everyone in the great hall especially Sorah and Altrus Varkelos watched in horror as they witnessed the wrath of the king and the power of the fire of justice. Althea was able to escape the soldiers' grasp and decided to die along with Aran. But King Satorex saw her running towards Aran and blasted her back, causing her to violently hit the wall and eventually knocking her unconscious.

Sorah was devastated seeing Aran destroyed right in front of her. All that was left of him were his ashes, while Altrus Varkelos cried in pain from losing his only son in a horrible death. Varkelos looked at the king, anger and hatred filled his heart. Athanax was contented with the outcome of his scheme. He was able to make the king inflict great pain to Altrus Varkelos that sparked the hatred between two friends. Now he is ready to execute the next phase of his evil plan, which would end King Satorex's reign.

Chapter Four

PACT OF DECEITS

The king ordered Althea to be taken to the prison chamber to later carry out her sentence as the people had already witnessed too much suffering that day. Sorah approached Aran's ashes. She picked up what remain of Aran and held him to her heart and still could not believe that he was gone forever.

"Why Aran, why? You promised to be with me forever, but you broke that promise. Why?" she cried as she held Aran's ashes.

Altrus Varkelos was shocked and in denial as he looked down his son's ashes. Both Sorah and Altrus Varkelos mourned for the loss of Aran. The king stood near Sorah and his best friend.

"We, the pillars of the Council, have the sacred duty of upholding the commandments that we created, to ensure order in the kingdom and the survival of our race." the king's voice shook as he spoke those words.

The king paused seeing the two in great pain. He turned his back and walked away.

"For losing a husband and a son, forgive me. But the law of the righteous must be followed." the King said before leaving.

Altrus Varkelos never once looked at the king as he spoke of those words. In his mind, he blamed him for the injustice and the death of his son. His heart was tainted with anger and hatred towards his friend and vowed justice for his son.

In the prison chamber, Althea woke up and felt pain in her abdomen. Blood ran down between her legs. She immediately knew that she had a miscarriage. She was agonized knowing that the life Aran gave her was lost together with him. Althea blamed everything upon herself, for the shame she brought to the kingdom and to her father, the sadness she left Sorah and Sarah, and for the death of the man she loves. She wanted to die and just be forgotten, but all she could do is wait for the Council to carry out her sentence.

She endured the pain and cleaned her body of blood and never told anybody of her miscarriage. As Sorah and Altrus Varkelos prepares for their journey back to Fostrum, Bronax approached and whispered words to Altrus Varkelos. He informed him that Athanax wanted to meet him in private to discuss something important that he may find solace for the loss of his son. He asked the escorts to bring Sorah back first and informed that he would follow later. Bronax escorted Altrus Varkelos to the Council room and there he met Athanax. Athanax approached Altrus Varkelos, took his hands and expressed his sympathy for the loss of his son. Athanax told Varkelos that he was surprised with the king's judgment towards Aran and finds it unfair.

Altrus Varkelos was somehow contented with Athanax's thoughts knowing he shared the same views regarding the king's judgment. Athanax wanted to discuss something with him but it needed to be in

28

secret. No one can know about the things he would reveal to him regarding the king, and it needed to be discussed somewhere outside Avetus, for it was not safe in the city. Altrus Varkelos was intrigued to know what Athanax wanted to reveal about the king, and demand that he tells him at that instant. Athanax knew Altrus Varkelos was weak at the moment after seeing his son put to death and used it to take advantage of Varkelos' emotions. He told him that he will help him avenge his son. Altrus Varkelos had mixed emotions on what Athanax just proposed, but his heart was already blinded with hatred and anger, shouting for vengeance. He then made a pack with Athanax and agreed to meet him at Fostrum. He revealed to him the secret passage route, which he secretly built to bring together Avetus and Fostrum. Using the passage, Athanax could move freely going back and forth to Fostrum without raising any suspicion from the warriors loyal to the king. Altrus Varkelos instructed Geonoz to escort Athanax and his party to the secret passage and informed that he will meet them at Fostrum on the next day.

Altrus Varkelos will play an important part in Athanax's evil plan. Athanax already hold half of the Arkan army at Avetus and gained the support of some of the civilian populace to join his cause of deposing King Satorex, but his numbers will not be enough especially that the twelve remaining strongest Warriors of the Light, and Sorah the brilliant stratagem, are there to defend the king and the kingdom. They still pose a big threat to his army. He planned to assassinate Sorah at Fostrum, let Altrus Varkelos betray the king at the right moment and use the Fostrum army to finish the warriors and the king.

When Altrus Varkelos arrived back at Fostrum, he was approached by Ghalatix. Ghalatix told him that he believed Athanax had something to do with Aran's misfortune that led to his death. Altrus Varkelos wanted to know more about Athanax's involvement. Ghalatix explained that he saw Bronax and Morsus eavesdropping at

Aran and Althea's conversation during the time she came for Aran. On that day, they noticed Althea was not in her usual self and seemed very scared to see Aran. He further elaborated that after Aran took Althea to the garden to have their talk, Bronax and Morsus suddenly disappeared, later reappearing from the garden and hastily left Fostrum without a word. He then explained that it all happened a week ago before Aran was summoned by the Council.

Altrus Varkelos knew that Athanax has deep influences on Bronax and Morsus. He knew that the two warriors had a deep animosity towards Aran for being appointed as general of the Fostrum army and also knew that Athanax secretly resented him for being the Altrus of Fostrum, which he desperately ambitioned to have. He then summed up all the events that took place and believed Athanax is planning to use him and his army to achieve his objective of deposing his brother, the king, and take the throne for himself. He was enraged at envisioning Athanax's plan and for thinking that he could make a fool out of him. He vowed to Aran that he will have his vengeance on both Athanax and the king no matter the cost.

That night, Sorah was in her daughter's room. She looked at Sarah who's being cheerful and bustling. She was still too young to understand the unfortunate events that happened to her father. Sorah held Sarah in her arms tightly and cried as she remembered memories of Aran and the thought of Sarah growing up not having the chance to meet her own father. Memories of Aran dying in front of her would haunt her forever. She could not understand how Aran could do such a sin. Then, image of Althea came to her mind. Her heart was divided. She harbored hatred towards Althea for what she had done, but she also pitied her for her tribulation and imagining the reality that she will die alone as a mortal. It saddened Sorah so awfully, as she lost not just a husband but a sister as well. But what is done cannot be undone.

It was a quiet night following the day of Aran's death. Athanax arrived at Fostrum together with Bronax and Morsus. They traveled through the secret passage Altrus Varkelos told them to use, escorted by Geonoz. He took them to the palace hall where Altrus Varkelos and Ghalatix were already waiting. As Athanax saw Altrus Varkelos, he immediately shook his hand.

"Please allow me to extend my deepest condolence for your loss." Athanax had to tilt his head down so he can hide his smirk.

Seeing Athanax and hearing those false words from him made Altrus Varkelos despise him even more than the king, but he played along with Athanax and hear out his plan. Altrus Varkelos sat in front of Athanax while the four warriors were in the background listening. Athanax revealed that he planned to revolt against his brother, King Satorex. He told Altrus Varkelos that his army and loyalists were already in place waiting for his command to move. Varkelos asked how he intend to win against the Warriors of the Light, to which Athanax immediately reply boasting that he held half of the Avetus army in his command and his army was already moving outside the city to the plain of Avetus where the battle will take place, but he needed Varkelos' help in order to win the battle. Athanax wanted to let the king believe that Altrus Varkelos was there by his side, loyal as ever to the kingdom. Having earned the king's trust, Varkelos could easily position his army near the king's ranks and, at the right moment, strike them where they very least expect it.

"In other words… you want me to betray the king?" Altrus Varkelos stood up and asked in a stern voice.

"Is this not what your heart desires? To avenge your son's death against an unjust king? He let his daughter live while your son died and all because of her petty love for Aran." Athanax sneered.

31

Altrus Varkelos hid his anger and hatred towards Athanax, especially that he was the one responsible for Aran's death by manipulating everyone to achieve his plan, but he promised Aran that he will have his revenge and he was determined to achieve it.

"What about Sorah? She can still defeat us. She is a great battle strategist," Altrus Varkelos asked.

Athanax had a special plan for Sorah. He revealed that he will send his men the night before the revolt.

"My men will … let me put it this way, they will dispose her here in Fostrum permanently" said Athanax looking at Varkelos, smiling derisively.

Varkelos knew what Athanax wanted to say indirectly. He would kill Sorah before she could join her father in Avetus. Because of his hatred towards his friend, the king, he turned a blind eye and allowed Athanax to carry out his plans. Athanax and Altrus Varkelos formed a secret alliance with the goal of ending the reign of King Satorex. Athanax informed everyone that they will attack the capital two days from that night. The meeting was concluded. Athanax and his party returned back to Avetus to start mobilizing their army. Before he left, he took Altrus Varkelos' hand.

"When the time comes, I will signal you to strike and you shall have your revenge." Athanax assured.

"You have my allegiance, and at the end of the battle you will stand victorious and I shall have my justice," Altrus Varkelos' voice shook with suppressed rage.

Athanax left Fostrum with full confidence and fancied himself as the next king of Treliseum. While they were traveling, Bronax and Morsus were secretly laughing at Altrus Varkelos for being wretched and pitiful. Part of their scheme was to eliminate him as well after the king is defeated. They took delight at the thought that he's playing according to what was planned. Athanax ordered them to send a small contingent of assassins to kill Sorah and everyone else at their house.

"And the baby?" Bronax asked.

"Leave no one alive," Athanax answered coldly.

Altrus Varkelos, Geonoz and Ghalatix were silently looking at them as they moved farther and farther away. Geonoz and Ghalatix then looked at Altrus Varkelos.

"What now my lord?" Geonoz asked.

"Now I will have my vengeance," filled with rage and hatred, he told the two.

A day has passed since the pact of deceit was sealed. In Avetus, the Council convened yet only the sound of silence crowded the room. No one spoke to another as they usually would. The atmosphere was cast down. Athanax announced that they would carry out Althea's sentence in the morning on the next day. King Satorex and Sorah were surprised by the sudden announcement he had made. The king faltered as he uttered his response. Athanax, yet again, reminded the king of the Arkan commandments that binds them all to follow since time immemorial. The king had no choice as the judgment has been spoken and the approval for Althea's sentence had been given. Sorah has accepted the fact that Althea was to be banished from Treliseum, but in her heart, all that lingered was apprehension. The day Althea's sentence will coincide with the revolt, but Athanax had planned to kill both Althea and Sorah on that very night. The Council adjourned, and both Athanax and Altrus Varkelos left the room.

"Tomorrow, you will wait for my signal and together we will finish the king," Athanax whispered.

"Yes. All of this ends tomorrow," Varkelos replied.

Sorah was left in the Council room with the king. She approached him and asked.

"Is this really the right path to take Father? Is it not yet enough that Aran had paid the price for their sins? Are we just going to sit down and wait until Althea dies too?"

"Forgive me my daughter, but this is the law that we created. It pains me so much, as it would to you to send your own daughter to her death." The king replied, struggling through his sorrows.

Sorah bowed down before the king. She left him alone and traveled back to Fostrum. Later that afternoon, Athanax ordered Morsus to send a platoon of assassins to Fostrum to eliminate Sorah, and two assassins to kill Althea at the prison chamber. The assassins were quickly dispatched. Two of them posed as soldiers, took Althea out from her chamber with her hands tied behind her back. They got out of the palace easily and brought her to a secluded place. Althea was baffled and demanded the soldiers an answer.

"What is the meaning of this? Why was I taken here?!"

The assassins laughed and thought that since she's going to die at that moment, they might as well tell her the truth. The assassins revealed the truth behind all of it, as well as her uncle's evil plan.

"Tomorrow, your father's reign will end. A new dawn for the Arkans is bound to happen. Your uncle will be the next ruler of Treliseum!" The assassin revealed.

"What do you mean 'end'? And what is this new dawn that you speak of?" Althea responded.

"Tomorrow, Athanax will plunge a revolt to eliminate the king, and as we speak now, another group was sent to kill your sister Sorah and everyone who carries the blood of King Satorex and we will start with you!" said the assassins, with a sinister laugh.

Althea's eyes widened and took a sharp breath after hearing the assassin's revelation, she realized that Sorah and especially Sarah were in grave danger. She need to do something to save them both. One of the assassins summoned his Serdeus.

"Would you be so kind to grant me my last wish?" asked Althea.

After hearing her question, the assassins were on their guard with anticipation that she might plan to escape so they asked her what this request was.

"I am pregnant with a child whose father was already destroyed. Seeing the man I love die slowly in front of me, I too, desire to die the same way." Althea replied, in a somber tone.

The assassins were confused and shocked to hear such a plea.

"And how do you want us to end your life slowly?" They wondered.

"Stab me in the abdomen... This will kill both me and my unborn child," Althea boldly said.

Again, the assassins could not believe she asked to die this way, but they granted her request anyway. As the assassin pointed his Serdeus at Althea's abdomen with her hand still tied behind her back, she took a deep breath and prepared herself for what is to happen. The assassin stabbed her and forcefully pushed his Serdius inside Althea. She endured the pain as blood gushed out of her wound. She lunged herself towards the assassin making the Serdeus pierce through her back. The assassins were downright shocked and amazed at her determination to slowly die. Suddenly, Althea used the pierced end of the assassin's Serdeus and cut her hands free from the binds and swiftly summoned her Serdeus to behead the assassin in front of her. The other one quickly summoned his Serdeus and fought with Althea. Wounded and profusely bleeding, Althea managed to kill the last assassin. Her face scrunched in extreme pain as she held her wound. Light then beamed from her hand. She immediately placed it over her wound and started healing herself. Althea wasted no time and hurried to reach Fostrum in order to save Sorah and Sarah.

At Fostrum, Sorah was beset with difficulties at the thought that she would never see Althea again the day after tomorrow. After all the things that Althea has done, she still loves her and her heart urged her to see Althea for the last time. Sorah decided to travel back to Avetus to see Althea. She asked Prea, her head chambermaid, to take care of Sarah while she was gone. She held Sarah and gave her a kiss before leaving. As she was about to fly, she looked at Sarah and saw her smiling and waving at her, which made Sorah feel hesitant to leave as if Sarah was begging her not to go. But she ignored that feeling and flew as fast as she could to reach Avetus in order to see her sister. Althea was trying to stop the blood from gushing out while she flew back to Fostrum. She had lost a lot of blood and for a moment lost consciousness. She fell from the sky, crashing in a forest. At the same time, Sorah happened to fly past her without noticing her sister. The two had crossed path and almost met, but Sorah did not see Althea as she plunged down to the vegetated forest. She continued on flying in full speed to reach Avetus.

Althea regained her consciousness and rested for a moment as she continued to heal her wound. She was very tired and about to lose consciousness again. Suddenly, images of Aran being burn alive and seeing Sorah and Sarah being killed flashed through her mind. Shaken, she woke up. She was determined to save them. She staggered as she stood up and expanded her wings. She flew towards Fostrum hoping that she could make it in time. Later that afternoon, Sorah arrived at Avetus and went directly to see Althea at the prison chamber. The chamber was empty and Althea was nowhere to be found. Sorah find it strange and went to see the captain of the guard. She learned that she was taken by two guards under the order of Morsus, but none of the guards knew where she was taken. Sorah went to see her father at the throne hall. As she entered the hall, she saw the twelve warriors of the Light in a discussion with the king. Everyone was hysterics and discussing over a serious and urgent matter. Sorah joined in and learned that there was an unauthorized movement of the army. Half of the Arkan army was taken out of Avetus and later found amassing outside the city, in the plains of Avetus.

Sorah asked who authorized the movement. Endemur, the captain of the warriors who succeeded Aran, informed her and the king that they do not have an idea on who spearheaded the movement. What he only knows is that the army that was moved belongs to the legions of Athanax, Bronax and Morsus. The king was confused about why his brother would move his legions outside the city, nevertheless, Sorah instructed to send scouts to observe the army. She then asked the permission of the king to muster the remaining Arkan forces and place them outside the city wall to prepare for the inevitable. The king agreed and gave the command of the army to Sorah. Sorah then sent two of the warriors, Elhir and Adiminor, to Fostrum to inform Altrus Varkelos of the situation and requested him to bring the Fostrum army to Avetus. She also instructed them to proceed to her house and protect everyone, especially Sarah. Elhir and Adiminor immediately left for Fostrum. Just then, a soldier came in and reported that they have found two dead prison guards in the city. The king was enraged to know that someone dared to spill blood within the city wall. He ordered them to find the culprits immediately. Sorah on the other hand instructed Endemur to send soldiers to find Althea. Faced with far too many uncertainties, Sorah started to feel uneasy.

The sun had set and the assassins sent by Morsus arrived at Fostrum. The soldiers at the gate have been instructed by Altrus Varkelos to allow them passage without questions. The assassins broke into two groups: one group proceeded to Sorah's house to carry out the plan of killing her and everyone in the house. The house was guarded by a handful of soldiers. The assassins surrounded the house and slowly moved in. The signal was given and they started their attack. It caught the soldiers guarding the house by surprise, but they were still able to fought back the overwhelming number of enemies. The assassins managed to break through the house and started searching for Sorah and the baby. Prea left Sarah in Sorah's room. She summoned her Serdeus and fought the assassins in order to protect Sarah. The assassins set the house on fire. Some of the Fostrum soldiers that were unaware of the commotion tried to rush towards the burning house but were blocked by the second group of assassins. The assassins were able to go into Sorah's room, but couldn't find her. Instead, they saw the baby crying. The assassin raised his hand holding his Serdeus and was about to strike Sarah, when all of a sudden, Althea smashed through the window, deflected the assassin's strike and killed him. Althea was just in time to save Sarah. She held Sarah in one arm as the other held her Serdeus fighting the assassins. She was trying to make her escape but the assassins were all around her. In order for her and Sarah to get out, she deliberately used her flame to cause a huge explosion, killing some of the enemy that attacked her. She immediately flew out of the house with the baby followed by the remaining assassins behind her. Elhir and Adiminor saw the explosion as they came near Fostrum and hurriedly flew towards it. Elhir saw that the Fostrum soldiers were fighting the assassins. They flew in to help the soldiers and were successful in eliminating them all. After the skirmish, they immediately proceeded to Sorah's house. The two were devastated to see that the explosion and fire had destroyed the house and everything was turned into rubbles.

Chapter Five

VENGEANCE

Elhir and Adiminor desperately searched through the rubbles for survivors, but all they've found were charred bodies. Then, the warriors saw Prea, staring at the rubbles and in a catatonic state.

"What happened here? Where is the baby?" Elhir frantically asked.

"Sarah was killed in the fire. I could not get to her in time. They're too many, I failed to rescue her," Prea was completely incoherent.

Witnessing the devastation, Elhir and Adiminor assumed that the baby perished in the fire. It was a very distressing moment for them knowing that not long ago, Sorah lost her husband, and now, they failed to save her daughter. Nevertheless, the warriors left the place of carnage together with the head chambermaid to take her to the healer and immediately seek Altrus Varkelos to relay Sorah's words. Upon arriving at the palace, Elhir and Adiminor were welcomed by their fellow warrior Ghalatix. They requested to speak with Altrus Varkelos -- immediately as they carry urgent message from Avetus. They were escorted inside and eventually met Altrus Varkelos.

"My Lord, we bring word from Supreme Commander Sorah, requesting your assistance to subjugate a possible threat that is amassing outside the city of Avetus." Elhir began.

Altrus Varkelos was surprised to hear that Sorah was alive and became the Supreme Commander of the army, a position he always held every time the king summons the army. He held a deep-seated grudge about it and secretly resented Sorah.

"Inform Supreme Commander Sorah that the Fostrum Army will come to the king's aid. Assemble the army! We march to Avetus tonight." ordered Altrus Varkelos.

Elhir and Adiminor were ecstatic from hearing Altrus Varkelos' words of dedication and loyalty. Elhir then informed Altrus Varkelos that the enemy already made the first move by attacking Sorah's house, which killed everyone including the baby. Elhir further presented him Prea in order to substantiate the treacherous attack. Varkelos was sickened to learn that even his granddaughter was not spared from Athanax's plan. He despised Athanax and his hatred grows even more; but he had to endure everything until he gets his revenge. Elhir and Adiminor excused themselves as they prepare to return to Avetus. Altrus Varkelos told them that he will have Ghalatix and Geonoz escort them. The two warriors declined the offer, but Varkelos insisted, pointing out that the enemy might still be somewhere waiting to attack them. Elhir and Adiminor were grateful for Altrus Varkelos' concern and agreed to take his offer. Prea was instructed to proceed to the healers to have her wounds treated. Elhir and Adiminor exited the room followed by Ghalatix and Geonoz. Altrus Varkelos whispered to them that Elhir and Adiminor must not reach Avetus. Geonoz and Ghalatix looked at him and nodded. Altrus Varkelos planned to eliminate Elhir and Adiminor to weaken the strength of the Warriors of the Light, putting Sorah's chances of victory in peril.

On her way to the healer, Prea stopped for a moment to grieve for the loss of Sarah. She somewhat felt responsible for her death. It was her obligation to protect Sarah and she failed. She felt devastated and struggles to regain her composure, when suddenly, she saw the four warriors leaving the palace. Prea wanted to thank Elhir personally for helping her come to her senses after the ordeal and decided to follow them. As the four warriors reached the gate, Geonoz suddenly stopped and turned around, while Ghalatix slowly moved behind Elhir and Adinimor.

"What is the matter brother?" Elhir asked.

Geonoz and Ghalatix gave a sinister smirk at the confused Elhir and Adiminor and treacherously stabbed them without mercy. The eyes of the two unsuspecting warriors widened and expressed an excruciating pain in their faces, as Geonoz and Ghalatix further lunge their Serdeus into their bodies, slowly killing them. Prea was horrified to witness the heinous crime committed before her. She quickly hid herself to avoid being seen by the murderers and thought that there may be other conspirators who could still be lurking inside Fostrum. She decided to leave the city for her safety and sought the help of Sorah in Avetus. Geonoz and Ghalatix ordered their soldiers to dispose the bodies of Elhir and Adiminor. Altrus Varkelos afterward, sent out messengers to Avetus to assure the king that he will come to his aid. Led by Altrus Varkelos, the Steward of Fostrum, the Fostrum army assembled and began their journey to Avetus.

Outside the city of Fostrum, Althea holding Sarah tightly, made it out of the burning house and flew beyond the Gate of Treliseum to escape the assassins that were chasing her. The assassins caught up with her and encircled her. She worried for Sarah's safety, knowing clearly that the assassins were after their lives, but she was determined to protect Sarah even if it cost her life. As the assassins attacked, she tried to fend them off using her Serdius and her body as shield to protect Sarah from the strikes, which repeatedly got her wounded. Althea was able to kill all the assassins, but the wounds gradually drained the strength that's left within her. Her vision was hampered by the blood dripping from her head. Fearing that there could be more enemies after them, she feebly stood up and searched for a safe place to hide. Althea continued to hobble until she found a small cave. She could hardly stay conscious as she entered the cave. Sarah fell asleep due to exhaustion from crying while Althea slowly put her down and immediately lost consciousness.

At dawn, the king's army was already in formation. Leading his army was his daughter Supreme Commander Sorah, backed by the remaining ten Warriors of the Light. As they waited, they saw the army massing at the other end of the field. As they approached, the army become more and more visible. Sorah saw the opposing army numbering far greater than their own. In the middle of the line they saw Athanax's flag being hoisted. The king was outraged to see his brother dared to revolt against him.

"What is the meaning of this Athanax?! Why is your army here in front of the city without my permission?" The king bellowed.

"Why do I need your permission? Today you will no longer be king! I will end your reign and I will lead the Arkans to a new era of order and power!" Athanax replied smugly.

. "Silence you fool!" the king shouted in anger

The whole army in the field were terrified by the king's voice. It was the first time to hear him rage like that.

Athanax was surprised to see Sorah still alive and immediately felt worried, knowing that a brilliant strategist such as her was in command of the king's loyalist army. The messengers from Altrus Varkelos reached the two sides; one messenger was sent for Athanax and forewarned him that Sorah's child had been killed, and that they will be coming from the west. The other messenger was sent to Sorah and cautioned her that the Fostrum army will emerge from their east. Since Altrus Varkelos' army will be surfacing from the east, Sorah moved half of her right flank in order to reinforce her center, as well as her left flank. She then placed three warriors of the light to hold the right flank long enough until the Fostrum army arrived. The king angrily commanded the rebelling Arkans to stand down or they will face death as judgment for their actions.

"Athanax, you as a pillar of the council, should be discerning to know better. The commandments we forged aimed to protect and unite our people. And yet you desecrated those sacred commandments right this moment and lead your followers to their demise!" said the king.

The rebelling Arkans felt terrified when the king spoke of their fate if they were to continue with their action. Athanax witnessed his followers falter as they heard the king's stern warning. He quickly countered the king's word.

"Fear not brave Arkans, as we are here today to end a tyrannical rule of King Satorex. This is exactly what he wants you to feel! He's trying to manipulate you by using our sacred commandments to impose terror! I, Athanax, promise you that I will forge a new commandment and liberate you from my brother's terror!" Athanax proclaimed.

Athanax's followers cheered as he spoke of the promise of liberation. He once again gained the morale of his army and instructed Bronax and Morsus to begin the attack. Bronax sound the trumpet in order to signal the troops. The king was saddened to see that his people chose to follow his brother Athanax who was blinded by his thirst for power. But as king of the righteous, he vowed to uphold the commandments and fight for the survival of his loyal people. He gave Sorah his permission to use the entire loyalist army under her command. Sorah knew that Athanax's army was larger than hers, so she planned to attack their center straight and ascertained that the enemy would reinforce less pressure on the left and right flank. She was putting her hope of victory on Altrus Varkelos's Fostrum army.

As Athanax's army began their attack, Sorah was in the middle of the loyalists' line. She led the attack of the center against the enemy's center. Every male and female Arkan, rebel or loyalist, summoned their Serdeus and flew towards one another, each side fighting a battle they have never fought before and an enemy they have never before faced: a battle against fellow Arkans. Accompanied by some of the Warriors of the Light, Sorah was the first to engage the rebels as they smashed the center and fought hard to break through. The rebels' center was shaken by the power and strength of Sorah and the warriors of the light, their defense begins to shatter. Bronax and Morsus saw the inevitable collapse of their center, immediately pulled out soldiers from their right flank to buttress the center.

Bronax and Morsus' decision to move their soldiers was exactly what Sorah had been anticipating. She planned to encircle Athanax's forces by holding her center and left flank. Once Altrus Varkelos' army arrived, she will have him attack from her right flank and shift some of her warriors from the center to the left flank in order to anchor and engulf the rebels from both sides. As the battle rages on, casualties and death mounted from both sides. Sorah was warned that her right flank was taking a heavy toll and the Fostrum army has yet to arrive. Fearing her right flank might collapse, she ordered some of the soldiers from the center to help the right flank. Despite having a larger army,

Athanax was still unable to destroy Sorah's line. Sorah proved herself to be the brilliant battle strategist of the Arkan kingdom.

The battle was beginning to shift its wind in favor of Athanax. His forces have managed to push back Sorah's line. Sorah clearly see the inevitable collapse of her center and could no longer wait for Altrus Varkelos's army to arrive. In a bold decisive move, she ordered her forces to push hard and break the enemy's center line at all cost. She fought with all her might and courage; her display of valor strengthened the morale of her warriors and soldiers. They've managed to break through the enemy's line and caused panic from the rebels' end. Athanax quickly sent his reserve to hold Sorah's forces from plowing their way to him and commanded Morsus to take the last reserve and attack them in their weak right flank. Morsus started attacking Sorah's right flank; the three warriors of the light in charge of defending the loyalist right flank, begins to shatter as the overwhelming strength of the rebels swarmed them. As the rebels about to overrun them and when all hope was perceived lost, King Satorex suddenly emerged, slashing the enemy and pushing them back. The king swung his Serdius so powerful, throwing the rampaging rebels like ragged dolls. Every blow the king makes, left the enemy in his path trembling with fear.

The king alone was able to repulse the attacking rebels, his skill in the Serdius, his strength, his powers and viciousness has instilled fear in the hearts and minds of the enemy. As the battle rages on, the king's army was slowly being pushed back by the sheer number of the rebels; the enemy's center that Sorah had broken through was blocked by another wave of reserves. The enemy was able to reform their line in time and held their ground. Sorah did not have reserve soldiers to replenish her ranks. The strength and determination of King Satorex, Sorah and the Warriors of the Light were the only hindrance that prevented the rebels from advancing further. Both armies were desperate to defeat each other.

Suddenly, the sound of trumpet of the Fostrum army was heard across the battlefield. King Satorex and Sorah looked to the east and saw Altrus Varkelos army slowly forming in the horizon. Athanax also witnessed his arrival and directed his army to continue attacking the loyalist army. King Satorex saw his best comrade Altrus Varkelos and waved at him, signaling him to support their right flank and attack the rebels at once. Altrus Varkelos and the Fostrum army remained standing and watched them from the high ground. The king was confused and tried once again to motion for support, but he was merely met with silence and inaction. The king stood stunned and a frightening thought raced through his mind – the chilling thought that Altrus Varkelos has abandoned them. Sorah on the other hand, continues to beacon the Fostrum army for rescue, but none reciprocated any intention to help. The Fostrum army remained in their position and watched the king's diminishing army be annihilated by the rebels. The Loyalist did not understand why the Fostrum army, their brothers and sisters, wouldn't want to come to their aid. Sorah clenched her fists and glared at Altrus Varkelos.

Realizing that Altrus Varkelos is no longer his friend but became part of the rebellion, King Satorex anticipated the inevitable defeat of his army. Out of desperation, he ordered all the female Arkans to return to the city and defend it until their last dying breath. He ordered Sorah to lead the defense of the city, but Sorah disobeyed her father's orders and swore to fight next to his side until the bitterest end. The king felt proud of his daughter's courage in the face of death. He ordered all the Warriors of the Light and the remaining male Arkan soldiers to rally behind him as they poised to make a final stand. In contemplation, King Satorex knew that his mission is to stop the rebels from destroying them, but their chances of victory was shattered by the betrayal of his friend Varkelos and the Fostrum army. The king then had a fearful thought of using the fire of justice to defeat Athanax. But he knew also that by using it, his hands will be tainted by the deaths of millions of his people. The king was lost, he falters and becomes indecisive. Sorah then took his hand.

"Father, I am with you until the end. We will share the burden together." she said bravely.

The king was grateful to his daughter. Her words urged him to do what he must for the survival of his people -- the righteous ones. Athanax on the other hand, could hardly contain his joy seeing his brother's pain from his own best friend's betrayal. He ordered all his remaining forces to charge and destroy those who opposes him. Altrus Varkelos witnessed and observed everything above the hill. He was waiting to see the final moment of King Satorex. Athanax's army charged to where the king's army would make their last stand. King Satorex raised his hand and mustered the destructive power of the fire of justice. Athanax and Altrus Varkelos saw the king's action and couldn't believe that he would go that far to win. Athanax ignored his brother's action and shrugged it off as a mere fear tactic. He ordered all of his forces to continue the charge and crush the loyalist army once and for all. As Athanax's army came near the king's line, King Satorex unleashed the power of destruction, the fire of justice, which destroyed half of the Athanax army.

Athanax and Altrus Varkelos were stupefied to witnessed the destruction unleashed by King Satorex. Athanax's body trembled in fear as he saw half of his army disappear in an instant and fazed at the thought of their total annihilation if the king unleashes yet another flame. He called out to Altrus Varkelos telling him that now is the perfect time to strike the king, while they are at the moment of weakness. But Altrus Varkelos turned a blind eye and ignored his plea.

Altrus Varkelos' reaction sent chills down Athanax's spine. He somehow pieced together the thought that Varkelos knew about his involvement in Aran's demise and that Varkelos had plotted this from the beginning. Athanax realized that, what greater joy could Altrus Varkelos get but to see the objects of his vengeance destroy one another while he watched from afar. Athanax clamped his jaw shut and gritted his teeth with rage seeing Altrus Varkelos up the hill, arrogantly looking down upon them. He vowed that no matter what happened, he will have his revenge against Altrus Varkelos and to his people.

King Satorex was greatly weakened after unleashing the flame of justice. After seeing the rejection of Athanax plea, Sorah knew immediately that Varkelos also betrayed Athanax. She rallied her warriors and soldiers, and prepares to make their final assault against the rebel. Athanax anticipated Sorah's move and without any warning, he summoned his own power of destruction; the power of decay, which he gained from being a corrupted Arkan. He hid this power from anyone, especially from his brother. As Sorah began her charge, the king saw Athanax mustering his power and knew immediately by looking at Athanax's gestures, that he too possessed a power similar to his. King Satorex hastily flew to reach Sorah, but Athanax unleashed his cursed power of decay, exposing all the warriors and soldiers including King Satorex. Sorah however, was embraced by her father in time and shielded her from the poison. The loyalist army started to wane as their bodies begin to decay. The shock robbed Altrus Varkelos of his logic after learning that Athanax also possessed a power similar to King Satorex. After being exposed, the king could no longer summon his flames as the poison has seeped through his body. This leaves Sorah to be the only one left to fight. The female Arkans defending the city wanted to go to her aid but were ordered by Sorah to remain behind the city walls. She did not want them to get near, fearing that Athanax, at any moment, could unleash another blast.

Alone and determined, Sorah ran towards Athanax to kill him and end the rebellion. Athanax saw her coming and blasted her with his poison, but this time, Sorah was prepared, she countered it using her flame as shield. She successfully reached Athanax and the two fought using their Serdeus. Clearly, Sorah was the more skillful combatant compared to her uncle. She finally subdued him and was about to strike him down when Athanax pleaded for his life. Sorah's hesitation cost her dearly, she was treacherously attacked from behind by Bronax and Morsus' flames. The two attacked Sorah ganging up on her. She tried her best to fight back, but she was already wounded heavily and tired. She was disarmed and held to the ground by Bronax and Morsus. Athanax approached her and struck her with his foot. The king begged Athanax to spare Sorah, but Athanax was persistence on kicking her. Athanax ordered Morsus to rally the remainder of his army and prepare them to fight the Fostrum army.

"You will never triumph with your evil actions. Altrus Varkelos may have betrayed us, but he will surely never bow to you either." rasped Sorah.

Athanax foamed at his mouth and hit her once again after hearing Sorah's jeers and mockery. Out of his anger, Athanax unveiled the truth about Aran and Althea; he told Sorah that he was the one who planned her husband's demised in the hands of her own father. Disgusted and in rage, Sorah struggled to stand up but was stabbed by Bronax's Serdius in the shoulder, pinning her back to the ground. Athanax wanted to savor Sorah's suffering some more by telling her that her sister Althea had been slayed by his men. Sorah gasped after hearing her uncle's revelation. Then, Athanax revealed to her the painful truth of all -- that her child was also killed when his men burned their house to the ground. Sorah was traumatized, she's so shocked and couldn't utter a word. The king stood up, ran towards Athanax and swung his Serdius to kill him, but Athanax blasted him again with his poison, throwing the king back violently. Athanax mercilessly ordered Bronax to slay all the wounded male Arkan loyalists, which the rebels immediately carried out stabbing and killing indiscriminately.

"You animals! You will pay for what you have done!" The king shouted.

The cruel fate suffered by her husband and her sister left Sorah detached from reality. Tears cascaded from her eyes as she saw in her mind her child Sarah crying and dying from the fire. Sorah had lost her sanity and screamed in agony. Athanax and the rebels were deafened by the frightening scream. Suddenly, Sorah's wings and armors slowly turned black as she continued to shriek. Athanax could not bear the sound of her terrifying agony anymore, he ordered his army to kill her, but Sorah flew above them and hovered while her body steamed with red smoke. She glowered at them fiercely and filled with rage. The rebels tried to destroy her but she slashed them all down killing them without difficulty with her Serdeus.

The king dreaded for this to happen to her. Her heart has been corrupted by hatred, turning her into a dark Arkan and gaining the power that he prayed would never befall in his children's hands. Sorah mercilessly killed the rebels like animals. Her eyes turned blood-red and a dark sensation sprang from her body, flames blazed from her hands. There she was set to make — the forbidden flame. The king tried to stop her but it was already too late; Sorah had unleashed the fire of justice and burned the entire rebels, including Athanax. Sorah's wrath and enormous power destroyed the rebellion. The king did not want to let his daughter bear the burden of killing thousands of their people.

"Sorah stop it!" King Satorex shouted, but he could not be heard.

"Aran, Althea and Sarah would not want you be the destroyer of life!" again he shouted.

When Sorah heard the names of her beloved, she immediately ceased her flame. She then descended to the ground, crying. Even after the king was exposed twice to Athanax's poison, he still managed to stood up and hold Sorah in his arms. The king shed tears upon seeing his daughter in such a miserable state. She had lost a husband, a sister and now a daughter. The king blamed himself for all of her suffering. Sorah did not utter a word and was unable to hold her tears back.

The battle was over. King Satorex nearly lost the kingdom but in the end, he still prevailed. The loud outcry of pain was heard across the battlefield. He was appalled to witness the burned and disfigured body of his brother Athanax and that of his followers. Altrus Varkelos was in disbelief after witnessing that Sorah defeated Athanax. He couldn't even believe that Sorah became a dark Arkan, something that he had never seen happen for an eon. Varkelos now felt frightened that the king's wrath would now befall him. Geonoz and Ghalatix urged him to attack now at their moment of weakness and before the king and Sorah could realize it. Altrus Varkelos was filled with conflicting emotions as his warriors urged him to attack. Then, King Satorex stood up and stared at him in the eye. Altrus Varkelos trembled as the king glared at him. He ordered his army to help the king's wounded soldiers. Geonoz and Ghalatix were surprised at the order and asked him to reconsider.

"Look at the king's eyes. If we attack now, we would surely suffer the same fate as those who already have." he told the two.

"Do not dare touch my men! We don't need any of your help. Instead, bring Athanax and his rebels to the court hall for them to face their judgment." King Satorex yelled at Varkelos and his men.

The king summoned the female Arkans instead to help his wounded men. He was holding Sorah and walked passed Altrus Varkelos without uttering a word. Altrus Varkelos knew that he too would soon face the king's judgment and now regret the choice he made. He dreaded what is to be laid ahead for him and his people because of his betrayal.

Chapter Six

CONTINUANCE OF LIFE

The civil war obliterated almost three quarters of the Arkan population. It was a monumental loss for this once proud race. King Satorex suffered a grave wound that even the healers could not cure. He put his arm around Sorah's shoulder as they walked into the throne hall to pass down the judgment to his brother Athanax, his friend Varkelos, and their followers for the failed rebellion. They brought forth his brother and his cohorts Bronax and Morsus. The three were severely burned, disfigured and groaning in extreme pain. The king glared at Athanax with unfathomable disappointment and handed down his judgment.

"Councilor Athanax, you of all Arkans, should have been most aware that desecrating the commandments is punishable by death and yet you defiantly led your followers against the kingdom." King Satorex stated.

Seeing them in their painful state, King Satorex thought they would not survive with their wounds.

"I therefore banish you from Treliseum, to be outlawed from returning and to die in dishonor," the king proclaimed.

The kind raised his hands towards the sky and opened the *Gateway of the Fallen,* with passages through unknown heavens where he would banish the rebels. The poison he was inflicted with, made him cough up blood for using so much of his power just to open the portal. As the rebels began to be pulled in towards the gateway, Athanax looked at his brother with vengeful eyes.

He then turned his gaze at Altrus Varkelos with anger and hatred. Athanax and his followers were engulfed by the power of the Gateway and were sent to the other side of the wormhole, to die in an unknown world.

"I vow on this day that I shall find my way back to have my revenge on all of you wretched righteous", threatened Athanax.

Terrified of the possibility that he too would suffer the same fate as Athanax, Varkelos immediately went down to his knees and begged the king for his forgiveness.

"Altrus Varkelos, why did you not come to our aid when the kingdom was in danger? Why did the Fostrum army, the army I entrusted you, did not heed our call for help?" asked King Satorex with much dismay.

Altrus Varkelos had nothing to justify himself and instead said,

"Forgive me my king. I was blinded by my anguish and thus abandon the kingdom."

The king was mournful towards him and was convinced that the reason for his betrayal was because he took away his son; the son whom he was proud of and loved so much. The king then contemplated on his judgment for Altrus Varkelos and his followers, while Sorah fiercely stood before them, frowned at them with displeasure and hatred in her eyes. King Satorex stood up and passed down his judgment.

"Let it be known to all that I, King Satorex, rightfully reclaim from Varkelos the title of Altrus of Fostrum. You and your followers are to be stripped of your Arkan powers and to be banished from Treliseum to world unknown, where you all will die as mortals." the king proclaimed.

Varkelos eyes widen after hearing the verdict and all of his followers protested with judgment.

"Silence you betrayers! You are in the great hall of the king! If you continue with such disrespect, I shall destroy each and every one of you filth." Sorah shouted in anger.

Flames ascended from Sorah's hands as the words were spoken. Varkelos followers were frightened of Sorah after they witnessed what she did to Athanax and his army. They bowed down and kept their silence. King Satorex raised his hand and took back the powers of Varkelos and his followers. All of their Arkan essence, immortality, strength, their flames, their wings and Serdius were stripped of from them. Varkelos' followers, as well as those that remained at Fostrum, faced the same judgment. Varkelos slowly turned around and watched in horror as his followers were being engulfed by the force of the gateway. He then turned to the king and looked him in the eye, but didn't utter a single word. He was the last to be hauled into the portal.

In the cave outside the Gate of Treliseum, Althea was still unconscious. She had lost a lot of blood and on the brink of death due to the grave wounds she suffered from her battle with the assassins. Sarah was already awake and crawled toward Althea. She held Althea's face, bouncy and bustling as she tries to wake her up. But Althea did not wake up. Sarah was trying so hard to shake her but she remained unconscious. Sarah became sad and scared. She hugged Althea and cried. As she cries, a bright golden light radiated from her body, the light enfolded Althea and her wounds were slowly being healed. As the last wound was completely closed, Althea suddenly opened her eyes, startling Sarah which extinguished her light abruptly upon seeing Althea awake. Still disoriented, Althea did not saw the light. She was mystified to learn that her wounds were all gone — not even a scar was left on her body. Althea then looked at Sarah who's being blissful and full of spirit. She held her and gave her a kiss and thankful that nothing bad had happened to her. She then remembered being chased by assassins.

As she frightfully anticipated potential attacks from the menacing assassins, she prepares to return to Avetus to her father and to Sorah so that Sarah could be out of harm's way. She carried Sarah and went out of the cave but was met with great shock. She gawked upon seeing the gateway, which she didn't realize her father opened, looming in the sky, and the people from Fostrum were being forcefully pulled in. She firmly held Sarah and tries to escape the power of the gateway but the force was too strong. Althea desperately clung to the boulders but miserably failed. In the end, she was pulled in with Sarah.

The entire court hall was quiet after the king's judgment was carried out. The king lifted his hand to close the gateway but suddenly collapsed. Sorah was able to hold him back up and sit him on the throne. The king was too weak. His power waned apace due to the poison throughout his body. Only King Satorex has the power to open and close the gateway. He was too weak and couldn't even stand up on his own. Sorah asked her warriors to bring her father to the healing chamber. Without the king, the gateway of the fallen was left open.

At the healing chamber, King Satorex saw that the male Arkans were tainted by Athanax's poison; their bodies including his, were already decaying rapidly and the healers could not do anything to stop it. He knew that if the entire male Arkan populace dies, their race will cease to exist. In order to stop that terrible fate from happening, he instructed Sorah to have all the male Arkans and himself put in a deep cold state of unconsciousness in order to stop the decay and preserve their life. To save the Arkan race from certain extinction, the king ordered the healers to carry out an unconventional method of reproduction to ensure the continuance of life; the healers would extract a drop of the male life-force and infuse it to the female womb to bear offspring. The king had foreseen that with this method of reproduction, the power of the newborn will be half compared to those that were born of normal birth. The king had no choice but to let go of his pride in order to save the race.

The male Arkans were put into a deep sleep, one after another. The king appointed Sorah to be the Altrus of both Avetus and Fostrum in his absence. Before his turn to be put to sleep, he apologized to Sorah for everything that has happened and hoped that someday, a miracle would come and save them from their accursed fate. King Satorex was then laid down while Sorah witnessed everything. Tears poured from her eyes as she watched her father and her people. Sorah bore hatred for what happened to her father and sister, to her people, to the kingdom and especially to her daughter. Remembering the people she loved brought her into a moment of sorrow and darkness. Sorah vowed before her father that under her reign, she will make the Arkan race prosper once again and make it a powerful kingdom – to be feared by all. As she made her promise, she held onto the pendant that her husband gave her; the pendant that hold Aran's life-force.

Inside the winding tunnel of the gateway, Althea held Sarah in her arms and carefully fly her way through the wormhole avoiding dangerous debris. She saw the Arkans that were pulled in were violently being tossed around and helplessly being killed by debris. They cried to her for help but she was occupied steering her way safely with Sarah in her arms. She was able to come out of the tunnel with Sarah unharmed despite the perils she faced inside the gateway. Sarah however, was having difficulty breathing in space. Althea frantically hovers to search for a star that would be suitable for them to dwell. After passing a small moon, she saw a planet from afar and dashed off towards it. As she got nearer, she found the blue planet. She was captivated by the beauty of the star. Sarah was already gasping for air, Althea had no choice but to go down hastily to the blue planet.

Althea landed on the planet surface and could immediately feel that the air is not as pure as in Treliseum, but finds it safe and breathable. She checked Sarah and saw her to be breathing normally now; their bodies seemed to have easily adjusted to the planet's atmosphere. Althea had a taste of its water and finds it's safe to drink. She began to search for a place where they could dwell on and found a mountain with a small cave just below its peak and finds it safe to stay away from the giant creatures lurking below. Althea went inside the cave and laid down her sleeping niece. She took a moment to rest, but the cries of the people that were left inside the gateway were haunting her. Her conscience urged her to save them. Althea decided to go back to the gateway. She lit a fire to keep Sarah warm while she sleeps soundly and closed the cave entrance to protect her from any harm while she was gone.

Althea flew back to space, back to the gateway and found groups of people clinging on to portions of large debris. They were very exhausted while most of them didn't make it. She pushed the debris where the people were holding, out of the gateway tunnel and into the calm space. She did it repeatedly to save as many people as she could. Althea asked them why they did not use their wings to save themselves.

She noticed that most of the people that she asked came from Fostrum and were forcibly pulled in similar to what happened to her.

"We do not know your highness. We suddenly couldn't use our wings nor summon our powers anymore, as if they were taken from us! We were helpless as we watched our family and friends die inside that wretched gateway," the people informed her.

Althea carried all the people that she saved down to the blue planet.

"What is that beautiful blue planet?" they asked.

"*ERES*," she replied instantly. It means "hope" in Arkan language.

As the people were safely brought down to the planet, she quickly attended to the wounded and healed them with her power. Suddenly, a woman approached her, begging for help.

"Please your highness! Please save my son!" the woman cried.

"What is the matter with him?" Althea asked.

"He would not wake up. He hurt his head and has been bleeding since then," the mother panicked.

Althea quickly went off with the woman and saw the boy heavily bleeding and unconscious. She tried to heal the boy but he has already lost too much blood and is now facing imminent death. To save the boy, Althea infused a drop of her blood into the boy to enable his body to heal itself. The boy suddenly opened his eyes and saw Althea smiling at him.

"What is your name?" Althea asked with a soft voice.

"*Ihram*," the boy replied, still staring at her in seeming infatuation.

The mother was so happy and relieved to see her son woke up from near death. The people expressed their deepest gratitude to Althea for saving their lives. Althea was in the midst of another group of survivors, when suddenly, she was attacked by a group of men. Without difficulty, she beaten the attackers but left confounded by the unexpected attack. She then saw Geonoz and Ghalatix came forward.

"What is the meaning of this? Do you not see that these people need help?" she demanded an explanation.

As she stood her guard, a man appeared from behind the mist. It was Varkelos. Althea felt even more confused at Varkelos' presence.

"Altrus Varkelos, what are you doing here? Are you not supposed to be with my father to stop the rebellion?" Althea wondered.

"It is because of you! Your father banished us and left us to die in dishonor. Because of you! I lost my son." Varkelos answered, while he stared at her with deep hatred.

Geonoz, Ghalatix and some of the surviving soldiers slowly approach her carrying whatever they can use as weapon to kill her. She ran back to the people she first helped. They saw her being chased by Varkelos' men and immediately came to her aid. They tried to stop them from harming her, but Varkelos was so determined to kill her.

"Please leave this place. It is dangerous for you!" Ihram's mother said.

Althea flew off, leaving her people behind her. Varkelos saw her escape.

"I will find you! wherever you hide I will have my revenge!" Varkelos shouted in fury.

Althea quickly returned to the cave shaken from her ordeal with Varkelos. She could not imagine why he was banished by her father. Althea was lost in her thoughts when suddenly, Sarah crawled to her side. She picked her up and cradled her in her arms, caressing her face. As she looked at Sarah, she remembered her sister Sorah and the pain she left her. She blamed herself for everything that transpired. Thinking back into everything that happened made her tearful. Sarah touched her face and smiled at her — Althea somehow found peace in that tiny smile. To atone for her sins, she swore to Sarah that she will raise her as her own daughter and protect her for as long as she lives, until the time she be reunited back with her mother.

Chapter Seven

THE NEW AGE

Three millennia has passed. The inhabitants of the blue planet prospered and multiplied a thousand fold. Through the passage of time, two great empires rose. The *Ithurian* and *Deodarian* empires. Although they originated from the same roots, they were each other's archenemy. The Ithurians were more technologically advanced people and most of their innovations were mainly for military use. They were heavily dependent on the planet's resources — extracting woods, steels and *Algios*, a source of energy that the Ithurians use to fuel their machineries.

The Ithurian held strong animosity towards the Arkans. For thousands of years, they were taught by their faith that the Arkan king and his kin were envious of their ancestor's intellect and resiliency. The Ithurians were made to believe that Fostrum, the city that their ancestors built and dwelled on, was made prosperous — their abundances were richer compared to Avetus. The Ithurian doctrines teach them that the Arkan king saw their ancestors as a potential threat to his reign, fearing that their power would outgrow his. The king ordered to suppress and unjustly banish them from Treliseum to die as mortals.

The Deodarians however, were the opposite of the Ithurians. This race embraced the Arkan commandments and swore obedience and loyalty to it. They lived and died by the commandments as their ancestors did. The Deodarians may be less advanced than their rival empire, but they were gifted with long life and self-healing powers. They could live around two to three hundred years, and possessed twice the strength of an ordinary Ithurian. The Deodarians were ruled by *King Zairel*, the wisest and strongest of all men in Eres. Together with his son *Prince Vasuril*, they led the Deodarians to become a powerful rival that the Ithurians could not disregard. Belief, was the main reason behind the conflict between the two empires; one side disowned their past, and the other embraced the truth. They waged war, countless battles were fought against each other from the time of the great exile until the present age. Numerous lives were lost from both sides until a peace covenant was adopted by the two empires. The covenant put an end to the battles but never the conflict. There were still small-scale disputes, but so long as both sides stayed within their realm, they managed to live a hundred years without war.

The Ithurian Empire was composed of five kingdoms: Ithuria, the central capital of the empire; *Enor* in the North; *Amara* from the West; *Minea* from the East; and *Sodaria* from the South. The Ithurians came from the bloodline of the exiled people of Fostrum, and were ruled over by *King Malkiem*, the direct descendant of Varkelos, known to his people as "the persecuted one". It was Varkelos who set forth the false doctrines about the Arkans. The Ithurians were great military inventors. They developed numerous weapons, ranging from air to land. The *Nephatron*, a giant human-like machine vehicle used to fight inland, the *Zelridar* air ship that dominated the sky, and the Ithurian's most prestigious invention – the *Zeltkova*. The Zeltkova is an armored suit with mechanical wings, which mimicked the power and strength of the Arkans. These were adopted into their infantry.

The Ithurians created the Alliance of the Kings, whose members are the rulers of the five kingdoms: King Malkiem of Ithuria; *King Turloch* of Minea; *King Ull* of Enor; *King Gileal* of Amara; and *King Kelon* of Sodaria. Because of this alliance, the Ithurian Empire held three quarters of the blue planet's land. But, even with the combined forces of the alliance and the technology they possess, the Deodarians still remained a formidable force to be reckoned with. The country of Deodara was the first place where the exiled people of Fostrum stayed, until the time when Varkelos and his followers decided to leave and formed the Ithurian kingdom to the North. The faithful however, remained and built the city of Deodara. Deodara was located at the southern end of the Ithurian empire. It was a magnificent city built on top of a hill. The Deodarians are a peaceful people, unless they are provoked and forced into a conflict, they are ready to fight. Both males and females were trained to be warriors at an early age – an Arkan tradition that they still followed, in order to prepare themselves to defend their faith and country against their enemies. Their loyalty to the commandments and their strong affinity to the Arkan culture was an expression of their undying gratitude to a beautiful Arkan noble that saved their ancestors during the exile. All of these were inscribed in the ancient texts. King Zairel and his people believed that their ancestors' savior is still in Eres, hiding and blending among the people. They prayed that someday, she would return to reveal and lead them to walk along the destined path.

It was an auspicious day in Ithuria when King Malkiem announced that the queen had given birth to their first-born son. The king was so jubilant for being blessed with an heir to his empire. He named him *Kiran*. All hopes and aspirations of the king for the future of the kingdom was bestowed upon his newborn son. As the Ithurian kingdom celebrate the birth of the king's son, far to the north, farther than the boundaries of Enor, the forest of Eres stood. The forest of

Eres was inhabited by vicious giant and man-eating creatures. It remained untouched and unexplored by the Ithurians.

Within the deep forest of Eres, a cry was heard, a cry of an infant white fox desperately fighting off predators from devouring its wounded mother. As the predators moved in for the kill, the infant fox discharged a breath of lightning shocks to repel back the predators. But the infant fox's power was not strong enough to kill the creatures. Suddenly, a young girl jumped in the middle of the pack and swiftly slashed and slayed all of the predators. The young girl approached the dying fox, while the young pup tried to push her back. She put the pup aside and tries save the mother fox, but it was already too late; the mother fox had succumbed to her wounds and died. The young pup nonetheless tried relentlessly to wake his dead mother.

"Hey little fellow, your mother has passed away. She fought bravely to protect you. Let her rest." consoled the young girl.

The pup howled in sorrow while the young girl stroked his head and sorrowed with him. She then buried the mother fox in a deep grave to prevent the predators from devouring her remains. The pup calmed down afterwards.

"Do you want to come home with me?" asked the girl.

The pup looked at her and wagged his tail, she picked up the pup and said:

"I'm going to name you *Sune*."

She held him in her arms and brought Sune with her, farther into the forest where she lived. They disappeared into the thick vegetation of the forest.

Twenty-five years has passed. Kiran, the son of King Malkiem, grew up to be a fine Ithurian prince and a kind-hearted person who looked after the welfare of his people. Kiran also had a younger sister named *Kina* who loved and respected him too much. Kina would follow Kiran anywhere he went and threatened any girls that dared seduce or flirt with him. Kina somehow developed a brotherly complex with Kiran. Both of them were also appointed by the king to lead the Zeltkova Armored wing regiment. One day, King Malkiem decided to call the Alliance of the Kings to convene in Ithuria to discuss a very urgent matter. He also summoned Kiran and Kina to join them. The four kings arrived in Ithuria and the Council, headed by King Malkiem, started the meeting. He informed the alliance that they are facing a crisis. Due to their rapid technological development, their supply of energy is slowly being expended. The supply of Algios within their territory would be depleted in the next five years. The alliance was alarmed by the crisis and brainstormed a solution immediately. King Turloch offered a proposition of asking the Deodarians to sell them some of their Algios, as the country of Deodara is known to have the most abundant deposits of Algios in the entire planet. King Malkiem hastily disapproved, stating that asking the Deodarians for Algios would alert them of their situation and they might use it to their advantage and attack the kingdom. King Ull then proposed sending out explorers to search for Algios outside the planet, a proposition that was immediately agreed upon by the Alliance.

It was a monumental task to be undertaken by the Ithurian Empire, as this would involve space exploration. The Ithurian inventors did build their ships to cope with space travel, but they never performed a conclusive test on that field. In the face of this grave situation, all they are left to do is to take that risk and push further the boundaries of the unknown. Before the Alliance concluded the meeting, Kiran also suggested that they should try to explore the forest of Eres in search for the energy. Their father cautioned them about creatures they failed to tame, but Kiran assured his father that they will take all the precautions and protection they need.

A month has passed and each kingdom sent out explorers to space out of desperation to search for Algios, the crucial energy that they need in order for their kingdom to survive. The Deodarians learned that each of the Ithurian kingdom sent out air ships to space; Prince Vasuril reported this to his father, King Zairel. The king ordered spies to be sent to Ithuria, to find out the reason for such a massive undertaking.

Meanwhile, deep in the forest of Eres, a wild boar was being tracked. A hunter's eyes were watching it from behind the thick lushes of bushes, slowly moving closer and closer. The boar sensed the predator and ran swiftly away from it. The predator emerged and chased the boar. It was Sune! Sune has grown to become a magnificent fox, with his beautiful silvery white fur to boast. He ran after the boar, purposely leading it to a narrow ridge. As the boar neared the ridge, Sune roared and suddenly, a beautiful girl appeared in front of the ridge directly in the path of the raging boar. The girl drew her sword and ran towards the boar at a lighting-speed rate. The boar charged towards the girl, and when she reached the contact point, she cut the boar down in one strike, killing it instantly. The girl and Sune took the boar back home.

"Mother will be delighted! It is going to be a feast tonight!" said the girl.

The girl and Sune walked deeper into the forest, until they reached a small clearing where a stone house was built. A woman could be seen harvesting vegetables in the garden. As the girl and Sune approached the house, the girl waved and shouted.

"Mother! We are back!"

The woman turned around and it was Althea who waved back at the girl. The girl told Sune to take the boar to the barn and that she would take care of it later. She hugged Althea and smiled.

"Sarah, where have you gone to this time to get that boar?" asked Althea.

And there she was – Sarah, who is now all grown up. She had just turned twenty, the age of adulthood. In Arkan years, she was twenty years old but one Arkan year is equivalent to one hundred and sixty years in Ithurian time. So in Eres, she was close to three thousand two hundred years old. When Althea asked Sarah, she was reluctant to give an answer.

"We got it near the river," Sarah lied.

Althea then turned at Sune.

"Sune, did you and Sarah go down the ridge again?" confirmed Althea.

Sune, without hesitation, nods his head, telling Althea the truth. Sarah turned around and mumbled.

"You traitor!"

Althea twisted Sarah's ear and pulled her back inside the house. Sarah was screaming in pain, Althea once again asked:

"Did you and Sune gone to the ridge?"

"Yes Mother we did. I'm sorry! I won't do it again! Please! Let go of my ear!" Sarah begged.

Althea released her grip and scolded Sarah.

"How many times have I told you to never wander that far! It is too close to the Ithurian border!" Althea remarked.

"But Mother, no one saw us. It was only Sune and I, plus the dead boar." Sarah reasoned with a silly grin on her face.

Althea once again twisted Sarah's ear.

"Do not get wise with me young girl. Promise me you will not go to that place again." Althea said in an assertive tone.

"Yes Mother, I promise. I promise. Please let go of my ear before it tears apart!" Sarah answered, now in extreme pain.

"Sarah, you need to understand that it is not safe for us to be seen by anyone. I have always told you. We are different from them. So please do not give your Mother any more worries." Althea reminded her.

Sarah promised her with a finger crossed behind her back. Sune saw her crossed fingers and barked. Althea told her to make the promise with her hands in front. Sarah looked at Sune and stuck her tongue out at him.

"I should have left you in the forest!" Sarah mumbled.

Althea was about to twist her ear again, but Sarah quickly replied "I promise I will not go there anymore", and made the promise while her hands waved.

Althea told Sarah and Sune to start butchering the boar, and to clean up afterwards for dinner. As Sarah walked to the barn with Sune, she kicked him from behind for telling her mother about the ridge. Sune kicked her back, which threw her into the mud. Sarah was furious and chased Sune to get back at him. Althea was happy seeing Sarah and Sune together. They were like siblings of a different kind and their bond was so strong. Sune for Sarah, was an irreplaceable brother, a partner and a member of their family.

Althea taught Sarah everything she knows. She taught her how to fight and trained her to be strong just like her mother Sorah. But she hid from Sarah the truth about their past, about her identity, her mother and especially her powers. She tried to raise Sarah as her own daughter and taught her to act as normal as possible. But as Sarah reached the age of adulthood, she started to exhibit Arkan powers, which she did not understand. All the same, Althea tried to guide her by teaching her to control her powers. She also strictly forbade Sarah to go to the city nor to be seen by anyone. She still vividly remembers Varkelos' threat and was concerned that if anyone finds out the truth, they would surely be hunted down. To avoid any form of danger, they secluded themselves from the people of Eres and lived as farmers and hunters in the forest of Eres, knowing that no one would dare venture that territory, all thanks to the giant beasts that lurked around the forest.

At dinner that night, Sarah told Althea that she again felt something strange about her body. Althea did not understand and asked her to explain what she meant. Sarah noticed that during the time she killed the boar, she slashed it with great ease. It was like slicing through water and her body was so light when she ran towards the boar. After hearing Sarah speaking about these changes, Althea knew that the Arkan powers within her were starting to awaken. Althea taught her everything she knew on how to survive but never did she warn her that the strength she possessed could never be matched, even by the strongest man on Eres. She also skipped teaching her about summoning her Serdeus and her wings. Althea was trying to hide the fact that she is an Arkan with a noble blood. She was afraid that if the people of Eres knew that an Arkan was living in the planet, they would certainly persecute them and kill them without mercy. Althea knew so much about the Ithurian Empire, because it was the kingdom that fronted the border edge of the forest of Eres. During the frequent visits Althea made to the land of the Ithurians while disguised as an old hermit, she discovered many things about the Ithurians, including their deep hatred towards the Arkan. It pained her to learn about the anti-Arkan doctrines that were being taught to the people. Lost in her thoughts, Althea didn't realize Sarah was calling on to her.

"Mother, are you listening to me?"

Althea was startled.

"I'm sorry. I was distracted by something." Althea replied.

Althea held Sarah's hand and told her that she would be faced with even more changes as time goes by. She also sternly warned her never to show her powers when people are around. Sarah inquired about the reason behind all the secrecy.

"Sarah, the people of Eres are physically and emotionally weak compared to us. They are easily swayed by fear about things they cannot explain." Althea answered.

Sune nodded in agreement with Althea. Sarah partly accepted the things her mother was trying to convey. Deep down, she wanted to go to the city. She believed that being different shouldn't be a barrier. If they meant no harm to the people of Eres, they could coexist with them. Althea felt that Sarah remained doubtful, but could not blame her for it. She was reminded of herself as she observed Sarah. She might have her mother's appearance, but Sarah's stubbornness was something she inherited from her. Althea went into the kitchen to bring out the roasted boar meat that Sarah and Sune had brought back and happily continued on with their dinner.

Chapter Eight

THE MEETING

The next morning, Sarah and Sune prepares to go out into the wild to do their usual hunting. As she looked at Sarah packing her things, Althea suddenly felt uneasy to let Sarah leave the house. She asked her if she could stay home and help her in the garden instead, but Sarah, who always prefers to be in the woods rather than in the house, refused Althea's request and hurriedly left the house. She tried to stop her.

"Do not worry Mother! I promise we will not go to the ridge!" Sarah beamed as she showed her hands.

Althea was still trying to reason with her, but she quickly jumped on Sune's back and rode off into the forest. Having used to worrying every time Sarah leaves for the woodlands, Althea couldn't seem to comprehend the anxiety she felt on that very day. She put her hand on her chest and hoped no harm would come to Sarah and Sune.

One the same day, the Ithurians organized a small expeditionary force to explore the forest of Eres in search of Algios. Kiran led the team with Kina. The expeditionary force consisted of examiners, a platoon of Zeltkova soldiers, and two Nephatron to protect Kiran,

Kina, as well as the examiners. Before letting them go, King Malkiem wished them luck in finding the supply and once again reminded them not to take too lightly the creatures in the forest too lightly. Kiran assured his father that they will heed all the necessary safety measures as they explore the forest. They bid the king farewell and boarded the air ship that will transport them to the forest of Eres.

Kiran and his party arrived at the edge of the forest and from there proceeded by foot to survey the land. He instructed Kina to set up a defensive perimeter to secure them while they work. Hours passed and the examiners could not find Algios in that area. Kiran decided to quest further into the forest hoping to find something in there. They searched from one area to another, however, to no avail. The examiners told Kiran that the forest may not hold the Algios and suggested that they turn back, but Kiran still determined to search through deeper grounds and went on. As they walked, a number of eyes quietly followed them. Kiran and his party hiked the forest for quite a while.

Kina then noticed that the guiding equipment hasn't been working for quite some time now; an unknown interference has caused some failure to the equipment. Everyone stared at each other, worried that they might be lost in the forest. Kiran tried to contact the pilots, but failed to reach them. Suddenly, a loud and frightening roar echoed throughout the forest. Kiran and his group were terrified. He immediately ordered his troops to make a defensive formation. The two Nephatrons were placed on their sides and were surrounded by the Zeltkova to protect them. The roar was getting louder and closer, they could clearly see that the surrounding vegetation was shaken by something that is moving from behind. Kiran prepares his men for the inevitable, when suddenly, hordes of giant predators rushed towards them. Kiran gave the command to open fire. The sound of weapons firing reverberated throughout the forest; Sarah and Sune, who were hunting near the explorers' location heard the sound. They were briefly startled by the continuous gun fire. Sarah decided to investigate. She rode Sune and dashed towards where the sound originated from.

All hell broke loose at the site where Kiran and Kina were. They desperately try to fight the creatures back, but there were too many of them. Everyone screamed in fear as the marauders destroyed the two Nephatrons. The Ithurians were in disarray as the creatures devoured the soldiers one after another. Kiran knew that they would die if they don't do something to escape. He ordered the remaining Zeltkova to protect Kina and head towards the high ground to re-establish communication with the pilots.

Kina ran ahead of Kiran with the Zeltkova soldiers, when suddenly, a creature emerged in front of Kiran, cutting them off into two groups. Kina was with the bigger group of Zeltkovas, attempted to reach her brother, but Kiran ordered them to leave and get to the high grounds. Kina flouted the order but the Zeltkova soldiers forcefully grabbed her and managed to escape. Kina ordered the soldiers to let go of her as she wanted to help her brother, but the Zeltkovas had to follow Kiran's order to save Kina. She felt devastated to leave her brother behind. Kiran and his small group ran back towards the forest, escaping the creatures that were chasing them. His men were being eaten one by one as they flee for their lives. Unfortunately, they got totally surrounded, they had nowhere else to go. Kiran ordered his remaining Zeltkovas to make a last stand and fight. The creatures slowly move towards them with watery mouths, snarling and ready to devour them. As the creatures attacked, Kiran gave the command to fight.

Sarah and Sune were almost at the place where the carnage was. They heard sounds of weapons endlessly being fired, until it suddenly stopped. These were punctuated by terrifying screams of people. As they reached the location, they saw creatures in a frenzy, consuming what looks like people. Then in a small clearing, she saw Kiran covered with blood, wounded and fighting the creatures with his sword. One of the creature attacked and bit Kiran, holding him through its mouth. Kiran closed his eyes as he anticipated his looming death. Before the creature could swallow him, Sarah swiftly jumped in and slashed the creature's head, severing it from its body. The head that had Kiran fell. Sarah and Sune wrestled against the creatures. Sune kept on lambasting his lightning shock, killing a mass of creatures, until the hordes retreated. Sarah asked Sune to check for any survivors while she went to see Kiran. Sarah found Kiran on the verge of death due to his injuries. Her eyes glistened with amazement when she laid her gaze upon Kiran. It was her first time to see another person aside from her mother. She instantly felt captivated to see a being of the opposite sex before her. Sarah asked Sune if anyone else was alive, to which Sune responded with a gesture that meant no one else. She then decided to bring Kiran home so she can nurse his wounds. Sune opposed the idea but Sarah insisted anyway. She asked Sune to carry Kiran on his back, but Sune dragged him instead. Peeved at how crude Sune was behaving, Sarah hit him on the head and demanded that he carry him properly. Sune obeyed her begrudgingly.

As Althea tended the garden, she heard Sarah calling out to her. She was surprised to see them back early that day, and from afar, felt confused that Sune seemed to be lugging a male person on his back. Althea immediately ran towards Sarah, asked them what happened and why they brought home an Ithurian. Sarah told her that they rescued him from the creatures that attacked and killed his people. Althea could not see the man behind the blood-spattered face. She told Sarah to send him back to the forest, Sune nodded in agreement, but Sarah quibbled.

"Mother, this person is hurt and could die at any moment if we do nothing! Can we at least help him before sending him back to his people?" Sarah pleaded.

Althea realized that they have the moral obligation to save the Ithurian or anyone for that matter, but most of all, she knew that she could not win over Sarah's stubbornness so she agreed to it. She told Sarah that once the Ithurian is healed, he would need to leave immediately – this agreement made Sarah happy and relieved. Althea asked Sune to bring Kiran inside the house to wash and to heal him. Sune laid Kiran down on Sarah's bed while Althea carefully disrobed him of his torn clothing. Sarah was still thrilled by Kiran's presence. She couldn't contain her excitement as she gawked at the bare figure. Althea caught Sarah gasping for air as she watched Kiran's body and instinctively twisted her ear.

"Ow! Ow! Mother, it hurts!" yelped Sarah.

"Go out and fetch me warm water" Althea demanded.

From the window, Sune couldn't help but crack up at the sight of Sarah being nagged for her funny thoughts. Sarah threw the bucket at Sune's face knocking him down as she went out of the house to get water. After examining Kiran's injuries, Althea knew that he would not last long unless she used her Arkan power to heal him. She stretched out her hands and light exuded. She hurriedly closed all the wounds and decided to clean him afterward. Sarah and Sune came in with the water and saw Althea using her power to heal Kiran. They marveled at such a rare sight. Althea told Sarah that it may take longer to heal him as his injuries were grave, but she will still try her best to save him.

After the long hours, Althea finally closed all of Kiran's wounds. The healing took a while before it finished; thus leaving Althea exhausted for using up much of her power. Althea asked Sarah to continue from where she had left off, and to clean the blood out of the Ithurian. Althea went into her room to rest, but before she has left, she ordered Sune to watch over Sarah and make sure she wouldn't do silly things with the Ithurian. Sune smirked while he glanced at Sarah.

Sarah carefully washed the blood from his body under the watchful gaze of Sune. She sure was charmed by his looks. She couldn't explain the feeling she was having as she ogled at his face. The feeling even grew fonder as she touched his face. Sune noticed Sarah was staring at his face too much and thought that she might be thinking naughty thoughts again. Sune hit her on the head as if to pull her out of the fascination.

"What was that for?" Sarah asked Sune angrily.

Sune barked at her, telling her to hurry up. Sarah then finished cleaning Kiran and left him in her room to rest.

The next morning, Althea woke up and saw Sarah and Sune sleeping in the common room. She went inside Sarah's room to check on the Ithurian's condition. As she walked towards the bed, the sunlight shone through the window and Althea could clearly see the Ithurian. Her eyes bulged staring in disbelief when she saw Kiran's face. He looked exactly like Aran. Althea suddenly trembled in fear seeing Kiran as it suddenly brought back memories of the past. Her heart began to pound as she remembered the tragic death of Aran and the sorrow she brought to Sorah. Such painful memories made her gasp for air. She dropped to her knees and crawled out the room. Sarah was awoken by the noise and saw Althea crawling out of her room breathing heavily, she went to Althea and hold her.

"What's wrong Mother? Why are you shaking?" Sarah frantically asked.

Althea could not utter a word out of shock. Sune was also awoken by the commotion and ran towards Sarah and Althea.

"Mother, what's happening to you? Please answer me!" But Althea lost consciousness.

Althea later woke up, seeing Sarah and Sune in front of her.

"Mother! Thank God you're awake! Are you alright? What happened to you?" Sarah asked worriedly.

Althea, still dazed from her shock, tried to stand up, but Sarah stopped her.

"Please Mother, take some more rest. You might still be drained from using your powers." She said.

"Sarah, the Ithurian must leave now. He cannot stay here with us," Althea's voice was underlined with panic.

Sarah was confounded at why her mother would say such a thing after they agreed to help him first before sending him back.

"Mother, the Ithurian has not yet healed. He is still unconscious!" Sarah reasoned, but Althea suddenly raised her voice in anger.

"I do not care. Send him away. Sune, take the Ithurian and send him to his people."

Sune couldn't seem to figure out whether to follow or not.

"Mother please calm down. I do not know what happened between you and the Ithurian, but if we send him away now, he may die and our efforts of saving him would only be in vain," Sarah once again pleaded.

After hearing Sarah's plea, Althea managed to calm her heart down and realized that she was right. She burst into tears, which alarmed Sarah and Sune as they had never seen her cry before.

"I'm sorry Mother for having disobeyed you about bringing an outsider here. If it will give you peace, we will send him off now," said Sarah.

As Sarah stood up to take Kiran, Althea took her hand.

"No Sarah let the Ithurian stay. I am sorry if I terrified you and Sune. But it is not about you… it's about me." Althea sobbed.

Althea then held Sarah in her arms, tears still streaming down from her eyes. Althea could not believe that the most dreadful day had come. She was worried by Kiran's presence; his absence in their land is certainly making his people anxious to locate him. If they did find him, their long hidden secrets would be unveiled. Sarah and Sune were very troubled about Althea's condition. Be that as it may, they respected her decision.

Weeks had passed when Kiran finally opened his eyes. The first person he saw was Sarah who was then changing his bandages. Sarah was ecstatic to see that Kiran had finally woken up from his long slumber. Sune rushed in to look at Kiran and growled at him. Sarah hit Sune with a pillow and told him to go away. Kiran was still trying to collect his thoughts. Sarah helped him sit. As Kiran looked around the house, he noticed a woman staring at him. He glanced at Althea, but she quickly turned to the other way.

"What happened? Why am I here?" Kiran asked, drearily.

"Me and Sune found you in the forest… You almost died from the attacks of the creatures! We brought you here and my mother saved you." Sarah answered.

Kiran then asked "Where are the others?" Sarah paused for a moment.

"I am sorry … we could not save them. It was too late when we arrived" Sarah replied with remorse.

Kiran cried for the loss of his comrades and blamed himself for their demise. Sarah tried to comfort Kiran.

"Please. It is not good for you to strain yourself. Take some rest and we will talk later." advised Sarah.

Sarah pitied Kiran for his despondent state. She looked to Althea for guidance, but Althea gave none as Kiran's mere presence makes her apprehensive.

Kiran recovered from his injuries after a month. He found himself alone in the house. He stood up and walked up to the door to search for anybody. As he went out of the house, he saw Sarah and Sune skinning a wild boar. Sune saw Kiran coming out and quickly ran towards him, snarling which terrified Kiran with his viciousness. Sarah threw a bucket, hitting Sune in the head and knocked him off the ground. Sarah approached Kiran.

"Do not mind that stupid brother of mine. He is just trying to scare you." said Sarah.

Kiran was confused when Sarah mentioned brother. How could a person have a fox for a brother? Sarah saw the confused look on Kiran's face and explained to him that Sune, for them, is an important member of their family. She treated him as her brother, since she didn't have any other siblings. She told Kiran that Sune was an intelligent and strong creature, that the only thing she didn't like about him is being more obedient to her mother than she is and hates him when he always goes against her. But at the end of the day, Sune was an important part of her life. Hearing Sarah's story relieved and impressed Kiran. Althea observed from the barn and couldn't help but be reminded of Aran every time she looks at Kiran -- the man she once loved and still love. The thought of him may bring bad memories, but she felt the need to find the will to face him. She kept on telling herself that it is just a coincidence that he looked like Aran, that he had nothing to do with her past. Sarah invited Kiran to have dinner with them since he has recovered from his injuries. Sarah called out to Althea.

"Mother, is it alright for the Ithurian to join us for dinner?" She cheerfully asked.

Sune stood up to disagree with Sarah, while Althea took a moment and hesitated to answer.

"Yes Sarah, but please have the meat ready before then." Althea stuttered.

Sarah was so happy that her mother gave her approval. She asked Kiran to go inside the house and that she will have dinner ready for them soon. Kiran dined alone in bed for a month and that night will be his first time to join them together for dinner. Sarah couldn't hide her excitement to have Kiran join them. Sune on the other hand was grumpy about it. Althea was still apprehensive about him, but repeatedly convincing herself that everything is but a coincidence. Later that night, the four of them had dinner. Althea and Kiran were quiet, Sarah kept on talking and tries to make the atmosphere livelier, while Sune just kept on yawning. Sarah went to the kitchen to prepare the pie for dessert. She seemed to have gotten tired from doing all the talking. She brought the pie on to the table and started talking once again.

"Oh, I am sorry! I just realized that we have not properly introduced ourselves yet. My name is Sarah. You already met Sune my brother and this is my mother Althea." Sarah told Kiran.

Kiran looked at Althea, his gaze made her feel uneasy.

"My mother saved you. We surely thought you were going to die, but my mother used her-" Sarah continued on blabbing.

Althea quickly gave her a dirty look lest she might tell him about the power she used to heal him. But before Sarah could finish her words, Sune suddenly pushed Sarah's head to the pie, abruptly stopping her from saying anything more. Sarah, with a face full of pie, stood up.

"What is wrong with you Sune?!" Sarah shouted.

Then, Althea slammed her hand down on the table which startled the three. She raised her voice.

"Quiet you two! Where are your manners? Do you not see that we have guest here?" Althea yelled angrily.

They felt embarrassed with their behavior. Sarah apologized while Sune bowed his head and tucked his ears back. Kiran however, unexpectedly burst into laughter. Althea, Sarah and Sune were all surprised at his reaction.

"I am sorry. I have never met a family like yours. You are too interesting," said Kiran as he tried to hold back his laughter.

After Kiran calmed down, he politely introduced himself.

"My name is Prince Kiran, son of King Malkiem of Ithuria. I, together with my kin, set out to search the forest of Eres for Algios, which our kingdom is in dire need of." Kiran explained.

"What do you mean by Algios that your kingdom needs?" Sarah frowned as she inquired.

"Algios is a source of energy that we use to fuel everything in our kingdom. Without it, we fear that we cannot protect our kingdom from the Deodarians." Kiran further explained.

Althea was curious about the Deodarians, she had never encountered them before. She asked Kiran who these Deodarians that he spoke of. He explained that the Deodarians were the archenemy of their kingdom and had always been for as long as they could remember. They are fearless people who trained both males and females to be warriors. They are fanatical about their beliefs. They live longer than them by more than a hundred years. They are twice as strong than they are and possess healing powers similar to the great Arkans. Althea raised a brow upon hearing about the Arkans. Sarah, on the other hand, had her interest even more revved up.

"Who are these Arkans" Sarah wondered.

But before Kiran could answer, Althea interrupted him,

"We should not concern ourselves with the Arkans. They are only fables."

Althea was clearly becoming uneasy about Kiran's story which in turn made Kiran secretly disagree with what Althea had said about the Arkans. He kept his silence for he felt that Althea did not want to talk about them. Disappointed that the story couldn't go on, Sarah, returned to the question about who the Deodarians were.

"I am sorry. We really do not know much about their history nor their ancestors. That is all what we know of them." Kiran answered.

"What about you? Do you know who your ancestors are?" Sarah unexpectedly asked Kiran.

"Yes… My family are the direct descendants of Varkelos, the persecuted one." Kiran answered innocently.

Althea's eyes flew wide open and her face turned paled upon hearing the name Varkelos. Her heart pounded with fear at the thought that Kiran was also a descendant of Aran. As Kiran and Sarah continued with their conversation, Althea could no longer muster the courage to face him. Painful images of Aran dying slowly in the fire were floating through her mind. She couldn't take it anymore. Althea then broke down and shouted.

"Enough!" Sarah, Sune, and Kiran were startled at Althea's burst of anger.

"Enough I say! Ithurian, you must leave immediately and go back to your people! You can't stay here anymore!" Althea got lost in her emotions while Sarah tried to reason with her.

"Quiet Sarah, I have been patient with you long enough. Now you have to obey what I say." she retorted. Sarah was stunned at the way Althea spoke to her.

"Please forgive me for being a bother, but truly, I am very grateful for the fact that you saved my life and took care of me for this past month. I am forever indebted to all of you. I shall leave tomorrow at dawn," Kiran calmly and politely responded. After saying this, he bowed and went outside the house.

The room was quiet. Sarah was upset and mad at Althea. She decided to leave the house to follow Kiran. Sune was left in the house with Althea. She sat down and began to cry. Sune approached Althea and put his head on her lap to comfort her.

Outside, Sarah searched for Kiran and found him in the barn. She immediately apologized for her mother's outburst.

"Kiran, please forgive my mother for what she said. She did not mean it. She might just be upset about my manners tonight. Please, I am sorry." Sarah explained, but Kiran only smiled at her.

"You and your mother have nothing to apologize for. It is I who needs to apologize for being a nuisance." Kiran replied.

"No, you were never a bother to me - uh, I mean to us…" Sarah quickly reverted.

Sarah told Kiran that she will take him to the edge of the forest, back to his people. Kiran was very thankful to Sarah for everything she had done for him. He told Sarah that she should visit the city sometimes and that it would be his honor to show her around, but Sarah knew that her mother would never allow her to go to the city and she already given Althea her word. At the thought of Kiran leaving, Sarah's heart was upset. She could not explain why she was having such feelings towards Kiran. She decided that it must be because she felt pity when she saw his agony for he lost his comrades… Or was it something else? A feeling or emotion like something she had never felt before.

Chapter Nine

A NEW WORLD, A NEW FEELING

It was dawn of the following day. Sarah and Sune prepare to leave the house to escort Kiran out of the forest. Althea was still in her room, hesitant to come out. Before leaving, Kiran approached Althea's room and knocked, but Althea remained inside.

"Before I go, I just wanted to say that I cannot thank you enough for all that you have done for me; for saving my life, for letting me stay in your house, and for having me as your guest from last night's dinner. I am much indebted to you for your kindness and I will surely remember it until the rest of my days" Kiran stated.

Althea wanted to face him before he leaves, but feels that she lacks the courage to do so. He walked away from the door. Althea then responded to Kiran from inside her room.

"Forgive me for my rudeness for not talking to you face to face, as my body does not feel well. My daughter and Sune will ensure your safety as they escort you out of the forest. Do take care of yourself and never return to the forest for you and your people's safety." Althea advised.

Kiran was relieved to hear that Althea was not mad at him and felt that he could leave their house without regrets.

The three left the house. Althea came out of her room and peered through the window to watch Kiran as they walked into the forest. It was painful for her to look at Kiran after learning the truth about him. She was being haunted by her past and blamed herself for all the conflict and suffering she brought to her family and to the Arkan kingdom. Memories of her father and Aran made her tearful. During those moments of sorrow, she longed to be with her sister Sorah for her strength, guidance and love.

Because Kiran hasn't fully recovered from his injuries, their journey exhausted him quickly and made him struggle to walk. Sarah asked Sune if he could ride on his back. Sune looked at Kiran and saw that he was panting, so he agreed to Sarah's request. Sune then bent down and Sarah told Kiran to get up onto Sune's back. Sune will carry him until they reached the edge of the forest.

"Is it really alright for me to ride you Sune?" asked Kiran. Sune responded with a growl.

"He said just this time only," translated Sarah.

They continued on their journey; Kiran riding Sune while Sarah walked beside them. Sarah felt uneasy around Kiran. If she had it her way, she would want him to stay and to know more about him. Sarah tried to strike a conversation with Kiran but could not think of any. Kiran noticed that Sarah was being restless.

"Are you alright Sarah? You seemed troubled by something." asked Kiran.

"No, no, no troubles here. It's just that I'll be missing you - Wait! What!" Sarah answered nervously.

Sune shook his head in awkwardness while Sarah's answer made Kiran smile.

"To be honest, I will also miss you all. Like I said before, you have an interesting family." Kiran told Sarah.

Sarah wanted to ask Kiran to stay a bit longer before going back, but after seeing her mother last night, it made her think that Kiran's being a prince might have made her feel uncomfortable. At the same time, it also worried her as she never seen her mother cry, nor be scared like that before. Sarah had always been a carefree person, but now, for the first time in her life, she was confused. Kiran noticed that Sarah still looked troubled.

"Sarah, if it is alright with you and your mother, you can visit me in the city anytime you want. I owe you a lot as well," Kiran said.

Sarah was so happy and excited to hear Kiran invited her to the city. She has never gone to any places other than their house and the forest. She has always dreamed of going to the city to see its people and their culture. But then, she suddenly remembered she promised her mother that she would not go where the Ithurians are. It made her feel frustrated. She wanted to spend more time with Kiran but was being held back by her promise to her mother. How she wishes she could have crossed her other fingers the day she made the promise and if only Sune did not tell on her. She gave Sune a fierce look, making Sune do a double take on her stare. As they reached the edge, Sarah and Sune stood stunned in seeing a large contingent of Zeltkovas and Nephatrons camped just outside the forest. The Ithurians were startled to see Kiran came out of the forest riding a large white fox. The soldiers rushed to Kiran with their weapons drawn, fearing that Sune would devour him. Sune roared and Sarah drew out her sword, ready to do battle against them. The soldiers were taken aback as they heard

Sune's frightening roar and saw Sarah. Kiran ordered them to stand down. The soldiers obeyed while Sarah and Sune were still on their guards.

"It is alright Sarah. They will not harm you as long as I am here. You can relax now," said Kiran.

Kiran got off Sune's back while Sarah sheathed her sword. Kiran, followed by Sarah and Sune, slowly approached the soldiers. A loud voice was then heard from the rear of the soldier's column.

"Out of my way! Out of my way I said! Where is my brother? Where is my beloved brother?" Kina shouted as she rushed to the front.

The moment she saw her brother Kiran alive, Kina immediately rushed towards him. Kiran smiled and said

"Hello Kina! It has been a while."

Kina then burst into tears upon hearing his brother's voice and seeing him alive. Kiran opened his arms to receive Kina. When all of a sudden, Kina punched Kiran hard in the face, knocking him down to the ground. Kina picked Kiran up holding him by his collars and shook him.

"Don't ever give that command to abandon you, ever again! Do you know how much I suffered leaving you in that wretched forest? Do you even have the slightest idea how much I worried not knowing what had happened to you? Huh, huh?" Kina angrily asked.

"It is also nice to see you again Kina" said Kiran. Kina could not hold her emotion back anymore and tightly embraced Kiran and cried like a little girl.

94

"I am so happy that you are now back. I am so happy that you are alive… I thought I would never see you again" Kina sniffled.

Sarah and Sune looked at each other, dumbfounded to see the young girl's reaction towards Kiran. Kina then saw Sarah and raised an eyebrow. She was astonished by her beauty, her tall slender body, her long black hair and her smooth fair skin were incomparable.

"And who is the girl?" Kina asked Kiran, with an irritated tone of voice.

"They saved me from the creatures that attacked us and let me stay in their house." Kiran replied. Kina pushed Kiran aside and walked towards Sarah.

"What?! you're the one who saved my brother?" asked Kina in disbelief.

"Yes we did. My name is Sarah and this is Sune. It is a pleasure to meet you," Sarah politely replied.

But Kina turned her back on Sarah and walked back to Kiran. Sune roared at her rudeness, but Sarah held him back. Kiran stood up and pulled Kina back to face Sarah and Sune.

"Listen Kina, without them I would have surely perished that day. I owe them my life, now you must show them some respect. Apologize to them," an angry frown creased Kiran's forehead.

"Please Kiran, it is alright," said Sarah, but Sune growled telling Kiran of his disappointment with Kina's attitude.

"No Sarah, my sister is wrong to treat you and Sune that way and I want her to know it." Kiran replied,

"Now apologize to them Kina." Kiran sternly told Kina. Kina was frightened as she saw her brother furiously mad at her for the first time.

"Please forgive me for my rudeness." Kina said hastily and bowed her head. Sarah felt awkward in that situation, but Sune raised his chin as if he wanted to tell Kina it served her right.

Sarah saw Kina still with her head down and noticed tears were dripping down her face. Seeing her tears made Sarah realize that Kina was not used seeing her brother being mad at her. It was the same feeling she had when she saw her mother get angry for the first time. Sarah approached Kina and took her hands.

"I know how you feel about your brother. He's mad because he cares about you so much. During the time he was with us, he kept telling us about you and how worried you must have been," Sarah explained.

Kina looked at Sarah,

"Really? My brother was worried about me?"

Sarah nodded and wiped the tears away from Kina's cheeks. Kina was very happy to hear what Sarah just told her. She stood up and shook Sarah's hand and smiled, while Kiran and Sune looked at each other, wondering what Sarah said that made Kina calm down.

The Captain of the search team informed Kina that they need to return to Ithuria immediately and that King Malkiem is waiting for Kiran's return. Kina relayed the word to Kiran and he gave the command to return to the city. The Nephatrons began to mobilize, while the Zeltkova soldiers flew in ranks as they head back towards the capital. Kina thanked Sarah one last time. Kina took a step back, spread her mechanical wings and flew to join her Zeltkovas. Sarah was amazed to the fact that they could fly. She envied them and longed to have those wings too.

"Well, I guess this is it. Thank you for everything. I really hope you would visit me in the city sometime." said Kiran.

Sarah could not give Kiran a straight answer but she really does want to visit him, she simply shook Kiran's hand.

"Take care of yourself," she said.

The two parted and went their separate ways. Kiran was taken to the air ship and flown back to Ithuria. Sarah waved at the ship as it gets farther away. There was sadness in Sarah's eyes upon seeing Kiran leave. Sune noticed and tried to comfort her. Sarah embraced Sune with teary eyes.

"Let us head back home," she said.

Sune suddenly felt something strange. Sarah asked what was wrong but Sune could not explain what it is. Sune just shrugged it off and headed back to the forest with Sarah.

Without anyone's knowledge, the whole event was being watched by Deodarian spies from a distance. The Deodarians decided to follow Sarah and Sune into the forest to gather more information about them.

Sarah and Sune reached their home and saw Althea working in the garden. Sarah felt awkward towards Althea for what happened last night and immediately walked towards the house.

"How is the prince?" Althea curiously asked.

"He was accompanied by his kin and safely returned to the city. May I be excused now Mother?" Sarah replied.

Althea was surprised at Sarah being so polite, it was very rare for her to be that way. She nodded and Sarah went inside the house. Sune approached Althea. She patted him and said:

"I'm sorry Sune if I was different last night. Please look after Sarah for me, alright?"

Weeks had passed and Sarah was still thinking about Kiran. She wanted to visit him in the city so bad but knew that her mother would not allow it. As the feeling of wanting to be with Kiran grew in her heart, she decided to go to the city without telling Althea. The only problem she has now was Sune. She knew that Sune would always follow her wherever she goes. She thought of lying to her mother and Sune about going hunting and afterward lure Sune deep into the forest to ditch him as she makes a run to the city. The next day Sarah decided to carry out her plan.

"Mother, me and Sune will go out hunting in the forest." She said casually, like always.

Althea was surprised that the formality was gone. It made Althea feel relieved, thinking that Sarah might have moved on from what happened that night with Kiran. Sarah rode Sune and headed into the forest.

"Do be careful now you two. And do bring home a big boar!" said Althea.

"I will Mother." Sarah replied.

Althea was happy that things had returned to normal between her and Sarah. After the two went into the forest, Althea started working on her garden, when suddenly, she felt the presence of intruders. She walked normally inside the house trying to avoid any suspicion from the intruders that their presence was already known. As Althea went inside, the intruders waited from a distance and quietly stalked the house. Out of nowhere, Althea suddenly attacked them from above. The intruders were caught off guard and started defending themselves from her relentless attacks, but the intruders were no match for her. Althea didn't want to kill them but instead inflicted wounds to their arms and legs in order to incapacitate them from fighting and from escaping. The captain of the intruders begged Althea for mercy and to allow them to tell her their intentions. Althea gave them a chance to explain themselves, but she was concerned about the wounds she inflicted on them. The captain revealed to her that they are Deodarians from the far south. Hearing the word Deodarians made her remember Kiran's story about them. She asked the Deodarians how they knew of her location and what their purpose was.

"What do the Deodarian want with a hermit? We have never done you any harm." asked Althea.

"My lady, we do not mean any harm. We were ordered to follow and watch the Ithurian army that came to this forest," the Deodarian captain replied.

"Follow them? But why? And how come you ended up here?" Althea retorted.

"Our people are the sworn enemy of the Ithurians. Since the days of long ago, we have been warring with them. Countless lives were lost in our battles, until the past king of Ithuria, which is Malkiem's grandfather, signed a pact with our king that made the two empires live in peace for one hundred years," the captain explained.

"Even if we are at peace at the moment, we cannot let our guards down. We have recently discovered a huge movement from the Ithurian. They sent ships to space and their army was scattered throughout the land for reasons that are still elusive to us. Our king sent out spies to watch their movements, in order to gather information so we can prepare ourselves in case they strike us. We followed the army that was sent here in the edge of the forest of Eres and we saw the prince emerged from the forest with a girl and a fox." added the captain.

Althea started to feel anxious and concerned, knowing that there were now too many people who knew of their location. She was worried that their secret might already been exposed. Suddenly, Althea was surprised to see that the Deodarians were healing themselves She was astonished after seeing that they possessed an Arkan-like power of healing.

"What are you people? Why do you have the powers of healing?" Althea's voice filled with curiosity.

"My lady, it is all thanks to your grace that we have these blessings." The captain answered, but Althea was confused and demanded a clearer explanation.

"My lady, when we followed the young girl and the fox here in the forest, we did not expect to find you living with them. Our people have been searching for you for so long, ever since the time of the great exile," the captain said.

Althea was getting more and more puzzled about what the Deodarian was telling her. She pointed her sword towards the captain for fear that they may have been searching for her so they could kill her.

"Are you looking for me to kill me as what Varkelos failed to do during the exile? Well, that's not going to happen." said Althea with a fierce look in her eyes.

"No my lady. Please, we are not from the line of Varkelos. They are our sworn enemies. Our people came from the line of Ihram." the captain pleaded.

"Ihram?" Althea clarified for she did not remember the name.

"Yes my lady. The boy you saved from death by giving him a drop of your blood -- the blood that now flows through our veins. With it, we inherited part of your Arkan powers. We are your people my lady and we as Deodarians are sworn to protect you and give our lives to your service." explained the captain.

The Deodarians approached Althea and kneeled before her, giving her their allegiance and word that they will offer their lives to protect her from the Ithurians. Althea was overwhelmed by the revelation. She asked how they knew that it was her who saved their ancestors. One of the Deodarians revealed that Ihram drew a portrait of what he remembered of her, and that portrait became their second greatest treasure.

"What is the first greatest treasure?" Althea wondered.

"The scroll of the commandments," the captain replied.

The Deodarians embraced the Arkan commandments as their ancestors did in the past. Althea was amazed to know that the commandments reached Eres and are being followed. The captain requested her to visit their kingdom to meet the people, her people, and their king; the direct descendant of Ihram, who had long been waiting for her return. Althea asked the Deodarians to return to their kingdom and to tell their king that she willfully accepts their invitation, and that she will visit their city when the need arises. The Deodarians were jubilant after hearing Althea's words and left the forest to return to their homeland. Althea was thankful that there were people out there who still followed the commandments.

In the forest, Sarah set out her plan of getting rid of Sune so she could visit Kiran in the city. They were stalking a wild boar when Sarah told Sune that they would do the usual strategy; Sune would chase the boar and lure it to the ambush point where she would kill it. Before they parted, Sarah told Sune to wait for her at the ambush point. After some time, Sune slowly approached the boar and started chasing it. He chased and lured it to the meeting point but Sarah was not there and nowhere to be found. Sune abandoned the chase and was confused at why Sarah was not there. He quickly realized that he was being deceived. He knew exactly where she was going. Sarah on the other hand, was so happy that she had finally got rid of Sune. She hastily made a run to the edge of the forest to travel towards the Ithurian city; thoughts of seeing Kiran made her so excited. She made it to the edge of the forest and began her journey to the capital. Suddenly, she was jolted with a small lighting shock. She fell to the ground, twitching. Once she came around, she saw Sune panting, glaring at her and extremely mad for being deceived by her. Sarah was surprised that Sune was able to catch up on her. She tried to talk her way out of Sune's anger, as Sune prepared to give Sarah another dose of lighting shock, Sarah went down to her knees and plead Sune to allow her to visit Kiran. Sune was taken aback to see Sarah begging.

"Please Sune, let me go see Kiran. I do not know why I feel this way but my heart is longing to see him." Sarah pleaded.

Sune did not understand Sarah's feelings. He had never seen her fixated like that towards anyone before. He was worried for her. He barked, telling Sarah that he does not agree with her going to the city.

"I do not understand myself either or why I want to see him. This feeling I have in my heart is something I have never known before and it won't not go away. I have tried many times to forget him but the more I try, the more I long for him. So please Sune help me." Sarah pleaded once more.

Sune was still uncertain about allowing her to go, but seeing Sarah implore put him in a difficult position. He saw that even Sarah was muddled about her feelings and he did not want to see her like that. In the end, Sune gave in to Sarah's plea. Sarah was glad that Sune allowed her to go, but he growled telling her that he was coming with her, which made Sarah even happier.

"Sune, you have to promise me never to tell mother about this. I do not want to worry her anymore because of my selfishness. So please Sune just this one time," begged Sarah. Sune did not have any other choice but to go along with Sarah on this. Sarah rode Sune and the two traveled to Ithuria.

After hours of traveling, they finally reached the city of Ithuria. Upon entering the city gate, the guards were alarmed to see a girl riding a large fox. The guards immediately drew their swords to stop both of them from entering.

"Halt! You with the big fox, state your purpose in coming here?" the guard asked in a commanding tone.

"I came to see Prince Kiran. Could you please tell him that Sarah and Sune are here to visit him?" Sarah replied.

Fearing what they were seeing, the guards disregarded Sarah's request and forcibly cast them out of the city. Sarah could not understand why the guards acted that why.

"Please. We are just here to see Prince Kiran. Let us pass," Sarah pleaded.

But the guards pushed Sarah violently, making her trip over and fall. Sune roared in anger. The guards were frightened by his roar and called for more soldiers to reinforce them in dealing with the beast. Sarah stood up madly.

"I have asked you politely and you dare push me?" the enraged Sarah told the soldiers.

The leader of the guard ordered Sune to be captured and to arrest Sarah for their defiance, but this time, Sarah did not hold back and fought against the guards. Word reached the captain of the Ithurian guards which is Kina. She, together with her elite Zeltkova bodyguards, went to the place of the commotion. Upon arriving at the scene, Kina saw Sune resting and Sarah knocking the last guard down. Kina's jaw dropped as she witnessed Sarah single-handedly defeated fifteen of her elite guards. Her Zeltkovas attempted to intervene but Kina stopped them and ordered them to stand down. After seeing Sarah's strength, Kina felt a bit intimidated.

"Sarah, it is nice to see you again. What brings you to Ithuria?" Kina stuttered.

"Kina! Thank goodness you're here. I just wanted to visit Kiran and these goons tried to take me forcefully." Sarah replied while she glared at the soldiers.

"My brother is doing fine and I personally thank you for that." Kina said.

Sarah was happy to hear that Kiran was fine. She wanted to see him but was too embarrassed to ask. She couldn't make up her mind whether to see him or not. To help Sarah with her hesitation, Kina decided to take Sarah to meet her brother. Sarah was relieved to hear Kina's words, which helped her overcome her confusion. Kina took Sarah and Sune to the inner city and to the castle to meet her brother. Kiran was having a discussion with his father, King Malkiem, when Kina together with Sarah and Sune came in. Kiran was happy to see Sarah and Sune and was grateful that they visited him. He quickly introduced them to the king.

"Father, these are the people whom I talked to you about. They saved my life and I truly am obligated to them. Allow me to introduce Sarah and her brother Sune." said Kiran. The king then approached Sarah and took her hands.

"Bless you my child for saving my son, my heir to the Ithurian throne. I, together with my people are truly grateful for what you have done for my son." King Malkiem said.

Sarah was honored to be thanked by the king and overjoyed to see Kiran again. At that moment, it was evident that Sarah was fascinated with everything she saw inside the castle because everything was new to her. The king noticed it and decided to personally give Sarah a tour of the castle. Sarah was delighted and likewise grateful to the king. Together with Kiran, the king showed her everything she wanted to see, which filled her heart with amazement. King Malkiem then took Sarah and Kiran to the castle's archive chamber to show paintings and scrolls and to tell Sarah the history of the Ithurian people. King Malkiem told the story of the Arkans, who they were and what powers they possessed. Sarah learned about the persecution of their ancestors under King Satorex the king of the Arkan, who later banished them to die, but they were saved by Varkelos who brought them to Eres and led them during those difficult periods. She also learned that with his perseverance and leadership, he was able to build what is now known as the Ithurian Empire. Sarah was made to believe the twisted truth about the Arkans as told by King Malkiem. Sarah was looking around the chamber when accidentally she saw a painting of a woman; a woman with black armor and wings. She asked King Malkiem who the woman in the painting was.

"She is the most ruthless Arkan ever to live. She destroyed many of my ancestors and came to be known as the slayer of a thousand souls. She is Sorah, the daughter of King Satorex." Malkiem answered with clenched fists.

Sarah was drawn to her. She felt that the woman was lonely, filled with sorrows and for an unexplained reason, she also felt a special affinity with her. Suddenly, flashes of memories came to her mind; the silhouette of a woman's face looking at her, holding her and saying words she could not understand. Kiran noticed that Sarah was totally immersed staring at the painting. He took her hand and pulled Sarah back to reality.

"Let's skip the rest of this tour and go to the city to have fun," said Kiran with a grin.

Kiran asked his father to excuse him and Sarah. He wanted to bring Sarah to town and show her around. The king graciously agreed, but before they left, the king thanked Sarah for taking the time to visit them. Kiran took Sarah outside where Sune and Kina were waiting; they saw Kiran holding Sarah's hand which made them both furious. Kiran took Sarah to town, closely followed by Sune and Kina. Kina was suddenly called by her Zeltkova bodyguards to attend another reported disturbance in the city. She did not want to leave Kiran alone with Sarah. Then Sune approached her and barked, telling her that he would keep a close watch on the two. Kina was at ease knowing that Sune will be with them. She left them to perform her duties. The three were walking down the street when Sune was distracted by the scent of roasted beef. Kiran secretly negotiated with the restaurant owner to feed Sune all the beef he wanted. Sune didn't hold back and started eating all the meat that was served before him. As Sune gobbled the beef, Kiran and Sarah made their escape from the backdoor.

"Finally! we got rid of those two," laughed Kiran.

"What? You planned this from the start?" Sarah sounded surprised.

"Well, you could say that. I wanted to spend time with you alone. Is that alright with you?" Kiran inquired.

"Huh…Yes it is totally fine with me," Sarah replied back, while her pale face turned pink.

He took Sarah to all the good places in the city. Sarah was so excited and was having so much fun with Kiran. It would seem that Sarah was starting to fall for Kiran. She still did not understand her feelings, but she was sure that she wanted to be with Kiran forever. Afterwards, the two took some time to rest. Kiran brought her to a garden and sat together on a bench.

"Everything I've seen here is amazing!" Sarah said in excitement.

"Then you should come here often," Kiran replied.

"I think I had more fun in the city than in the castle. Oops! No offense to your father," Sarah blurted.

"None taken! And for that I would like to apologize." Kiran responded.

"Apologize for what?" she wondered.

"Well, about what my father told you about the Arkans and our people." said Kiran,

"Why is that?" Sarah asked. She was confused about Kiran having different views with his father.

"To be honest with you, it is difficult for me to believe that the Arkans were bad. I mean, our temple priest kept on preaching those stories countless times, but the more I hear about them, the more doubt it casts in my mine. The Deodarians the people I spoke of before, embraced the Arkan law, which is also the reason that the conflict between our two empires started. They are fierce and brave warriors. They would only react if they were provoked, but otherwise, they are a peaceful people," Kiran explained.

Sarah was not paying attention to what Kiran was saying. Instead, her heart raced as she discovered Kiran's gentle side. She was getting confused about the emotion she's feeling towards him and unwittingly slide closer to Kiran. Kiran then turned and their eyes accidentally met. The sound of Sarah and Kiran's hearts pounding can be heard and Kiran was momentarily enchanted and drawn to her beauty. In the heat of the moment, Kiran slowly moved his head closer to kiss Sarah. Both eyes closed and as their lips were about to touch, a loud belch was heard that startled the two. They saw Sune looking at them, steaming mad. Sarah suddenly felt embarrassed towards Kiran.

"I'm sorry. It is getting late and I think we should be heading back home. I had so much fun today. Thank you very much for showing me around." said Sarah as she hid her blushing face. She hurriedly got up on Sune's back.

"Wait Sarah, ah … thank you also for visiting me today. Please do come back again," said Kiran.

He tried to approach Sarah, but Sune gave him a piercing look, which made him step back. Sarah and Sune left the city and headed back to the forest. Their sudden departure made Kiran thought that he might have offended Sarah by his actions. Kiran was perplexed and regret trying to kiss her. Sarah and Sune finally arrived home. It is rare for them to come back home late and without a boar in their hands.

"I am sorry Mother. We did not get any wild boar today. We will try tomorrow," Sarah wearily said.

Sarah immediately went to her room to rest, while Althea looked at Sune and wondered if anything interesting happened that day. Sune simple shook his head and then quickly fell asleep because of exhaustion.

That night, a storm came thundering down the forest. While Sarah and Sune sleep soundly, Althea was restless, she was having a dream, and in her dream she saw her sister Sorah coming at her wielding the Fire of Justice. She woke up startled at the sound of the thunder. She was panting and frightened. She imagined that the dream may be a sign of something to come -- something bad that was about to happen. Tears slid down her cheeks as she remembers about the dream and hoped that what she saw doesn't turn into a reality.

Chapter Ten

THE ENCOUNTER

Six months had passed since the Ithurian started their space exploration in search of energy outside the planet Eres. Five air ships were launched from each kingdom and so far none yielded a favorable result. Most of the explorers had already lost hope amidst the search. The space explorers traveled farther away into the outer realm with hopes of finding new stars that could house rich deposits of Algios.

One day, a group of explorers from the kingdom of Ithuria embarked on further searching the space for new planets, when all of a sudden, they were caught in a strong and violent turbulence in space. They struggle to maneuver the ship behind an orbiting moon to shield them from the turbulence. They were astonished to see that a wormhole was the source of the turbulence. The force of the wormhole was so immense that lightning fields surrounded the whole funnel of nebula. The ship's scanner suddenly indicated Algios readings in the other end of the wormhole. The explorers had finally found the Algios they'd been long searching for, but they need to cross the dangerous path to get to it. The crew of the ship bravely gone through the wormhole to the other side. They were all but too happy to finally get a hold of what they had been searching for – though they need to move really fast because they're running out of time.

The ship started to enter the funnel. The force was getting stronger and stronger as they traveled further within the middle of the hole. Tremendous force shook the ship but it managed to hold up until they were able to escape the uproar and finally came out on the other end. The commander was relieved that they made it through in one piece. The scanner spotted high concentrations of Algios in that star system. It pointed to the coordinates of a particular planet which they immediately set their ship's course to. Upon reaching, the explorers were again stunned to see the origin of the signal. They saw the green planet and how magnificent it looks from afar. It was ten times bigger than Eres. The crew confirmed that deposits of Algios were identified on that same planet. The commander immediately ordered his men to land the ship and to start investigating the surface.

Upon arriving at the green planet, one of the crew member confirmed the location of the Algios. They took samples to test and discovered that the Algios they found was the purest form of energy, it can fuel a ship and last for decades. Right in that instant, they brought out their Nephatrons for security, as well as huge drilling equipment to excavate the Algios. As they were about to start drilling the ground, a huge fire ball blasted towards them and destroyed the drilling machine. The crew members were caught off guard. They began to panic until the commander ordered his men to take arms and prepare to defend the site. They positioned themselves in a defensive formation and waited for the enemy. As the smoke receded, they saw winged beings walking towards them. As they approached, the explorers noticed that all of the winged beings were female, their hands glowing and forming what seemed like a sword. The commander ordered to open fire. And right there, the battle began.

They flew in swiftly and attacked the Ithurian explorers to no end. The Nephatrons got destroyed easily. The explorers tried their hardest to stop them from pulverizing their equipment. Clearly, they were no match for the winged beings. The commander then gave the signal to retreat and head back to the ship. Everyone ran in panic as they fear for their lives. Everyone boarded the ship and hurriedly launched into space. They were chased by the winged beings who continuously blasting their ship with fire. After seeing that most parts of the ship were destroyed, the winged beings let the Ithurians go. The commander ordered to proceed to the wormhole and back to Eres. They had to inform the king about the events that happened in the green planet.

The planet that the Ithurian landed on was Treliseum; the home world of the Arkans. The captain of the Arkan warriors sent a messenger to Avetus to inform Altrus Sorah about the incident. When the word reached Altrus Sorah, she was perturbed at the fact that someone dared to trespass their domain – especially that it has remained peaceful for three millennia. She immediately ordered her warriors to investigate who or what race invaded their land, and deployed more warriors to protect Fostrum. Suddenly, a voice called on to Altrus Sorah.

"Mother, may I have a moment with you?"

"Yes *Narie* what is it?" Sorah answered.

Then from the shadow where the voice was heard emerged a young girl. She was Sorah's second child and her name is Narie. Narie was three Arkan years younger than Sorah's first born. She was a strong and wise warrior who possessed an ardent sense of justice just like her mother. Narie offered to lead the probe to hunt down the intruders. Sorah consented to her request on the condition that the elite warriors were to accompany her. All of the elite warriors during the new age of the Arkan were female; in fact, Arkans who were born after the Great War were females. This was the effect of the abnormal way of reproduction. Since then, the Arkan race became predominately female second age warriors.

Narie bid her mother farewell to go to Fostrum. But before she left, Sorah approached her and gave her a hug.

"Be careful out there now. Come back immediately once you find something," warned Sorah.

"Yes Mother I will, and I promise you I will find them and make them pay for their transgression." Narie answered sternly.

Narie then met with *Heres, Kinara, Una, Antra, and Aril,* the five elite warriors that will accompany her on the mission. They proceeded to Fostrum to begin the search.

After Narie and the warriors left the court hall, Sorah went to her chamber to reflect on the incident. It has been ages since they went to battle. She suddenly remembered the Great War and it pained her to think of the bitterness it brought. She brought out and opened her precious chest and took out a painting of Aran together with her holding their first born. She never told Narie about her sister Sarah, she thought that it was best for Narie to never know about the pain and sorrows of the past. Sorah blamed the war for the death of her child. It made her cry every time she thought about her first born's unfortunate fate.

Because of the miseries the war brought, Sorah became more protective of her second child. She loved Narie so much and promised herself to never lose anyone she loves again. With the unfortunate fate her first born suffered, it worried her so much of Narie's safety each time she goes on a mission. To ensure Narie's safety, Sorah will always have the elite warriors accompany her wherever she would go. Upon putting the painting back, she accidentally dropped the chest and everything that was inside scattered all over the floor. She hurried to gather her things. As she scrambled through the items, she saw the painting of herself and her younger sister Althea. Sorah couldn't make out what she felt: it was a mixture of both love and hatred. Love -- because Althea was her one and only sister whom she promised to protect and hatred for the betrayal she committed that led to her sorrows. She hastily put the painting away and tried to compose herself before returning back to her duties.

Narie arrived at the scene of the battle and quickly noticed that the objects that were left behind by the intruders seemed foreign to them. Eager to find out where the enemy came from, Narie touched one piece of the object and used her ability to see through the past. She saw that they came from the gateway of the fallen and their home world was a small blue planet located somewhere at the other side of the gateway. Everything that came after then became vague. She asked Prea, the captain of the elite warriors, to personally handle and lead the defense of Fostrum while she and her five warriors would travel to the other side to find the enemy. She and the five warriors transformed to their armored forms, spread their wings and flew towards the gateway of the fallen to begin the hunt.

The explorers barely got out of the wormhole; the lightning fields further damage and broken their already crippling ship, which made it impossible for them to return back to Eres. The commander decided to land on the orbiting moon and try to salvage whatever they could. As they landed, they began to do the repair while the commander attempt to establish communication with Ithuria. Suddenly, the crew noticed that the air tank was damaged. Time was running out for them as well. He recorded all of his findings and sent the message into space and hoped that it will reach Ithuria as soon as possible.

Three days had passed and the message of the doomed explorers reached Eres. As the Ithurians analyzed the message, they were amazed to learn that the explorers were able to find the energy they needed, but awe turned to shock as they continued to analyze it. Without any more delay, the researchers handed the message to Prince Kiran. Kiran then called forth the Alliance of the Kings to relay the crucial findings.

Similar to the reaction of the researchers, the kings were exultant to learn that they finally found the supply of energy, but as Kiran continued, he explained that in order to reach the planet where the energy was, they would have to cross a wormhole which would take a month to reach. Kiran further discussed the inhabitants of that planet. He showed orbital images of the green planet's surface and saw two huge cities: one city had a wall and a gate in the middle. After seeing the cities, the kings stared at one another with mutual unease. Kiran afterward, presented the disturbing images taken by the explorers during their battle with the unknown beings. Everyone in the Council room looked harrowed to see how easily the Nephatrons were decimated. They could not believe the strength and speed of the attackers, until they saw that they had wings and wielded the power of fire. As they see it unfold, King Malkiem stood up and pointed his finger to the image.

"Arkans! The Arkans! We have found the Arkan planet!" King Malkiem shouted.

Everyone in the Council room was shocked to realize that the Arkans were the inhabitants of the newly found planet. They never imagined that they were real. For the longest time, the Arkans were perceived as merely fables and legends. But, upon seeing those images, the truth could no longer be denied.

"Then, we stumbled upon the Arkan planet, the planet Treliseum, as written in the ancient text," King Turloch's voice trembled.

"This is bad. They might attack us at any moment as we speak. King Satorex was written to be a vengeful king." King Ull spoke with fear.

"Nonsense Ull, we are ready to face the Arkan. Our technology was created specifically to combat them if the time comes, and that time is now. I say we go to war with the Arkans!" King Gileal said proudly.

"Silence you old fool, have you not seen how easily they destroyed the Nephatrons, how easily they repulsed our soldiers?" King Ull replied angrily.

"You are the fool and a coward Ull. Our soldiers didn't expect it when they were attacked. They were unprepared. But if we face them in the battlefield, our strength and numbers will surely overthrow those cursed Arkans." King Gileal answered back.

"Who are you calling a coward you old bigot!" King Ull retorted.

"Enough Both of you! We are facing a crisis here and we need to be united as one and not divided," King Kelon reprimanded.

The Alliance's views were clearly at odds. King Malkiem knew that they need the crucial Algios for the empire to survive, but he also knew so well the hatred he hold towards the Arkans for the injustice they committed against their ancestors. He wanted revenge and he had been waiting for the chance to finally face the Arkans in battle.

King Malkiem wanted to let the people know of their situation and desires to win their support to go the war. The kings will then vote based on what their constituent want. Kiran did not support the idea of war and believed that they should look for other alternatives than force. He pleaded to the Alliance to consider negotiating with the Arkans, but King Gileal and Kelon only laughed at that idea.

"Prince Kiran, surely you cannot reason with savages. Did you not see what they did to our soldiers? They just attacked them! And we should negotiate with them? Absurd!" said King Gileal.

"But we are the ones who trespassed their domain. They had every right to defend their territory!" Kiran responded.

"Varkelos the persecuted one, had written in the ancient text that Fostrum belongs to our ancestors which we Ithurians, the seed of Varkelos, have every right to reclaim it." King Kelon said in support of King Gileal.

"But-" Kiran tried to respond but was stopped by his father, King Malkiem.

"Enough Kiran, we the Alliance of the Kings will decide what is best for our kingdoms and I ask you my son to stand down," King Malkiem advised.

Kiran was still adamant on convincing the kings. Kina on the other hand, held him back.

"Brother, let us wait for the votes and deliberation. For now, we cannot convince them yet since their views differ." Kina said.

Kiran agreed with Kina and decided to be patient instead.

Meanwhile, Narie and her warriors had exited the wormhole. She used the memories she saw from the object she touched to locate the intruders' home planet. As she saw the vast galaxies from the other side, she realized that it would be difficult to find them. One of her warriors discovered that the intruders' ship had crashed at the nearby moon. They hastily went down to investigate the vessel. Narie went inside to see if there were survivors left hiding inside, but all they found were lifeless bodies floating around. The explorers evidently ran out of air and eventually died.

Narie saw the commander still strapped to his seat. She approached him and took his hand to look into his past. She clearly saw from the commander's memories the location of their home planet, their people and their city. Narie and her warriors exited the ship and swiftly flew to where the blue planet was.

In Eres, word about the existence of the Arkans was made known to the people across the empire. The kings deliberated and tried to gain the support of the people to go to war against their ancestor's oppressors. The people from the kingdom of Amara and Sodaria are in full support of the war. Minea and Enor on the other hand, remained cautious and conservative, while the rest Ithuria was divided. One group believed that war is the answer, while the other wanted to seek peace with the Arkans. The empire was divided and King Malkiem wanted to have a unified stance of his people before making a decision.

King Gileal and King Kelon encouraged King Malkiem to decide right away before it is too late. The two told him that they need to mobilize the entire army immediately since it will take a month of journey to reach Treliseum. They couldn't afford to have the Arkan make the first move. They reminded King Malkiem that he has the sacred duty to avenge their ancestors for the injustice the Arkans had done to them. King Turloch and King Ull remained silent.

"I know how you feel. Gileal, Kelon my old friends, what more can a descendant of Varkelos yearn for but to avenge their ancestors. But as your supreme king, I also have an obligation to our people. If we go to war with them, I want the people to be with me with all their hearts and loyalty and would sincerely sacrifice all that they have -- their lives included -- to defend this cause"

"This is the Arkans that we are talking about here! They have powers that we cannot comprehend, with strength far stronger than the strongest of the Deodarian and their valor to die for their king is unmatched." King Malkiem stated.

King Gileal and King Kelon soon realized that it was indeed a huge gamble to face the Arkans in battle and that he was right about needing the support of the entire people for them to claim victory. The kings convened and returned to their respective kingdoms. For the days that followed, King Kelon and King Gileal began to launch a black propaganda, painting the Arkans as evil in order to gain the sympathy of the people so that the war that they have long yearned for could be justified.

The Deodarian spies lurking within the four kingdoms were able to gathered all the information they needed and sent a messenger back to Deodara to report everything to King Zairel. King Zairel was jubilant to know that the Arkan home world has finally been found. He could never imagine that their belief in the Arkan and their acceptance of the commandments would someday prove to be the right path. The king informed his people of the good news and everyone was overjoyed. Prince Vasuril then asked his father what their stance going to be. The king contemplated for a moment and said:

"We will wait for our savior to come and she will guide us to the right path that we need to take."

Chapter Eleven

THE FEELING OF KINSHIP

arie finally found the blue planet where the intruders originated from and swiftly soared through the atmosphere and below the clouds to observe the surface from above. Narie and the warriors saw six cities built throughout the cardinal points of the planet and the biggest of them all was Ithuria. They called it the middle city. Narie wanted to avoid being seen by the enemy, thus, she decided to land somewhere away from the cities, away from the Ithurian eyes and from there travel by foot. She and her warriors chose to land near the forest of Eres and began to examine its atmosphere. One of the warrior tested the air and found it breathable and safe. They transformed themselves into their normal appearance, sealing their wings and armored form.

Narie wanted to investigate as much ground she could, she decided to divide her warriors into two groups. She took Una and Aril with her, while Heres, Kinara and Antra made up the other group. Heres asked which side they should take. Before Narie could answer, she suddenly felt something strange, something familiar yet unknown voice was calling on to her. She turned around and the voice grew stronger when she faced the forest of Eres. She told Heres to take her group and head towards the city while she takes the forest to investigate. The warriors looked at one another.

"Are you sure Narie? The enemy's city is this way," Una reminded her.

"I know but there is a strange feeling that tells me to go this way," Narie replied.

Una and Aril clung to each other frightened after hearing what Narie said. Heres hit the two on the head.

"You two are part of the elite warriors and are tasked to protect Narie and you easily got scared by this?" Heres mocked.

Narie instructed Heres to bring her group and make haste to the city and find out as much as she can about its people. Afterwards, she instructed them to meet at the middle city (Ithuria). She strictly forbade the warriors to use their powers in front of the inhabitants and ordered them to disguise themselves and blend in with the people in order to move around freely without raising suspicion that might alarm the enemy. After Narie's final instructions, the two groups went their separate ways.

After hours of walking, Heres saw the city of Ithuria from a distance and reached their first goal. They dressed themselves like locals and walked together with the people. The three successfully passed the guards and entered the city unchallenged. They proceeded to their next objective, which is to start gathering critical information about the enemy. Meanwhile, Narie and her group had walked for hours exploring the forest.

"Narie, do we have to go this far? There is nothing here but trees, trees and trees! The enemy would not live here," Aril complained.

"I agree with Aril. Let us head back to the city together with Heres," Una said in support of Aril's proposition.

But Narie was completely entranced by the sensation and the voice that kept calling her. They went deeper and deeper in to the forest until they reached the point where Narie could no longer sense it anymore.

"What's wrong Narie?" asked Una.

"It stopped -- the voice. I can't hear or sense it anymore," Narie replied.

As they continued talking, they suddenly felt that they were being stalked. They quickly summoned their Serdeus and took a defensive stance. An eerie silence settled in the forest as they stood on their guard waiting for the prowlers to make the first move. When suddenly, the surrounding trees were shaken. They became restless after realizing that they were being surrounded by enemies they couldn't yet see. Then, giant predators rushed in and attacked them. Seeing the ferocious giant predators, Narie ordered Una and Aril to use their Arkan power to fight the creatures. They transformed into their armor form and flew straight to the creatures without fear, killing as many they could. Narie and the two warriors stumbled across the monsters' nest, which triggered a horde of creatures rushing in to them. Narie knew that they can't hold the creatures for long.

"Una, Aril, retreat and make a run for it. I'll try to hold them back!" shouted Narie.

"No Narie! We stay and fight together," Una countered.

"We need to move out quickly or else we will die here! You and Aril make an escape path and I will follow you as soon as you move out!" Narie yelled back.

The two warriors combined their strengths and start carving their way out of the nest, while Narie stood her ground, holding back the hordes from moving forward. Una and Aril fought hard to create a crack in the creature's encirclement until they managed to break through.

"Let's go Narie! This way!" shouted Una.

Narie heard Una and as she turned around to run to them, a creature suddenly lunged forward and whipped Narie with its tail, hitting her in the head, knocking her unconscious and thrown off in a deep ravine. Una and Aril were distraught to see what happened to Narie. They tried to reach for her but the ravaging hordes blocked them. Aril then pulled Una out.

"We can't leave Narie behind," Una's voice trembles in panic.

"Yes, we will come back for her later. For now, we need to get out of here or else all of us will die," Aril replied while pulling Una's arm.

Aril and Una hurriedly flew to escape the hordes, but could not fly high enough as they were gridlocked by the long reach of the giant predators. They used the cover of the trees to escape the seemingly unending chase of the creatures. Narie falls down the ravine, hitting the rocks tumbling over and over until she fell into a river that carried her downstream, further into the forest.

On the next day, while Sarah and Sune were bathing in the river, Sune saw something strange further up by the riverbed and quickly ran to check it. His eyes bulged as he saw a young girl bruised, bloodied and lying half-dead. Sune immediately called the attention of Sarah who was still bathing. Sarah did not answer. He called to her again and again, but was ignored. Sune then released a small dose of lighting shock into the water, giving Sarah a painful jolt.

"Ouch! Sune what are you doing?!Are you crazy? You could have killed me!" yelled Sarah angrily and twitching.

Finally, Sune got Sarah's attention and made her come to him. Just the same, Sarah stood motionless and in shock to see a young girl lying there.

"Is she still alive?" asked Sarah.

Sune gesturing that she is alive but barely. Sarah saw her badly bruised and that her leg was dislocated. She decided to bring her home with them but Sune faced Sarah with a look telling her, "What about your mother?"

"We cannot leave her here like this. We need to help her," Sarah urged.

Without any argument, Sune agreed for the first time. Sarah gently picked the young girl up, placed her on Sune's back, and returned home straightaway. Althea was at the barn when she heard Sarah calling on to her. She went out and once again was shocked to see Sarah bringing home another injured person.

"Sarah! Did I not tell you to stop bringing-" Althea abruptly stopped as soon as she saw Narie's face. She immediately felt a distinct affinity towards her.

"Quickly Sune, take her inside the house. We must treat her wounds." said Althea hysterically.

Sarah and Sune looked at each other, dumbfounded after seeing Althea's reaction. Surely they expected her to blaze in anger but it was the opposite. Sarah laid Narie down on her bed and Althea asked her to fetch some water to clean the wounds. Althea looked at the young girl's face and for a brief moment, she saw Sorah's face in her youthful years.

Althea started to worry again about unknown people staying with them. But every time she looked at the young girl, she sensed a different, yet familiar feeling about her. Sarah came back in with the water.

"Can you heal her Mother?" Sarah asked with concern.

"Yes, I must try, but I can sense that she is strong," Althea replied.

"Sarah, would you be kind enough to take Sune with you into the forest and find out if she has any kin with her," Althea requested.

"Sure Mother. I will leave immediately," Sarah responded urgently.

"Sarah, take warm clothes with you. You and Sune might need to spend the night out there and please do be careful." Althea reminded Sarah.

"Yes Mother we will."

Sarah rode Sune and dashed into the forest to find the girl's kin. Althea went back to her room and started healing Narie. She kept being reminded of Sorah every time she looked at her face. Then, Althea remembered her dream, the dream seeing Sorah coming towards her wielding the fire of justice. It frightened her with the thought that Narie could be a sign of something to come. Nevertheless, Althea used her Arkan powers to heal Narie's injuries.

The next day, Narie woke up feeling dazed and confused. She looked around and found herself in an unfamiliar place. The door opened and Althea came in to bring medicines for her. Althea was startled to see that Narie had woken up so soon after obtaining those injuries.

"Oh, you're already awake," said Althea in amazement.

"Where am I? Who are you?" Narie was still bemused and scared.

"You are in our home. Sune found you injured and unconscious at the riverbed" Althea replied.

Narie tried to get up but was too weak to do so.

"Don't force yourself. You need rest. Your wounds have not yet healed and your leg still needs time before you can stand up and walk," Althea warned.

"What happen to my leg?" Narie curiously asked.

Narie pulled out the bed sheet and saw her dislocated leg. She sat upright on the bed and tries to recall what happened before she got to Althea's place. Suddenly, she remembered being attacked by the creatures, and that Una and Aril were still out there.

"I need to go. My warriors are still out there, fighting the creatures!" Narie blurted.

"Warriors?" the confused Althea asked.

Narie remembered that they could not tell the inhabitants who they were.

"I meant my aide. There were three of us that set forth to this forest and I'm afraid that the creatures might have, might have…" Narie cried at the thought that her warriors may have been killed. Althea then approached Narie and hold her in her arms patting her head.

"Come now. You do not have to worry about your friends. I sent my daughter and Sune to find them. They will be back soon, together with your friends. I promise." She soothed with a gentle voice.

Narie was surprised when Althea embraced her and hearing her gentle voice made her remember her mother's calming touch. Narie was about to hug Althea back when she realized that it was not her mother she was talking to. Instead, she leaned back to escape the caring arms of Althea.

"I am sorry. I just remembered someone." said Narie while wiping the tears away.

"It is alright my child. You do not have to worry about anything as long as you're with us." Althea assured her.

"Pardon me for saying this, but you sent your daughter to look for my aide in the forest. It is very dangerous out there. The creatures that attacked us almost got me killed," said Narie, very concerned.

"You do not have to worry again about anything. My daughter is strong you know. She can take care of herself and find your friends. Now, rest my child and we will talk again later," Althea replied.

Althea put the blanket around Narie to warm her, and tucked her back into the bed and went outside the room. Althea was confused about the feelings she was having towards Narie. She did not know anything about her and yet she sensed that she's part of her -- a feeling she had not felt for a long time.

In the forest, Una and Aril were still being hunted and chased by the creatures. They were so tired from escaping and evading the predators. They sealed their armors away as those were just slowing them down. Both were wounded from battling the creatures all night, but the persistent creatures kept on coming.

130

"I'm sorry Aril, but I think I have reached my limit. Please go on without me... I will hold them off," said Una exhaustedly.

"No, we will fight together and die together." Aril shouted.

"What a waste... we just got here and now we are about to die," Una said grimly.

The two smiled and held on to each other to make their last stand. As the creatures were about to devour them, Sarah appeared and slashed the creature that was about to kill the two. Una and Aril were surprised to see that someone suddenly jumped in to save them. They saw Sarah's back as she slowly walked towards the hordes, then Sune appeared.

"Sune, protect them. I'll deal with the hordes," Sarah told Sune.

Sune stood guard near Una and Aril. The two were daunted seeing a creature like Sune. They could not do anything due to their injuries and compels them to sit down near a tree were Aril tended to Una's wounds. The hordes ran towards Sarah and in turn she attacked the creatures head on, slashing and killing them easily. Una and Aril were amazed to see Sarah's strength and speed. They could not believe that she was killing the creatures with great ease. After killing many of the creatures, the horde finally retreated.

"Look Sune, we killed a lot of the baddies today. We will have a feast tonight," said Sarah playfully.

Una and Aril gawked seeing Sarah and still could not believe that she defeated the horde all by herself. They never had thought that the inhabitants of that planet were that strong. Sarah then approached the two.

"Come! I will take you to our house and treat your wounds." said Sarah.

"We thank you for saving our lives, but we need to go back there. One of our kin was left there in the creatures' nest," Una panted.

"Your friend is safe and she is in our house. My mother is treating her injuries. Sune found her yesterday near the river," Sarah explained.

The two warriors were so happy to hear the news from Sarah and were relieved to know that Narie was alive and safe. The two burst into tears.

"I thought we lost Narie! How would we explain it to her mother if something bad happened to her?!" Aril wailed.

"It is alright now Aril. Narie is safe and so are we," said Una.

"We thank you for saving Narie and both of us today. We owe you our lives and will be forever grateful to you."

"Come, we must go. We need to treat your wounds immediately." Sarah replied.

Sune took Aril on his back, while Sarah picked Una up and carried her as well.

"By the way, I am Sarah and this is my brother Sune. We live here in the forest with my mother. How about the three of you. Where did you come from?" Sarah inquired.

"I am Una. This is Aril and the other one under your mother's care is Narie. We came from a city farther from the North and were looking for the middle city." Una lied.

"Middle city? What is that?" Sarah asked again.

"The largest among the six cities we saw when we came here." Una cautiously replied.

"You mean the city of Ithuria! Well, indeed it is the biggest city here in Eres," Sarah answered.

"This star is called Eres?" Una's eyes widened upon hearing what she said.

"Yes. I am surprised you did not know that even though you were born here," Sarah sneered.

Eres, which meant hope in the Arkan language, was the first thing that came to Una's mind. She was wondering whether there was any relation to them or was it just pure coincidence. Due to their exhaustion, Aril already fallen asleep while Una tried to keep her thoughts awake, but Sarah told her to take some rest for it will be a while before they could reach the house. Una did not hesitate in taking Sarah's advice.

The four finally arrived home and were met by Althea who was waiting for them at the porch. She saw Aril and Una still asleep. Althea asked Sarah and Sune to bring them to her room to clean them and treat their wounds. Althea gave Sarah and Sune a hug for making it back safe and thanked them for finding Narie's kin. They let the three rest for the meantime.

The next morning, Una and Aril woke up and saw Sarah putting bandages over their wounds. Sarah already cleaned them up with fresh clothing to wear and was now finishing up on the bandaging. Una asked if they could see Narie, so Sarah escorted both of them outside the bedroom and saw Althea preparing breakfast in the kitchen.

"Good morning! It is good to see that both of you are fine," said Althea cheerily.

Una and Aril felt awkward towards Althea, for they did not know who she was or how to address her.

"Let me introduce you to my mother. Mother, this is Una and Aril," said Sarah.

"It is an honor to meet the mother of the one who saved us," replied Una while bowing her head.

"Please let us see Narie." Aril requested urgently.

Althea then took the two inside Sarah's room, and there they saw Narie still resting. They quickly ran towards Narie and embraced her out of happiness.

"Narie! Narie! we thought we lost you. We're sorry for not being there when you were in danger," the two said.

The emotions of the two suddenly woke Narie up from her sleep. She got stunned to see Una and Aril by her side. The three burst into tears for surviving such a terrible ordeal and for finally being reunited. Narie then saw Sarah for the first time and could not take her eyes off her.

"Forgive me for my rudeness as I have not introduced myself yet. My name is Narie and these are my kin, Una and Aril."

"We are foreigners from this land and we came from the south." Narie said.

Una and Aril wanted to tell Narie about where they were from but it was already too late.

"The South? I thought you came from far north. Una told me yesterday," asked Sarah, confused.

Narie looked at the two and they nodded.

"I am so sorry. I may still be dazed. Yes, we came from the far north," Narie quickly corrected.

Althea approached Narie while holding Sarah.

"Well it is a pleasure to know all of you. My name is Althea and this is my daughter Sarah," said Althea.

Sarah approached Narie and offered her hand. Suddenly, after shaking her hand, Narie felt an immense power within Sarah. Right in that instant, she also saw a silhouette image of a woman speaking of words that could not be understood. She accidentally saw vague memories of Sarah, even though Sarah didn't know anything about her past after Althea kept it from her. As she looked into Sarah's memories, Narie gazed at her and unwittingly squeezed her hand with force – thing that made Sarah take it as if Narie was trying to challenge her on purpose.

Narie then felt pain in her leg. Althea knew that she and Sarah need to put her leg joint back into place. Althea asked Una and Aril to step outside for a while as she and Sarah will have to treat her leg.

"Sarah you put the leg back while I hold Narie," said Althea.

"Wait, is this going to hurt much?" asked Narie, worried.

"No, you won't even feel anything." said Sarah. Narie somewhat felt reassured.

Althea held Narie's hands while Sarah positioned herself holding Narie's leg. Sarah abruptly twisted Narie's leg back in place, which gave Narie a pain that she never felt before.

"That hurt! You said I wouldn't feel any pain! You lied!" screamed Narie while she grimaced in pain and crying.

"Well sorry princess. I guess it slipped my mind," said Sarah with a grin.

Una and Aril heard Narie's scream and wanted to go inside but were stopped by Sune who stood at the door preventing them from entering. The two decided to sit down and wait after looking at Sune's daunting face. Sarah came out of the room and called Sune to join her go hunting.

"Is Narie alright?" asked Aril.

"Yeah She's fine, but she's such a crybaby!" Sarah replied.

The two went inside the bedroom, while Narie still nurse her pain. Althea walked out of the room and left the three alone.

"Thank you very much for all the help you have provided. We will surely repay you for all your kindness," said Una.

"You don't have to. It is our obligation to help those in need." Althea said.

Althea came out of the bedroom and staggered to her feet. She grabbed a chair and sat down, frightened by what she saw through Narie's memories when she held her hands. She saw her home world Treliseum, their city Avetus and the image of her sister Sorah. For a moment, she suspected that Narie and her two friends could be Arkans, but she may be wrong. It made her restless, confused and scared at the thought that her dream is turning into a reality. Even though Althea already knew that the three were Arkans, she took great caution not to let Narie know about her and Sarah's past. She will do anything to protect Sarah from the people whose only wish is to harm them.

They were having dinner with Una and Aril that night while Narie still resting in bed.

"By the way, where were you headed before you got lost here in the forest?" Althea tried to know their motives.

"We were supposed to go to the middle city to meet our friends," Una somehow stuttered in answering.

"She mean the city of Ithuria." Sarah clarified.

"May I ask what's your purpose of going to Ithuria?" Althea once again asked.

"We are travelers from far north and we wanted to do trade with the city," Una answered.

Althea could clearly see that the two were tense as they answered, so she stopped asking any more questions.

"If you would permit, could we still stay here until Narie's leg is healed and able to walk?" Aril pleaded.

"You could stay here for as long as you want. I mean, we seldom get to have guests anyway. Right, Mother?" said Sarah.

Althea stared at Sarah for deciding on her own and knew that she could not take back Sarah's words, for it will be rude. In the end, she just gritted her teeth and went along with Sarah.

"Yes of course, you could stay here until Narie fully recovers and when that time comes, my daughter Sarah and Sune will escort you out of the forest safely." Althea replied.

"Thank you very much for your kindness. Truly, we never thought that people like you still existed in this world," said Una with teary eyes.

"Please don't cry! Now, let us eat before the meal gets cold." said Sarah.

Sarah was very happy and excited to have made friends with people who were close to her age. Althea on the other hand, was doubtful of the three and hoped that she could hold on to hiding their secrets until the time they leave.

Back at Ithuria, Heres, Antra and Kinara learned that the Ithurians were the descendants of the Arkans who were banished by King Satorex after the Great War thousands of years ago. They were surprised to learn that they managed to survive the exile and have long been thriving on that planet which they called Eres. They also learned the reason they came to Treliseum and the threat of war that awaits the Arkans. Heres ordered Antra and Kinara to return to Avetus immediately and inform Altrus Sorah of what they found, while she will stay behind to gather information and wait for Narie's return. Antra and Kinara hurriedly left the city and then Eres for the journey back to Avetus, bearing the news that would surely ignite the flame of hatred between Sorah and the seeds of Varkelos.

Chapter Twelve

SEEDS OF THE BETRAYERS

everal days has passed since the three warriors took refuge in Althea's house. Narie is now able to walk again with the aid of a crutch. Una was helping Althea with the everyday house chores while Aril took care of Narie as they sat by the porch and basked in the peace and tranquility of the forest,

"Good morning crybaby! How's your leg?" Sarah intentionally tries to annoy Narie.

"Well, I'm doing fine. Thank you very much monkey girl" Narie countered with a smirk on her face.

Aril told Narie that Sarah jumped out of trees a lot when she saved them from the creatures. It made her furious when Narie called her a monkey. Sarah turned to face Narie and confronted her with a threatening stare.

"What did you just call me?" asked Sarah.

"You heard me monkey girl!" she repeated. She wanted to give Sarah a dose of her own medicine.

"You better take back your word crybaby or I'll…" but before Sarah could continue, Narie stood up, stared at her close in the face and said:

"Or you'll what?"

The two engaged in a close stare down while Aril and Sune tried to break them off.

"What is all the commotion about?" asked Una.

"Don't mind them. They're just kids being kids," Althea sighed then continued her chore.

The quarrel between the two has continued to go on every time they cross paths. Althea and the others had to put up with Sarah and Narie's little feud every day and it has been like that ever since. Narie's leg was completely healed and was able to walk on her own. She plans to leave for Ithuria as soon as she completely recuperates. During dinner that night, Sarah was seated across Narie. Sune, Una and Aril kept glancing from left to the right as they observe the tension building up in the room. It was quiet at the start. Althea was enjoying her dinner when suddenly:

"Could you please pass me some water?" Narie asked Aril.

"I'll get it." Sune, Una and Aril were all struck to hear Sarah.

Sarah slowly poured the water down Narie's cup while everyone took a deep breath. Sarah pulled back with the water jug and Narie picked up the cup to drink. The three heaved a sigh of relief after seeing both of their gestures and believed that it could be a quiet dinner after all. All of a sudden, Sarah sneezed and pushed the table, hitting Narie's arms thereby splashing the water onto her face.

"I'm sorry princess! Pardon my sneezing! Where are my manners!" Sarah was being sarcastic towards Narie.

"You did that on purpose you, monkey girl!" Narie stood up, fuming in anger.

"I said I'm sorry didn't I crybaby?" Sarah sneered.

A fight broke. Sune, Una and Aril tries to separate them. Althea, who wanted to have a quiet dinner was already at her limit in dealing with Sarah and Narie's little feud until she couldn't hold her anger anymore. She stood up and slammed the table.

"I've had enough putting up with both of you! Could we at least enjoy a quiet dinner together without this kids' fight? For once, grow up and start acting like adults! Now, sit down and eat your vegetables!" said Althea in a loud commanding tone.

"Yes Ma'am!" everyone replied in unison and immediately started eating together.

After Althea's outburst of anger, Sarah noticed that Narie was again crying for being scolded by Althea. At first, she thought that she really was such a crybaby, but what she saw in that moment was a different tear. Guilt started to creeps into Sarah, she felt responsible for Narie.

After dinner, Narie was outside the porch, looking at the clear night sky filled with stars. Feeling burdened by her guilt, Sarah thought of apologizing to Narie. When by coincidence she saw her outside, Sarah felt awkward and paced forward and back. She was undecided whether to go back in or not. She swallowed her pride and said,

"Look Narie, I know we got off on wrong footing here. I know, I've been mean to you and you got scolded because of me, but when I saw you cry tonight, it felt different. It pained my heart and I wanted to apologize. So here I am, I'm sorry and I promised that I will never annoy you anymore,"

Narie looked at her and smiled.

"I cried not because I was scolded by your mother, but because I miss my own so much. Althea reminded me of her so much every day that I spent here -- how similar the two are and the way they get mad is really scary," Narie said as she looks at the stars.

"Don't be scared. My mother only did that because she cares for us" said Sarah.

"I know that and I do not hold any grudge towards her. Actually, I like your mother a lot," Sarah felt Narie's sincerity.

"So can we call it even between us and start over again?" she stared at Narie's eyes in a manner that reciprocated her sincerity.

"That would be nice!" Narie replied.

The two shook hands and a new friendship between them began. They shared stories the whole night and became closer to each other as the days goes by. She took Narie out to hunt and taught her the secrets of the forest. Sune, Una and Aril looked at one another in surprise as they saw the sudden change between the two. Standing at the window, Althea crossed her arms and smiled. She was happy to see that the two were now getting along so well and developed a bond that is similar to sisters. It was not known to anyone however, that they were indeed sisters who were separated by the tragedy of war.

Sarah and Narie became inseparable and their friendship grew stronger for the entire three weeks that Narie and her kin stayed. They spent most of their time together at the riverbed where Sune first found her and together they lay down under the shade of the tree. Narie was enjoying herself too much as they talked about Althea when she remembered her mother Sorah and the reason why she was there -- the mission that still needs to be carried out. Her mood shifted from gleeful to serious. She walked towards the river and stood gazing upon it. Sarah wanted to know if something was troubling her. Narie knew that the day would come for them to part ways. Unable to devise an excuse, Narie, with clenched fists, faced Sarah and told her that it is time for her to leave to fulfill her mission. Sarah stood in disbelief as she heard her leaving. One could hear the sound of the breeze and swaying trees as the two couldn't utter any words. Sarah has been preparing herself for that day and yet, she still finds it difficult to say goodbye. Narie decided to leave at dawn of the next day, together with Una and Aril. She thanked Sarah for the things she has done for her. Sarah on the other hand, remained quiet and motionless as she stared at the river. Narie wanted to talk to her more but Sarah just left without saying a word. Narie understand what Sarah was going through. She gave her time for herself and went back inside the house to prepare for their journey to the city.

On the next day, Narie talked to Althea.

"Thank you very much Althea for all the kindness you shown to us. I promise you that we will find a way to repay you," said Narie while she made a side glance at Sarah who stood beside Althea.

"You already did, by giving my daughter here something she never had before and that is your friendship," Althea replied.

Narie extended her hand to Althea. She looked at her hand and hesitated for a moment. Althea feared that she might involuntarily look into her memories. Instead, she held Narie's shoulders and gently pulled her in to embrace her.

"Be safe on your journey," Althea whispered.

Narie, Una and Aril bid their farewell one last time to Althea, while Sarah and Sune ushered them by taking the safe path out of the treacherous forest. Sarah walked and didn't utter a single word during the journey. Sune found it extremely peculiar. Narie walked towards her side, tapped her shoulder and said:

"Are you alright? You seem surprisingly quiet today."

"Do you really have to go? I mean you can stay here as long as you want to." Sarah asked while she kept her head down.

"I'm sorry Sarah, but I have something important that I must do. It saddens me as much as you do to leave but I have been entrusted to fulfill something. I hope you understand" Narie replied.

Sarah remained quiet. She seemed to be walking aimlessly in the forest. She could not even start a decent conversation with Narie.

"Ran out of words to say monkey girl?" Narie raised her voice, startling everyone, especially Sarah.

"Who are you calling monkey girl you crybaby!" Sarah rushed towards Narie and grabbed her by the collar.

Their eyes met menacingly. Una, Aril and Sune held on to each other and braced themselves for a fight that was about to erupt. The two stood still, stared at each other and then laughed loudly. Sune, Una and Aril were relieved and then giggled along with the two. Afterwards, Sarah returned to her usual self and started talking once again. After an hour of walking, they finally reached the edge.

"Well, I think this is it. I guess this is good bye," said Narie with a shaky voice.

Sarah however, was not paying attention to Narie and the others. She grinned as she looks towards the city of Ithuria, her eyes were wide open while Sune raised an eyebrow and felt that trouble was about to happen once more.

"Sarah are you alright?" asked Narie.

"I have a great idea. Let us all go to the city. Sune and I know the prince!" clenching both her fists excitedly and in anticipation of seeing Kiran again.

Sune let out a sigh of disappointment. He has seen it coming and knew that whatever Sarah decides she wants, she always gets. He shook his head knowing that there's no point for him to argue with her but to go along with her plan. Narie was glad that Sarah would accompany them to the city and could spend a bit more time together. Sarah, Narie and the rest arrived at Ithuria. The guards remembered Sarah and Sune from the last encounter and immediately allowed them passage without questions. Sarah took Narie, Una and Aril to town and showed them around to have fun but the three was on their guard and on high alert. Their eyes shifted from left to right, observing everything in their surroundings. She instructed Una to find Heres' group and meet up later.

Kiran happens to be in town, conducting talks and speeches to his people when he saw Sarah by chance. It was an awkward moment for the two -- meeting again. Kiran still remembered the last time they met when he tried to kiss Sarah.

"Hello Sarah! What a surprise to see you here!" Kiran stuttered while looking above Sarah's face.

"Hello Kiran. It's been a while. How are you doing?" Sarah lowered her head as her face visibly turning red seeing and hearing Kiran again.

Aril's brows furrowed seeing Sarah and Kiran's greet each other. She asked Sune if that's the usual way of greeting there. Sune simply tilted his head sideways and shrugged his shoulders. Narie on the other hand, was intrigued to see Kiran and couldn't stop gazing at him. It took some time for Sarah and Kiran to be at ease with each other again and somewhat tried not to think about the kissing moment.

"By the way Kiran, this is my friend Narie and Aril."

"They wanted to come here to do some trading," Sarah grabbed Kiran's arm and pulled him in front of Narie.

"It's a pleasure meeting you Narie and Aril. I hope you enjoy your visit to our city" the mild manner Kiran said,

Narie's heart beats in excitement after knowing Kiran, she finds that Sarah was really close to him after seeing her holding Kiran's arm in that manner. Narie can't explain her emotions, why she envied Sarah with her relationship with him. Narie started to have a feeling unknown to her growing in her heart towards Kiran, but she tried to suppress the feeling she's having for the sake of her friendship with Sarah.

After the long day, Narie asked Kiran if there is a place they could settle in for the night; Kiran asked one of his bodyguards to escort them to the town's inn.

"It was nice meeting you Kiran and thank you for sending your aide to escort us," said Narie who shook his hands while intensely looking at Kiran's admirable face.

"The pleasure is mine. A friend of Sarah is also a friend of mine," Kiran replied.

"I do hope to see you again Kiran" she said in a flirtatious tone and slowly let go of Kiran's hand.

Sarah's eyebrow raised and her mouth slightly gawked upon seeing Narie's gesture and tone, but she didn't give much thought about it. Afterwards, she embraced Narie and wished her success in her mission and hoped of seeing her again. Narie likewise look forward to that chance. As Narie walks away from them, she quickly turned her head and took a glance at Kiran for the last time. She put one hand over her heart and could feel the pounding. She was confused about the feeling she's having every time she looked at him. She wanted to know more about Kiran but realized that he already has Sarah, she slowly turned her gaze and walked away.

Kiran was left with Sarah and began to feel awkward once again. Sarah however, has already forgotten about the kiss and acted normally towards him.

"So Kiran what are you doing in the city? You look very occupied," Sarah casually chatted with him.

"Yes, we are facing a crisis right now and I'm trying to convince the people to resolve it peacefully." Kiran answered in a voice to which Sarah sensed urgency,

"What do you mean crisis and convincing about what?" Sarah was brows furrowed,

"We found the Arkan planet and my father is deciding either we go to war with them or not depending on what the people want," Kiran replied.

"The Arkan, you mean they are real?" Sarah jumped in excitement upon hearing it, she got confused of her emotion as to why she felt that way and the obsession she developed for the dark-winged woman she saw in the portrait.

"Yes, I was surprised about it too, but it is saddening to know that some of my people are pursuing war and revenge, which I greatly opposed and will do everything I can to stop it," Kiran sounded desperate.

Sarah otherwise admired Kiran's great conviction in stopping the war and she never saw this side of him before, a prince that values the lives of his people and the future of his kingdom. She suddenly felt the urge of holding Kiran in her arms and her heart hammering, telling her to kiss him, but after she gathered the courage to follow her heart, Kiran was called by his aide reminding him of their next consultation with the people.

"I'm sorry Sarah but I have to go. I hope you would visit me again next time" said Kiran.

"Yes I will. Don't overwork yourself," clasping her wrist behind her back as she replied.

The two parted ways. Kiran was escorted by his aide while Sarah rode Sune and headed towards the forest back to their home. She felt defeated for missing the chance to kiss Kiran.

That night at the inn, Narie met Heres and learned from her that the people of the planet were the sons and daughters of the betrayers of the Arkan kingdom. They were able to survive the great exile and settled here in what they call the planet Eres. Narie frowned in disbelief upon hearing that they named the planet Eres or "hope" in their native language. She was infuriated after hearing Heres' report. The Arkan likewise held animosity to those who betrayed their king and the commandments. She saw all of the people of Eres as enemy of the Arkan kingdom, all of them which include Kiran, Sarah and Althea.

"Narie, I've also found out that the Ithurians are planning to go to war with us. They are in dire need of an energy which they found in Treliseum and their Council are currently deliberating about reclaiming Fostrum," said Heres.

Narie stood up and her aura of rage was evident after learning the Ithurians' plan of claiming the land for which her grandfather fought.

"If it is a war they want, then a war we will give," she crossed her arms and stood up.

After hearing Heres' report, Una and Aril's faces looked pinched and were murmuring among themselves.

"What is wrong Una and Aril? What is troubling you?" the curious Heres asked.

"If what you said is true about them being the descendants of the banished one, then why do they still possess Arkan powers?" Una replied.

"Impossible! Their powers were taken by the king himself before they were damned," Heres was in awe.

"Why did you say they still have the Arkan power?" Narie looked narrowly at Una.

"Because we saw it with our own eyes! We saw her strength and speed, which surpassed even me and Aril," Una's lips were set in a grim line.

"Where did you see this power and who is this that you are referring to?" Narie demanded to know.

"It is Sarah, the girl from the forest, the girl who saved us all. We saw her how she alone easily killed the horde of creatures! The same hordes that almost ended our lives," Una answered.

Narie knew that all of her warriors were truthful to what they say, but still in her heart, she could not believe that Sarah had Arkan powers. She was told by her mother herself that the king took back their powers before they were cast out of Treliseum, but the odds of that story being true was high since they just learned that the banished Arkans, who were supposed to have died in the exile, were alive and thriving. Narie thought that the only way to prove if what Una and Aril witnessed was real is none other than to test Sarah's powers in actual combat.

"Heres, I want you to take Una and Aril and continue to gather whatever you can find about the Ithurians," Narie instructed.

"What about you? Where are you going?" Aril asked with a worried glance.

"I'm going back to the forest to challenge Sarah in combat to confirm if she indeed has Arkan powers," Narie answered.

"I'm coming with you. It is dangerous to go back there," Una's heart leaped into a gallop.

"Do not worry Una. I will take the safe path Sarah used when she took us out of the forest," Narie replied.

Una understood what Narie wanted to achieve going back to the forest. She wanted to make sure if the Ithurians still possessed their

Arkan powers, and if indeed they do, the road to victory against the Ithurian will be difficult and perilous.

Chapter Thirteen

THE TRUTH REVEALED

On the next morning, Narie returned to the forest taking the safe path that Sarah showed them before. She was determined to know if Sarah really possessed Arkan-like powers. Sarah became her close and only friend and wanted it to remain that way, but after learning that they came from the seeds that betrayed her grandfather, she was thrown into confusion on how to face her when they meet.

Narie safely came out of the forest and reached the river where she saw Sarah and Sune resting after finishing a day of hunting. She picked up a stick and crept towards them. She was about a foot away from Sarah when she swung the stick and intentionally struck her. Narie's jaw dropped after seeing how swift Sarah evaded her attack. Sarah's body reacted on impulse and was still half asleep when she dodged her attack.

"Who's there?!" Sarah shouted.

Sune stood up after being startled with Sarah's voice and saw Narie in front of them.

"Narie? what are you doing back here and why did you just strike me with that stick?" she turned to face her with narrowed eyes.

Narie circled around Sarah and Sune and began to tell her the real story about the Arkans — who they are and what power they possessed.

"Narie, what are you talking about? I don't understand," said Sarah.

But Narie went on with her story, telling her about the great betrayal that was committed against the Arkan king and that these betrayers were defeated and banished from their home world. Sarah frowned upon the things Narie said, but it caught her attention after hearing about the Arkan and wanted to learn more. Narie revealed that before the king banished them, he took back their Arkan powers and left them to die on the other side of the gateway of the fallen.

Suddenly, Narie clenched her fists and trembled in anger with the thought that the betrayers managed to stay alive after all these years and were thriving in this planet they called Eres. Sarah was somehow getting a clearer sense of what she was trying to convey. Narie hated these people for what they committed against the Arkan kingdom and vowed to seek justice for the king.

"But why Narie? why do you hate these people so much?" Sarah demanded.

Narie stopped circling Sarah and gave her a fierce stare and said:

"Because they betrayed my grandfather, King Satorex!"

Sarah was astonished to hear what Narie just revealed, not just that she is the granddaughter of the Arkan king but also the daughter of Sorah, the dark winged woman. Gazing intently, Narie slowly walked towards Sarah.

"I never knew that our friendship would turn out this way. But I promised to avenge my family," Narie said. She was determined to fulfill her promise.

"Nari wait! I don't know what our past had done to your family. You are my friend and I will never hurt you!" Sarah responded as she took a step back to avoid confronting her.

Narie suddenly ran towards Sarah, raising her forearm with her fists clenched. Sune jumped in front of Sarah and let loose a breath of lightning shock to repel her. Narie however, raised her arm forward with her palm open and easily deflected Sune's bolt of lightings. Both Sarah and Sune gawked while they witnessed how powerful she is. Sarah then told Sune to stand down and to never meddle with their fight after she decided to deal with Narie alone. The two circled around and sized up each other's strength.

"Are you ready?" asked Narie while sliding her right leg back, raising her fists near her chin and lowered her body.

"Let's get it on!" said Sarah with a smirk.

They ran towards each other and the battle began. Both engaged in hand-to-hand combat. Even though Narie was more knowledgeable in the art of the warrior, Sarah was much stronger, skillful and fast. Narie was being the aggressor; she kept throwing punches. Sarah on the other hand, was keeping her pace and fighting smartly. Sune didn't like being told to just sit down and do nothing while watching Sarah fight on her own. Be that as it may, it was his first time to see Sarah's serious and fierce side. He wanted to help but Sarah bound him to obey. He then decided to rush back to the house to call Althea for help.

Narie unremittingly threw strikes against Sarah, but could not land any; Sarah was so fast in dodging them all. Narie was starting to be annoyed. She felt that Sarah wasn't being serious. Narie just kept punching until she did a spin kick which caught Sarah in the abdomen, smashing her far back into to a boulder. Narie did not stop there. She ran towards Sarah and kept on punching her. Then, she swung with her fist and Sarah took a big blow on her jaw, pushing her back as she staggered sideways. Narie was getting tired, she began to breath hard and rapidly. As the sun was setting, Sarah slowly stood up with blood dripping from her lips. Sarah raised her arm and wiped the blood off. She faced Narie and scowled at her savagely. A trail of dust was left flying behind as Sarah ran towards Narie in god-like speed. Sarah unleashed a barrage of fast and relentless punches which caught Narie several times as she couldn't keep up with Sarah's speed. She tried blocking the punches but only to no avail. She realized now that Sarah does have Arkan powers. Unable to do anything anymore to escape her blows, Narie felt frustrated.

Because of the consistent blow she's receiving from Sarah, Narie unwittingly pulled her arm back and summoned her Serdeus – with the tip of the sword directed at Sarah. Sarah gasped as she saw a sword appear out of nowhere; she froze in amazement and lost her balance. As Narie was about to stab her, Althea jumped in the middle of the fight and swerved Narie's Serdeus with her own while Sune pulled Sarah away from Narie. Both Narie and Sarah were in awe to witness what Althea did. Narie couldn't believe that she had a Serdeus, whereas Sarah was marveled to see that power of Althea for the first time.

"Please Narie, leave this place and don't ever come back," Althea pleaded.

"How were you able to summon the Serdeus? Only an Arkan warrior can summon it!" Narie's brows furrowed as she regarded her Serdeus.

"What is your real name" Narie demanded.

"What my name is, is inconsequential. Please leave me and my daughter alone," Althea turned her back at Narie and slowly walked up to Sarah and Sune.

Narie truly despised the Arkans who betrayed her grandfather and her mother and wanted to take revenge for them. She accused both of them as traitors of the Arkan kingdom. Althea stopped and faced Narie.

"What are you talking about? Who is this grandfather of yours that you said we betrayed?" Althea asked with a puzzled look.

"She is the granddaughter of the Arkan king, King Satorex and the daughter of Sorah, the dark-winged Arkan," Sarah blurted out.

Shocked by the revelation, Althea inhaled a sharp breath. Her body trembled and her heart pounding. She just heard the names of her father and sister from Sarah's own mouth. Sune abruptly turned his head towards Sarah who just stood stiff after her slip up. Althea turned to face Sarah and approached her.

"Sarah, how did you know of these things?" she pressed her lips together.

Nervous and tense, Sarah hesitated to reply because she knew that she'd be in trouble if Althea finds out that she's been secretly going to the city.

"How did you know about her grandfather and her mother? Answer me!" Althea glared.

Sarah took a deep breath and eventually confessed that she has been visiting Kiran in the city and his father, King Malkiem, told her about the Arkans.

Althea pursed her lips, raised and threw her hand hard and hit Sarah in the cheek. The sound of the slap could be heard throughout the forest. Shocked, Sarah stared at Althea in disbelief while holding her fire-red cheek. It was the first time that Althea laid a hand on her. Narie was startled and instinctively put her hands over her mouth. Hurt and embarrassed, Sarah couldn't do anything but stand there and sob.

"How many times did I told you never to go to the city because it is dangerous out there? And yet you disobeyed me. You played me for a fool and you betrayed my trust," Althea spoke with a quivering voice.

"But Mother, I'm tired living like this – I feel like I'm living in a cage! Stripped of my freedom! I have no one else to talk to other than you and Sune. I too, longed to explore the world, meet other people and soar high above the skies with wings like the Ithurians do!" she answered with teary eyes.

Althea did not know that this was how Sarah felt after all this time.

"I'm doing this to protect you because I love you," she grabbed her daughter's shoulders.

"I don't need you to protect me. I can protect myself. I want to be free! I don't want to spend the rest of my life living the kind of life you lead," Sarah yanked Althea's arms to release her grips.

Hurt, Althea once again hit Sarah. All she wanted was Sarah's safety. Narie felt like a little child who just sat at the corner, scared and embarrassed.

"I hate you! I wish you never been my mother!" Sarah wailed and ran off to the forest.

Althea could not believe what Sarah had just said. Sune shifted his gaze between Althea and Sarah. He did not know whether to go after her or not – though Althea told Sune to go after Sarah. Althea just stood frozen. What Sarah wished for was the truth: she is not her real mother.

Narie bowed her head down and quietly sneaked away.

"Don't move!" Althea shouted,

Narie pulled her head inward and down, and yielded without hesitation.

"Could you come by at the house? I want to talk to you," Althea requested.

Still frightened, Narie couldn't muster to say anything. She simply nodded and followed Althea to the house. Upon arriving, Althea heated the food and tries to busy herself, but it was visible that she was wiping her tears away. Narie was again reminded of the feud earlier and now felt awkward.

"Narie, would you be kind enough to prepare the plates?" her voice was soft but a bit strained.

"Yes Ma'am," Narie politely answered.

Narie just furtively glanced at Althea during dinner.

"What's wrong Narie?" Althea noticed that she seemed restless.

"Is Sarah going to be alright out there?" she worried for her best friend as she looked outside the window.

"There's nothing to worry about. She will be fine. Sune is with her," Althea calmly replied.

"How is your mother doing? What is she like now?" Althea leaned forward while sitting on the edge of her chair.

"My mother is doing fine. As overseer of two cities, she is occupied most of the time. My mother has always been strong and brave. She loves her people so much and always remained firm," her eyes crinkled as a small smile appeared on her face.

"May I ask who your father is?" she held her chin with one hand; her eyes are in search for answers.

"I have none," Narie quickly replied.

She explained that after the Great War, most of the male Arkan either died or fatally wounded. The surviving male Arkans, including the king, were put to deep sleep to preserve their lives. She shared that in order to continue the cycle of life, they've been extracting the life force of the male Arkans and infused it with the female ones for them to bear children.

"My mother just told me that she used the life force of the man she has always loved in order for me to be conceived," as she uttered this, she looked down the table and crossed her hands.

Althea knew for certain that it was Aran's life force that Sorah used to conceive Narie. She realized that she and Sarah are true sisters. Narie then asked why an Arkan like her is living with the traitors.

"Well, you can also say that I'm a traitor as well," Althea replied.

Narie did not understand what she meant. Althea explained that long ago, when she was still living in Treliseum, she betrayed her beloved elder sister. She amenably told Narie the truth – that she loved the man whom her sister married and committed a forbidden love – which ended up causing the death of her sister's husband.

"I may have tricked him to fall for me but his heart still solely belonged to my sister." She was evidently in distress and brushed her tears away.

Narie was speechless and tearful as she listened to Althea's bitter past. She also revealed to her that because the war broke out, there were evil men who wanted them dead so he took her sister's baby in order to protect her. She added that it was her way of repentance for the sins she committed against her beloved sister.

"Why did you bring the baby here?" asked Narie.

"That is something I could not explain myself either. Things just happened so fast. The next thing I knew, we were already here," Althea replied.

Narie realized that Althea and Sarah have been living in Eres for almost three millennia. It thrilled her to know that they have been in existence since the beginning of the planet's history.

"Why didn't you go back to Treliseum?" Narie wondered.

"There is nothing for me to go back to anymore," she stood up by the window and looked from afar.

Narie briefly paused, trying to muster enough courage to ask the next question.

"Who is your sister Althea? I give you my word that I shall find her and reunite you both," Narie promised.

"There is no need for that anymore, because to my sister, I'm already dead," Althea replied in tears.

"Is Sarah the daughter of your sister?" Narie queried.

"Yes she is. She may have my stubbornness, but she truly has her mother's essence in her," Althea grinned.

"So, she is an Arkan after all!" she was both pleased and amazed.

Narie wondered if she ever wished for Sarah to meet her real mother back in Treliseum. But Althea didn't want to rush things for now and told Narie that in due time, and if chance permits, they will be together again. After the talk, she begged her to keep it a secret and to never spill it to any soul, especially Sarah. Because the truth will only hurt Sarah and seeing her upset is the last thing she wanted to happen. Althea knew that it was only a matter of time for Sarah to uncover the truth about her past, but until then, she vowed to be by her side for as long as she needs her to be. Narie on the other hand, gave Althea her word of honor to keep it a secret and vowed to help her unite Sarah with her Arkan mother.

Chapter Fourteen

THE EVIL RETURNS

Another group of Ithurian explorers from the kingdom of Minea stumbled across an unfamiliar space in search for Algios. They entered a realm filled with treacherous dark nebula surrounded by perilous lightning fields. The crew of the ship was suddenly shaken by a force and tossed them violently in all directions. The ship was caught in an undetected solar storm and compelled the pilots to take an emergency landing. The pilots were terrified as they struggle to regain control of the ship, tightly griping the yoke and steering it out of that stomach-churning wave. They frantically scanned the area and found a planet that was closest to their position. As they approached the coordinates, the crew were repulsed to see a black charred planet where the sun denies its light. As terrified as they were, the pilots didn't have much choice but to land the ship on the planet due to the imminent danger the violent turbulence pose.

The explorers examined the surface for any signs of life and energy but could not detect either of the two. Everyone hopes for the solar storm to clear soon so they could leave that hideous planet the soonest time possible. All of a sudden, the scanner detected multitude of life signatures coming towards them in great speed. The commander was alarmed to the unknown life source approaching them and immediately ordered the Nephatrons and his crew to take arms and defend and hold their position. The creatures were nearing from where they stand but nothing visible could be seen in front of them. Everyone was sweating profusely out of fear and anxieties. Then without warning, the ground quaked and man-like creatures emerged from underneath and started attacking them. The Ithurians fought back but the creatures were faster and stronger than them. The commander ran inside the ship and immediately sent out messages back to Eres to signal for rescue. The creatures easily broke through inside the ship and destroyed their equipment. The transmission was abruptly cut off. One of the creature grabbed the commander by the neck and dragged him outside. He looked out the window and saw most of his men had been killed easily, while the others himself included, were held in captivity.

The captured Ithurians were taken to their captors' main city and were brought inside a huge dome – which seems to be the central stronghold. The commander saw the inhabitants of that charred planet numbering by the millions. The Ithurians were horrified and sickened to witness their dead comrades being cannibalized, their organs being eaten by the monsters and their limbs being infused into their own disfigured bodies.

Then, there was silence in the dome. The creatures bowed down as the patriarch arrived and walked towards the throne. As he was seated, the patriarch saw the captured Ithurians,

"What are these creatures?" the Patriarch asked.

"My lord, they are our captives; they trespassed into our domain", one of them responded.

The Ithurians stared in shock and disbelief hearing the creatures spoke eloquently. They groveled before the patriarch and begged for their lives after having witnessed the fate of their dead comrades.

"How do their meat taste like?" the arrogant patriarch asked while checking his nails.

"Their meat is good and their limbs are similar to ours, my lord." Their mouths were now visibly watering.

The commander of the Ithurian stood up and walked towards the Patriarch.

"Stop this sacrilege or our mighty army would come down upon you and destroy all of you monsters!" boldly said by the commander.

"And who might you be if I may be permitted to asked?" the patriarch said in a soft tone.

"I'm the commander of this expeditionary force of the Ithurian army, the mightiest army in the galaxy," the commander proudly announced as he looked directly in the eyes of the patriarch.

"Mightiest Army you say? Good! It means more food for my people. Bring that insect to me!" the patriarch glowered.

He gripped the forehead of the commander and looked into his memories. He then crushed the skull of his head, threw the body to his minions and savagely devoured it in just a matter of seconds.

"My lord, what about the rest?" eagerly asked by one of the creature while his stomach growled.

"Well, don't play with your food!" the patriarch answered coldly.

The captured Ithurians groaned in pain as the creatures slowly gobbled them alive piece by piece.

"Prepare the army. We just found ourselves a new planet to feed!" said the patriarch. The inhabitants cheered in euphoria.

"Long live the king! Long live King Athanax!" the creatures applauded.

The black planet that the unfortunate Ithurians discovered was the stronghold of the Fallen Arkans; burned and disfigured male and female Arkans who also survived the great exile. They managed to multiply a thousand fold, they survived by conquering neighboring stars and fed on the inhabitants of that galaxy. Athanax saw from the Ithurian's memories the location of their planet and ordered Morsus to take a small contingent of the warriors to scout ahead the blue planet in preparation for their invasion. Morsus took fifty *Draakab* or dragon riders in his command and left the black planet towards Eres.

Back in Eres, the message sent by the doomed explorers reached Minea. King Turloch was informed about it and immediately called the Alliance to convene. During the meeting, King Turloch presented to the Council a terrifying message they received from the explorers. They warily paid attention to the message and heard the commander in panic. They heard him say "being attacked by monsters", "with unimaginable strength and speed which they could not match". They heard horrifying screams in the background, then the message abruptly ended.

After hearing the whole message, the Council was left in great shock and immediately King Kelon insisted that the Arkans attacked them again, inciting the same incident they faced at Treliseum. Kiran disagreed with King Kelon's insinuation. He was firm in his belief that the Arkans have nothing to do with it and argued that they may have trespassed yet again and made new enemy for the Ithurian kingdom. King Kelon and King Gileal warned the Council that the Arkans have made their first move and pressured King Malkiem to decide quickly before it is too late. King Malkiem asked the alliance to give him two days to contemplate and afterwards, he will formally address the people about his decision to go to war or not with the Arkans. King Kelon and King Gileal were jubilant, while King Turloch and King Ull remained skeptical. Kiran knew that his father might have been swayed in favor of the war. He and Kina immediately left the Council and went straight to the people to convince them to join his call for peace with the Arkan. He knew that his father will always listen to what the people will say. He planned to divide the people's judgment to buy him some more time as he tries to further convince the Council of negotiation rather than war.

Days after Morsus and his Draakab left the black planet, they finally located and reached Eres. He saw the forest of Eres as a strategic location to hide his soldiers and dragons. He picked twenty of his warriors to accompany him in the city to spy on the Ithurians, while he ordered the remaining Draakab to stay hidden and wait for his return. Morsus and his band of twenty took the dangerous path of the forest where they met and attacked by vicious giant predators. But because the fallen still hold remnants of their Arkan powers and with their sizeable number, they were able to slay the predators without difficulty and made their way through with ease. After exiting the forest, he scattered his men throughout the Ithurian kingdoms and ordered to gather whatever they can find regarding the enemy's military power. In the still of the night, Morsus and his group silently infiltrated a small village outside the Ithurian capital. They killed all the villagers, cannibalized the body parts and used the dead villagers' faces to hide their hideous appearances. They made their way towards the capital and secretly entered the city without the guards noticing them.

Dawn of the next day, hundreds of thousands of people from all over the Ithurian kingdom arrived at the capital to hear King Malkiem speak about the impending war with the Arkan. Heres, Una and Aril eagerly waited for the king's decision -- a decision that will change the fate of both the Arkans and Ithurians. King Malkiem slowly walked out to the balcony and immediately cheered by his people upon seeing their proud king. King Malkiem raised his arm with his palm open to greet his people. He paused and took a deep breath before he started with his speech. The people slowly settled down and awaits the king's word.

"My people, I come before you bearing words of impending perils that we, as Ithurians, have to face. For thousands of years, our struggles to achieve greatness remained unbroken; the resiliency of our people brought us to where we are now. We have thrived and built magnificent cities, which became the very foundations of our mighty empire.

But this blessed greatness comes with a price; through centuries of technological progression, the repository of the crucial Algios that fuels our empire's military might is rapidly diminishing and we only have a few more years of sustainability before it is completely depleted. And if this inevitable day comes, our kingdom will be vulnerable to our enemies. Time is running out for us, therefore, we, the Alliance of the kings, have decided to send explorers to search the energy we need outside our planet. For months we waited, slowly and painstakingly charting the stars in the galaxy, until we made a great discovery -- a discovery that left us all astounded. We found the energy we need, the purest form of energy crystal that we have never seen before -- one small core could power our machines and last for a decade. But alongside this new discovery, we learned that this energy was located at the planet where our ancestors once dwelled, Treliseum, as written in our ancient text and Fostrum, the city our ancestors built. Then, our old nemesis stopped us from reaching the Algios -- they who are afraid of our ancestor's knowledge and resiliency, fearing that someday, our ancestors would rise above them; they who oppressed and took away our ancestor's honor and cast them out of Treliseum to die in an unknown world; they are known to us all as written in our ancient text; and they are none other than the Arkans! Yes, my people, the Arkans are real. And after many decades, our path has once again crossed. These Arkans attacked and killed our brave explorers without mercy. So now, my people, I come to you today to seek your support. Our empire is in peril. We have no one to help us except ourselves. In light of this, the alliance has agreed that we will once again reclaim Fostrum, the city our ancestors built, for it is our right as children of Varkelos, the persecuted one. Ithurians, are you with me to go to war with the Arkans?

Most of the Ithurians cheered in support of their king, while some were against it. Heres, Una and Aril were appalled to hear what King Malkiem told his people. Heres had enough of the lies and wanted to take matters into her own hands but was restrained by Una and Aril. Within the huge crowd of people, Morsus and his group were blending in with the locals. Morsus learned that the Ithurians were the descendants of Varkelos; he knew that King Athanax will be pleased if he finds out that these people are the sons and daughters of their betrayers. This is the moment they had been waiting for a long time -- to finally have their vengeance on both the Arkans and Varkelos' seeds. Morsus immediately ordered one of his men to take the fastest dragon and return to the black planet and inform King Athanax about what they have discovered from the Ithurians. The messenger left the city in haste to return to the forest and rode the fastest dragon out of Eres.

Meanwhile, Morsus's soldiers that were left in the forest became impatient and hungry. They decided to scavenge the forest for food. After a while of searching, they arrived at a clearing and found Althea's house. The creatures immediately smelled something familiar -- a more delectable scent that made their stomach rumbles and their mouths watery.

Narie had spent the night in Althea's house before heading back to the city. Before leaving, Althea once again begged her to keep all that she had confessed a secret between the two of them. Althea approached her and embraced her, which made Narie felt awkward.

"Take care of yourself Narie and don't give your mother a lot of worries alright?" Althea advised her in a motherly tone.

"I will Althea, and I hope you and Sarah would make up soon," she embraced her back.

As Althea walked Narie to the door, both instinctively felt presence of intruders coming in close. Suddenly, the creatures sped up to attack them. Althea and Narie clenched their fists as the flames slowly formed their Serdeus. They ran outside the house and crossed swords with the creatures. From each blow the creatures made, Althea felt the strength and speed of the creatures different from the Ithurian and the Deodarian she had fought before. Althea and Narie's bodies shone -- the light surrounded their bodies and changed them to their armored forms, leaving the enemies in shock as they realized that they were fighting an Arkan. The creatures became even more desperate and eager to kill both of them. The leader of the pack ordered his men to attack, they ran towards Althea and Narie with their crude swords raised and taunting and shouting like wild animals. The two Arkan scowled at the approaching enemies. Trail of dust blown from behind them as they swiftly flew towards the enemies, swinging their Serdius and slashing the creatures one by one until none was left standing. After the battle, Althea approached one of the dead creatures and learned that these were neither Ithurians nor Deodarians. She has never seen these soldiers before.

Narie on the other hand, was still in shock to see Althea in her full Arkan form. She could not take her eyes off her armor. At the back of her mind, she knew that she has seen it before but could not remember where.

"Narie, you have to leave the forest and return to Treliseum immediately," said Althea while she examined the dead creatures with great curiosity.

"But are you going to be alright if I leave you here alone?" Narie's was deeply concerned.

"You do not have to worry about me. I can take care myself. Now hurry! Go!" she tries to ease Narie's worries with a smile.

Narie was hesitant to leave Althea alone but realized soon after, that she still has an important mission to fulfill. She heeded Althea's advice and hastily left the forest towards the city to meet her warriors. After Narie left, Althea approached one of the dead creatures and saw that each of their limbs were different as if it was fused together. She removed the armor mask and saw a burned and disfigured face of a man. She extended her hand and touched the forehead to looked into his memories. She was astounded to see herself in the middle of a great battle that happened in the past. She saw Sorah hovering the sky with dark wings and unleashing the fire of justice, which blinded her with its flames. Althea instinctively closed her eyes and released her grip. She felt the pain of Sorah's flame while she was deeply attached to the soldier's memory. She was puzzled on how her sister could have possibly used the power that only their father could wield. She thought that the only way to know the truth was to travel to the creature's home planet and continue the search there.

Meanwhile, the thought of the disagreement with Althea left Sarah walking aimlessly, shoulders slumped and sobbed as she thought about her mother. She didn't want to return back home yet because of the guilt and shame she felt in her heart. Her aimless walking brought her in front of the Ithurian capital without realizing it. She passed through the gate and saw hundreds of thousands of people in congregation at the castle courtyard. They were shouting and arguing about the war. She then saw Kiran standing on a podium and was about to speak to the king standing on the castle balcony. She told Sune to wait for her at the gate and quickly ran towards Kiran. She saw Kina at the foot of the podium and reach out to grabbed her arm.

"Sarah? What are you doing here?" Kina gawked at the sight of her.

"What is going on here Kina? Why are there so many people here?", turning her head and looking at all the people around her.

"My father has made his decision to go to war with the Arkans, but Kiran is trying to stop him. The people are in deliberation," Kina sounded pessimistic.

At the same moment, Narie arrived at the city and rejoined with her three warriors. Heres informed her that the Alliance have already decided to go to war with them and will take Fostrum by force. Narie tried to hold her emotions back after learning about what the Ithurians were planning. Her heart pounds in anger and hatred. Then, Narie and Sarah heard Kiran's voice speaking to the king and the people, telling them to negotiate with the Arkans rather than going to war.

"My King, my people, please calm your emotions and be rational about this. We must not dare walk the path of war with the Arkans. Instead, we must negotiate with them." His supporters lauded him for his steadfastness for peace.

"Nonsense Kiran! The Arkans have always been our enemy since the time of our ancestors. How would you expect to negotiate with them?" said King Kelon with a disdainful attitude.

"By trying my lord. If we don't try, we would not know," Kiran quickly replied.

"But they attacked us first and killed our soldiers," King Gileal joined Kelon.

"We invaded their land and took their resources on our own accord. What would have you done if someone did the same thing to your own kingdom?". The two kings were silenced by Kiran's wit.

"But still, they attacked us twice and killed our soldiers! How do you expect to negotiate with those barbarians?" the enraged King Gileal pointed his finger at Kiran.

"Death to the Arkans!" the people bawled.

Narie' had heard enough lies, insults and mockery from the Ithurians. Her heart couldn't take the anger anymore. She balled her fist as her Serdius gradually formed and walked towards the balcony to strike the leaders of the Alliance. Una was shaken to see the Serdius almost in complete form. She quickly grabbed a hold of Narie's hand and hid the sword.

"Narie, please suppress your anger. We cannot fight here, not with this multitude," Una gasped in fear and held Narie's trembling hand.

Narie felt Una's heavy grip and saw her worried eyes. She realized that her rash action almost put her warriors' lives in danger. She decided to return back to Avetus immediately before anything bad happens and to tell Altrus Sorah of the coming war.

After Kiran heard King Gileal's words and the people's applause, he stood quiet and became weary. King Kelon and King Gileal smirked at this sight of Kiran's frustration. Sarah and Kina on the other hand, stood with the crowd and wanted to go up the podium to help the beleaguered Kiran whose hope now waned. As he aimlessly looked at the crowd, Kiran met Sarah's eyes which happens to be staring at him intently. In Sarah's eyes he felt the flame of hope, telling him to continue the good fight and never be defeated by small obstacle that blocks his way. Somehow, a brand new hope and determination burned in his heart. He clenched his fists, took a deep breath and faced the leaders of the Alliance once more.

"There is no proof that the second attack was carried out by the Arkans, for all we know, we might have yet again trespassed another group's domain and made new enemies for ourselves," Kiran refuted. His strong passion was felt by everyone that listened.

King Gileal and King Kelon fumed in rage with Kiran's defiance and demanded King Malkiem to deal with him.

"How are you going to act on your rebellious son?" King Kelon struck his fist at the armrest of his chair.

King Malkiem stood up and looked at Kiran.

"Kiran, we the Alliance of the kings will decide what is best for our people. As your king, I ordered you to stand down." King Malkiem spoke softly; he was trying to convince Kiran.

"My lord, I will not stand down. As future king of Ithuria, it is also my obligation to protect our people." It was the first time for Kiran to defy his father,

"Kiran, as your father, please don't," the king tried to convince him once again.

"No father I cannot let you blindly lead our people to their death," the strong-willed Kiran was very firm in his belief.

"Be careful of your words Kiran. You may be my son and heir, but I can hold you liable to your words," the words burned in his tongue as he raised his voice at Kiran.

"Then, so be it Father. I will not stand down for sending our people to an inevitable defeat against the Arkans."

"Hear me my fellow Ithurians: the teaching of our forefathers and what they attested in the ancient text tells us that the Arkans possessed powers beyond our reach. As what the King from Sodaria and Amara repeatedly tells you, with the power of our technology, we can beat the odds and fight the Arkans at their capacities. And yes, they may be right in saying so, but many lives will be at stake. Or worse, many will be lost just to even that odds. Even if our technology is at par with their powers, it is still a hopeless battle to go against the King of the Arkan, King Satorex, who is known to have annihilated thousands of Arkan souls in an instant by unleashing his power of destruction as witnessed by our ancestors, by my own forefather Varkelos himself. We must not give in to our hatred because this will only result in death. We must not challenge something that is unbeatable because this will only lead to our kingdom's ultimate failure. So my people, what I propose to you all is to negotiate with them. We don't have the

175

*strength nor power to go against the Arkan king. And if negotiation
fails, we will move to the next planet and to the next until we find
the energy without losing a single life."*

The people cheered at Kiran's speech and those that favored the
war previously were now at doubt. They were enlightened by the fact
that going against the Arkan is futile.

"Malkiem, your son speaks the truth. If we go to war, we might
lose everything," King Turloch urged.

"Absurd! With our current military power, we can conquer them
even if they put their king on the frontline," the pompous King Kelon
refused to accept Kiran's words.

"What does it take to make logic get through your thick skulls?
Kiran spoke with proof – our ancestors imprinted them in the ancient
text! And you two? on which do you base your logic? From the dice
you played with your concubines?!" King Ull slammed his fist down
the armrest and stood up.

"How dare you say that you old goat" King Kelon triggered King
Ull into a heated argument.

"Enough!" King Malkiem shouted.

King Malkiem stood up and looked down at Kiran. He also agreed
with Kiran. He let his emotions cloud his judgment that almost made
him lead his people towards misery. Kiran reminded him of their
obligation to their people and for the empire.

"Kiran, I approve your proposal of negotiating with the Arkans.
You have only a month to put together productive results," said King
Malkiem.

Kiran eyes and nose crinkled and raised both of his fists in the air as he heard his father's decision. But then, he realized that the time period his father gave him would be impossible.

"But my lord, the time you have given me is not enough. It will take a month to reach Treliseum," pressure can be felt from Kiran's tone.

"That won't be a problem anymore." King Turloch assured Kiran.

His astronomers have managed to find and plotted a new and shorter route to Treliseum and with King Ull's builders, they were able to develop and build a powerful engine that can travel three times the speed of their conventional airship. The engine can be retrofitted to any ship with simple modifications needed -- all in all, the total amount of time to reach Treliseum was now three days. King Turloch and King Ull had been anticipating this moment to come from the time they found the location of the Arkan planet. The two kings have planned from the beginning to help Kiran with his crusade of peace and took into their own accord to provide him all the means to accomplish this important mission.

"King Turloch and King Ull, you have my utmost appreciation and gratitude for this. I promise you and my father that I will try my very best to bring the good news upon my return." Kiran stepped back and put his hand to his heart.

Kiran went down from the podium, while the people clapped their hands in appreciation. He was then met by Kina and was surprised to see Sarah with her.

"You look great out there -- speaking like a true king. We're so proud of you," Sarah said as he patted Kiran's shoulder.

"Thank you Sarah, but the real work starts now. I just hope that I will be able to reach the Arkan king's heart to consider negotiating with us," said Kiran.

"I know you can Kiran. I always knew that you can accomplish great things!" Sarah encouraged him.

He held Sarah's hand and took her away from Kina and the crowd for them to have a quiet moment together.

"Sarah, I will be gone for a while. I need to fulfill this important task for my people. I'm scared Sarah. What if I fail and let my people down?" Kiran's eyes were clouded with doubt.

"You don't need to be scared of failure Kiran. You have already done something great today. You have stopped an impending war and bloodshed. Just do it one step at a time. Don't take a big leap just yet. Just do what you always do and you will be fine," she held Kiran's hand and put a warm smile.

Kiran held Sarah in his arms, happy and thankful for the trust she had for him. Sarah's face flushed bright pink and bit her lips. She also wanted to hold him but didn't have the courage to do it. Then by chance, their eyes met and briefly stared intimately at each other, Kiran slowly moved his head closer until their lips finally met. Kiran told her to wait for his return and he will bring her the good news. Kiran then parted with her to get on with his preparation. Sarah paled, she raised her hand to cover her pounding heart to calm herself with what just happened. It was her first time to be kissed by a man she deeply falls in love with. After that meeting, she felt the need to go back home to settle things with her mother. Sune's brows furrowed and tilted his head to the side seeing Sarah coming out of the city swinging her arms, skipping and spinning loosely. She held Sune's face and told him that they were going back home. She jumped at Sune's back and the two headed back to the forest.

Meanwhile, Althea gathered all the dead together and used her flame to burn the creature's body, until nothing was left but their ashes. She thought that it is the least she could do for them. Althea was determined to find out the truth behind the attack -- what relation do they have with her sister Sorah and their reason for coming to Eres. But before she proceeded, she remembered Sarah, thinking that she might worry if she is not home. She left Sarah a note telling her that she will be gone for a while and will be back as soon as she can. Althea went outside the house. She looked above the sky and light came out of her, enfolding her body and transformed to her armored form. She stretched out her wings and flew to the sky, to space and towards the black planet.

As soon as Althea flew off, Sarah and Sune happened to come back. She opened the door and called on to her mother but no one answered. She searched the entire house and found that Althea was not there. She was frightened by the thought that Althea might have left her for good after the harsh words she said. Sune pushed his snout at Sarah's back to get her to pay attention to a note that was left on the table. Tears rolled down her cheeks after reading the letter. She hoped that Althea could still forgive her for her disrespect and wished everything would return back to how they used to be.

In another part of the galaxy, the messenger sent by Morsus arrived at the black planet and immediately told King Athanax everything they learned from Eres. Athanax's hands shook violently in rage as he clenched his fists after learning the truth about the Ithurians. But his mood suddenly changed upon learning the impending war between the two of his most hated people: The Arkans and the seeds of Varkelos. From this conflict, he began to scheme his evil plan of achieving his vengeance by making the Arkans and Ithurians destroy each other. He swore that he would do everything he can to make the war happen.

"Bronax, assemble the entire army!" Athanax commanded.

"Yes my king. What are your plans?" asked Bronax.

"We will make the Arkans and Ithurians destroy each other, burn Eres where the betrayers dwell and take back Treliseum for ourselves," said Athanax as he stared from afar with glaring eyes and a sinister laugh.

Chapter Fifteen

DESPERATION

Narie and the three warriors arrived safely back to Avetus. She immediately went to see Altrus Sorah to present the results of her mission, together with the nine warriors of the light. She informed her mother that the enemy who invaded their realm was a race called Ithurians and are dwelling on a planet called Eres at a galaxy found on the other side of the gateway. Sorah's brow raised in intrigue as she heard that the planet was called Eres.

"Eres -- they named the planet hope?" Sorah stared in disbelief.

"Yes Mother. They used our own language to named it," Narie replied.

Narie revealed that the Ithurians are the sons and daughters of Varkelos and the banished traitors. Sorah's clenched fists gripped so tightly that her knuckles turned pale. She couldn't contemplate how the traitors were able to survive the exile without their powers. She also learned that the population of the Ithurians outnumbered them by more than three to one and their military power relies mostly on machineries and their proud Zeltkova warriors.

Narie then spoke of the war that the Ithurians will wage against them, as well as their plan of taking Fostrum by force in order to acquire the energy they desperately need. She also reported the lies that Varkelos has imparted to his seeds — that Fostrum belongs to them. Sorah was enraged about the lies and arrogance of the Ithurians.

"If it is war they want, then we will give them the war they wished they never had," declared Sarah. The warriors raised their fists and cheered in support.

Sorah called her warriors of the light, Prea, the captain of the warriors and one of the remaining few primordial Arkans: Heres, *Kinara, Anthelia,* Una, Aril, *Antra, Fereal* and *Vijera* to prepare the Arkan army for war. Narie did not tell Sorah about the two Arkans who were secretly living with the Ithurians. She did not mention about Althea and Sarah for she was bound by her word she sworn to Althea. After the meeting, Sorah walked towards Narie and embraced her.

"Welcome back my daughter and congratulations on the success of your mission," Sorah enveloped Narie in a warm embrace.

"Thank you Mother. This was indeed, the most difficult mission I have faced so far," Narie said. She yearned so much to be with her mother.

Sorah linked her arms with Narie's and together walked the great hall, when all of a sudden, Narie asked about the great Arkan war and wanted to know more about it and the relation between them and the Ithurians. Sorah was not surprised that Narie became intrigued about the past after what she had seen and learned from her time in Eres. She also believed that it was the right time for Narie to know about the truth.

"The Great Arkan war was about a love that failed," Sorah tilted her head down as she told Narie whose eyebrows only knitted together. Sorah told her everything from the time before the war started and after the banishment of the Arkan rebels and the betrayers. She told Narie that the Great War weakened the Arkan for it almost destroyed their race -- most of the surviving male Arkans were gravely wounded in the war, including her grandfather the king. They were put into deep sleep to preserve their life in order to continue the Arkan race. They extract the life force from the male Arkan host and infused it with the female to reproduce new lives. However, the process was slow. They could only extract the life force every five years to prevent straining the host, otherwise, the host will die.

Sorah also revealed that because of this process, the power of the newborn was only half compared to the primordial Arkans.

"Mother, I do not understand why we only inherited half of the Arkan power," asked Narie with her eyes still perplexed.

"It is because of how the reproduction of life was being carried out that made the newborn's power's half and became a second-age Arkan," she replied, but Sorah could still see bewilderment on Narie's face.

"You see Narie, the full power of an Arkan comes from the love between two people" Sorah elaborated.

Narie suddenly raised her hand and touched her heart. She remembered Kiran as the word "love" was uttered. Her eyes sparkled and the corners of her mouth slid upward. Sorah did a double take on Narie after seeing her smile. She saw as if a ray of sunshine was shining all over her face. After knowing the entire story, Narie somehow vision the hardship and pain her mother faced every single day to keep the kingdom and the Arkan race from dying. She finally understood why her mother seldom smile or even happy. She held Sorah's hands and softly spoke:

"Thank you Mother," said Narie as she leaned on her chest.

Sorah smiled and patted her head.

"Mother, if it is alright with you. May I know from whom did you acquire the life force to conceive me?" She leaned back and looked at Sorah with inquisitive eyes.

Narie's question caught her by surprise. Sorah gave a quick bark of laugh and then stared into the void.

"It was from the man I loved and still love," Sorah answered.

"Is there any picture of my father that I can see for me to get to know him?" Narie asked as her heart raced.

Sorah knew that this day would come and thought that it is the right time for Narie to know. She took her into her room, the room which she forbade anyone from entering. Sorah took out her hidden chest and pulled a portrait of Aran and her carrying their first-born.

"This man is your father Narie. His name is Aran," said Sorah as he pointed to Aran in the portrait which brought back bittersweet memories of him.

Narie somehow saw a resemblance of his father and Kiran, but cast that thought aside after seeing the baby.

"Who is the baby Mother?" Narie sat on the edge of the chair and pulled the portrait near her face.

"She is my first-born, your sister, but she died a long time ago during the Great War," Sorah slowly took the portrait away from Narie. She vaguely smiled and looked at the baby with mournful eyes.

Narie saw tears from her mother's eyes as she spoke of the baby in the portrait. She felt her mother's pain and her undying love for her first-born. She held her mother by her arms to give her comfort. Narie saw another portrait protruding on one side while the other end was covered. She saw her mother on one end of the portrait with another woman. When she pulled out the portrait, her face turned white and put her hand to her beating heart when she saw on the other half of the portrait.

"Who is the woman in this portrait?" she asked with a trembling voice.

Sorah's emotion suddenly changed upon seeing the portrait Narie was referring to. She saw her mother's eyes turn cold.

"She is my younger sister, Althea, but she also died during the war," Sorah took the portrait from Narie and hastily put it back inside the chest.

It was devastating for Narie to know the painful truth about her mother's past with Althea and the baby who is Sarah. It left her completely speechless, scared and reluctant to tell Sorah that they are alive. She thought that her mother deserved the right to know the truth, but remembering her promise to Althea put her in a difficult situation. She was confused whether to tell her mother the truth or not and this disconcertment only burdens her heart more.

Meanwhile on the other side of the galaxy, Althea successfully located the black planet and carefully landed on the surface without being seen. It was quiet and the inhabitants were nowhere to be found.

She probed the surrounding area and saw the wreckage of the Ithurian airship. She touched a part of the airship and saw memories of the creatures that destroyed it – they were the same group that attacked them on Eres. Suddenly, she heard crowd of people cheering from a distance. She walked further up the hill and the sound was getting louder and louder until she reached the top where she saw the inhabitant's city. In the middle of the city was the huge dome where all the people are gathered. Althea secretly infiltrated the city and stealthily made her way through the dangerous streets towards where the people were gathered. Upon reaching the place she flew on top of the dome to have a better position to hear and watch what was going on inside. Inside the dome, Althea was taken aback to see a great gathering of people, creatures and dragons numbering by the millions. They were cheering at a man who was about to deliver his words to his people.

"Hail the patriarch, our savior!" the people cheered.

Everyone then kneeled and bowed their head as their patriarch entered and made his way towards the center. Althea quietly listened and watched the event unfold. The patriarch looked at his people and start delivering his will.

"My children, it has already been three thousand years since we were casted out of our beloved home world by the self-righteous King Satorex and his daughter Sorah -- Sorah the one responsible for our pain and suffering; the one that took away our beautiful form and made us into these hideous disfigured creatures as we are now; and Varkelos, he who betrayed us and left us to be destroyed in the hands of our enemy. We were thrown out of Treliseum and left to die in this forsaken star. Many of us perished and some were made to sacrifice so that others may live. We struggled and we managed to survive. We conquered stars and fed on its people to make us strong once again. We took their women to bear our seeds to multiply and

today, we became a powerful force that made the galaxies tremble in fear. But my children, today I bear to you all good tidings, the seeds of Varkelos the betrayer, which now call themselves Ithurians has finally been found and thriving on the blue planet they called Eres. And with great fortuity, they are going to war with the Arkans. This is the moment we been waiting for thousands of years. This is the time to finally have our revenge. This is the time to smite both the Arkans and the seeds of our betrayers."

The people cheered and voiced their support.

"Hail the patriarch! Long live King Athanax!"

He divulged to the people his plans of making the Arkans and Ithurians go to war and destroy each other. He would then send his main army to burn the Ithurian planet and move on to Treliseum to finish and destroy what remains of the Arkan and Ithurian war and finally claim the ultimate price, which is the Arkan kingdom.

Althea was thunderstruck by this revelation, knowing now that these people were once Arkans banished by her father and the reason behind their hideous appearances was because of Sorah's wrath. But the things that shocked her the most was knowing that her uncle Athanax was leading these Fallens on a path of vengeance and towards the destruction of both the Arkan and Ithurian. Fear started to find its way through Althea's heart as she thought the outcome of the future in case her uncle succeeds. She thought that she needs to protect Sarah and inform her sister of the impending danger.

Althea decided to leave the planet immediately. Unfortunately, she became careless in her haste to escape. Her heart was pounding with fear which was greatly felt by Athanax. He followed the emanating fear and looked up and saw someone moving on top of the dome. He quickly took his dragon and flew above to stop the fleeing intruder.

Athanax's eyes bulged out and his mouth gape upon seeing Althea in front of him.

"You! You're supposed to be dead!" Athanax exclaim.

Althea was also startled by her uncle's sudden presence. Her stomach churned unpleasantly as she saw the Draakabs immediately surrounded her.

"Isn't it ironic my dear niece? I was just telling my people about my plan of destroying your father and sister and then you happen to drop by!" he glared at Althea with a smirk on his face.

"You will never succeed! You failed once and I will make sure you do so again!" she held her head straight up and faced him with a clenched fist.

"Well, I think that would be hard to believe my child, because today you'll meet your end. Kill her!" he pointed his finger at Althea and commanded his Draakab.

Lights radiated from her body and immediately transformed to her armored form and fought the Draakab. Her powers were much stronger compared to the Fallen since they lost half of theirs when they were burned by Sorah's flame. But her singular strength was not enough to fight the enemies that relentlessly attacking her. She swung and slashed her Serdius, killing as many she can but her body started to become heavy for every attacks she made and her consciousness was starting to ebb away. She was getting exhausted. The Fallens kept on coming and were able to inflict several wounds on her, but even so, she fought with all her heart and determination to escape that place no matter what.

While she was busy fighting the enemy in front of her, Athanax saw a chance and treacherously attacked her from behind; he stabbed her in the back with his poisoned Serdeus. The sword tore her skin and plunged deeply into her back, sinking right through her organ. Her eyes rolled in the back of her head and screamed in pain as Athanax twisted his Serdius further into her. A horrible and excruciating burning sensation was felt by Althea who fell down to her knees. She turned around and saw her uncle's disfigured face. Athanax holding his Serdeus still impaled at Althea's back. He then grabbed her forehead to see through her memories. He saw images of Sorah, Narie and Sarah but before he could dig deeper into her memories, Althea slowly balled her fist as her flames came out of her palm. From a small fireball, the flame grew quicker and larger. Athanax saw her flames building up and cowardly jumped away as far as he could to take cover. Out of desperation, Althea unleashed a devastating fire explosion that killed all the Draakabs surrounding her. Athanax was lucky enough to survive the blast. As the cloud of smoke dissipated, Althea was nowhere to be found. Athanax ordered his soldiers to search for her and never let her leave the planet. Althea however, has already flown out to the sky and out of the black planet. She was badly wounded and the poison that Athanax stabbed her with was beginning to take its toll. Nevertheless, she was determined to return to Eres, to Sarah, before it was too late.

The soldiers informed Athanax that they could not find Althea and believed that she might have escaped the planet. He knew that she would not last long with the poison he infused in her body. But Athanax did not want to take chances, he told Bronax that he will travel to Eres and personally deal with the Ithurians.

"Bronax, I shall bring three thousand of our warriors with me to Eres, I want you to prepare the main army and wait for my message to move," Athanax commanded.

"Yes my king, I shall wait for your word," Bronax obeyed.

Athanax then assembled his three thousand Draakabs and left the black planet toward Eres. He could almost taste his revenge for the Arkans and Ithurians, and longed to once again set his foot back in Avetus.

Althea has been losing a lot of blood and barely holding on to consciousness as she flew back to Eres. She endured the pain and the fatigue. All she could think of was to return to Sarah at all costs before it is too late for her. She made it back to Eres and desperately flew to reach home. As she saw their house, Althea suddenly lost consciousness; she fell from the sky and violently crashed into the barn, startling Sarah and Sune who were sleeping inside the house.

Sarah and Sune got up and saw the barn was on fire. They went outside to see what happened or what hit them. They quickly grabbed the bucket and fetched water to douse the fire out, but before they could get near, they saw a person in armor bloodied and wounded, staggering coming out from the fire. They didn't realize right away that it was Althea.

"Stop! Who are you? What have you done to our barn?" asked Sarah.

But Althea was still too dazed, she couldn't hear Sarah's voice. Sune stood in front of Sarah to protect her. Sarah saw the trail of blood as Althea walked towards them.

"Once again, I'm warning you! What business do you have here?" asked Sarah sternly.

Then, Althea's armor slowly dissolved into steam, revealing her true appearance that left Sarah and Sune astonished. They could not believe that Althea has the power to change forms. Barely conscious, Althea collapsed.

"Mother, Mother, are you alright? What happened to you? Who did this to you?" Sarah whimpered.

"I am sorry Sarah for hurting you." Althea's voice quavered in pain,

It was the first thing that Althea uttered before losing consciousness again.

"Mother, Mother stay with me!" Sarah yelled.

She carried Althea inside the house and to her bed. She saw Althea's body sustained so many wounds, including the fatal stab at her back. She was also repulsed to see Althea's body decaying; Sarah was in panic.

"Mother, please wake up! Tell me what to do?" Sarah pleaded.

Sarah and Sune were so dumbfounded as to what happened to Althea. She tried her best to stop the bleeding and patched her wounds but her greatest worry was seeing her mother's body decaying rapidly. She did not know what do. There was no one she could turn to for help. All she could do was to be with Althea and pray that she wakes up to guide her what to do.

Chapter Sixteen

THE PAST MEETS THE PRESENT

t the Ithurian capital, Kiran together with Kina prepares to board the royal airship that will carry them to Treliseum and fulfill his mission of achieving peace with the Arkan king. He was escorted by emissaries and a small number of Zeltkova soldiers. King Turloch and King Ull were the only members of the Alliance that were present to officially send them off.

"Kiran we will pray for the success of your mission," King Turloch shook his hand.

"Only you can stop this looming war Kiran," King Ull added while standing at the side of King Turloch.

"I will do my best my lords," the determined Kiran replied.

As Kiran turned around to board the ship, he saw in a distance his father King Malkiem watching them; their eyes met and the king slowly nod his head once to which Kiran reciprocated with the same act. The people of Ithuria shrieked in support as the ship ascended towards the sky.

"Come back to us safely my son." King Malkiem whisper as he watched the ship go farther away towards space.

Kiran and the rest of the crew watch Eres from orbit and bid their farewell as they prepared to travel in hyper speed. The pilots fire the engines and Kiran gave the command to initiate the jump. It took Kiran and his crew days to reach the location of the worm hole. He ordered to terminate the hyper drive engines and switch to normal cruising speed. They voyaged for a brief moment and arrive at the coordinates. Suddenly, the pilots call Kiran attention. As Kiran arrived at the helm, his mouth gaped to see the worm hole in front of them. Everyone in the ship had the same reaction. As they make their approach, everyone grew wary while treacherous thunderclouds and lightning field surrounded the wormhole. The ship was shaken by strong turbulence as they begin the entry and became more and more violent, lightning struck the outer haul of the ship as they go further within the wormhole's treacherous lighting fields. Yet, the ship came out safely with only a minor damage.

Finally, they saw the planet Treliseum home world of the Arkans. It took them a few moment staring at the magnificent green planet in astonishment. Kiran ordered the descend to enter the planet's atmosphere. As the ship came out of the atmosphere, Arkan sentries patrolling the skies suddenly attacked them.

"Prepare for battle. Open the hatch. Shoot them down," Kina panicked as she gave the order.

"Belay that order," Kiran countered.

"But Kiran, they're attacking us! We need to defend the ship!" Kina was evidently tense.

"No, we entered their domain without warning. It is natural for them to defend their skies. No one opens fire without my command!" Kiran said in a defiant tone.

Kiran then asked the pilots to open the channel and pleads to the Arkans.

"This is Prince Kiran of the Ithurian kingdom. We do not want to fight you and we come in peace," Kiran repeatedly broadcasted on the channel.

The Arkan sentries ceased their attacks and signaled the pilots from the window to land their ship away from Fostrum. Kiran told the pilots to follow the Arkan instruction to avoid further confrontation. The ship landed outside the gate of Fostrum. He and his group disembarked and made their way to the gate by foot. As they neared the gate, they saw the Arkan army for the first time standing guard and looking daggers from the top of the gate.

"Do not dare make another step on our sacred ground if you value your lives," said Prea, the captain of the warriors of the light.

"Please, we come to make peace with you. We seek an audience with your king," Kiran implored as he made a few steps forward.

"Altrus Sorah reigned this land in the king's stead and you are not welcome here. Go back to where you came from and never return, or else face death," she menaced.

"Please, we do not want to go to war with you. We only want to negotiate for peace between our race," Kiran replied.

A loud and raucous laugh echoed from Prea and the Arkans.

"Negotiate? Peace? Who would dare negotiate with people whose ancestors were traitors of the kingdom?" Prea answered back in rage.

Kiran and everyone looked at one another with their eyebrows knitted together after Prea called their ancestors traitors, but before he could respond, Kina blurted in repulse.

"Liars! Our ancestors suffered injustice and oppression from your king!" her teeth gritting while she points her sword at Prea.

"Silence you fool! What do you know about your ancestors' sins? You know nothing!" Prea's voice roared in fury as she faced Kina with an icy stare.

Kina's body trembled as she couldn't hold the anger anymore. She flipped her mechanical wings and flew directly towards Prea. Kiran ran towards Kina to restrain her but didn't make it in time to grab her. Light appeared behind Prea's back forming her wings and summoned her Serdeus. With the speed of a peregrine falcon, she dove head on towards Kina. The two warriors clashed and Prea humiliatingly pushed Kina back. She was no match to the overwhelming strength and speed of Prea. Kina was easily defeated in battle, the Zeltkovas immediately ran to her aid,

"Stand down all of you!" Kiran commanded his Zeltkova.

"How can we make peace with the Arkan if we ourselves are acting like barbarians?" the anger in his voiced echoed the field.

Kina tried to reason with her brother but Kiran told her to lay down her weapon and never go against his orders. She was disheartened by Kiran's anger and merely lowered her head and stood down. Prea raised an eyebrow as she heard what Kiran told Kina and his soldiers.

"It is wise of you to tell your warriors to stop this futile act for I alone could have destroyed you all if I wish to," Prea's voice sounded cold.

Up above the gate wall, Narie suddenly walked in and looked down to see the disorder. Upon seeing Kiran, her heart raced and instinctively covered her wide open mouth. She quickly flew down to stop Prea.

"That is enough Prea!" she held Prea's shoulder from behind.

"Narie, what are you doing here?" her eyes glistened.

"I was informed by the messenger that an Ithurian ship entered our domain and Altrus asked me to investigate," Narie replied but her eyes were transfixed at Kiran.

Kiran held his chin, intensely staring at Narie as he strives to remember her. Her heart's beat faster seeing Kiran again. As Narie walked towards Kiran, he finally remembered that she's Sarah's friend. His puzzled look quickly changed to surprise upon realizing that she is an Arkan. Narie on the other hand, had confused feelings upon seeing the Ithurian prince. She knew that she should hate him after discovering the truth but her heart was telling her otherwise. Secretly she felt excited to see Kiran again.

"If I remember correctly you are Sarah's friend, Narie is it not?" Kiran asked.

Narie's eyes sparkled and her cheeks flushed at the thought that Kiran still remember her.

"Mind your manners Ithurian. You are not allowed to act so casually in front of Narie, the daughter of Altrus Sorah," said Prea who has become irritated by Kiran's rudeness.

Kiran didn't blink as he learned yet another revelation.

"Pardon my rudeness your highness and please forgive my sister for her rash action. We came here to seek the audience of Altrus Sorah and we want to make peace with the Arkans," Kiran and his party tilted their heads down and on bended knees.

Narie was uncertain to either grant Kiran's request or not, knowing that her mother would never make peace with the people whose Varkelos' blood flows within their veins, but Narie's heart felt throbbed as she saw Kiran beg.

"Wait here Kiran. I will convey your words to my mother," words fumbled in Narie's tongue.

"But Narie, they are traitors! They don't deserve peace." Prea stared at the Ithurian savagely.

"I clearly know that. Let my mother Altrus Sorah decide for their fate and not us," Narie knew that her decision would only rile her mother but she wanted to help Kiran in any way she can.

Kiran was grateful to Narie for considering his request. She was about to fly back to Avetus when Kiran blurted that he will be waiting for her return. Kiran's words melted her heart. She quickly turned her back from everyone to hide her crinkled face. She instructed Prea to watch over them until she's back, but to act accordingly if the Ithurians make a foolish move. Narie flew back to Avetus to speak to her mother. She found Sorah still in discussion with the Council for some matters of the kingdom. Asking Sorah to meet Kiran will surely infuriate her as Narie thought it would. She requested to speak to Sorah in private. The two left the council room and walked down the hall. Narie's palms were sweating, her heart began to speed up and her eyes kept making side-glances at Sorah. She gathered all her courage and informed Sorah that the Ithurian sent their prince to seek an audience with her to talk of peace. Her eyes sharply opened and saw the scowl in Sorah's face. Her mother resented the Ithurians for the betrayal committed by their ancestors. She immediately denied Kiran's request and asked Narie to send them back to where they came from. She added that she will not accept any peace with them. Sorah then walked back to the council room in a quick pace when Narie rushed to her and grasped her hand and begged her to give the Ithurian a chance. Sorah pulled a baffled look at Narie's defiance. She had always thought that she would hate those who betrayed the kingdom and the commandments. She looked at Narie with extreme focus and tries to un-puzzle the reason that made her change her belief. Sorah raised an eyebrow and became intrigue with the Ithurian prince.

"Alright Narie, I will meet this Ithurian but bring only him," said Sorah.

"Thank you Mother. I will immediately bring him to you," she answered in a polite manner.

Narie was very happy about the decision but she hid her excitement in front of her mother. She excused herself and left Avetus in haste to bring Kiran back with her. Sorah on the other hand, had clearly saw through Narie. She took a deep breath in an effort to calm her uncertainties for Narie. She wanted to see for herself this Ithurian prince that greatly influenced her daughter. Narie arrived back at Fostrum and told Kiran that her mother would meet him and only him. Kina and the soldiers did not agree to let him go alone, but Kiran insisted and told them that he will be fine. Narie wrapped her arm around Kiran's waist and flew back to Avetus. Her pale face suddenly turned red as rose while she holds Kiran close to her during their journey.

"Your Highness, I really didn't expect you to be an Arkan. At first I thought you were Sarah's sister." said Kiran.

She became agitated to hear Kiran started talking about Sarah.

"Please just call me Narie. I am not used to being addressed with nobility anyway." Narie diverted.

"Alright Narie. Anyway, you have my thanks for helping us meet your mother, my people will surely be grateful to you," Kiran sounded overwhelmed with gratitude and appreciation.

The conversation with Kiran fills Narie's heart with exhilaration all throughout the journey back to Avetus. Once they arrived, Kiran was visibly amazed to see the great city of the Arkans. It was truly magnificent as what was written in their ancient text. He was the first Ithurian to ever set foot on the city. He quickly noticed that most of the Arkans he saw were females and the men were nowhere to be seen. He didn't ask Narie about it for he was still gawking at the city's splendors. Narie took him inside the palace and brought him to the Council where the warriors of the light were waiting. Everyone inside the room stared coldly at Kiran.

"Narie, what is this traitor doing here?" one of the warriors asked.

"He is here to present his plea to Altrus and she approved it," Narie responded in an assertive tone.

She left Kiran alone in the council room to fetch her mother. Kiran was baffled as to why the Arkans kept calling them the descendants of traitors. He wanted to ask but Kiran was hesitant to even approach them. Altrus Sorah made her way to the Council escorted by Narie. Everyone in the room including Kiran bowed down to her. Sorah greeted the Council and everyone raised their heads afterward. As Kiran slowly raised his head to face Altrus Sorah, her eyes widened in shock and covered her gaping mouth with both hands upon seeing Kiran's face. She thought she saw Aran in front of her. She trembled as she tries to keep her composure.

"Mother, let me introduce to you the representative of Ithuria," said Narie with a big smile plastered on her face.

"Greetings your highness! I am Prince Kiran, son of King Malkiem of Ithuria. We are from the star called Eres. I and my people came here to beseech peace with the Arkans," Kiran humbled himself before Sorah.

Sorah could only gaze at Kiran in astonishment. She could not believe that he has the exact same face as Aran. Narie noticed that her mother was unresponsive and intently staring at Kiran.

"Mother are you alright?" Narie whispered.

Suddenly, Sorah's amazement turned to anger as she remembered the betrayal Aran committed in the past. It was painful for her to look at Kiran.

"Leave now Ithurian! You will never gain what you seek here. Leave now and never return!" she harshly told Kiran.

"Mother, could you at least give him a chance to hear what he has to say?" Narie importuned.

Sorah's mind was constantly being flashed with the memories of Aran and Althea's betrayal, as well as her husband's death.

"Please your highness, I beg of you to reconsider. Thousands of my people's lives will be at stake...." said Kiran but before he could finish his word he was abruptly interrupted.

"Silence! you betrayed my trust, there will be no peace" shouted Sorah covering her ears and struggles to catch her breath,

Narie and Kiran were puzzled by Sorah's emotional outburst; both didn't understand her claim about Kiran betraying her trust, for that moment was the only time they've met. Sorah holds back her tears and hurriedly left the council room; Kiran fell down to his knees with his palms resting on the floor, he was devastated about Sorah's decision and fearful that the impeding war will come into a grim reality. Narie was startled by her mother's harsh words but already expecting her decision. She saw Kiran on his knees with tears of despair. She holds Kiran's arm and helped him to stand up, there is nothing more that they can do. Clearly, Sorah will never accept peace with them. Narie escorted Kiran out of the council room where the warriors were smirking at him. Kiran was lost in despair and mumbling incoherently as they walked the hall, she can hear him saying about the lives that will be lost if the war happens,

"Tell me Kiran, why did you choose to seek peace with us knowing fully that we will never forgive your ancestors for their treachery" asked Narie with a tone that contain curiosity,

"I been wanting to ask you this earlier Narie, all of the people here kept calling my ancestors as traitors and I do not understand why" Kiran thirst for the truth,

They walked further along the hall and passed by the portrait of King Satorex, Narie stood in front staring her grandfather with sadness in her eyes, she began to tell Kiran the real story behind the war and his ancestors banishment. She revealed that the Arkan king most trusted friend betrayed him during the great war,

"During that time when my people was about to be destroyed by the rebellious Arkan, my Grandfather call unto his best friend for help, but that friend just stood by and watched them be annihilated" her fists trembles in anger,

"That is truly despicable and cowardly act by that friend" said Kiran with an expression of disgust,

"Yes indeed, and that best friend who betrayed my grandfather was Varkelos and his people, your ancestors" facing Kiran with a cold stare,

Kiran's brows furrowed and his jaw dropped hearing what Narie said. In his heart he felt naked and being displayed publicly after learning the truth about the sin that their ancestors committed against the Arkan king. He slammed the wall with his fist in anger for the lies and deceits that he and his people were made to embraced for thousands of years. He asked Narie the reason why his ancestor chose to betray the king, but Narie could not give him the answer to that question, only her mother and the primordial warriors knows the truth behind it. Once again, Kiran begged her to help him convince Altrus Sorah for another chance to speak to her, he will do everything he can to make Sorah reconsider peace and stop the impending war. He revealed that the Ithurian kingdom is facing a time of difficulties and danger, they require the Algios found in Treliseum to save their kingdom and to ensure the unceasing survival of his people. Narie clearly saw what Kiran was trying to achieve, he does not believe war should be the solution for this long time conflict between the two race, he specifically came to Treliseum hoping to seek peace with the Arkan. Narie somehow find similarity between Kiran's noble effort of stopping the war and saving his people to the burden that her mother is carrying in order for the Arkan to exist. She was moved by his resolves, his courage and saw him to be a great man, a good leader with a kind heart. Seeing these attributes from Kiran, she suddenly felt a thud pounding her chest, her faced flushed bright pink and felt giddy.

She got scared and confused from the feeling that growing stronger every time she look at Kiran,

"I will talk to my mother again to hear your plea, please wait for me at the council room" said Narie with her chin down to avoid his glance. Kiran got ecstatic after hearing Narie and unwittingly pulled her into his arms,

"Thank you Narie for believing" said Kiran,

The warrior escorts were appalled seeing him holding her like that, while Narie was savoring every moment of it,

He suddenly realized his rudeness and loosen his arms around her. Narie however quickly turned her back at Kiran and hold her cheek with one hand and the other to her chest,

"Please forgive me for my discourtesy" Kiran said embarrassingly,

The two eyes met and gave each other a smile, Kiran was escorted by the warriors back to the council room while she made her way to her mother's quarter. Upon entering the room, she saw Sorah looking at the portrait of her father,

"Did you send the Ithurian back" Sorah asked while she wiped the tears from her eyes,

"No mother he is in the council room waiting for you to hear his plea" her voice shook as she answered Sorah,

Sorah was enraged by Kiran's defiance and called the warriors to cast him away, but Narie countered her order which stunned Sorah. Narie goes down to her knees and begged her to reconsider about peace. Sorah tilted her head to the side looking at Narie with a face plastered with confusion; she couldn't understand her actions and emotions anymore,

"Why do you favor the Ithurian so much Narie?" asked Sorah, eager to find out the answer,

"Because Kiran reminds me so much about you mother, your sacrifices, your burdens and hard work in keeping our race from dying, he too will do everything to protect his people and those that he cares just like you" Narie calmly answered,

Narie begged her to give the Ithurian another chance to correct the mistakes and atone for the crimes committed by their ancestors in the past. She also believed that under Kiran's leadership, peace between the two races can be achieve. After hearing Narie's answer, Sorah slowly walked up towards the window and turned her gaze to the sky. She realized that it's not only that Kiran has the same face as Aran but he also has the same kind heart, the one who looked after the interest of others before himself. It was painful to remember the past, but it also gave her solace as she remembered Aran's warm smile. Sorah took a brief moment to collect herself and afterwards expressed her intention of talking to Kiran once more. Narie was happy and thankful that her mother had a change of heart.

"Why do you believe so much on this Ithurian?" asked Sorah.

"I do not know why Mother but there is a feeling inside me wanting to," she replied holding her chest.

Sorah knew that Narie was infatuated with Kiran and feared that she may have already fallen for him -- something that she will have difficulty accepting. But the thing that worries her the most is to see her getting hurt, a feeling she wouldn't want Narie to go through and endure.

"Bring the Ithurian to the throne hall and I shall speak to him there," said Sorah.

Narie left the room and hurriedly returned to the Council room. She was excited to inform Kiran that Altrus Sorah has agreed to meet him once again. They entered the hall and saw silhouette of Sorah sitting on the backlit throne.

"Leave us Narie. I want to speak with the Ithurian alone," said Sorah.

A cold and eerie silence filled the room after Narie left. Sorah stared at Kiran intently from behind the shadows.

"Answer me this Ithurian: why should we make peace with you, whose forefathers were traitors of our kingdom?" she asked in a scathing tone.

"Your highness, I do not know the answer why my ancestors betrayed your king. Indeed, it is an unforgivable act, but that was the path they chose to take. I am entrusted to find a way to ensure the survival of my people and that's the path I choose to take right now, even if it costs me my life," he retorted softly as he tightened his fists and looked Sorah with a fixed eye contact.

Watching Kiran speak, she constantly seeing Aran in her memories, begging her father to spare Althea's life in exchange for his. It was absolutely reminiscent of Aran. Kiran was also willing to sacrifice his life for his people.

"What will the Arkan gain from this peace that you seek from us?" asked Sorah. She was putting Kiran to a test.

"Your highness, the Arkan will gain nothing from us. We do not have anything to offer you," he bluntly answered.

Sorah laughed at Kiran for not being tactful with his words and straightforwardly said that peace will not be an option for them. Sorah told Kiran to go back to Eres and to warn his king never to challenge the Arkan again. Faced with frustration, Kiran refused to accept failure and will do everything to deny the fate of war from coming.

"From the time of our forefathers, we were told to believe that the Arkans were an oppressive and envious race, and that they are the embodiment of injustice," Kiran uttered, mystifying Sorah.

"Even if these were the teachings passed down through the ages, I find it difficult in my heart to embrace it and have always believed that there is something good and great about the Arkans" he added.

"And why do you think of that?" she leaned to one side of the armrest of the throne touching her chin as she asked.

"How could the Arkans be like what my ancestors taught us if the Arkans already have everything," Kiran answered, perplexed.

He has always believed that the Arkans have lived in abundances. They possessed powers that defy logical understanding. They were blessed with wings to soar the skies freely. And above all, the Arkans were given the gift for which any living creature would envy -- the gift of everlasting life. So it only left him with great doubts towards the teaching that the Arkans envied their ancestors.

Sorah was fascinated with Kiran's keenness to seek the truth and felt his genuine intentions for peace. He went down to his knee and asked Sorah for her forgiveness for what their ancestors had done in the past. He also begged for her to save his people in exchange for his life -- a gesture which made her remember Aran's final moments before his death. Sorah shed tears seeing Kiran crossing the same fate as Aran. The throne hall was quiet, Kiran was still down on his knee and Sorah in deep thought. She then told Kiran that she would contemplate about peace and instructed him to wait for her answer. Sorah called Narie in to escort him to the Council room. As the two walked down the hall, Narie expressed joy because her mother was reconsidering about peace and praised Kiran for his great effort. Sorah went back to her quarter and took Aran's portrait once again.

"Is this what you truly wanted?" said Sorah while looking at Aran's portrait.

She cried in pain remembering the betrayal but when she looked at Aran's eyes in the picture, she suddenly remembered something that Aran said to her,

"I will always be there for you to protect you and I will always love you"

Sorah felt the warmth and comfort in Aran's words and thought that this might be his way to atone for his sin. Then, the sound of trumpets was heard in the palace. Narie and Kiran, as well as the warriors, proceeded to the throne hall where Sorah will make her pronouncement. Sorah informed the Council that she will give the Ithurian a chance for peace. All the Arkans except for Narie, were taken aback by the decree. Kiran however, heaved a sigh of relief and felt triumphant that war has finally been averted. The warriors demanded a reason for Sorah's decision. She explained that for all the hatred she kept in her heart and the belief that the traitors will always be traitors, it all changed when she heard Kiran's plea. Through him, she saw hope for the Ithurians' penance for their wrongdoing. The warriors were reluctant to accept Sorah's decision but did not dare challenge her. Instead, they put their trust on Sorah's wisdom. Narie and Kiran were full of joy about Sorah's decision. She looked at her mother from afar and felt that Sorah has somehow found peace in her heart. After the declaration, Altrus Sorah and Narie asked Kiran to extend his stay for a day or two in order to discuss plans and preparations needed to start the talk of peace between the Arkans and the Ithurians.

Chapter Seventeen

THE REVELATION

n the forest of Eres, Sarah was desperately patching Althea's wounds. Her hands were stained with Althea's blood, cloth after cloth, there were spills of blood all over the floor. She made all effort to stop the bleeding. Shaken by fear on the thought that her mother would never again wake up, Sarah wept uncontrollably. She wiped the tears away, smearing her face with blood while she continued working on Althea. Sarah was able to stop the bleeding, but couldn't do anything about the rapid decaying of Althea's body. She has never seen that kind of wound before. Sarah's face manifested distress; she was helpless. She kneeled beside the bed, placed one hand on her head while the other held Althea's hand.

"Mother please wake up. Please forgive me for what I said before. It was disrespectful of me to treat you in that way. Please Mother wake up!"

"I promise to be good and obedient and I will never go against you anymore, so please open your eyes Mother," Sarah pleaded while squeezing Althea's hand.

Sarah had hoped for either Narie or Kiran to be by her side in that moment of her desperation. But she knew that there's nobody there to help her. Suddenly, Althea slowly opened her eyes and heard Sarah's cry. She was able to come back to her senses and touched Sarah's head, startling both Sarah and Sune.

"Mother! thank heavens you're awake!" Sarah and Sune were ecstatic to see Althea had woken up.

Sarah and Sune heaved a sigh of relief after she was able to come around despite the injuries she obtained. Althea immediately uttered the danger that was about to come. Sarah however did not understand what Althea been mumbling.

"Mother, please save your strength. Help me and tell me what do to stop this wound from spreading!" she asked while she focused on Althea decaying body.

"There is nothing that can be done for me now Sarah. This poison is unknown to me and I have no cure for it," gasped Althea.

Sarah cried fearing of losing Althea forever.

"Listen to me Sarah. You need to be strong on your own now. Remember what I have taught you. A great war is again coming," Althea uttered.

Sarah shook her head and weep as she refused to listen anymore to what Althea was saying. She tries to stop her from continuing but Althea knew that her end was near and wanted to tell Sarah the truth before it was too late.

"Sarah, there is something you need to know," said Althea.

"Please Mother stop! You need to rest," Sarah broke down.

"My time is almost over, but before I leave you, I need you to know the truth." Althea paused.

"Sarah, I am not your real mother." Tears gush down her bloodied eyes as she confessed to Sarah.

Upon hearing this revelation, Sarah froze and speechless. She hoped that what she heard was a lie but Althea continued on to reveal everything to her.

"Sarah, I've always loved you and treated you as my own flesh and blood, even if you despise me now for what I had just revealed to you. I will not blame you and I will always love you as my daughter," Althea wailed as she extended her arms to reach Sarah.

Sarah forcefully took Althea in her arms and hold her tightly. It was an act Althea was not expecting her to do. Both weep as they held in each other's arms.

"Please forgive me Sarah for hiding the truth from you. You were in danger at the time and all I wanted was for you to be safe" Althea sobbed.

"Mother, forgive me also for saying those cruel words. I did not mean them. I love you so much and I promise I will be a good daughter from now on," Sarah assured.

"You do not have to apologize to me. I knew that this day would come but I did not expect it to be under these circumstances."

"There is greatness in you my child. You are an Arkan Sarah, with the blood of nobility flowing through your veins and you can wield unimaginable powers at your will." Althea revealed as she fought for her breath.

"Who is my real mother then?" she asked softly.

"Your true mother is Sorah, my sister," Althea's voice choked with emotion.

Sarah was overwhelmed by the last truth she revealed. Althea still trying to speak but she was already coughing blood. Sarah tried to stop her and did whatever she could to help ease her pain but Althea seemed to have reached the limit of her endurance. With her last breath, she mumbled:

"Forgive me Sarah, I love you!"

"Sorah"

Althea's eyes slowly closed and falls into silence. She whispered her sister's name one last time before succumbing to her death. Sarah was paralyzed from shock seeing Althea died in her arms, she felt her heart bursting into a million pieces. Her world appeared to have suddenly stopped. Everything moved slow as her gaze was fixed at Althea. Her body stiffened and felt heavy. Sune could not hold his tears either. He approached Sarah and sat beside her and together they mourned for Althea.

A moment has passed. Sune was trying to tell Sarah to let Althea rest but she was unresponsive. Sune tried pulling Sarah back to her senses when suddenly she called out to Althea.

"Mother you need to wake up! Mother wake up!" she grabbed Althea's shoulders and shook her like a rag doll.

Sarah cry in anguish as she repeatedly spoke those words. Sune couldn't bear seeing Sarah like that anymore, he pulled her away from Althea's lifeless body once again. But then, Sarah had a gush of memories of joyful moments she spent together with Althea, from the time she was young up to the present age. She finally realized that everything Althea did was to love her and to protect her. It fills her heart with guilt. After all the love Althea gave her, she couldn't believe she said those cruel things to her. She grabbed Althea tight and forcefully shook her.

"Wake up Mother! Wake up! Wake up!" Sarah retorted from a soft voice that piped up to the extent that she was already yelling at Althea.

In the end, Althea didn't answer her back. She didn't wake up. Sarah stared at Althea's lifeless body and refused to believe that she was not coming back anymore. She wrapped her arms around Althea tightly. Tears pouring down her eyes unceasingly and mumbled.

"Please don't leave me alone Mother."

As she held her mother's lifeless body, she detached herself from reality and from her despair, she screamed in agony and uttered.

"Wake up Mother!"

In an instant, Sarah's body emits a powerful force of blinding light, which pushed Sune back as he struggles to find something to hold on due to the immense power Sarah was unleashing. Sune was in a state of openmouthed astonishment as he saw Sarah's true power. Sune shed tears upon witnessing wings of light forming behind Sarah's back, as she holds Althea in her arms tightly. The light started to enwrap the lifeless body of Althea. The wounds in Althea's body slowly disappear and the poison that plagued her body was cleansed by the light. Sarah's wings become clearly visible, while Sune still holding onto dear life as he trembles in fear. Then, Sarah screamed her lungs out,

"Wake up!"

A powerful pillar of light burst out from her body and quickly spreads throughout the planet which even rippled across the galaxies. Her light passed through the body of Athanax who was about to reach Eres. He quickly felt the power of the light and saw that some of his wounds have disappeared. It baffled him and made him more eager to reach Eres. Sarah's light also travelled through the other side of the wormhole and reached the planet Treliseum. The light passes through all the Arkans on both Fostrum and Avetus. The warmth of the light pass through Sorah's body and gave calmness in her heart, a sensation she never felt for a long time. Sarah's light miraculously stretched to the chamber of the sleeping Arkans. It passed through King Satorex's body and was reciprocated by a small twitch of his finger.

Sarah's light slowly fades away. She was still holding on to Althea as she cries unceasingly. But then, Sarah felt an accelerating thud in her chest. At first, she thought it was her heartbeat, she then looked at Althea and saw her took a deep breath. Sarah and Sune were aghast to see her alive again. Althea slowly opened her eyes.

"What happened to me?" asked Althea with a bewildered look in her eyes.

"Mother, you were unconscious and we tried to wake you up and you did!" Sarah stuttered.

With creased brows, Althea raised her hands in front of her and turned it side to side. She noticed that all of her wounds disappeared, even the poison that consumed her body were cleansed away. With a blank stare, she remembered a similar happening when Sarah was still a baby back in the cave at Fostrum. Althea knew then that she should have died from the wounds she sustained from her battles with the assassins and yet she miraculously survived, akin to what just happened at that moment. Althea looked at Sarah and started to believe that she might have inherited the power of life, which was believed to have been lost after the Queen Vasilia passed away.

"Tell me what happened Sarah. What did you do?" she eagerly asked.

"I was so scared Mother. I thought we've lost you!" Sarah stuttered and shivering.

"What did you do Sarah? Answer me!" Althea raised her voice to calm Sarah down.

"When you closed your eyes, I tried calling you many times to wake you up but you never did. I felt scared and angry with myself, then I felt a burning sensation in my heart. I don't know what happened next," Sarah evenly answered.

Althea confirmed that Sarah inherited the Queen's power of life. Like her, she too has the ability to heal people, but Sarah inherited much more, a power that is much stronger than her.

"Sarah listen to me. A great danger is coming and we need to do something to stop it," said Althea.

Sarah didn't understand what Althea was saying.

"Mother, you have said this too many times before, this great danger. What is it?" asked Sarah with a slack expression.

"The coming of the second war, a war that was left unfinished. It's an inevitable war of revenge," she grabbed Sarah's arms and stared brazenly in her eyes.

Still, Sarah's face was painted with confusion as she struggles to grasp what Althea was saying, but seeing how desperate and worried Althea was, her heart couldn't help but to tremble in fear as she hears about the second war. Althea finally told Sarah the entire truth about the Arkans, who she is, her parents, her birthright and the truth behind the war.

"You are the lost princess of the Arkans, the granddaughter of King Satorex," Althea revealed.

"Then, this means that Narie is my sister?" said Sarah with an upturned face.

"Yes, she is your younger sister" Althea replied.

It made Sarah very happy to know that Narie was truly her sister; she always felt the kinship she had with her during the times they spent together. Althea then confessed about the betrayal she committed against her mother Sorah, a betrayal that led to the death of her father Aran. But she told Sarah that her father loved her mother so much, which is why he sacrificed his life. Upon hearing Althea's past, Sarah was in tears realizing that Althea has been burdened by this guilt for a long time.

"We need to stop Athanax's plan. He is the king's brother who has deep hatred towards us and he is bound to destroy both the Arkans and the Ithurians with the army of the Fallen," Althea was clenching her hands together.

"Mother, is he the one that gave you that poison?" she inquired.

"Yes, I went to their planet and learned all of his plan. He is the one who stabbed me with that poison. He is coming here to Eres to make the Ithurians wage war with us." Althea's eyes were tight and worried.

Sarah gasped after learning about Athanax's plan. She knew that Kiran was in the Arkan planet making peace with her mother and if

218

Athanax's plan succeeds, Kiran might be killed by the Arkan for being a betrayer.

"Mother we need to act now. Kiran went to see my mother Sorah to seek peace," Sarah panicked.

"Sarah you need to understand that we as Arkans, have the duty to stop the war and to stop Athanax. Are you ready to take on those tasks?" she asked Sarah with a daunting stare.

"Yes Mother with all my might," Sarah answered, full of determination to save Kiran.

Althea instructed Sarah and Sune to immediately proceed to the Ithurian capital and inform everyone, especially the king about the danger that is coming to Eres and the coming of the Fallen. Without any more hesitation, Althea finally decided to go back to Treliseum to Avetus and talk to Sorah about the impending evil that was looming. Sarah was concerned about her plan of returning to Avetus, fearing the uncertainty that awaits Althea when she faces the Arkan and her mother Sorah. But Althea has made up her mind. She knew that she need to set things right with Sorah someday and that day has come.

"Don't worry about me Sarah, I will be fine. Besides, Narie will be there. But I'm afraid of leaving you here alone," the concerned Althea expressed.

"Don't you worry about me Mother. Sune is here to protect me and we will do our best to convince the Ithurians," Sarah replied.

"No matter what happen wait for my return and together with your mother, we will fight this battle together," Althea vowed.

Lights enfold Althea's body and became her armor to show Sarah their true powers. She slowly balled her fists to grasp the light that was emanating from her palm. From there, her Serdeus appeared. Sarah and Sune's eyes widened, marveled by her power. Althea reminds Sarah that she too has that power and she needs to learn it soon, to be able to fight the battle that lies ahead. She guides Sarah with the most important thing she need to know and that is the summoning of her Serdius. Sarah quickly grasped what Althea was teaching her but because it requires more time to learn the summoning techniques. She was only able to call upon the incomplete form of her Serdeus. Althea was somehow satisfied with what Sarah has accomplished so far. At least, using her Serdeus it will allow her to have a weapon that will never break as long as she's alive.

The moment has come and the three prepares to go their separate ways and fulfill their missions. Sarah and Sune hastily traveled to the Ithurian capital to warn the people of the invasion. Althea was about to leave Eres to deal with Sorah, but worries for Sarah being left alone in Eres. If the Fallens could make their way into the planet, Sarah will be fighting the battle alone against Athanax's army, and in order to defeat the Fallen, she will need both the Arkan and Ithurian forces to fight together. But Althea foresaw that there was a poor chance that the Arkan and Ithurian will join forces to fight Athanax. With these uncertainties in mind, she feared for the Ithurian and Sarah's safety if she fails to return with Sorah. Althea was contemplating of a way to protect the people of Eres in her absence, when suddenly, something came across her mind, a thought that would somehow give Sarah some time until she returns with or without the Arkan army.

Chapter Eighteen

LIES AND GREED

A thanax finally reached Eres with his army and proceeded to the forest to hide their dragons as what his advance party had done. Before he could enter the city, he needs to disguise himself and his army to hide their hideous appearances. The messenger informed him that they found a village with a military outpost outside the city of Enor, Athanax immediately ordered his minion to head towards the village to acquire the disguises they need. The messenger tilted his head to the side with crinkled brows as the small contingency of Morsus' forces hiding in the forest earlier was nowhere to be found. He simple shrugged his shoulders and assumed that they might have joined Morsus' group in the city.

Athanax and his army arrived at the village. He surrounded the area and ordered to attack and kill all the villagers and soldiers at the outpost. They slaughtered them without mercy, even women and children, were not spared from their heinousness. Athanax's minion ate the dead and cannibalized their body parts especially their faces. Most of the Fallens used the Ithurian soldiers' uniforms and armors, which they pillaged from the dead and the outpost armory.

After a hearty meal at the village, the Fallens then moved to Ithuria to begin infiltrating the city and to execute their evil plan of making the Ithurians wage war with the Arkans. As they reached the Ithurian capital, Athanax ordered his army to spread throughout the city. He was immediately met by Morsus and reported to him that the war was halted because the prince was able to convince the people to negotiate with the Arkans. The Alliance of the kings will not decide until the prince return in three weeks' time. Athanax grinned in anger as he heard about Kiran's intervention. He had expected that the Ithurians were already preparing for war by now. He ordered Morsus to bring some warriors and stop the prince from coming back to Eres,

"He must never return to Eres. Kill them all," he told Morsus.

Morsus hurriedly left the capital with his group, took their dragon from the forest and flew to the wormhole to await Kiran's return. He instructed his men to prepare for an ambush with the intention of stopping the prince from ever reaching Eres.

Athanax learned that the root of all of this conflict between the Arkans and the Ithurian was because of the Algios, the energy that the Ithurian desperately needed for their survival. He knew that in order to convince the Alliance of the kings to go to war, he needed to convince the people first. And from the Ithurian desperation, he saw a perfect chance for him to get on with his plans. Athanax ordered his men to spread lies to the entire kingdom that would propel the Ithurians to change their stand against the war. The Fallens spread their lies to the Ithurians, telling them that Treliseum, the planet of the Arkan holds abundant supplies of Algios that could last for eternity and there are riches more than enough to sustain every single Ithurian. The lies spread like wildfire. The people were quickly blinded by the riches. Slowly, as greed bred greed one after another, the Ithurians started to change their view about the war. With an evil laugh, Athanax was amazed to see how easy it was for these Ithurians to be deceived and to forsake their principles once riches and power were involved. He continued exploiting their greed to corrupt them and to manipulate them to move according to his wishes and plans.

Athanax was successful in creating a division within the kingdom. Many of the Ithurians have expressed agreement to go to war with the Arkans. He succeeded the first stage of his evil scheme and now turned his eye to the Alliance of the kings. He, together with a handful of spies that earlier infiltrated the palace escorted him to the Council room. During that time the Alliance was facilitating talks with their temple priest, military advisers, politicians and merchants. It was a perfect chance for him to poison these people with his lies. The Council members were in deliberation. King Turloch and King Ull, the temple priests, and some merchants were not in favor of war, believing that they were not strong enough to challenge the Arkan king. It was also their belief that the aftermath of the war would surely weaken or destroy the kingdom. While the opposing party would still argue about the birthrights they hold as descendants of Varkelos,

"My lords, friends, I already gave my son my words. We will wait for his return and if he fails in his mission, then will think of our next move," said King Malkiem.

Suddenly, with his chin high and shoulders back, Athanax walked in and made his presence known to the Council.

"Greetings your highnesses, my lords and gentlemen" he bowed his head and politely greeted.

"Who are you and how did you enter this council meeting?" King Kelon walked towards Athanax in haste and blocked his path.

"My lord, I am just an ordinary citizen and a merchant of this great kingdom. As a merchant, the faith of my business relies on your decisions about the war," the lying Athanax said with a hidden smirk in his face.

"Then, take your sit among the merchants there and speak only if you are asked," King Kelon pointed his finger to the merchant's seats as he glared at Athanax,

Athanax lowered his head once again to show his obedience but on the inside, he was gritting his teeth and his eyes were full of hatred for taking orders from a mere mortal. He endured and swallowed his pride so he could move freely inside the Council room. The kings and other Council members debated about their views and opinions. They could not arrive at a common stand and decision, but instead to wait for Kiran's return. In this internal turmoil, Athanax saw his chance and was not hesitant to take it. He lifted his hand and expressed his intention of addressing the Council. King Malkiem raised an eyebrow and focused on Athanax. He asked the other kings for objection but none was heard. He then allowed Athanax to speak.

"My lords, let me properly introduce myself. I am *Feirul*, I and my people came from the line of Ghalatix, which is one of the closest aids of our revered savior Varkelos."

"I can assure you that the reason why the Arkans will not consider peace with us is because they are hiding the riches and abundances the planet Treliseum holds," Athanax stated.

The Council was perplexed. It was the first time that the Alliance heard of such revelation. He continues on with his lies telling them that Fostrum itself, the city their ancestors built, holds unlimited supplies of not just Algios but also precious rocks and gold deposits. He further added that the most precious and guarded treasure the

Arkan hold lies in the holy temple of Avetus which houses the scroll of power that unlocks the secrets of the Arkan powers. The Council members were at the edge of their seats, their eyes rolled from side to side, while some members were visibly craving for the gold and precious stones he mentioned. He plans to manipulate the Council using greed and it was working in his favor.

"How did you know of these things? We the Alliance didn't even know about these!" King Ull asked inquisitively.

"We have scrolls of evidence left by my ancestor Ghalatix as he was one of the builders of Fostrum. And from these scrolls it tells us about these abundances, my lord," Athanax answered confidently. His confidence made his lies even more convincing.

He told the Council that the reason for their descendants' banishment was due to the Arkans' greed and selfishness. They didn't want to share it with anyone. King Satorex was worried that Fostrum has become a powerful city and feared that if they used these riches against him, it will surely end his reign. After Athanax's revelation, some of the council members who previously opposed the war had a sudden change of heart. Athanax was insistent on instigating that these riches were more than enough for every man in Eres and with these riches, they would have the power to conquer and destroy their enemies.

Athanax could see that some of the members were still reluctant and doubtful. He realized that he need to have one final push to put them under his total control. He concocted a story that the Arkan king knew that their ancestors held the power of ending his reign. The Arkan king then sent his army to suppress them, but they fought back to stop the oppression which in the end triggered the Great War of the

Arkans. Athanax claimed that because their ancestor fought back, they were able to inflict great loss to the Arkan army.

"Going to war with the Arkan king is unthinkable. Haven't your ancestors told you that he annihilated one-fourth of the Arkan rebel's army in the blink of an eye?" King Turloch glowered at Athanax.

"Yes indeed. It is written in history and also proves how ruthless King Satorex is," Athanax answered, his nostrils were flaring and the vein in his temple was visibly throbbing. That is how immense he hated his brother.

"Then going to war with them is absolute death for us" King Turloch retorted.

"My lord, we should not be frightened of King Satorex anymore," Athanax scowled at the council.

"And why is that?" the curious King Malkiem asked.

"Because my lord, King Satorex is dead. He died a long time ago during the war," Athanax replied with a psychotic smirk.

Mouths fell open. Everyone had incredulous looks plastered on their faces. They couldn't believe how an immortal and powerful king could have died. Athanax further explained that the king sustained a grave wound which was inflicted by his own brother, leading it to his death. King Malkiem demanded Athanax to show proof of what he claim. As he didn't see it coming, Athanax decided to divert the retort to King Malkiem.

"My lord, you will know I speak the truth once you learn that your son is already dead in the hands of the Arkans," Athanax dared King Malkiem back.

King Malkiem was taken aback. Fearful that what he just heard might be true, he became worried about Kiran and regretted sending him off to Treliseum. The Council was utterly deceived by his lies. The Ithurians started to gain confidence and became arrogant as they thought that they could now fight the Arkans and reclaim Fostrum. King Turloch and King Ull, who remained anti-war, was concerned of being outnumbered by pro-war Ithurians.

"Malkiem, now you realize that it was a mistake to allow your son to talk with the Arkans. Now, what is your stand?" King Gileal demanded Malkiem to address the matter hastily.

"But Kiran is there! We need to wait!" King Malkiem nervously replied.

"For how long are we going to wait? He might be dead already for all we know!" King Kelon said. King Malkiem turned pale, lifted his hand and took a hold of his chest.

"How dare you say that! Even so, we still need to consult the people before we, the Alliance could decide," King Ull lashed out at Kelon.

"We shall then seek the people's opinions!" Athanax quickly interrupted.

Sarah and Sune arrived at the capital and saw chaos in the city. A group of people supporting the war was lashing out violently against a group that was against it. The Zeltkova soldiers intervened to break the fight and tries to restore order. Sarah was boggled as she searched for answers about the pandemonium. She heard people saying about riches that Fostrum hold, then about King Satorex being dead and about Kiran being killed by the Arkans.

"Who told you this?" Sarah forcefully pulled one or two citizens to the side to interrogate.

The people she asked however, gave different answers. Some said that it was the Alliance who told them, while some said that it was already written in the ancient text and that they had simply not seen it yet. The people were completely fooled by the lies Athanax and his minions had disseminated.

Then, the Council made their presence at the palace balcony to once again address the people, only to see that the crowd were in chaos and disorder. Athanax's spies fueled the anger and greed of the people. Their opinions clashed with the remaining few who still opposed the war.

"Cease these actions at once and listen to me!" King Malkiem slammed his fist against the balcony as he ordered his people.

The violent uproar was quickly pacified by the Zeltkovas, but before King Malkiem could start addressing the people, most of the Ithurians had been shouting, expressing their favor of war against the Arkans. King Malkiem and even Sarah were in disbelief. They turned their heads and looked at the people who singularly expressed their desire for war.

"My people, I come to you once again to seek for your stance against the Arkans. The Council has a reason to believe that my son Kiran and my daughter Kina are in danger."

"I know that as king, I must honor my word to my son and to my people, but I could not simply turn my back at the possibility of losing Kiran, the heir to the throne of the Ithurian Empire, who is now in the hands of the Arkans."

"My people, are you with me as I set off to Treliseum and claim my son, your prince, back to us?" King Malkiem voice trembled in apprehension.

Many of the Ithurians supported the war. Those who opposed were silenced by the majority. The people were corrupted by greed and only thought of personal gains alone. They blindly agreed and gave King Malkiem their support to fight the Arkans.

"Now Malkiem, this is the will of the people. You must not ignore it," said King Gileal, with his palm open directed towards the people who wildly cheered below them.

"The people have spoken and decided to support this cause. What do you say Malkiem?" asked King Kelon.

"Perhaps we should wait for Kiran. It is also possible that he might have successfully negotiated peace with the Arkans," said King Turloch who remained true to his word to give Kiran enough time after he come back from his mission.

"Enough Turloch and Ull! We listened to you when we sent Kiran to the Arkan, and now you play by our rules because the people have decided," King Gileal said arrogantly.

Glaring at Kelon and Gileal, King Ull took a step forward to confront the two but his arm was pulled back. King Ull turned around and saw King Turloch shaking his head. King Malkiem sought the opinions of the Council members before he makes his final decision. The commanders of the military were eager to go to battle against the Arkans to avenge their ancestors' honor, while the merchants only agreed because of the riches of Treliseum. King Malkiem then turned to the last branch of the Council, the temple priests. King Turloch and King Ull were confident that the priests would never agree to war. The four kings and the other members fixed their gaze at the temple priests. Everyone nervously and painfully waited for the decision. Then the head temple priest stood up, covered his mouth with his fist as he cleared his throat and gave their approval to go to war. King Turloch was pushed back to his seat as he collapsed in shock. King Ull smashed his palms on the table and looked daggers at the priests.

"Your holiness, how could you approve such an endeavor?! Many lives will be lost if we go to war," King Ull was both in fury and dismay.

"We the temple priests, believed that it is our spiritual and moral obligation to stop the tyranny and injustice of the Arkans and to save our beloved Prince Kiran; thus, we gave our approval to King Malkiem," expounded the head priest.

The lies Athanax told regarding the scroll of power was the real reason the temple priests changed their judgment. They were blinded by their hunger on unlocking the knowledge of the Arkan as well as their godlike powers. Now, King Malkiem was left with no choice but to approve the war as the whole Ithurian kingdom demands it. He then walked back towards the balcony where the people down the courtyard cheering and shouting. He faced them and proclaimed his decision.

"Ithurians, the Council has spoken! We fight the Arkans and claim back our land!" King Malkiem bellowed.

"Death to the Arkans!" the people shouted.

Hiding behind the cloak of deception was Athanax with an evil grin on his face. He was exuberant to see that he had successfully manipulated the Ithurians and that his plan was finally working well according to his expectations.

Chapter Nineteen

THE REUNION

It took Althea thousands of years to finally return back to Avetus and face Sorah. As she reached Tresileum, she couldn't stop her tears from falling upon seeing her beloved home world again. As she flew to the clouds, she saw heavily armored sentinels patrolling the skies of the Arkan realm. Avoiding confrontation, she decided to land outside the city of Fostrum and make her way to the great wall by foot. Althea bravely walked across the open field of Fostrum towards the wall. The Arkan warriors above the gate saw Althea and ordered her to stop, but she defiantly continue her way to reach the gate. Then, three Arkan warriors transformed into their armor forms and flew down to confront her. They blocked her path and warned her of grave consequences if she dares to continue.

"I am here to see Altrus Sorah on urgent matters," Althea stood tall as she faced the three warriors.

"State your name. Are you with the Ithurians?" one of the warriors asked, pointing her Serdius at Althea.

"My name is irrelevant. Let me see Sorah," she hastily replied.

"How dare you plainly address Altrus! Turn back! Your rudeness is not welcome here!" the three warriors approached and scowled at her.

But Althea ignored the warning and walked right through them. The three warriors looked at one another in confusion after witnessing her defiant attitude. The three felt insulted and ran after Althea to restrain her. They clutched both of her arms and blocked her path. But Althea easily escaped their firm grips which compelled the warriors to resort to their Serdius. Althea had no choice but to fight her way through. The three Arkans ran towards Althea holding their Serdius and ready to strike her down. Althea stood her ground, easily parrying and dodging their attacks. After a brief moment of battle, she defeated the three Arkans without even breaking a sweat. The other warriors above the wall gaped in disbelief at the sight of their brethren falling easily from the speed and strength of the mysterious stranger. One warrior quickly flew back to the palace and informed Prea the captain of the warriors, about the situation they were facing at the wall. Prea immediately flew down to personally handle the matter.

Upon arriving at the wall, Prea looked down too see the disturbance below. The first thing that caught her gaze was Althea, her face turned pale as if she had just seen a ghost. Prea's shocked expression drew fear among her fellow warriors. She flew right down in great speed to stop Althea from further engaging her warriors. Althea saw Prea flying down like a ball of light. The ground shook and sank, creating a crater as Prea landed in the middle of the battle with one knee and both of her knuckles touching the surface. Althea leaped back away from the crater in the nick of time. Prea slowly stood up and stared at her.

"Althea, is that you?" asked Prea.

"Yes Prea it is me. It's been a long time," Althea answered in surprise.

"You're alive? How is this possible? They said you were killed during the war!" Prea stared in disbelief.

"I can explain later, but right now I need to speak to my sister," said Althea urgently.

The warriors gawked at Althea after hearing that she is the sister of Altrus. Prea denied her passage and audience with Sorah. As a member of the warriors of the light, she was tasked to uphold the commandments and one such law denies all the rights and honor for a banished Arkan.

"I am sorry Althea. I'm afraid I can't let you in. You are no longer one of us. Please leave this place in peace," she told Althea.

"I need to speak to Sorah. This involve the survival of the kingdom. A great danger is coming!" All the Arkans looked and mumbled as they heard Althea's warning.

But Prea stood firm and ignored her plea. She once again asked her to leave. Althea sighed and frowned upon Prea's stubbornness. Faced with frustration, she balled her fists and glared at Prea,

"If you won't let me see Sorah, then I'm afraid I just have to go through you," she told Prea in a stern voice.

The warriors were angered by her transgression and flew down to stop her, but Prea ordered them to stand down knowing that second-age warriors will be a no match for her. Only a primordial Arkan such as herself could stop Althea.

"All of you stand down. I will deal with her alone," Prea commanded her warriors.

Prea was determined to stop Althea no matter the odds. She summoned her Serdeus and pointed it at Althea. An action that tells Althea that diplomacy has failed and Prea together with her warriors will not listen to reasons anymore. It compelled Althea to summon her Serdeus and prepares to fight Prea. The two eyes met as they circled around each other, gazing fiercely. There was a brief silence in the field. It was so quiet; all they could hear was their own hearts pounding. A soft gust of wind then swooped down their faces. Each paused for a moment and took a deep breath, as the howling wind passed. The two warriors swiftly ran towards one another and the battle commenced.

Even though Prea was a primordial Arkan, she still could not equal Althea's strength and powers since King Satorex's blood flows within her veins. Prea kept on attacking but because of Althea's speed, she easily evaded her strikes and fails to even lay a finger on her. Prea suddenly transformed to her armored form in order to match Althea's powers and speed. The other warriors stood still and intently watching the battle, they were astounded to see Prea struggling to fight the mysterious stranger that could wield a Serdius. They couldn't even believe that she had to use her armored form to stop Althea. One of the warrior sent a messenger to Avetus to inform Altrus Sorah and requested her presence immediately.

Using her armored form, Prea was able to match Althea's strength and speed. She persistently chased and attacked Althea, driving her back away from the gate. Althea felt the power of Prea's armored form against which she couldn't take lightly anymore. Prea flew towards Althea in godlike speed, raised her hand and swung her Serdius, wounding Althea in the arm making her lose her focus. Prea then turned around and kicked Althea, throwing her down to the ground.

"You better leave Althea, if you know what's good for you," Prea warned her.

Althea slowly stood up, raised her head and gave a deadly glare, which daunted Prea and the other warriors.

"If you really don't want to listen to my plea, then I have no choice but to kill you," Althea sternly affirmed.

The warriors were deterred. They saw in her eyes that she would do everything to get past them.

"Then come on, show me what you got," Prea challenged her.

Althea's body was then enfolded with light and slowly transforming into her armor. As the light diminished, Althea was in her complete armored form. Everyone stood still and watched in shock seeing that the mysterious stranger was indeed an Arkan. Prea's hands trembled and her heart pounding in fear, realizing the full power of Althea. Althea spreads her wings and flew towards Prea to finish her once and for all.

The messenger arrived at Avetus and quickly informed Altrus Sorah of the situation at Fostrum. Sorah was told that a renegade Arkan at the gate was causing a problem. Sorah was still in a discussion with Kiran and Narie and instructed the messenger to speak to Prea and let her deal with the matter. But the messenger quickly replied that Prea was currently fighting the renegade Arkan and was having trouble stopping her. Sorah looked at the messenger with her brows furrowed at the thought that Prea as a primordial Arkan, the strongest Arkan second to her, was having difficulties.

"Prea is having trouble stopping the intruder?" asked Sorah in disbelief.

"Yes Altrus Sorah. The warriors of the light believe that we may need your strength," the messenger replied.

"I will depart immediately to personally deal with the intruder," said Sorah.

Sorah abruptly finished her discussion with Kiran and asked him to return back to Eres for now and will resume their talk in the next meeting.

"Altrus Sorah, again I couldn't thank you enough for giving our two races a chance for peace. I and my people are eternally grateful to you and I look forward to our next meeting," Kiran politely said.

"Yes indeed, we're also looking forward to seeing the new dawn of peace and forgiveness. I will send our emissary to inform you of our next discussion," Sorah replied in haste.

Sorah instructed Narie to finish up with the minor details before sending Kiran back to his crew. Sorah left the throne room escorted by Antra and Anthelia and hastily flew to Fostrum. On her journey, her mind began to filled with curiosity on the thought about the mysterious Arkan that even Prea's strength and power could not stop. Upon arriving at the top of the gate, Sorah noticed that everyone was standing infixed attention and their eyes were in deep worry. As Sorah took a step forward, she was appalled to witness Prea being miserably defeated by the renegade armored Arkan. She turned her gaze at the unknown Arkan and instinctively covered her mouth upon seeing Althea alive. Sorah couldn't move as her body shuddered.

"Altrus, Prea is losing and being driven back by the intruder," said Antra with great concern.

Sorah was distracted by her emotions after seeing Althea again. She couldn't believe that after all these years, she was alive and wasn't killed by Athanax,

"Altrus, what is your command?" Anthelia frantically shouted, seeing Prea inevitable fall.

Althea relentlessly attacked and pushed the battered Prea back. She was clearly a no match for Althea. As Althea was about to deliver the final strike, Sorah immediately jumped in the middle of the battle and blocked her strike.

"Sorah," the surprised Althea said.

Althea trembled seeing Sorah up close. Deep within their hearts they were happy to see each other again. But suddenly, Sorah remembered the betrayal. She immediately became spiteful towards Althea and began attacking her.

"Sorah stop! Listen to me!" Althea pleaded.

Althea tried to defend herself against Sorah but Sorah was way stronger than she is. Nevertheless, Althea put up a valiant battle and managed to hold her ground.

"Listen to me Sorah! The kingdom is in danger! Where is father?" she asked as her voice quivered.

"Silence! you don't deserve to see the king! For all of us, you're already dead!" Sorah blurted out in anger.

Pain pierced through Althea's heart after hearing Sorah's words. Even so, she still tries her best to reason with her, but Sorah seemed to have been clouded with pain and anger.

"Please! A great danger is coming and you need to know about your..." Althea was abruptly interrupted.

Before she could finish what she wanted to say, she was pushed back by Sorah's punches. Althea's body became heavy, gasping for breath and dragging her body after a long brutal battle with her sister. Finally, Sorah delivered the final punch that knocked Althea unconscious to the ground. Sorah ordered her warriors to bring Althea back to Avetus and to put her in the prison chamber.

The warriors looked at Sorah in shock upon seeing her catching her breath. It was very rare for them to see their Altrus fight a long battle and to be wounded like that. Sorah however, didn't mind what her warriors think, all she felt was a great relief knowing that Althea was alive. Sorah still finds it difficult to forgive her. Pain may still linger in her heart, but the love for her only sister outweighed everything. Sorah vowed to protect her this time and will make sure that she will not go anywhere alone anymore.

As Sorah and the other warriors flew back to Avetus carrying Althea and the wounded Prea, Narie and Kiran arrived at Fostrum to send him and his party back to Eres. Narie immediately noticed that there was a commotion above and below the gate but didn't pay much attention. She brought Kiran back to his group and met Kina and the Zeltkova waiting for them.

"Kiran! we're glad you're alright!" Kina was joyful to see Kiran again.

"I bring good words. The Arkans have agreed for peace. We need to bring the good news to Father and to our people," said Kiran with an upturned face.

As Kiran and Kina continued talking, Narie couldn't help but notice the bewildered faces of her kin. As she kept shifting her glance at the gate, damages on the wall caught her attention and knew that a battle had just occurred. She immediately interrupted the two and asked Kina if she saw any unusual event that happened before they arrived. She learned from Kina that a battle did occur and just ended minutes after they came.

"What battle are you talking about?" Narie asked.

"We saw a lone Arkan walking towards the gate and requested for passage, but your warriors denied her and she forced her way in. Then, a battle broke out," Kina shared.

"What lone Arkan?" Narie became more anxious.

"She singlehandedly defeated four of your best warriors," Kina smirked with a little sarcasm in her tone.

Narie bit her lower lips and held her chest.

"But the lone Arkan was defeated by a warrior they called Altrus Sorah," Kina added.

Narie was surprised to hear that her mother fought the intruder, which was a very rare thing for her to do.

"Where's the lone Arkan and my mother?" asked Narie.

"They flew back to your city together with the lone Arkan," she answered.

Narie told Kiran to return to Eres for the meantime and that she would send words for him about their next meeting. The jubilant Kiran and his group boarded the royal ship and departed Treliseum on route back to Eres to deliver the good news. Narie already had a feeling who the lone Arkan was and worries for the consequences that might befall on her. She hurriedly returned to Avetus in order to confirm the lone Arkan's identity.

Upon reaching Avetus, Narie immediately searched for her mother and found her in the throne room where the healers tend to her injuries. Her brows drew together as she saw her mother inflicted with wounds, even though she is the most powerful of all the Arkans,

"Mother, where is the renegade Arkan? How is she?" Narie asked anxiously.

Sorah looked at Narie with a baffled face after hearing her ask the question. She was expecting Narie to ask the intruder's identity first, but instead she wanted to know where she is and somewhat felt concerned for her condition.

"The intruder has already been taken care of," explained Sorah.

"Where is she mother? I want to know," her eagerness conveyed suspicion.

"She's in the prison chamber for now and we will decide her punishment later," Sorah replied, while intently observing Narie's behavior.

Narie hurriedly walked towards the door to go to the prison chamber to see the lone Arkan. But because of her growing suspicion, Sorah stopped and confronted her.

"Stop Narie! Why are you so eager to meet this Arkan? Do you know anything about who she is?" Sorah bluntly asked.

Narie's heart raced and her stomach churned unpleasantly with her mother's questioning.

"Did something happen to you when you were in Eres?" Sorah added.

"No Mother. Nothing happened. It's just that I wanted to know who this Arkan that defeated our warriors and even injured you," she uneasily defended herself.

For the first time Narie lied to Sorah. It was difficult but she thought it was necessary. She wanted to be sure if Althea was indeed the intruder. She excused herself and rushed to see the prisoner. Down at the prison chamber, she was stopped by the soldiers guarding the gate.

"Let me pass. I need to see the prisoner," Narie said in a commanding tone.

But the soldiers denied her of passage and told her that by the order of Altrus Sorah, no one is allowed to neither see nor speak with the prisoner. She strongly felt that the prisoner was none other than Althea, which explained why the chamber was heavily guarded. She became concerned for Althea thinking of the injuries she sustained from the battle with her mother. She once again returned to Sorah and sought her permission to be allowed in the chamber.

"Mother may I be allowed to see the prisoner to question her?" she asked in a soft voice as she struggle to calm herself.

"That won't be necessary Narie. I will personally undertake that task," Sorah hastily replied.

"But Mother, this is a such a small task for it to take your precious time," she insisted.

"You don't need to worry about that Narie. Just focus on the negotiation with the Ithurian and leave this matter to me," Sorah told her in a stern voice and gazed at her with suspicious eyes.

Narie frowned at her mother's decision and realized that she need to be careful of what she would say and do, to further avoid attracting her mother's suspicion. She left the throne room in haste and contemplated on other ways to see the prisoner. Althea on the other hand, still unconscious inside the prison chamber and being treated by the healers sent by Sorah.

Narie wanted to find out the truth about the prisoner. She thought that the only way to know about her identity was for her to travel back to Eres and find out if Althea and Sarah are there. She secretly left Avetus and began her journey to Eres alone, a journey she's eager to take after knowing the truth about who Althea and Sarah were.

Meanwhile, Sorah was reluctant to see Althea down at the prison chamber, fearing that hatred towards Althea might overcome her emotion. Deep inside her heart, she still has love for Althea and didn't want to lose it completely. Confused of what must be done with her sister, she went to the sleeping chamber of the male Arkans to seek for her father's help. Sorah entered the cold chamber and saw her once proud father now frozen in time, waiting to be awaken by a miracle. She approached him and touched the glass, she shed tears talking to the king seeking his guidance.

As she sat in the quiet chamber, she remembered the time when Althea was still a child. She saw Althea sad and crying about their mother's passing. She held Althea's hand and remembered saying:

"Don't cry Althea, I promise to protect you and I'll always be here for you."

Her words confronted her. Sorah cried as she saw memories of them together and the promise she made. She looked up to her father and saw for the first time -- tears coming out of King Satorex's eyes. Her pain and confusion was felt by her father even in his deep slumber.

Chapter Twenty

THE DEATH OF PEACE

arah and Sune were in the palace courtyard listening to King Malkiem's announcement as the people continuously cheers for war with the Arkans. The Ithurians were easily deceived by the lies of Athanax about the riches and power Treliseum holds. Thus fueling the people's greed and making it easy for them to be corrupted. Sarah and Sune forced their way up the podium while King Malkiem was still giving his speech.

King Malkiem announced that the Council has reached a consensus. He then declared war with the Arkans.

"We will reclaim what is rightfully ours! We will reclaim the land of our ancestors!" King Malkiem shouted while raising both of his fists to the sky.

King Turloch and King Ull remain opposed to the war but did not dare say anything anymore since it was futile to argue with them for they're already been blinded by greed. As the people applauded, all of a sudden, with great courage Sarah stood up the podium with Sune.

"You are making a big mistake!" Sarah shouted.

The people immediately went quiet and gave her a bewildered stare. Athanax rushed to the balcony to know who dared said those words and got the surprise to see that a young girl with a fox was brave enough to challenge the king. Athanax, with a scowl on his face, stared at Sarah and felt that he has seen the her before but couldn't remember where. King Malkiem saw Sarah and remembered her as the person who saved Kiran.

"How can you say our decision is wrong young girl?" King Malkiem demanded.

"My lord, a great threat is coming to Eres and it is not from the Arkans. Our people are in danger and you must act upon it with haste," Sarah warned.

Confused to she said, everyone looked and mumbled with each other.

"And what is this danger you're implying that's coming to us, young girl?" King Kelon sneered.

She revealed to the people that a war against the Fallen Arkans is coming to Ithuria. They're already bound for Eres with the sole purpose of annihilating the Ithurian race. Athanax froze and stared wide-eyed as he heard about Sarah's revelation. He did not expect anyone from Ithuria would know about his plan. Then, he remembered Sarah, he remembered seeing her in Althea's memories. The Ithurian laughed when Sarah mentioned about the Fallen Arkan.

"The Fallens were already destroyed thousands of years ago by the Arkan king himself!" Athanax's voice trembled in panic.

Athanax pointed his finger at Sarah and accused her of being an Arkan sympathizer, but Sarah stood tall with her chest thrust out boldly and warned the people to prepare for war with the Fallens and that they would need to seek the aid of the Arkans if they were to survive against the Fallen.

"The Fallens were not entirely destroyed by the Arkan king, some of them survived and for three millennia, they managed to thrive and increase their numbers, devouring planets and feeding on the inhabitants. For thousands of years, they also nurtured hatred towards the Arkans and Ithurians." Sarah looked into the eyes of the confused Ithurians as she exposed the Fallens.

"Lies! There are no account or evidence that the Fallens are still thriving. For some millennia, the planets were peaceful until the Arkan drew the first attack," Athanax frantically countered.

Everyone agreed and cheered what Athanax said. To further cast out the people's doubts, he constantly spoke of the riches found in Fostrum to further entice the people's greed and divert their attention away from the Fallens. Sarah was trying her best to convince the people about the coming danger but none would believe her. Instead, she was accused as an Arkan sympathizer. Athanax influenced the king to arrest her for being a traitor to the Ithurian Empire. King Gileal and King Kelon concurred and immediately gave the order to seize her. The soldiers rushed to arrest Sarah but were thwarted when Sune discharged a strong lighting field that repulsed them back. Sune roared at the Ithurians and gave them a menacing stare. He was ready to kill anyone who would hurt Sarah.

"Is there anyone among you who believes in my words? Is there anyone still faithful to defend the Ithurian race?" Sarah asked the people in desperation.

None responded to her plea and instead she was reciprocated with ridicule and insults. Sarah had no choice but to leave the city. King Turloch and King Ull quietly left the Council and immediately sent their agent to follow Sarah and request a secret meeting with her. As Sarah and Sune were about to step out of the city gate, the agent suddenly approached them.

"The faithful of the Ithurian Empire is requesting to meet with you in secret," the agent informed.

"What faithful?" Sarah's eyebrows furrowed.

"Come to this place and you shall know them," the agent replied and immediately left.

Sarah and Sune decided to go to the place where the agent told her to be. As she turned around the corner, she gawked at King Turloch and King Ull escorted by a few of their bodyguards already waiting for her. Sarah was confused and asked them the reason for the meeting.

"What is the meaning of this?"

The two kings introduced themselves and told Sarah that not all of the members of the Council believed that war with the Arkan was the solution. They stood by and supported Kiran's belief that making peace with the Arkan was the right path to choose.

"So, do you believe that the Arkans are not our enemy and it is the Fallens that we need to face?" Sarah eagerly asked,

"My child, we may have enough reason to believe your story about the Fallens," King Ull was about to reveal an important information to her.

"Why is that my lord?" Sara's forehead crinkled in confusion.

"We received a terrifying message from one of our explorers we sent out to space. The message tells us that they were attacked by monsters and hideous creatures, which we now think were the Fallens. We believe none of the explorers survived that attack," King Turloch was sadden.

"Then why did the Council still insist going to war with the Arkans if you already have this evidence. You know that you're putting Kiran's life in danger, don't you?" she balled her hands in anger.

The two kings told Sarah that they tried to stop the decision but a man from the south, whose name was Feirul, influenced the Council, revealing a history of their ancestors which even they didn't know exist. They described the man as very eloquent in his words and when he speaks as if he was there during the great battle that sealed the fate of their ancestors. Sarah was also told that not all the people in Eres despised the Arkans. There were the Deodarian people from the far south who embraced the teachings and culture of the Arkan.

"Then maybe we can ask them for help?" she raised her eyebrows and gave a questioning gaze.

"That my child would be impossible. The Deodarians are the sworn enemies of the Ithurians. Even if we asked them, I'm not sure if they would be willing to help us," King Ull answered.

The two kings learned from Sarah that when the time the Ithurian army left Eres to wage war with the Arkans, the fallen will exploit that chance to attack since only a handful of soldiers will be left to defend Ithuria.

"How did you know of this?" King Ull asked with a puzzled face.

"My mother Althea. She was able to infiltrate the Fallen's planet and acquired all of these information," Sarah replied.

"Your mother? How was she able to go there?" King Ull was confused even further.

"It's a long story my lord, but what we need to think right now are the Fallens. They're real and they're coming for us," she glared at the two kings.

King Turloch and King Ull knew that they're going to take a big risk in believing her story, but they put their judgment on the message they received from the explorers. King Turloch decided to stay back on Eres with his army to defend the kingdom, which was contested by King Ull.

"If you're going to stay here to fight the Fallen, then I as well will stay here," King Ull said.

"No my friend. You need to go with Malkiem or it may raise suspicion that we are Arkan sympathizers and we could face harsh consequences," King Turloch raised his hand and touched his shoulder.

"But Turloch, if what this young girl said is true, how could your army fight with that multitude?" King Ull was concerned for his friend.

"We still don't know how strong the Fallen army is and even so, I'm counting on you to continue convincing Malkiem to stop the war," King Turloch remained hopeful that they can still convince Malkiem once Kiran returns.

"If that is your decision then I shall abide, I will leave half of my army here under your command," King Ull decided.

King Turloch ended the meeting and told Sarah to return to the city once the entire Ithurian army leaves Eres. Sarah agreed and the three parted ways. Sarah and Sune left the Ithurian capital for their safety and set their camp outside the city to wait.

The decision was final, King Malkiem ordered his generals to prepare the Ithurian army and set course for Treliseum. All the Ithurian military arsenals and Zeltkova soldiers boarded their battleship and started their journey towards the Arkan planet. King Turloch approached King Malkiem and requested that he be allow to stay behind to guard and defend the Ithurian kingdom against the Deodarians, which was easily approved by King Malkiem.

Unknown to the Council, Athanax's warriors disguised as Ithurians soldiers were able to board the ship without suspicion. The citizens cheered and celebrated as the Ithurian Armada ascended to space to finally wage the long awaited war against the Arkans. Sarah and Sune saw the sky filled with battleship and couldn't help but worry. She wished that Althea and Kiran would be able to reach through her mother Sorah before everything is too late.

Meanwhile, Kiran and his group finally came out of the wormhole and headed back to Eres. His heart race and eyes sparkled in excitement as he couldn't barely wait to tell his father about the success of their mission. But unknown to them, Morsus and his men were already on the other side of the wormhole, waiting to ambush and kill them. As Kiran's ship passed by the moon. They were suddenly attacked by the Fallen from behind, the creatures grabbed a hold of the ship and forced their way inside. Kiran and his crew were caught off guard by the attack. He quickly ordered his pilots to fire the engine boosters and make a run for it. He was determined to stop the war and bring the news back to his father no matter what happens.

As they traveled in extremely high speed, the creatures were still clinging outside, using their claws and crude weapons to ripped the outer haul of the ship. Kiran, Kina and the Zeltkovas fought the Fallens that penetrated inside, but they were too many for them to handle. One by one, the soldiers fell until the creatures broke through the front of the ship killing both the pilots, sending the ship spiraling out of control in hyper speed. The remaining Zeltkovas forcefully pushed Kiran and Kina inside the escape pod and ejected them in time before the ship hit a meteor which instantly disintegrated, killing everyone inside including the Fallens.

The emergency pod was violently thrown out of the ship and crashed on a nearby asteroid rock. Inside the pod, Kiran and Kina were wounded and unconscious. Morsus and his remaining warriors arrived at the crash site and confirmed that everyone onboard the ship had perished. He took the ship royal emblem to show as proof that the prince was eliminated. Luckily, he didn't notice the escape pod that survived the crash. Morsus immediately left to rendezvous with Athanax.

Not far from the crash site, Morsus saw the main fleet of the Ithurian warships making their way towards the wormhole. He sensed that Athanax was with the royal flagship along with the Council. He was secretly let in by the spies aboard the ship. Morsus then gave Athanax Kiran's emblem to show that his mission was a success. A sinister grin on Athanax's face was apparent as he saw the emblem. He wasted no time and hurriedly called the attention of the Council, especially King Malkiem to pass on the news that Kiran and his party were mercilessly attacked and killed by the Arkans and that no one had survived. He then presented to the Council the ship royal emblem, where Kiran and his party rode as a proof that he was, indeed killed.

"How did you acquire this?" King Kelon gasped.

"My lord, I have sent my scouts ahead to guard our route against any ambush the Arkan would make and not far from here they found pieces of the prince's ship," Athanax lowered his head to hide the smirk on his face.

King Malkiem fell down to his knees and broke into tears upon seeing the emblem. His heart was crushed from learning that his children, his son and heir to the kingdom were killed by the Arkans. King Malkiem clenched his fists and tremble in rage as he glared at his generals and ordered them to make haste to Treliseum to avenge the killing of Kiran and Kina. Athanax excused himself and left the king's chamber for he couldn't hold his evil smile anymore, knowing that everything was going smoothly according to his plan. With the prince eliminated in the picture, the flame of peace that he carried died along with him. And now with hatred and greed, he finally has the Ithurians completely under his control. After King Malkiem learned about Kiran's fate, his mission of securing the future of his people and the kingdom was suddenly changed to revenge and the destruction of the Arkans.

Narie meanwhile came out of the wormhole and swiftly flew back to Eres. On her way, she happened to pass by floating wreckages and immediately recognized Kiran's ship. Narie's face turned ashen and her heart pounded like a drum as she tries to decipher what happened. She was suddenly struck with the idea that there's a connection between Althea's returning to Treliseum and Kiran's fate. Narie felt a profound pain in her heart thinking of Kiran's demise. She covered her faced with her hands and sobbed in distress. It was her first time to feel such pain of losing someone she truly fallen in love with.

She wandered around the wreckages coping with grief and the loss. Then, she accidently touched a piece of the wreckage and caught a glimpse of what happened. She saw Kiran and his group fighting the creatures -- the same creatures -- that she and Althea fought against before in Eres. Then her eyes widened to see Kiran and Kina being thrown out of the ship. Narie frantically searched the area for the pod that she seen in her vision and successfully located it in one of the asteroids. She saw both Kiran and Kina inside, still unconscious, bleeding and need to be treated immediately. Narie knew that it was too far for her to return to Treliseum. The closest planet that she can go to was Eres. Concerned with Kiran and Kina's condition, she pushed the pod back to the Ithurian planet.

As Narie steered clear some dangerous nebula clouds, she unexpectedly came across the Ithurian armada in full speed on route to the wormhole. She gasped for air as she saw the entire fleet. She was puzzled as to why the Ithurians would send their warships to Treliseum. She wanted to return to Avetus and warn her mother, but leaving Kiran and Kina now will surely put their lives in danger. Narie looked back to the direction of the wormhole with her brows drawn together and with a heavy heart, she turned her back and chose to save Kiran instead.

Back at Ithuria, after the whole Ithurian fleet left Eres, King Turloch sent out messengers to all the soldiers that remained in the five kingdoms to prepare for battle and to defend their city. The soldiers were mystified by the order.

"My lord, what are we preparing for? We are at peace with the Deodarians," one commander asked.

"Commander, let us be prepared and hope that no harm comes our way," King Turloch replied, with his eyes tight and worried.

The commanders didn't understand what the king meant but obeyed his order. A small number of Athanax's spies and warriors remained in the city with the intention of killing the king and raised havoc before the main Fallen army arrived on Eres. The leader of the spies sent out messenger to Bronax to inform him that the city was ready for the taking.

As the Ithurians were occupied in preparing their defense, the Fallens have made their move and decided to kill King Turloch. They treacherously attacked the soldiers by slashing them with their claws and crude weapons, killing many of the unsuspecting soldiers. They ran towards King Turloch with fierce eyes of a predator that's ready to devour its prey, but the Zeltkovas were able to sprint to his side and surrounded him with their guns drawn shooting the attacking Fallens.

They were able to stop the attack and killed some of the creatures. The defiant King Turloch and his Zeltkovas angered the remaining Fallens for putting up a futile battle. The Fallen then ripped the skins covering their bodies with their claws to reveal their true form; the hideous and disfigured appearances repulsed the Ithurians. King Turloch couldn't deny anymore the fact that everything Sarah said about the Fallens was true after all.

The Ithurian soldiers fired their weapons sporadically in panic. Many of them were stricken, King Turloch ordered his men to rally beside him and reform the defensive line.

"Stand fast! Draw your swords and fight to the bitter end!" King Turloch shouted in desperation.

King Turloch instructed his soldiers to form a defensive line with their shield locked in front and weapons behind to push back the monsters. He managed to bring the morale and spirit back to the soldiers. The Ithurian line was able to kill and drive back the creatures, but because the Fallens possessed remnants of their Arkan powers, they were stronger and faster than the Ithurians. The leader of the Fallens ordered his last platoon of creatures to attack and waste no time to kill King Turloch. The creatures snarled at the Ithurian and went berserk as they ran towards the soldiers, ramming them and shattering their line. The Ithurian line was broken and many Zeltkovas died in the rampage of the creatures. King Turloch was separated from his troops; the remaining Zeltkovas tries to go to his aid but were blocked by the creatures. Claws protruded out of the leader's hand and immediately ran toward the king to finish him off. King Turloch stood up and drew his sword to fight the Fallen.

The creature swung his claws to cut King Turloch down, but the king was thrown away by the power of the creature's blow as he blocked the strike. Still in daze, King Turloch staggered to stand up, he raised his head and saw the creature walking and grinning up at him. The creature slowly raised his claws and swung at him once again, he closed his eyes and prepare himself to meet his end. Suddenly, Sarah appeared and blocked the creature's strike. King Turloch saw the back of Sarah with sun rays passing through her sides.

"My lord, gather your men and kill all the remaining enemies. I'll take care of this," said Sarah.

King Turloch rushed back to his men and rallied them. The creature stared at Sarah in disbelief and laughed.

"Little girl, are you lost?" he taunted.

"I know exactly where I stand and that is here to destroy you!" Sarah sneered at the creature,

"Such bold words! I shall kill you and eat your flesh!" the creature snarled.

Sarah and the leader of the Fallen engaged each other in a vicious battle. As an Arkan that carries the blood of King Satorex, Sarah was more powerful than her opponent. After realizing that he's getting a beating from a young girl, the Fallen was infuriated and attacked her savagely. Sarah summoned her Serdius and ran towards the creature and slashed him in one strike, severing his head from the body. King

Turloch and his men on the other hand, were still battling the remaining Fallen, when Sune jumped in to help them. He ran towards the Fallens and unleashed a breath of destructive lighting shock that killed all the remaining creatures.

King Turloch and the soldiers fought for breath and fell down to their knees with eyes wide open, trying to fathom what had just happened. They couldn't believe that the Fallen Arkans were alive and has infiltrated the city as well as Eres -- just what Sarah has told them.

"Now you understand the danger. Now the threat has come true," Sarah looked at the eyes of the Ithurians.

"What are we going to do?" King Turloch asked, still shivering from his ordeal.

"Send out messengers to all the villagers in the kingdom. Get all the able men! We will need all the people we can get to fight them!" Sarah sternly answered.

King Turloch sent out messengers and ordered his generals to assemble the army and all the military arsenals in their possession to prepare for the fight of their lives.

"King Turloch, we must send message to the Deodarians to help us in this fight," Sarah urgently told King Turloch.

"But I don't think they will help us," the doubtful king said.

"We must try, as inhabitants of this planet. They must fight with us to defend not with anyone's kingdoms or empires but for Eres," Sarah sounded in desperation.

Fear found its way inside Sarah and Sune's heart after seeing the evil has finally shown its face. Both were scared knowing that this will be their first time going into a battle and without Althea by their side.

Chapter Twenty-One

THE SECOND TREACHERY

arie finally reached the orbit of Eres. Pushing the pod carrying Kiran and Kina inside made her a little exhausted but nonetheless, she was relieved knowing that Kiran and Kina will be alright once they arrive at the city. From afar, Narie saw something strange in the stars ahead. She noticed the rapid displacements of light as if the stars were moving. She momentarily left the pod floating in orbit and flew towards the strange sighting. As she came near enough, she was shocked to see the massive army numbering to a million heading towards Eres. The banner that they carry is the same as those carried by the creatures she fought before. Her brows knitted close together as she stared with vacant eyes at the event that was unfolding. She need to get Kiran and Kina back to Eres immediately and warn his people about the army that was about to come down.

Narie flew back to the pod and safely carried it back to the Ithurian capital. As Narie descended, the Ithurian soldiers surrounded her with their weapons drawn mistaken her for another Fallen. Narie put down the pod, summoned her Serdeus and readied to defend herself.

"Stand down! Put your weapons away!" a loud commanding tone was heard from King Turloch.

Both Narie and the Zeltkova soldiers stared at each other, dumbfounded by the king's order.

"What business does an Arkan have with us?" King Turloch looked at Narie from head to toe with his mouth gaping.

"I've brought Kiran and his sister back and they need to be treated of their wounds immediately," Narie answered.

King Turloch gasped as he saw the ship's emergency pod with Kiran and Kina inside unconscious.

"Prince Kiran, Kina! What happened to them?" King Turloch's voice stuttered in panic.

"I found them on my way here. Their ship was ambushed and destroyed by the creatures and only Kiran and Kina survived," Narie shared.

The soldiers quickly rushed to the pod, took Kiran and Kina out and brought them to the infirmary to treat their wounds. King Turloch asked Narie why an Arkan such as herself would want to help the prince.

"Because he made peace with us and I am obligated to help him," Narie answered in a straightforward manner.

Blood drained from King Turloch's face when he heard Narie. They have learned that Kiran's mission of peace was successful and yet, they pursued to wage war against the Arkans.

"Why is the Ithurian armada heading towards Treliseum after we have made peace with you?" she stared at the king with her innocent eyes.

King Turloch fell to his knees. He struck the ground with his fist as he began to cry about the wrong path the empire had taken. Seeing the king on his knees and in tears cause the Ithurian soldiers to lose their morale and spirits. Then suddenly…

"Narie!" someone called on to her.

Narie felt a chill ran up her spine after hearing that very familiar voice calling her name. She slowly turns around and saw Sarah and Sune. No words came out of her mouth as she gawked at Sarah in astonishment and at the thought that there she was – her long lost sister. Sarah walked towards Narie while trying to hold back her tears. As they stood in front of each other, both didn't know how to react or where to begin. No words were uttered by the two of them. They just stood there and looked at each other.

Sarah was overwhelmed with so much happiness and couldn't hold back her tears anymore. Narie likewise, became teary seeing Sarah, but the main reason for Narie's tears was the thought that Sarah was separated from them. They were made to believe that Sarah had died during the great war and the fact that she was separated from their mother who still yearned for her. Sarah couldn't hold back her emotions anymore and quickly held Narie in her arms tightly. Narie was carried away by the emotions and embraced her back.

Sune was crying at the side seeing the sisters finally reunited from a period of long separation.

"Mother would be happy to see you again," Narie whispered.

"I have always yearned for a sister and it finally came true," Sarah cried. Her voice was shaking.

As the two savored their special moment of sisterhood, Narie suddenly remembered the reason why she came back to Eres.

"Sarah, where is Althea?" Narie held Sarah on both shoulders as she leaned back.

"She went back to Avetus to talk to Mother to warn her of the coming danger," Sarah replied.

Narie confirmed her hunch that the imprisoned Arkan was indeed Althea. Sarah grew very concerned as she saw Narie's reaction.

"Didn't you meet her? What happened to her in Avetus?" Sarah gave a worried glance.

"I haven't met her in Avetus, but she was imprisoned by Mother," Narie hesitantly answered.

Sarah begged Narie to take her to Avetus to talk to their mother into freeing Althea, but Narie told Sarah that it would be impossible for now as the Fallen army is making its way into Eres.

"When are they coming and how many of them?" King Turloch raised his voice in panic.

"I saw a million-strong creatures or more flying towards your planet. They'll be coming from the north and will be here a day from now," Narie announced the shocking news.

"A million-strong! How could we fight with that multitude?" King Turloch staggered back and pressed the heel of his palm to his forehead.

Sarah told King Turloch to enlist all the able Ithurian men and move all the soldiers of the five kingdoms to Enor where the battle will take place. She specifically asked the king to send words to the Deodarians begging them to come and help in this fight. She instructed the soldiers to evacuate all the villagers near Enor and head to Ithuria for shelter. All the soldiers boarded their ships and traveled towards the city of Enor, leaving the other kingdoms defenseless as they made haste to reach Enor and fortify the city's defense in time.

Sarah and Narie went inside to check on Kiran. Suddenly, Sarah inhaled sharply and stood rooted to the ground as she saw both Kiran and Kina in their condition.

"What happened to them?" Sarah stuttered as she asked.

"They were attacked by the creatures on their way back here to Eres. The same creatures that are now coming," Narie replied while standing in front of Kiran's bed.

Sarah and Narie finally understood the events transpiring. They knew that the Fallens were behind everything, they were successful in deceiving the Council to have them go to war with the Arkans and even attempted to kill Kiran to make sure that the peace he carries will die along with him. Sarah told Narie and King Turloch that the Fallens were bound to destroy both the Arkans and Ithurians to fulfill their revenge and to take Avetus as their price.

As Sarah and Narie continue their talk, Kiran suddenly opened his eyes and called on to Narie's name. Narie unwittingly rushed to Kiran's side, kneeled down and held his hand.

"I'm here Kiran" said Narie with teary eyes.

Sarah stood stunned and speechless as she saw Narie and Kiran and felt that a special bond has grown between the two. She was hurt seeing Narie and Kiran, but endured the pain and quietly walked out of the room, leaving the two alone. Narie slowly turn her gaze at Sarah as she left the room.

"Narie what happened?" asked Kiran, still in daze.

"Your ship was ambushed by the Fallens," Narie replied.

"Kina! Where is Kina? Is she safe?" panic started to engulf Kiran.

"Yes, she is here safe and resting," Narie answered him with an assuring tone.

King Turloch nervously informed Kiran that his father took the whole Ithurian army and waged war with the Arkans. Kiran was enraged upon knowing what his father did, after all the hardship he went through to finally attain peace with the Arkans. Kiran was in despair to hear what his father and the Council have done.

"We will be betraying them once again," Kiran cried, covering his face with his hands.

Everyone didn't understand what Kiran said but King Turloch further reported that the army of the Fallen is heading towards Eres and were to arrive a day from that moment, to destroy all the inhabitants of the planet. Kiran couldn't believe the unfortunate events unfolding before him. He turns to Narie and gave her a worried glance.

"Forgive me Narie. Forgive me for failing to make peace between our races and now, the sin of our ancestors will again be repeated," Kiran held his head down, covering his face in shame.

Narie held Kiran in her arms to give him solace. With the warmth of her arms, Kiran regained his composure.

"Narie, you need to go back to Avetus immediately. It is dangerous to stay here," said Kiran.

"No, I will not leave you now. You will need me here to fight beside you," the defiant Narie answered.

Kiran was grateful to Narie for her decision to stay. With a stern voice he ordered to send out messenger to his father and inform him that he is alive and that Eres is in danger. He instructed King Turloch to send not just one messenger as he knew that the Fallen would do everything to stop anyone from interfering with their plan. King Turloch immediately sent out a platoon of messengers with the crucial mission of carrying the message and to reach King Malkiem and King Ull no matter the odds.

Kiran staggered to stand and asked for his armor. Narie stopped him and told him to take some rest.

"There is no time for me to rest. Our punishment is coming here and we as Ithurians have to face it," Kiran boldly said.

"You can count me in brother," Kina gave her brother her support as she woke up.

Narie realized that in order to stand a chance, she would need Sarah's power to fight the Fallens together with her. She excused herself and went outside to look for Sarah. She found her standing with Sune, looking at the sky and in deep thought.

"Sarah I need your help," said Narie.

But before Narie could continue, Sarah walked strongly towards her, pushing Narie a couple of steps back.

"Are you in love with Kiran?" Sarah stared at her and blatantly asked.

Narie was caught off guard by Sarah's sudden question. Nonetheless, Narie wanted to be honest with her feelings and especially towards Sarah.

"Forgive me Sarah, but yes I do love him," said Narie guiltily.

Sarah then turn her gaze back to the sky.

"You don't need to apologize Narie. There's nothing between us to begin with," Sarah's voice was soft and a bit strained.

Nevertheless, Narie still felt guilt in her heart and tried to hold Sarah but was abruptly stopped when Sarah looked at her.

"Take care of him for me will you? And I promise to protect you both," Sarah told Narie with a warm smile in her face.

Narie smiled back at Sarah and the two sisters embraced each other. Narie knew that Sarah need to use her Arkan powers to be able to stand a chance with the Fallens. Narie asked her to summon her Serdeus. Sarah remembered what Althea taught her and did it in front of her. Narie frowned in frustration after seeing that she could only summon an incomplete form of her Serdeus. She asked Sarah to transform into her armored form.

"Sorry Narie, but I still haven't been taught to summon my armors nor my wings yet," she grinned while scratching the back of her head.

Narie showed her how it is done. However, since the Arkans were taught of these skills starting from childhood, it would take quite a while for Sarah to grasp the knowledge. Even so, Narie was satisfied enough to see that Sarah could use her incomplete Serdeus. Both of them continued on with their training, while the Ithurian army made haste to Enor in preparation for the battle that looms ahead.

Back in Avetus, Sorah finally decided to confront Althea. She looked at her father and asked for his guidance before proceeding to the prison chamber. Althea was sitting on the floor facing the prison cell door, when she suddenly heard someone coming and immediately rushed towards the door.

"Please! I beg of you! Let me speak to Sorah! The kingdom is in danger!" Althea shouted and pleaded.

Then, from the shadows emerged Sorah looking at her. Her presence pushed Althea a few steps back.

"Sister," Althea uttered.

Sorah walked towards her with a fierce gaze that daunted Althea.

"They said you died during the Great War and yet here you are. Where have you been hiding from all these years?"

"It is your fault that our people suffered. You have shamed our family and dishonored our father," Sorah spoke in a deep, dark voice.

"Father -- how is Father? Where is he? I need to speak with him," Althea ran towards the bars and pleaded.

"You are not worthy of seeing our father!" Sorah's rage echoed within the chamber.

Tears flows down Althea's cheeks after hearing what Sorah said, it made her remember their tragic past. It broke Sorah's heart to see Althea cry. She was trying to take a hold of her emotions towards Althea but she would then remember the betrayal which slowly fills her heart with hatred. Unable to control her emotions anymore, Sorah rushed to get out of the chamber.

"I'm truly sorry for what I have done. If I could turn back time to undo all of this I would, but I can't. I'll be carrying this shame and pain for the rest of my life," Althea's voice was shaking.

Sorah stopped and hear what Althea wanted to say.

"Listen to me Sorah. Aran was a good and honest man and he loves you so much," said Althea.

"Love me? What does love have to do with it when both of you betrayed me?" Sorah angrily confronted her.

"I betrayed Aran-- I tricked him into believing that I was you," Althea confessed.

Sorah stood motionless and in shock as she hears the revelation from Althea.

"Stop it Althea! Don't dare say another word!" said Sorah while she tried to walk away from her.

"Listen to what I have to say sister, for this may be the last time I could tell you the truth," Althea stared at Sorah in desperation.

Althea admitted that she was carrying Aran's child at that time and the terrible guilt she endured alone forced her to tell Aran everything. Aran was dismayed about what she did and was concerned for the child. He knew that the Arkan commandments will put her to death if the Council finds out.

"Aran sacrificed his life to save me," Althea cried.

Sorah felt devastated to hear the truth. Althea added that she lost the life inside her when she tried to stop their father's flame from destroying Aran.

"Why Althea? Why did you do this to me?" Sorah begged for an answer.

"I loved him first, but his heart has always yearned for you," Althea voice crackled in anger and couldn't hold her tears back.

Althea then spoke about her firstborn. Sorah slowly turned around and walked towards her and said.

"What about Sarah?"

"She is also alive and all grown up to be a fine Arkan," Althea smiled as she told Sorah.

Sorah couldn't contain her happiness.

"How could that be? Athanax killed her," Sorah's eyes glistened with hope.

"I saved her from uncle's assassins and we were accidentally pulled in to the gateway, together with Varkelos' people."

"I took her to the blue planet that I called Eres and saved the banish ones, which eventually started the Ithurian race," Althea explained.

Tears of happiness streamed down Sorah's face as she hears that Sarah is alive. She starts asking a lot of questions about her.

"She is fine sister. She is so much like you – except for her stubbornness, which she got from me," Althea smiled.

Althea also revealed that Athanax is alive and plotting another war -- a war of revenge against both the Arkans and the Ithurians. Sorah was again confused on how possibly the rebels could have survived. They were half-dead when they were casted away. But Althea assured her that they are alive and thriving. She had seen Athanax, which almost got her killed. Athanax would do everything he could to destroy them and will finish what he failed to accomplish back then.

Meanwhile at the gateway of the Fallen, two Arkan sentry were patrolling the sky when they saw an unusual silhouette forming from the nebula clouds inside the gateway. As they came closer to investigate, they were shocked to see the Ithurian warship heading towards them. King Malkiem was informed that they spotted Arkan scouts. Still in anguish, he ordered to shoot them down in an instant. The two Arkans were startled when the Ithurians opened fire. They tried to evade and escape, but one of the Arkans was hit and instantly killed, while the other was shot and gravely wounded.

The wounded Arkan managed to reach Fostrum. Prea was there to receive her words.

"The Ithurians -- the Ithurians are coming … They betrayed us once again --" said the wounded Arkan before succumbing to her death.

Prea turned red with fury as she heard that the Ithurians betrayed them once again. She called on to all the warriors to prepare to defend Fostrum and send words to Altrus Sorah that she need to bring the main army immediately to fight the traitors.

Sorah and Althea's talk was suddenly interrupted by Anthelia who informed her that the Ithurians have trespassed and already killed two of their kin. Sorah's eyes narrowed in confusion as to why the Ithurian would attack them after agreeing peace with their prince. She then thought that the prince might have acted as a diversion to talk peace while they sent their army and strike them where they least expect it. Anger and resentment towards Kiran and his people flashed through her eyes. She was furious that the Ithurian resort to such a ploy. She knew she should have not trusted those traitors in the first place. Altrus ordered to sound the trumpets of war and assembled the Arkan army. She will personally lead them to Fostrum and deal with the traitors once again.

"Sister, it is Athanax's doing! Please let me fight with you," Althea pleaded.

She ignored Althea's plea. She didn't want to put Althea in harm's way again and vowed to protect her within Avetus this time. Althea was insistent but Sorah immediately left the chamber, leaving her still behind the bars. Altrus Sorah went to the Council to address the Arkan army.

"It was wrong of me to have believed and to give those Ithurians a chance for peace. This only proves that the descendants of traitors will forever be traitors," her voice was filled with rage.

The entire Arkan army cheered and rallied behind Altrus Sorah. She ordered the army to set forth to Fostrum in order to destroy the invaders. Sorah asked for Narie but no one had seen her. She got worried for Narie but that thought need to be set aside for now. Sorah expands her wings and flew to the sky. Behind her was the entire Arkan army heading towards Fostrum to face the inevitable war against the Ithurians.

Chapter Twenty-Two

UNLIKELY ALLIES

As the Ithurian prepares for war against the Fallen on Eres, Kiran formed his own war council which was joined by Sarah, Narie, Kina and King Turloch. They accessed their forces and discussed their battle plan. King Turloch reported that the number of infantry soldiers left in the entire kingdom was about a hundred thousand regulars and that they were able to enlist citizens which numbered up to around eighty thousand. Kina reported that they had a battalion of Nephatron at their disposal, plus two hundred Zelridars on standby and ten long range heavy artilleries already on their way to Enor.

The Council knew that their strength was not enough to defeat the Fallens. Kiran plan to hold the defense of the city long enough until his father return with the main army, but he knew that they will be taking a risk on waiting for his father to come back. He asked King Turloch if there's still anyone out there whom they could call for help. Sarah stood up and told the Council about the Deodarians. They need to send word and ask them to fight with the Ithurians. Without hesitation, Kiran agreed with Sarah's proposition and instructed his aid to send a messenger to Deodara and inform King Zairel that prince Kiran of Ithuria is seeking for his help in fighting the Fallens.

As the messenger prepares to leave, a soldier came running in the Council room, panting. He informed them that they detected a massive army moving in from the south. The Council was alarmed and didn't expect the Fallens have already arrived.

"No your highness! It is not the Fallens that are marching towards us" said the soldier.

"Then who and what army is it?" King Turloch eagerly asked.

"It is the Deodarians my lord. The army of Deodara has come," the soldier replied.

Alarmed and worried, Kiran and King Turloch thought that the Deodarian might have used this moment of their weakness to attack. Suddenly, the sound of horns from the Deodarian was heard. Kiran and the Council members hastily went up to the wall and saw hundreds of thousand Deodarian soldiers standing in the horizon.

"What are we going to do?" King Turloch's voice began to tremble.

Paralyzed with fear and confusion, Kiran couldn't think properly. His shock robbed him of his speech and began to falter. Seeing Kiran's reaction, Sarah took the initiative and suggested to stand down.

"Are you out of your mind child? they could attack us at any moment!" King Turloch screamed as he pulled his hair.

"Then why didn't they attack? What are they waiting for?" Sarah challenged King Turloch's assumption.

Narie and Kina agrees with Sarah and asked Kiran to stand down and wait.

"They're testing us if we're going to draw the first blood," Sarah glared at the Deodarian army.

After regaining his composure, Kiran followed Sarah's suggestion and ordered his army to stand down. The soldiers stared at him in confusion and were reluctant to follow his instruction. Kiran faced his men and raised his voice in repeating his order to stand down. It was quiet in the field, where one side the Deodarian army stood and another side where the Ithurians shield themselves behind their walls. It was a terrifying moment that the two armies faced each other and waiting for any provocation.

Then, they saw a lone rider coming out from the Deodarian line and heading towards the wall. The Ithurians within the wall trembled in fear as they saw the lone rider stop at the foot of the gate.

"I am Prince Vasuril, son of King Zairel of the Deodarian Empire. We were sent here by order of our king to fight alongside the Ithurians," Prince Vasuril's voice echoed throughout the plains.

Jaws dropped inside the Ithurian wall after they heard what the prince of Deodara announced. They couldn't believe that a miracle just happened. Help came at their moment of desperation. Kiran ordered to open the gate and allowed the Deodarian passage. Prince Vasuril entered the city and was escorted to the Council room. Everyone stared in amazement at the sight of Prince Vasuril's physique. The Deodarians were much bigger than the tallest men in Ithuria and possessed a stronger body. Kiran approached Vasuril and shook his hand.

"I'm Prince Kiran, son of King Malkiem. We're truly grateful for your coming here to help us," said Kiran.

After shaking Kiran's hand, Vasuril turned his head from side to side, looking at the people inside the Council room. He was looking for somebody.

"Is Sarah here amongst you?" asked Prince Vasuril.

Everyone was surprised by Vasuril's question and raised an eyebrow as to why the Deodarian prince knew and was looking for Sarah.

"My lord, we would like to apologize if she caused you and your people any troubles and let me assure you that we will watch over her to never again cause any problems," said King Turloch, knowing Sarah's strong sense for justice, had assumed that she might have caused problems with the Deodarians.

"No trouble was caused by her. I only need to meet her," Vasuril replied.

"My lord, I'm Sarah and I thank you for your coming here to our aid," Sarah stepped forward and faced Vasuril.

"You are wrong. It is us that should be honored and grateful to have finally met an Arkan princess." Vasuril went down to his knee and bowed his head.

Kiran and the Council stood still with bewildered faces as they heard that Sarah was also an Arkan. Sarah's forehead crinkled in confusion as she tries to figure out how the Deodarians knew about her secret.

"My lord, may I ask how you know about me?" Sarah was eager to hear the answer.

"It was all thanks to your mother. She came to us and told us about you and the danger that is coming. She guided us to the path that we must take," Vasuril answered in a soft tone of voice.

"My mother? you mean Althea?" Sarah clarified.

Prince Vasuril told Sarah the story when the time Althea came to them, seeking their help and warning them of the great danger that was to come.

A Recollection of Althea's journey to Deodara:

After Sarah and Sune left the forest to warn the Ithurians about the coming of the Fallens. Althea was very worried for Sarah, knowing that if she failed to convince Sorah to come and help the Ithurians, Sarah will be left with the Ithurians alone. It was a difficult decision to return to Avetus, but she need to do everything she can to convince Sorah to help. She planned to unite the strength of the Arkan and the Ithurian to defeat Athanax and his minions, but doubt also came across her mind knowing the deep hatred Sorah held in her heart for Varkelos and his seeds. Althea couldn't bear the thought of seeing Sarah fighting and dying alone in the battlefield of Eres.

She suddenly remembered the Deodarians -- a race of people who were blessed with fragments of her Arkan powers. The Ithurians were to stand a chance if she could make the Deodarians fight with them. She immediately set forth to the far south, to the realm of the Deodarian Empire. After passing the Ithurian city in the south, she flew further more to cross the borders of Ithuria to Deodara. Her eyes glistened as she watched in amazement that the Deodarian indeed followed and embraced the Arkan culture. Their architecture was the same as the Arkan which somehow made her feel like home. She soon found the main city, which the Deodarians modeled and built to resemble the great city of Avetus. Althea slowly descended in the city square. All the people went down to their knees upon seeing her presence.

"Please rise. I am here to see your king," said Althea.

A group of Deodarian warriors walked towards her and escorted her to the palace to see the king. Inside, she was greeted by the people with royalty. Everyone bowed as she made her way to the king's throne hall. She was met with King Zairel and his son Vasuril together with the Council elders.

"Your highness, finally you came! We've been waiting for your return in the land where it all began," King Zairel greeted her with teary eyes.

Althea frowned, puzzled by King Zairel words.

"Land where it all began? I do not understand" said Althea.

"Your highness, do you not remember this land? It is the place where you saved our forefathers from death. It is the place where you blessed us with your powers, which made our people what we are today."

"It was because of you that we embraced the teachings of the Arkan and devoted our lives to the commandments. To us, you're our savior and we owe you our lives," King Zairel expounded a powerful truth.

Althea couldn't help but feel overwhelmed on how the Deodarians looked up to her. But she was still confused as to how they were able to acquire the knowledge of the Arkan. She was then presented a vast chronicle of the Arkan history written before the Great War that survived during the exile. From then on, the Deodarian forefather Ihram continued writing journals after the exile, recounting every memory he had with Althea and the struggles of Deodarians from the time they lived as nomads to becoming a mighty empire. After Ihram passed away, his journals were bound together and became the book of truth for the Deodarians. It was the book that reminded them of their past.

Althea finally understood the history of the people and admired their devotions. She then told King Zairel the purpose of her coming.

"King Zairel, I came here today to seek your help to aid the Ithurians in stopping the Fallen Arkans from destroying Eres."

"I know that you have been bitter enemies long before your empires were forged, but I say this to you today: the danger is coming and it will not just destroy the Ithurians, but your people as well -- all because you once carried the blood of the Arkan. These enemies are the Arkans that rebelled against my father and they were banished as well. They became the Fallens -- with deep hatred towards the Arkan and to your people. The one leading the Fallen is the king's brother, Athanax. His army is heading towards Eres and will be here four days from now. I embarked myself on a mission to return to Avetus to ask my sister Sorah the Light of Strength, to come to your aid and together we will destroy the Fallen once and for all. But, there is also a chance that my sister would abandon you in facing the Fallens. The Arkans still bore hatred towards the seeds of Varkelos, the one who betrayed the king. All I can do is to try. With this, I'll be leaving my daughter, or in truth, my niece here in Eres alone. She is also an Arkan granddaughter of King Satorex, but her powers have yet to be fully awakened. I know I'm being selfish with my plea, as this will surely

279

put many of your people in danger and many will surely perish, but I have no one else to ask for help but you. So please help us. Lend me your strength to stop the darkness from extinguishing the light."

Althea lowered her head and pleaded to the Deodarians.

"Your highness please, you do not need to plead. As I said before, we've been waiting for a long time for your return. Our forefather Ihram wrote in his book of truth that one day you will return to us and guide us to our true path. Here you are -- fulfilling that prophecy," King Zairel replied.

Althea slowly raised her head and saw the Deodarian faces. They were smiling at her -- happy and not a single Deodarian showed fear. Her eyes slowly opened up in amazement, seeing that the Deodarians would even embrace death to remain truthful to their belief.

"Your highness, we the Deodarians are with you. Our lives are for you to command," said King Zairel and the entire empire cheered.

"Thank you very much for your devotion and forgive me for putting your people in harms' way" said Althea.

"No your highness. We were born to follow you, to die for the commandments and it is we that need to thank you for it is our honor to fulfill that task," the proud King Zairel said.

Althea was grateful to King Zairel, to his people for the bravery and resolves they shown and for being truthful to the commandments. Prince Vasuril then asked about her plans.

"Look for Sarah. She will be at the capital to convince the Ithurians about the war against the Fallen. You need to meet with her there," said Althea.

"It will be done," Prince Vasuril replied.

King Zairel then faced his people and announced:

"My people, our prayers have been answered. The savior written in the book of truth has finally came back to us. She is exactly what the book foretold and she is here to guide us to the path we have long been awaiting. The path is treacherous. Some will face pain and some will perish but it is a path that we chose to walk and it is finally revealed. Now the time has come for us to act. We will march straight towards the heart of evil and we will make our stand to fight to the last warrior alive and stop the Fallen from destroying the people of Eres. Are you with me, my people?"

The entire Deodarian people shouted, voicing their whole-heart support to the King and to Althea. Every warrior -- man, woman and the elderly -- that could still fight wore their armors, sharpening their weapons and prepares themselves for the coming battle. The people were jubilant rather than scared. In the mind of the Deodarian this was what they've been preparing for since the day they were born -- to serve the savior and to die by the commandments. Regrets was a thing the Deodarians were not accustomed to.

Afterwards, Althea shook King Zairel hand.

"Please look after my daughter for me. I'll leave everything up to you and I promise you that no matter what, I will return and join you in the battlefield," Althea asserted.

Present time at the Ithurian Council:

"Those were the last words of your mother Althea before she left for Avetus," Prince Vasuril recounted the story for the Council,

Sarah's eyes filled with tears after she learned that Althea still looked after her even though she's somewhere far away. Kiran and the Council stood up and thanked the Deodarians' bravery for coming to help them and promised them of everlasting peace if they could get past the ordeal. Finally, the Ithurian and Deodarian armies began their journey towards Enor to face the Fallen. It was a battle that will decide the faith of the people of Eres -- a battle between the forces of light and darkness.

Chapter Twenty-Three

THE WAR OF REVENGE

The Ithurian army finally reached Treliseum. King Malkiem saw that Fostrum was heavily defended by the Arkans from land to the sky. He positioned his entire army outside of Fostrum, began unloading their arsenals and mobilizing the infantry. Athanax couldn't hold his joy to finally set his foot back on Treliseum, the land of the Arkans. The only thing that stands in the way of achieving his evil plan is the gate of Fostrum.

The Ithurians put up their camps and began planning for the invasion of Fostrum. King Malkiem was still in despair about Kiran's demise in the hands of the Arkans which made him unstable and irrational with his decisions. He wanted to hasten the preparation of the army and attack straightaway, but because of the massive number of soldiers and equipment they brought, it would take a day to finish the preparation. All King Malkiem could do is to wait.

Altrus Sorah and the main Arkan army arrived at Fostrum and was told that the Ithurians were still making their preparations.

"We should attack them now Altrus, before they could even prepare for battle," Anthelia firmly suggested.

"No, we will not stoop down to their treachery. We will face them honorably in battle," said Sorah, looking down at the Ithurian as they prepare for war.

Sorah called forth her elite warriors Prea, Anthelia, Heres, Kinara, Una, Antra, Aril, Fereal and Vijera, the strongest Arkan warriors of its time. Each of the elite warriors command an army of Arkans. Altrus Sorah ordered Una and Aril to bring their warriors back to Avetus to guard the city and protect the sleeping Arkans Altrus Sorah and her army waited for the Ithurians the first move to begin the war of revenge. Another matter however deeply concerned Sorah is Narie, she had not yet been found even in Fostrum. Sorah sent out her warriors to find her immediately before the battle began.

Meanwhile, Athanax mustered his army of three thousand Fallens and led them to the secret passage that he once used to meet with Varkelos on the eve of the Great War. The passage was secretly built by Varkelos as a means of escape route for the Arkan and it leads directly inside the city of Avetus. He instructed Morsus to lead the army and wait for his signal to attack. Athanax will be staying back with King Malkiem and the Council to make sure that everything goes according to his desire.

Back in Eres, as the sun set in Ithuria, Kiran was updated by his commanders that they were able to add three hundred thousand Deodarian warriors into their force totaling around four hundred thousand. Kiran consulted with Sarah about their battle plan. She firmly told the Council that they have to stop the Fallen from reaching the walls and make sure to hold them back.

Kiran appointed King Turloch to command the long range artilleries and turrets and defend the wall of Enor at all costs. He ordered the Zelridar squadrons to be the first line to engage the enemy and attack the Fallens from above to prevent them from coming even close to their line.

Narie shared to the Council her experience fighting the creatures and revealed to them that the Fallen may have the advantage of numbers, but they still hold the technological upper hand by utilizing their Nephatrons and projectile weapons. The Fallens were still using crude weapons like swords and spears. Having learned this information from Narie, Kiran decided to put the Nephatron battalion on the second line, supported by the artilleries from behind to prevent the line from being swarm by the creatures.

"I will take my Zeltkova soldiers and stand behind the Nephatrons," Kina volunteered.

"Please allow me and my warriors to take that place my lady. Let your soldiers defend your city," Prince Vasuril pleaded.

"But it will put your people directly in front of danger," Kiran countered.

"As Deodarians, we have already accepted our fate. This is the path shown to us by our savior, the path that we need to take and it is an honor for us to walk on this destined path," Vasuril answered without traces of fear in his voice.

The Council knew that the Deodarian warriors were stronger than the Ithurians. Coupled with their power of healing, they're more suitable to take the third line. Narie volunteered to join the Zelridar in their air assault, while Sarah and Sune will be with the Deodarians to fight on the ground. The idea was strongly disagreed by Kiran.

"It will put you and Narie directly on the belly of the beast. This is our battle, our retribution and I wouldn't want the two of you getting hurt," Kiran appealed.

285

"This is not just your battle Kiran. Your ancestors and our people started this war and we intend to finish it once and for all," said Sarah with Narie by her side.

Hearing Sarah speaking in that manner made Narie remember their mother. Sarah's resolves, firmness, voice and her essence bore a striking similarity with Sorah. Kiran was left silence to what Sarah said, he knew he had no choice since he also need their Arkan powers for the fight. Kiran was left with no option but to agree with their plans.

After the Council meeting, Sarah and Sune hurriedly left the room to prepare for the coming battle when Kiran hastily ran after them.

"Sarah, may I have a word with you?" Kiran asked.

Kiran wanted to be honest to Sarah about his relationship with Narie.

"Sarah please forgive me, but I'm in love with Narie," said Kiran, bearing a guilt feeling.

"You don't need to apologize Kiran. I know you're a good and honest man and that's what I like about you. Please take care of my sister," Sarah answered.

Kiran was puzzled when he heard that Narie was her sister.

"Your sisters? What? -- how did it happen?" he stuttered.

"It's a millennium-long story," Sarah said with a grin.

Narie approached Kiran and held his hand. Sarah was already at peace. She already accepted Kiran and Narie's new found love.

"After all of this, both of you will be the bridge between our two races and I promise you that I and Sune will protect that bridge," Sarah gave her word to both of them.

The three looked up to the sky as they watched the approaching dark cloud -- the sign of the coming of the Fallens.

Meanwhile at Treliseum, the Ithurian army has finally been assembled and ready for battle. They marched towards the gate of Fostrum and leading them from the center was King Malkiem. Nearing the gate, they saw the Arkan army standing outside of Fostrum. The Ithurians stared in disbelief as they saw the entire Arkan army were female.

"What is this farce! Are your men that scared to face the Ithurian army and sent their women to do their job?" King Malkiem sneered.

Then Altrus Sorah came out at the center of the line and slowly walked towards the enemy. Unwittingly, the Ithurian were stepping back at the mere presence of Altrus Sorah the destroyer of thousand souls as written and told in their ancient text. As Sorah walked towards them, red aura was visibly steaming out of her body. The Ithurian line trembled and was subconsciously being pushed back by fear.

"Stand your ground! This land belongs to our ancestors, to us! They are the oppressors and we will drive them out!" King Malkiem raised his voice in anger.

But before King Malkiem could continue, he was abruptly interrupted by Sorah.

"Silence sons of traitors! Your ancestors were mere caretakers of this land -- the land fought and won by our king. For the kindness my father gave to your ancestors, you repaid him with treachery," Sorah's rage echoed across the field.

King Malkiem and his army were daunted by Sorah's voice. Athanax slowly clenched his fists and stared openly at his niece. As he gazed at her, immense hatred emanated from within him. He can still feel the pain of her flame that turned them into hideous monsters.

"Don't falter with her lies. They know our ancestors could stand up to their cruelty and matched their powers. This is why they suppressed and stripped them of their Arkan honor and sentenced them to death," Athanax's face was contorted with rage and fury.

The Ithurian regained their spirits back and shouted "Death to the Arkans!"

"You can try taking this land, but mark my word, this land will be your grave," said Sorah with a fierce gaze.

The Ithurians were suddenly silenced by Sorah's warning. King Ull once again asked King Malkiem to reconsider before everything is too late, but Athanax used Kiran's death to further fuel his hatred, his anger and to cloud his logic and judgment. King Malkiem gave the order to his generals to attack the Arkans. And finally, the battle between the Arkans and Ithurians began. Squadrons of Zelridar and battalions of Nephatrons started their assault at the gate.

Altrus Sorah stood bravely at the center of the Arkan line together with her warriors. A gentle breeze of wind blew at Sorah, which pushed her hair back. She closed her eyes and felt the wind touching her face. As the wind passed by, she opened her eyes and glared at the rushing Ithurian enemy. She slowly balled her hands and light came out forming her Serdeus. She expands her black wings and with pride she conceals her armor form believing that the Ithurian were not worthy to use it upon and believed that she can destroy the enemy even without it.

Altrus Sorah ran and then flew directly to the center of the Ithurian line, followed by her faithful warriors in full armored form. With incredible speed she's the first Arkan to reach the enemy's line and smashed the Ithurian center like a battering ram, sending the frontline soldiers flying in the air. Sorah kept on pushing forward until she easily shattered the Ithurian line. A squadron of Zelridar fires missiles towards her to stop her from advancing, but even the rain of missiles didn't stop Sorah. A legion of Arkans ascended to the sky with their Serdius raised and battled the Zelridars from above.

The Ithurians were being driven back by Sorah's relentless attacks. King Malkiem ordered the Nephatrons to advance together with the Zeltkova warriors to even the battlefield. King Malkiem ordered the Zeltkova soldiers to move forward to challenge the Arkan strength. The Arkans were overwhelmed by the Ithurian arsenals and didn't expect that the Zeltkovas could mimic their powers, this somehow prevented the Arkans from advancing further. Altrus Sorah and the elite warriors overpowered the Nephatrons and destroyed a number of them, but because the Arkan population was few, the Ithurian was able to counter them with forces numbering far greater than their own. Sorah rallied the warriors to her and led the charge.

Meanwhile on another battle that will soon unfold, the Fallen armada finally reached Eres and lands in the north as told by Narie. They began their march towards the city of Enor, where the Ithurians and Deodarians were already waiting for them. The Fallen army was visible on the field of Enor. Bronax led the army and assessed the wall of the city. His scouts informed him that a line of Ithurians was standing below the wall.

"Devour the inhabitants of this planet!" Bronax pointed his finger at the wall and gave the order to attack.

The creatures raised their weapons and start charging and running towards the Ithurian line like wild beasts without battle formation. The Fallens were faster and stronger than the Ithurian, but the Deodarians' strength matched them in every way. Kiran saw that hell was unleashed, he immediately signaled the squadrons of Zelridar to attack the rushing creatures. The Zelridars flew in lines and began their attack from the sky, firing missiles towards the Fallens. Narie flew down to block those who were able to pass the aerial bombardment. The aerial attack was effective, Kiran thought that the Zelridars alone could hold back the enemy. Sarah and Sune were watching the battle unfold at the third line, her palms were sweating and she had her gaze fixed at Narie.

Narie stood her ground and prevented the enemy from moving forward. This was supported by the Zelridar from above. A terrifying scowl was painted on Bronax's face seeing his army couldn't move forward because of the effectiveness of the Zelridars. He signaled his commander to unleash the Draakabs (dragon riders) to counter the Zelridars from the sky. The Draakab swiftly flew to the sky and attacked the Zelridar line, shooting fireballs from their mouth. The Zelridar formation was shattered; the pilots fought the Draakab individually, leaving Narie alone on the ground. Sarah saw that the Zelridar was being occupied by the Draakab and one by one being destroyed which left Narie fighting alone on the ground. Because the Zelridar line was broken, many of the creatures were able to cross over and put Narie in a dangerous situation. From the third line, Sarah gave a worried glance seeing Narie's predicament. She immediately jumped on to Sune's back and rushed towards the first line to get Narie out.

"Sarah, it's dangerous to be out there! Stay behind the line!" Prince Vasuril warned.

"I will be back. I need to help Narie. Prepare yourselves! The enemy will be coming here soon," Sarah replied.

Narie slayed as many creatures she could but they still kept on coming. She fought in her armored form using her Serdeus and shooting flames from her hands. But even with her great advantages, she still couldn't stop the sheer number of creatures from coming, Narie was then pushed back and accidentally fell from her back. The hordes of creatures were about to strike her, when in the nick of time, Sarah and Sune jumped in and rammed the creatures directly, pushing the enemy back to give Narie enough time to stand up. Sarah balled her hand and lights came out forming her incomplete Serdeus. She fought with Narie while Sune aided them with his lighting blast. Kiran was at the top of the city wall watching the battle. He felt helpless that he couldn't join Sarah and Narie below. He need to stay back within the wall to coordinate the defense of the city.

Somewhere on the other side of the galaxy, Athanax nearly fell over in elation after seeing the event unfolding. Everything was going according to his scheme. He was able to make the Arkans and the Ithurians destroy each other, while his main army attacked the Ithurian city on Eres. He acted as the conductor that orchestrated two battles at the same time. He could already taste his revenge from the Ithurians whose ancestors deserted him and the Arkans that tried to destroyed him. He put an evil grin on his face as he watched two of his most hated enemies slaughter each other.

Altrus Sorah used her flame, shooting fireballs, burning and killing many of the Ithurians. Suddenly, a platoon of Nephatron carrying a thick-layered metal shield slowly moved towards her, another Nephatron line followed from behind firing their missiles at Sorah. She was pushed back by the overwhelming barrage of missiles that exploded one after the other. Even her fireballs were being deflected by the Nephatron shield. The elite warriors were also being driven back by the Zeltkovas. They continuously rained the warriors with their projectile weapons, which killed a lot of Arkans during the Ithurian onslaught.

Prea gasped as she saw from the top of the gate that the Arkan line was being driven back. She quickly ordered her battalion to summon their bows and arrows to aid their sisters fighting below, shielding them from the Ithurians' advance. Prea and her warriors released volley of arrows to the Ithurians and killed many of their them. As Prea continued to unleashed the Arkan arrows, they managed to halt the enemy's advance and gave the Arkans on the ground enough time to recover the line.

The Arkan warriors saw Sorah fighting alone in the middle of the battlefield, away from their line and trying with all her might and courage to repel the Ithurians. The warriors' heart was completely embolden by her bravery and valor. The elite warriors sound the horn to charge and move to where Sorah was standing. All the Arkans' wings glowed in bright light and together cheered their battle cry.

"With all my strength and courage! For the King!"

The Arkan warriors gritted their teeth and glared at the enemy as they attacked and fight their way to reach Altrus Sorah. Prea from above the wall, continued to shoot arrows to aid the warriors at the frontline. Sorah's bravery only proved that she was indeed, worthy to be called the Light of Strength. She kept on pressing forward to reach and destroy King Malkiem, but was facing too many obstacles because of the overwhelming firepower of the Nephatrons. King Ull, after witnessing the carnage of the battle, has secretly ordered his faithful soldiers to stand down. King Malkiem however, saw that his army couldn't further advance and was being thwarted by the Arkans' arrows. He calls out his long-range artilleries to blast the Arkan archers on top of the gate. Massive-size artilleries rolled to the front and King Malkiem gave the order to aim at the gate. Then…

"Death to the Arkans!" King Malkiem voice crackled in anger.

All the artilleries fired at the same time towards the gate. The loud thundering noise of the artilleries being fired rippled across all corners of the battlefield and caught the attention of Sorah. She turns her gaze to the sky and followed a trail of smoke from the artillery shells.

"Oh no!" whispered Sorah as she gawked.

Her eyes opened wide in horror and didn't blink as she saw the explosions destroyed the top of the wall where Prea and her warriors stood. The explosion and fire killed many of the Arkans who were defending the wall. Prea's battalion was shattered by the endless bombardment of the Ithurian artilleries, she ordered her warriors to take the wounded and dead and take cover. Sorah was enraged as she watched the gate being destroyed and her warriors dying. A red dark sensation again steamed out of her body and flames covered her fists. Athanax saw it and realized immediately that she intends to unleash the fire of justice to destroy the entire Ithurian army, similar to what she did to his army in the first war. He knew that once it happens, his plan would ultimately fail. With the remnant of his Arkan power, he swiftly ran towards Sorah from behind while her gaze was occupied by the destruction of the gate. Athanax's hand released a green smoke, which afterwards formed his Serdius. He took a big step forward and treacherously plunged his poisoned Serdius into Sorah's flesh. There was a sickening sliding sound as it penetrated Sorah's back. Sorah cried out in pain and agony as trickles of blood slid down from the corner of her mouth. She slowly turned around to face the one who stabbed her. Her eyebrows raised, her jaw dropped and gasped when Athanax revealed his face to her. She saw the disfigured face of her uncle with a sinister smirk staring at her. Sorah stared back in disbelief as she saw Athanax alive. Athanax's eyes filled with hate and anger.

"Now, let's see if you can still use your powers," Athanax whispered and swiftly pulled his poisoned Serdeus out of Sorah's back.

Blood gushed out from Sorah's back and was gravely wounded. She looked at her hands and saw it decaying. She knew right then that it was the same poison that King Satorex was inflicted with during the first war. Athanax quickly disappeared in to the crowd of Ithurians, rushing towards Sorah. Because of her wound, she was pushed back and inflicted with numerous wounds from the Ithurian attackers. The elite warriors saw Sorah staggering and struggling to defend herself against the rush of enemies. Using their powers and sheer courage, they forced their way through the Ithurian line in order to reach and aid Sorah.

With their determination, the warriors were able to reach the wounded Sorah and quickly surrounded her to protect her from the enemy. The Ithurians continued firing their artilleries at the gate. Prea refused to abandon the wall knowing that once they did, the Arkan casualties at the battlefield would be catastrophic. She ordered what's left of her battalion to continue firing their arrows in order to help the warriors below. Prea bravely stood up the wall and blocked the incoming artillery shells by using her flame as shield.

Sorah knew that the gate wouldn't last long if the artilleries continues to fire. She ordered her brave soldiers to charge the Ithurians and destroy the artilleries no matter the cost. Heres asked Sorah to retreat and seek treatment for her wounds, but Sorah refused to leave the battlefield even though the poison was already spreading throughout her body. Together with her warriors, they forced their way towards the artilleries, using their flames and every ounce of their courage to break through. They were determined to destroy the guns in order to save Prea and the warriors who's defending the gate. Suddenly, Heres and Kinara were able to break the line and reached the artilleries but were immediately cut off from the rest of the warriors. The two struggles to fight the Ithurians defending the guns. They put all their strength and power to reach the artillery. As Heres and Kinara struggles to destroy the first canon, they got hit and wounded continuously by the Ithurian's guns and swords. The determination of the two elite warriors made them succeed in destroying three of the artilleries, but by doing so they were mortally wounded. Heres tries to destroy the fourth gun, while Kinara fends off the Ithurians. Kinara couldn't hold back the overwhelming number of the enemy. One Ithurian soldier raised his weapon and aimed at Kinara. He pulled the trigger hitting her in the head and killed her instantly. Heres saw Kinara slowly fell to the ground and knew that she doesn't have much time left either. With her last breath, Heres cried:

"With all my strength and courage, for the King!"

Heres grabbed the fourth artillery and concentrate all of her energy as she clings to it. Flames began to come out of her body until the energy build up became unstable. The Ithurians continued shooting Heres as she stood her ground to the bitter end. She looked at the sky and tears slid to the side of her face. She slowly closed her eyes and her intense energy triggered a huge explosion, destroying the artillery and killing the Ithurians surrounding it. She sacrificed her life by blowing herself to destroy the fourth gun. The two elite warriors were killed and their lifeless bodies were still being stabbed and shot by the Ithurians. Sorah and the remaining warriors saw the bodies of their fallen brethren being desecrated. Fueled by rage, Sorah fought her way through, repelling and killing the Ithurians that stood on her way just to reach Heres and Kinara. She carried the two bodies away from the Ithurians, while being continuously struck and wounded by the enemy.

The warriors came to her aid and again shielded her from the enemy. The Ithurian line that defending the artilleries were shattered. Sorah took this advantage and quickly ordered her elite warriors to destroy the remaining guns.

Athanax had foreseen that the Arkans' defeat will not be long, as Sorah could no longer wield her destructive flames of justice anymore. To further amplify the odds of victory for the Arkans, he gave the signal to Morsus and his Fallen warriors hiding and waiting below the city of Avetus to attack. The Arkans inside Avetus were caught off guard as the Fallens stormed their way into the city. Some of the Arkans managed to sound the alarm and blow the horn of battle, which alerted the warriors in the city. Next thing the defenders of Avetus realized was that many of their kin had been killed by the treacherous raid of the Fallens. Afterwards, the enemy forced their way into the palace in order to kill King Satorex. Una and Aril arrived just in time to fight and defend the palace.

At the battlefield, Sorah heard the sound of the horn from Avetus. She knew that her father and Althea are in grave danger. She flew to the wall and instructed Prea to take charge of the defense of Fostrum, while she returns to Avetus in order to stop the invaders. Sorah immediately flew back to Avetus in great speed, hoping to reach the city on time to save her father and her sister Althea.

Chapter Twenty-Four

DESPERATION

nside the prison chamber, Althea was startled to the sound of trumpets blown from within the city. She grabbed a hold of the prison bars and squeezed her head between the bars, in an attempt to find out what's all the commotion about. She saw warriors and soldiers running and panicking. She frowned, puzzled by what she's seeing outside. She begged one of the guards to open the cell door and let her fight, but the guard ignored her and ran outside, leaving Althea alone in the chamber. She tries breaking the door but couldn't because the prison chamber was protected by the *Will* of King Satorex, which sealed away the power of an imprisoned Arkan. Morsus and his minions had already broken through the city's defense and entered the palace. The Arkan warriors struggle desperately to fight and hold back the ravaging Fallens. The Arkan main army was sent to Fostrum to deal with the Ithurian incursion and only a handful was left in the city, which made it difficult for them to stop the overwhelming numbers of the creatures.

Clearly, the odds were against the Arkans as they never expected to fight two battles at the same time. They're fighting two armies and their forces were suffering heavily. Althea was busy breaking her way out when suddenly, a group of Fallen breached the prison chamber. A small group of Arkan warriors came to stop the creatures. The battle lasted for a while, they were outnumbered yet they managed to eliminate most of the creatures, until only one warrior from each side remained. The last Arkan warrior was mortally wounded while the creature slowly walked towards the wounded Arkans with his sword raised and ready to smite her. But as the creature about to strike, Althea reached out her arms and grabbed the creature's neck from behind, breaking it and killed it instantly. Althea threw the creature's body and begged the dying Arkan to release her so she could fight with them. With the remaining strength left of the wounded Arkan, she crawled towards the cell door and released Althea. Althea immediately reached out her hand to the wounds of the dying Arkan to heal her.

"The sleeping chamber... The king is in danger..." Blood spewed out of the wounded Arkan's mouth as she told Althea.

"What sleeping chamber? What about my father?" Althea frantically asked.

"King Satorex is in the sleeping chamber ... you need to save the king ... I beg of you!" The warrior grabbed Althea's collar, pulled her head closer and stared at her. Those were her last words of the brave warrior before she succumbed to her death.

Althea's heart won't stop pounding; she could feel her body shaking thinking about her father. She realized that she needs to go to him immediately. A blinding light enfolds Althea and quickly transformed to her armored form, summoning her Serdeus as she exited the prison chamber. She saw the Fallens heading towards the sleeping chamber. She flew swiftly towards the enemy with her Serdius raised. The creatures saw her and started attacking her, with her skills in combat and her powerful flame, she fought hard to forced her way to her father. After a while of gruesome battle, Althea finally reached the sleeping chamber and quickly barricaded the door. She turned around and saw for the first time after three thousand years, her father the king sleeping in a glass like coffin. She drew a sharp breath as she staggered to approach her father. She covered her mouth in shock and tears streamed down her eyes. She kneeled at the foot of the king and asked for his forgiveness. Then, Morsus and his minions broke through the barricaded door, saw the king and all the male Arkans sleeping.

"So, this is where you have been hiding all this time?" said Morsus with an evil grin.

"You will have to go through me first before you could lay your filthy hands on my father and my people," Althea lifted her Serdius and was ready to battle Morsus.

Una and Aril made it to the sleeping chamber in time and saw Althea facing the Fallens alone. They hurriedly stood beside her.

"No your highness! They will have to go through us!" added Una and Aril.

Althea looked at Una and Aril and was startled to see them again. Together, the three stood in between the Fallens and the sleeping Arkan.

"We came here to destroy you and your people. And destroy you I shall! Attack!" Morsus ridiculed the three.

Althea and the two warriors ran towards the Fallens and fought them bravely. They were determined to stop them from destroying the male Arkans. Sorah however, arrived back at Avetus staggering as she makes her way to her father. Blood was trailing behind her. She was weak and badly hurt. Nevertheless, she still has enough strength to plow her way through, killing all the creatures that stands in her way. Sorah entered the sleeping chamber and saw Una and Aril fighting the creatures. She was surprised to see Althea inside, swinging her Serdius, slashing the enemy and fighting with all her might defending their father from Morsus and his minions. Sorah rushed towards Althea and jumped in to join the fight. Both stood side by side and catch a glimpse of each other.

"What are you doing here?" asked Sorah.

"What family should do. We stand and fight together," Althea replied with a smile.

Althea 's eyes bulged and in the depths of her gaze as she saw Sarah's blood and her decaying hands. She knew right away that it was Athanax's doing. Sorah was becoming weary. She was dragging her feet, moving slower than usual and her vision hazed. Morsus and his creatures were able to push onward nearing the chamber. Althea, Una and Aril desperately holding the enemy back using what remains of their courage and strength.

Meanwhile at the battle of Enor, Sarah, Narie and Sune were still fighting at the first line, but they knew that the line would not hold anymore as the Zelridars acting as their aerial cover were occupied fighting the Draakabs. Sarah decided to fall back to the second line where Prince Vasuril and the Nephatrons' stood. Narie flew out of the battle, while Sarah rode Sune and retreated to the next line.

From the top of the wall, Kiran ordered King Turloch to prepare the artilleries to support the Nephatrons and the Deodarians' line. He also ordered the tower turrets to fend off the approaching Draakabs. As the Fallens continued their incursion towards the wall of Enor, Narie had reached the second line while Sarah and Sune dashed off towards them. Narie gave the command to the Nephatrons to lock their shields, while another rank of Nephatrons formed from behind pointing their guns towards the enemy. Prince Vasuril prepared his warriors for the inevitable if the Nephatrons line breaks.

Sarah and Sune leaped off the last step and finally reached the second line. Then:

"Fire!" Narie shouted, commencing the Nephatrons' assault.

Ranks of Nephatrons fired their cannons and guns aimed towards the rushing Fallens and one after the other, the creatures fell to the ground. Even with the wall of shields and barrage of firepower of the Nephatrons, the Fallens still kept on coming until they reached the line. The Fallens rammed the shield wall relentlessly to break through the line. The Nephatrons tried to push the creatures back using their shield as they struggle to hold their ground.

"When the Fallens breaks through that wall, we will stand our ground and fight until the end," said Prince Vasuril, pointing his sword at the Fallen,

Sarah and Narie looked at each other and prepared themselves to face yet another fight. Then the inevitable happened, the Nephatrons' line was shattered and swarm of Fallens rushed towards the wall.

"Prepare to fight!" Sarah shouted.

Sarah, Narie, Sune and the Deodarians waited eagerly as the enemy approached.

"With all my strength and courage, for the king!" Narie shouted.

"With all my strength and courage, for the king!" Sarah and the Deodarians cheered together.

The Deodarian line clashed with the Fallen. Kiran saw the Nephatrons' line was broken. He gave the command to fire the artilleries to aid Sarah, Narie and the Deodarians. Volleys of artillery fire rained down at the assaulting Fallen, explosion after explosion, ripping apart and decimating the creatures. The artilleries somehow slowed down the Fallens and gave the Deodarians a fighting chance. Bronax saw that the Ithurian artilleries were hampering the movements of his army. He called out his Draakab and ordered to attack the artilleries. As the Draakabs approached the wall, Kiran already prepared and countered it with the numerous turrets positioned above the wall firing at the dragons. The turrets proved to be very effective in keeping the Draakabs at bay.

On another front of the war, the platoon of messengers sent out by King Turloch finally reached the wormhole and were immediately attacked by Draakab sentries placed at the wormhole by Morsus to prevent anyone from interfering with the battle at Fostrum.

"All right men this is it! No matter what happens, one of us must to go through that hole and deliver the message to King Malkiem and King Ull. God speed!" the platoon commander announced to the radio.

The messengers valiantly fought the Draakabs and forced their way towards the wormhole. One by one the Ithurian messengers were being killed, until two ships were left to fight. The commander knew that the situation doesn't look good for them. He ordered his last men to follow him from behind, shielding him from the enemy. The commander sacrificed himself by ramming his ship to the Draakabs that blocked their way. The explosion created a gap, which allowed the last pilot to fly inside the wormhole and successfully came through the other side. The surviving messenger hurriedly set course for Treliseum to deliver the crucial message. The messenger hovered the sky of

Treliseum and watched in horror as he witnessed the battle engulfing the field of Fostrum. He lands his ship near the Ithurian camp and immediately sought for King Ull to relay to him Kiran's message. King Ull's face turned pale when he learned that Kiran's mission of peace with the Arkans was successful. The next line of the message further shocked him as he learned about the grave situation Kiran was facing on Eres.

King Ull quickly ran to see King Malkiem to inform him about Kiran and what's happening in Eres. He went up the front line and talked to King Malkiem, King Kelon and King Gileal, as well as Feirul.

"Malkiem, cease this incursion at once. We have made a grave mistake," King Ull said in urgency.

"What nonsense are you talking about?" King Gileal demanded.

"Kiran! Kiran is alive and he is on Eres. His mission of peace was successful." King Ull stuttered.

"What? But how can it be? His ship was destroyed!" King Malkiem asked. He was unable to absorb the news.

"This could be a trick, your highness. We confirmed that the prince's ship was destroyed by the Arkans!" Feirul claimed as his voice trembled.

"Then, what do you have to say about this?" said King Ull as he glared at Feirul.

King Ull showed the Council Kiran's message. Kiran was alive and was speaking to his father, pleading him to stop the war and return to Eres as the Fallen Arkans had invaded the planet. Everyone, especially Athanax whose evil plan was exposed, were shocked.

"Now you believe me Malkiem? Your son is alive and is begging us to return immediately to stop the Fallens!" King Ull said.

The Council was in disarray from the sudden turn of events and the urgency on Eres. King Gileal and King Kelon were not in favor of pulling out their army from Fostrum. They knew that Fostrum will be in their hands soon and this was not the best time to retreat. But King Ull reminded Malkiem that he gave his word to Kiran and Kiran fulfilled his end of the deal. As king of the Ithurians, he has the sworn duty to stay true to his word and uphold justice. Athanax's brows drew together and bit his lower lips with the thought that he came so close in achieving his revenge and suddenly will end in failure. He vowed that no matter what happened, he will have his revenge.

"Malkiem, open your eyes! Order the retreat at once! Our kingdom, your children are in danger!" King Ull begged.

Deep within his heart King Malkiem was happy to know that his children are alive. King Ull continued to plead, while King Kelon and King Gileal disagreed. King Malkiem then decided to head back to Eres to stop the Fallen before everything is too late -- a decision that shattered King Kelon, King Gileal and Athanax.

"But Malkiem, we almost have Fostrum within our grasp. Imagine the riches and power that we can hold!" King Gileal growled aggressively.

"My friends, our planet is in danger. Our people are in danger. Does that hold no importance to you?" King Malkiem answered irritated.

"Who cares about Eres if we can have Treliseum and its riches? We can start all over again in here," King Kelon said.

"You bastard! You would sacrifice your people for your greed!" King Ull retorted.

"Be careful of your words Ull! You are a traitor and an Arkan sympathizer! Guards, seize this man!" Kelon shouted.

"Enough all of you! I'm still the supreme king of the Ithurians and don't you dare forget about that. I hereby order all the Ithurian armies to cease the attack and return to Eres immediately" King Malkiem stated in a rough commanding manner.

The Council was silenced. King Ull had never been so happy for his friend, but the rest were angered by the decision. Unknown to the Council, Athanax was plotting a way to salvage his plan.

"Then, if the king would permit, I will take my army and head back first to Eres to help Kiran, while the main army prepares to withdraw," said King Ull.

King Malkiem didn't wait anymore for the Council's decision and approved King Ull's request without hesitation.

"Ull, please tell my children to wait for my return. It will take quite some time to send the army back to Eres, but we will try to get there hopefully in time. And please tell Kiran that I promise to atone for this dreadful mistake," said King Malkiem in a firm reassuring tone.

King Ull left the Council's camp and swiftly mobilized his army for the journey back to Eres. King Kelon and King Gileal once again tries to convince Malkiem that it is a mistake to leave Treliseum, but Malkiem had already made up his mind and no one could ever change it. King Malkiem was about to step out of the camp to order the retreat when suddenly, a sword pierced through his heart. The king yelp and gave a grimace of pain. He turned his gaze and saw Feirul's eyes glaring at him after stabbing him from behind. The two kings gasped and quickly drew their swords. King Malkiem looked at Feirul in horror. Feirul further lunge his Serdeus into King Malkiem,

"I shall have my revenge on all of you!" Athanax whispered as he watched Malkiem's life extinguished.

"What have you done Feirul? What is the meaning of this?" King Kelon and King Gileal demanded an answer.

"Isn't it a waste to leave this planet's treasures for it is almost within our reach" said Athanax.

"Why did you have to kill Malkiem? Now we are lost!" the two kings panicked.

"Malkiem is weak and that is why he needs to be eliminated. We are not at lost yet. I will lead this army and defeat the Arkans and have their riches and power to ourselves. Are you with me" Athanax sneered.

Greed outweighed the two kings' morals and logic. They looked at one another and grinned sinisterly. Without hesitation, they agreed with Athanax's proposition.

"But how would we lead the army without Malkiem? The generals will only heed his command." King Gileal asked in panic.

"Do not worry about that. I shall take care of it," Athanax scoffed.

Athanax called his Fallens to dispose King Malkiem's body. He then used his power to take King Malkiem's appearance. Both King Gileal and King Kelon stood in amazement as they witnessed his transformation. King Ull and his army hurriedly depart Fostrum and passed through the wormhole, racing against time to reach Eres in order to aid Kiran with the battle taking place at Enor. He hoped that

Malkiem would be able to stop the war immediately and return to Eres in time with the main army. But, without knowing that his friend had just been murdered by the Fallen king.

"What about Ull?" King Kelon asked.

"We don't need to worry about him. He only has a small army for us to worry about," Athanax replied.

Athanax took command of the entire Ithurian army and ordered the generals, commanders and soldiers to push through with the attack and kill all the Arkans. King Kelon and King Gileal just stood behind Athanax.

As the battle rages on at Fostrum and Avetus, the Arkans were facing an impending defeat from the Ithurian. Prea had ordered the Arkans to retreat within the Fostrum wall and from there will make their last stand to hold the gate no matter the odds. Squadrons of Zelridar, battalions of Nephatrons, legions of Zeltkova advanced towards the Fostrum gate and the Ithurian artilleries continues to bombard them. Even with the sheer number and firepower of the Ithurians, it was still difficult for them to conquer Fostrum because of the fierce determination of the Arkans to defend the city down to the last warrior standing.

"My sisters, whatever happens we will not yield to the Ithurians. Defend the city at all costs!" Prea shouted.

"With all my strength and courage, for the king!" the Arkans cheered.

The Arkans' battle cry was heard by Athanax and the two kings.

"Persistent are they! When are they going to give up?" said King Gileal, with a smirk on his face.

"Patience my friends. Soon the Arkan will be no more. I had sent my army within Avetus the main city and at this moment, they too will fall," Athanax boasted.

The two kings were unaware that he brought his army with him, but that doesn't concern them anymore as long as they could have the riches and powers of Treliseum, King Kelon and King Gileal will follow Athanax even in the pit of hell to satisfy their greed.

Back in Avetus, Sorah was getting weaker by the minute due to the poison she was inflicted by her uncle. She suddenly collapsed and luckily Althea was close by her side and was able catch her.

"Una, Aril hold them back. I need to help Sorah," said Althea.

Una and Aril battled the creatures, while Althea do everything she can to heal Sorah. The situation became grim as Athanax's main army was unleashed in Eres with the sole purpose of destroying the planet and the annihilation of its inhabitants. Sarah and Narie were the only Arkans that dared to stand in the way against his army.

Chapter Twenty-Five

THE LIGHT OF SORROW

small group of Arkan warriors came to reinforce Altrus Sorah inside the sleeping chamber. Althea grabbed Sorah's arm and wrapped it around her shoulders, took her near their father's chamber, away from the battle to heal her. Althea put her hands over Sorah's wounds and lights began to radiate.

"It was uncle who did this to you wasn't he?" Althea grimaced at the sight of Sorah's decaying hands.

"I saw him in the battlefield at Fostrum. His eyes tell it all -- full of hatred and determined to destroy us. I should have seen this coming from the moment Kiran came here," Sorah grumbled.

"You've met Kiran?" Althea asked with curiosity in her voice.

They stared silently into each other's eyes and both were reminded of Aran, the man they both loved. Althea couldn't stop the poison from spreading throughout Sorah's body. All she could do was to slow it down.

"It's too late for me now. No one can stop this poison -- not even Father," Sorah's voice quavered in fear.

"There is one who has the power to cleanse this poison. She saved me from this same filth once and brought me back from the dead," Althea revealed.

"Who is this person you speak of that has this power?" a glimmer of hope resounded in Sorah's voice.

"It's your daughter Sarah. She inherited Mother's power of life," Althea answered, holding Sorah's hand and smiling.

Sorah's eyes gleamed with tears of joy and was proud to hear what Althea told her. But she soon realized that it was still hopeless for her since Sarah was on another side of the galaxy. As more Fallens entered the sleeping chamber, Sorah and Althea stood up together, summoned their Serdius and went back to battle the enemies, defending their father and the male Arkans to the bitter end.

Back in the city of Enor where another battle was taking place, the Deodarian line was holding strong, thanks to the strength, bravery and the healing power of the Deodarians. The line was further strengthened by Kiran's artilleries which shielded the Deodarians from the rush of the Fallens. The turrets also proved to be effective in fending off the Draakabs. Amid the battle raging on at the second line, a bloodied Ithurian soldier came running towards Sarah. The soldier was gasping for breath and informed Sarah and Narie that a division of the Fallen army was approaching to the far left, where villagers are still being evacuated. Sarah knew that she couldn't send any of the Deodarian warriors to help, for they are crucially needed to hold the enemy at the front line. Sarah and Narie stared at each other and could clearly see the determination in their faces. Without second thoughts, they decided to proceed to the village to fight the Fallen while the villagers escaped. Sarah instructed the wounded soldier to ran back to the city and inform Kiran about the village. Sarah approached Prince Vasuril and tapped his shoulder from behind.

"Prince Vasuril, I together with Narie and Sune need to help evacuate the villagers from the far left. I will leave you in charge here," Sarah asserted.

"I will do my best," Vasuril replied.

"With all my strength and courage, for the king!" both Sarah and Vasuril said to each other.

Sarah, Narie and Sune immediately rushed to the village to help evacuate the remaining people. Upon arriving, their mouths gaped seeing how bad the situation was in the village. The Ithurian soldiers were about to be overrun by the creatures and the villagers were being slaughtered along the way. Flames began to come out of Narie's hands. She flew towards the creatures and unleashed a devastating fire, burning many of the Fallens. Sune also jumped in and breathe lighting shocks, killing as much as Narie. The combined power of Narie and Sune were able to gradually hold back the Fallens, giving enough time for the Ithurian soldiers to regroup. Sarah instructed the Ithurian commander to lead the villagers to the capital while they hold the enemy back. The surviving Ithurian soldiers at the front line pulled out and helped carry their injured kin to make a desperate run for the capital.

Sarah summoned her Serdeus and quickly ran towards the enemy to help Narie and Sune. They lured the Fallen in a narrow ridge which prevented the creatures from overrunning their position and to have a better chance of holding them back until all soldiers and villagers completely evacuated. The wounded Ithurian soldier sent by Sarah reached the inner city of Enor and went directly to see Kiran. The soldier reported that the left flank was swamped by the Fallens and only the two Arkans and the fox were holding it back. Kiran knew that Sarah and Narie are in danger of being overrun, he immediately directed one of the cannon to fire at Sarah and Narie's location to give them artillery support to shield them from the Fallens.

Bronax tremble in rage as he saw the Ithurian artilleries still firing and preventing his army from moving forward. His Draakabs couldn't do much in stopping them either. Determined to destroy the Ithurians, he ordered the release of the *Diurox* (*Diurox* are blobs of creatures that have limbs and a mind of its own. they can identify their target and explode at will), squadrons of Draakabs flew to the sky carrying the Diurox aiming to destroy the artilleries.

As the swarm of Draakabs approaches the city wall, Kiran and King Turloch saw strange creatures being carried by the dragons.

"Shoot down those dragons, Don't let them get near the cannons no matter what!" Kiran shouted.

The turrets aimed at the incoming Draakabs and continuously fired, shooting down as many they can to prevent them from getting near the wall. But because of the sheer number of the Draakabs approaching at the same time, the turrets couldn't stop all the dragons of that magnitude. Some of the Draakabs managed to slip through the turret's tracers and were able to drop the Diurox at the top of the wall. The Diurox immediately ran towards the artillery, attached itself and violently exploded, destroying the cannon. Kiran and King Turloch were thrown a meter away due to the force of the blast. Sarah and Narie heard the thundering sound of the explosion and saw that the cannon burning at the wall.

Still in shock, Kiran stumbles to stand up. As another group of Draakabs approaches, he ordered all his soldiers to shoot down the Diurox and prevent it from touching the wall. All the Ithurian gun

312

blazes as they shoot the Draakabs and Diurox down, but a wave of dragons was again able to land on the wall, destroying yet another artillery cannon. Situation became grim as the strength of the artillery fire supporting the Deodarian line dwindles. The cannon that aided Sarah and Narie was also destroyed by the Diurox.

The Fallens were gaining ground as the Diurox continues to destroy the Ithurian artilleries. Many of the Deodarians were being killed by the onslaught of the Fallens as the line couldn't hold them back much longer. Kiran saw the inevitable collapse of the second line and immediately ordered to sound the horn of retreat for the Deodarians. Kina instructed her Zeltkova on top and below the gate to push the creatures back and give enough time for the Deodarians to make their retreat to the inner city.

Sarah, Narie and Sune were still fighting at the village on their own when they heard the sound of the horn.

"Narie, fly back to the city and join Kiran!" Sarah told Narie in an urgent tone.

"I'm not going to leave you here," Narie countered.

"Sune and I will be right behind you, now hurry!" Sarah assured Narie.

Narie spread her wings and retreated to the city. She turned around to take a glance at Sarah and Sune below and saw them running behind her. Suddenly, Narie saw another group of Draakabs trying to land another batch of Diurox at the wall. Her heart raced, thinking if Kiran was alright on top of the wall.

"Sarah, I'm going to stop those Draakabs from dropping those creatures at the wall," Narie panicked.

"Go, be careful and we will meet you back at the city," Sarah shouted.

Narie flew towards the Draakabs with her Serdius drawn and slashed as many she could to stop the Diurox from destroying another gun. From the ground, Sarah and Sune dashed to reach the city of Enor when suddenly, the Fallen appear out of nowhere and completely surrounded them, they walked right into the creature's ambush. Sarah fought with the Fallens still mounted on Sune's back. She tried desperately to reach the safety of the wall. One of the Draakab saw Sarah fighting their brethren below and decided to attack. Narie saw the rider heading towards Sarah, targeting her with the Diurox. She immediately chased the Draakab to stop it from harming Sarah and Sune, but before she could reach to kill it, the rider already released the Diurox down to the ground and ran towards Sarah and Sune. Sune spotted the Diurox and immediately unleashed a breath of lighting strike, killing the Fallens that surrounded them and made the Diurox explode prematurely. Because of the close proximity of the blast, Sarah was thrown from Sune's back and fell down on a hill separating her from Sune. She hurt her head as she hit the ground. Still daze, she stood up and staggered to walk.

"Sune, where are you?" Sarah held her bloodied head and cried out in the forest.

It was a first time for Sarah to fight without Sune by her side. Overwhelmed with fear, she lost her balance and fell down in a swoon. Then, the creatures came and starts to surround her once again. She staggers to stand up with the aid of her Serdius and prepared herself to battle the Fallens. Hungry for Arkan blood, the creatures' mouths watered. They were eager to devour her body, Sarah could hear the heavy breathing and snarling of the creatures as they ran towards her with their weapons pointed. Sarah gathered all her remaining strength to fight the Fallen, parrying, slashing and killing the overwhelming enemy just to stay alive. On the other side of the hill, not far from where Sarah was, Sune frantically searching for her. His heart wouldn't stop pounding, his eyes darted from side to side hoping to find Sarah. As Sune continue his search, he was repeatedly being blocked and attacked by the Fallens. But with his lighting breathing power and his superior strength, he managed to slash the enemy with his razor-sharp claws and plow his way through.

Sarah's body became heavy, her strikes and movement were slower than before. The blood from her injured head flows down to her left eye, hampering her vision. She was gasping for breath after fighting alone against the never-ending rush of creatures. The Fallens were able to inflict many wounds on her body, but even so, it didn't stop her from fighting. Because of her weary state, one creature managed to sneaked behind her and pierced his sword deep into Sarah's back. Her face was a grimace of excruciating pain and fell one knee down to the ground. The wound was grave, blood gushed like waterfall. Her vision started to get bleary and she was on the verge of collapse. Yet, she endured the pain and still determined to reach the city to be with her sister Narie.

·Sune's eyes sprung open in horror after he found Sarah bloodied and wounded, fighting with one knee on the ground as the Fallen continues to surround her. Another creature took advantage of her exhaustion and attempted to strike her again from behind while she was distracted fighting his brethren in front. The creature pointed his sword and ran towards Sarah to deliver the final blow and finish her off for good. Sune rushed to save Sarah, ramming all the creatures that stood in his way, disregarding his own safety from the Fallen's swords that repeatedly slashing and stabbing his body as he ran through them. The creature's blade was about to pierce Sarah's back, when Sune leaped in desperation biting the creature's neck and bumping into

Sarah throwing her out of the kill zone. Sune's bite tears the creature's neck and killed it instantly. Sune then unleased his most devastating breath of lightning shocks ever, killing all the creatures that surrounded them. The Fallens were shaken by power of the fox and retreated for the meantime to regroup. Sune stood in front of the fleeing enemy, while Sarah was behind him, lying on the ground and briefly unconscious. Sarah regained her senses, staggered and saw Sune's back.

"Let's go Sune! We need to reach the city!" Sarah groaned. She was exhausted and in pain.

Sune remained standing, facing the direction of the enemy.

"Come on Sune, they're coming again! We need to go now!" Sarah repeated.

Yet, Sune stood still and pant heavily. Sarah noticed that Sune's legs were trembling, when suddenly he collapsed. Frozen, Sarah didn't blink and in the depth of her gaze at Sune, she quickly ran to his side and held his head. She stopped with a gasp after seeing that Sune was fatally stabbed and the sword was still impaled in his heart. Sune's silvery white fur was stained by his own blood.

"You will be alright Sune. You will be alright," she quivered.

Sune was breathing heavily and coughing too much blood. Sarah couldn't do anything to ease Sune's pain.

"Stay with me Sune. You're going to be alright. Please, please! Don't leave me," Sarah cried.

Sune watched Sarah's crying face. Even with the crushing pain, he somehow managed to give Sarah a smile to calm her down. The pain became unbearable. Sune was already gasping for breath. He knew that he would not last much longer. Tears slid down his eyes knowing that he will be leaving Sarah alone. Suddenly, the gasping stopped and he was not moving anymore. It became quiet at that moment. Sarah just stared at Sune's lifeless body in disbelief. Seeing Sune lying on the ground from afar, the Fallens once again took the chance and rushed to attack Sarah. Narie was still fighting the Draakabs in the sky when she suddenly felt a piercing pain in her heart. She looked down and saw Sarah crying, holding Sune's motionless body in her arms. A dreaded feeling crept up from the pit of Narie's stomach as she saw the swarm of Fallens running towards Sarah with their swords drawn, eager to kill her. Paralyzed by shock, Sarah couldn't command her body to move and remain to the ground holding Sune's body. Narie felt that Sarah might have given up the will to live and wanted to embrace death. She hastily flew down to reach Sarah before the Fallens does.

"Sarah get out of there! The Fallens are heading towards you! Sister listen to me! Please!" Narie pleaded.

But Sarah remained lost in her anguish, still couldn't grasp the reality of Sune's demise.

"This is not happening! This can't be happening! No, no, no!" Sarah mumbled.

She looked up and saw Narie telling her something. But because of the physical and mental pain she was suffering, she wasn't able to comprehend Narie. Sarah turned her gaze at the Fallens that were about to kill her and held Sune tight in her arms.

"No!" Sarah's scream echoed throughout the forest.

A sudden powerful blinding light burst out of Sarah's body. The creatures and Narie were thrown violently out of control because of the immense blast force of her light. The light was seen by both Bronax and Kiran across each side of the battlefield. In Avetus, both Sorah and Althea felt a sharp pain in their chests and stumbled down briefly.

"Something happened to Sarah. I felt her pain," Sorah instinctively said.

"Yes sister. I felt it too," Althea concurred.

Sarah's light was becoming extremely powerful as she watched Sune's lifeless body. All she could think of was for Sune to come back to her, until subconsciously, she unleashes the power of life to bring Sune back from the dead. She screamed and a blinding pillar of light more powerful than the time she unleashed with Althea, and her wings came out on its own. Sarah's light spread throughout the battlefield in Eres and rippled across the galaxies, reaching both Fostrum and Avetus.

The light passed through the bodies of all the living and healed their wounds. Athanax and his minions at Treliseum felt the warmth of the light and noticed that some of their scars were slowly disappearing, while the Arkans at both battlefield, were fully healed of their wounds and gained a renewed strength. The light also penetrated the chamber of the sleeping male Arkans where Sorah and Althea was at. Already familiar with the sensation she felt with the light, Althea knew immediately that it came from Sarah – no less.

"Althea, what is happening to me?" Sorah's voice cracked with fear.

Althea turned her gaze at Sorah and was speechless to see the light engulfing her. Sorah witness that the light was cleansing her of the poison.

"What is this light? It's healing me of my wounds," Sorah said in awe.

"It is Sarah's light. She found her way back to you," Althea couldn't hold her tears. She felt that Sarah was with them during that desperate moment.

Sorah's wounds were completely healed and the poison in her body had finally been cleansed. Her powers were restored – she had never felt such renewed strength in her before. Althea on the other hand, was worried that something bad might have happened to Sarah for her to use that power.

"Sorah, I need to go to Sarah. She might be hurt!" said Althea worriedly.

"Then, we shall go together," Sorah replied.

Sorah slowly turned to face the Fallen inside the sleeping chamber and flew right through them, throwing the creatures away and single-handedly pushed them back out of the sleeping chamber. The Fallens were shocked to have felt the strength of Sorah.

"Now you will pay for your transgression," Sorah glared at Morsus and his minions.

Fear crawled up to the spines of the Fallens upon hearing Sorah's stern voice, but Morsus knew that he couldn't go back to Athanax cowering. He is fully aware that Athanax would show no mercy to those who falter.

"Attack her! Destroy all of them!" Morsus commanded his minions.

Flames began to emanate from Sorah's hands as she walked towards the attacking creatures. The other Arkan warriors took a step forward to follow her but was stopped by Althea.

"Stay where you are. Sorah will handle this alone," said Althea.

Out of desperation to fulfill his mission of destroying King Satorex and his kin, Morsus made a last attempt to attack the Arkans, but as they neared Sorah, the fire of justice was unleashed, annihilating all the Fallens inside the city of Avetus. Althea and the Arkan warriors were shaken as they witnessed the power of the forbidden flame, while some turned their gaze away for they couldn't bear to watch the horror and intense pain of the Fallen as they burn slowly to their death. As Morsus' life was about to end, he took one last glance at Sorah and Althea.

"You may think you have won, but Athanax will come and continue what we have started!" Morsus groaned in extreme pain.

"You're wrong! He doesn't need to bother himself to come here for I am coming after him and we will finish what he started!" Sorah retorted.

Sorah, Althea and the rest of the warriors watched as the Fallens were finally destroyed and turned into ashes. She ordered Una and Aril to follow her and Althea while the remaining warriors stays in Avetus to protect the king. They immediately left Avetus to reach Fostrum and hoped that Prea and the warriors still managed to hold the city's defense against the Ithurian invaders.

Chapter Twenty-Six

THE THIRD WIELDER

The pillar of light slowly faded after Sarah opened her eyes and saw Sune lying in her arms motionless. The Fallens, disoriented and shaken by the force of Sarah's light, momentarily stopped their attacks as they stood in awe seeing their old scars were partially healed and their bodies rejuvenated. Sarah was still rooted to the ground holding Sune in her arms bewildered and confuse. She clenched her fists and shook her head in anger, wondering why her light didn't bring Sune back. After a brief moment of enchantment, the creature's attention was once again diverted to Sarah. They saw her sitting motionlessly and holding the lifeless body of Sune in the middle of the field. The Fallens drew their swords once again, snarled and began charging towards Sarah and this time to destroy her for good.

Sarah's heart was filled with sorrow and anger for Sune's fate. She still couldn't accept the truth that Sune was gone. The creatures close in on her and their blades were about to slice through her body, she lifted her head and screamed in agony. Her scream sent shivers down the enemy's spines and her body suddenly fumed a visibly red aura. The creatures stood in terror as they saw Sarah walk towards them, leaving a trail of red smoke. The leader of the Fallens ordered his men to resume the attack. Sarah felt like being stabbed by a dagger over and over again as she kept the thought of Sune's death. The pain was becoming unbearable and Sarah couldn't take it anymore. Without warning, Sarah suddenly unleased the forbidden fire of justice and instantly burned all the creatures surrounding her. The flame spreads throughout the forest reaching those creatures on the open field laying siege to the city. Bronax was petrified as he witnessed his army annihilated by the flame in an instant. He couldn't believe he would once again witness the destructive power of the fire of justice being wielded. He knew exactly about the devastation and consequences if they continue to go against whoever the wielder was. He quickly ordered the entire Fallen army in full retreat before being completely decimated by the flame.

Narie rose from the rubbles. She shook her head and collect her thoughts after being thrown by the immense force of the light. She suddenly remembered Sarah and quickly search for her. She found her sitting in the middle of the field, surrounded by charred bodies of the Fallens. Narie's breathing and heartbeat began to race as she approached Sarah still holding Sune's body. Sune didn't wake up from her light because his heart was destroyed by the creature's sword and no power could ever heal it.

"Sarah are you hurt?" in a soft voice she asked.

Sarah didn't respond. Narie saw that even Sarah's wounds were completely healed. Narie gawked at the thought that Sarah hold this much power in her -- a power that exceeded even hers.

"Sister, we need to go to the city now," she touched Sarah's shoulder and whispered.

But Sarah remained motionless and hesitant to leave Sune.

"We can't do anything for Sune anymore. He gave up his life to save you, so please sister let us now go," Narie pleaded.

Tears slid from Sarah's eyes as she finally realized that Sune was not coming back anymore. Narie fell on her knees and held Sarah in her arms, trying to console her.

"Could you help me bury Sune?" Sarah requested.

Narie couldn't hold her tears back anymore and cried together with Sarah.

"Of course sister. Anything for Sune," Narie sniffled.

With their bare hands, they buried Sune in a shallow grave. Narie and Sarah stayed for a few moments with Sune before heading back to the city. Back at Enor, the Ithurians and Deodarians rejoiced after the defeat and retreat of the Fallens. Everyone patted each other's back and felt relieved and thankful that they had survived the ordeal. Kiran on the other hand, felt happy that his people survived, however, it also surrounded him with a haze of fear and uncertainty. Seeing the scale of devastation of the power of the flame, he feared that it could also annihilate them if the wielder whoever it might be chooses to.

"We truly are lucky Kiran. If the siege continued for another hour the city would surely fall," said the exhausted King Turloch.

"I do hope we are my lord," Kiran replied with uncertainty.

Kina and Vasuril came by to give Kiran and King Turloch their thought after the siege.

"Kiran, the city walls sustained heavy damage from the Diurox attack and will need days to re-fortify. We are left with only two artillery cannons. Our Nephatrons were reduced to only a handful platoon. We have so many wounded soldiers and others whose morale's hang by a thread at this very minute," Kina stated.

"Prince Vasuril, what is the voice of the Deodarians? asked Kiran.

"I lost many of my warriors today and many others gravely wounded. It will require us a long period of time to heal this kind of injuries. Only the powerful healers in Deodara could hasten the rejuvenation of my warriors," Vasuril shared.

Kiran then knew that the city of Enor was already lost. If the Fallens launched another attack, they would surely be overrun and perish if they stay. With a heavy heart, Kiran decided to abandon Enor and move all of their remaining forces to the capital.

"We're leaving Enor and move everyone to Ithuria. Prince Vasuril, we truly are grateful and forever indebted to your people for coming to our aid, but I could no longer bear to see your people suffer even more. Even though I am desperately in need of your strength, the lives of your warriors should come first. Please return to Deodara and heal your warriors. My ships will take your injured warriors back. We will hold the Fallens in Ithuria," said Kiran.

"I'm sorry Prince Kiran, but I might have to take that option," Vasuril sighed.

King Turloch and Kina felt disheartened as they learned about the Deodarians' departure. Nevertheless, they understood the decision Kiran made. It was the Deodarians that suffered the most in the battle for holding their ground in preventing the Fallen from breaching the wall. The Ithurians prepares to move for the capital, but before they left, Kina ordered to burn the city down to prevent the Fallen from acquiring their technology and using it as their stronghold. Kiran went up to the wall and gazed across the field of Enor looking for Sarah and Narie. He grew uneasy thinking what could have happened to them.

"Kiran, we're running out of time. We need to move now!" said King Turloch as his voice rose in panic.

He was left with no choice but to leave without them. He ordered some of his scouts to search for Sarah, Narie and Sune as soon as possible and to escort them to the capital.

Meanwhile back at Treliseum, the battle at Fostrum rages on. The Ithurians remained relentless in their assault on the wall, but because of the pillar of light that passed through their bodies, the Arkans were miraculously healed of their wounds and gained renewed strength, they were able to push the Ithurian army back. Then, Sorah and Althea together with the reinforcing warriors arrived on top of the wall.

"Cease this incursion at once and remove yourselves on this sacred ground or face the full wrath of the Arkans!" Sorah's voice echoed throughout the battlefield.

The weary Ithurian army felt unsettled by Sorah's stern warning. Some of the soldiers had lost hope and footing in the battle. They wanted to return back, but Athanax who took the appearance of King Malkiem ordered to continue with the attack.

"Fire those cannons and destroy them all!" Athanax shouted in rage.

The Ithurians aimed their cannons at the wall where Sorah and Althea stood. Prea and the warriors gawked at the sight of the barrage of artillery shells coming down at Sorah. As the warriors rushed to save her, Sorah raised her hand towards the incoming shells and burned them with her flame, destroying all the incoming projectiles in one blast. Everyone stood motionless in fear after witnessing the devastation of Sorah's flame. Both the Arkans and Ithurians were shocked. But the one who got the most shock was Athanax, he couldn't think of how Sorah could have used her flames after he had poisoned her. He suddenly thought of the light that he felt earlier. He realized that surely enough, if the light healed him, Sorah and the rest of the Arkans were no exception.

Athanax's blood boils seeing Sorah looking down on him from the wall. He ordered the Ithurian to attack but the soldiers had lost their spirits to fight anymore, fearing that Sorah's flame would definitely destroy them all. Athanax insisted that they attack and promised them the reward of riches if they follow his order. The Ithurians were reluctant but the call of greed was too overpowering for them to resist. The soldiers resumed their hopeless attack and marched towards the gate, but this time, Sorah will not exercise restrain anymore. She decided to destroy the entire Ithurian army. That was Athanax's plan, that's what he wanted Sorah to do and that was the moment he's been waiting for a long time -- his revenge to the seeds of Varkelos.

"No sister. You are playing exactly in favor of his evil game. This is what he wanted you to do -- to destroy the Ithurians!" Althea warned.

Sorah realized that Althea speak the truth as she had ever since she came back to Treliseum and from the time she met Athanax on the battlefield.

"Please sister, I beg of you! Don't destroy the Ithurians. They are being tricked by uncle," Althea once again pleaded.

Sorah looked down from the top of the wall and watched the Ithurians fueled by their greed, make a desperate assault towards the gate. She raised her hand once again – this time towards the rushing Ithurians, while Althea persistently begged her to spare them. Athanax saw Sorah's gestures and knew that she would unleash the fire of justice and destroy the Ithurians. As Althea tries to stop her, she was restrained by two warriors and prevented her from interrupting Altrus Sorah.

"Death to the Arkans!" Athanax shouted.

Athanax was trying to provoke Sorah. Sorah's hand emitted light as her flames intensify. Athanax laughed sinisterly as he anticipates the end of the Ithurian. Suddenly, Sorah remembered Kiran and the peace he seeks for his people. After seeing Kiran in her thoughts, she unleashed a wall of fire directly on the path of the attacking Ithurians. The force and extreme heat of her flames sent the soldiers running back. Sorah spared the lives of the ignorant and greedy Ithurians. Althea heaved a sigh of relief knowing that Sorah didn't fall into their uncle's evil plan. Athanax on the other hand, glared at Sorah from afar. His anger turned into violence as he wrecked the council tent. His body trembled in rage knowing that his plan of revenge failed.

"If you dare choose to continue with this futile attack against my people, I assure you that I will not be merciful the next time and I will surely send you all to the abyss," Sorah warned the Ithurians in a daunting tone.

The Ithurians were terrified to see the flame in her hand. Even Athanax couldn't make the Ithurians follow his order anymore. The Ithurians were already convinced that fighting the Arkan was futile. Athanax threatened the soldiers with the consequences of death if they don't follow his orders to attack. The field commanders however, argued that the soldiers have had enough and told him that if he further insists of the attack, there will be mutiny within the army and a move to overthrow him was inevitable.

"It is wise to heed the commanders' words Malkiem," King Kelon stuttered.

"It's over. We've lost. We can't send our men to a hopeless battle," King Gileal said with a defeated tone of voice.

Athanax was furious. Even Morsus and the army he sent to Avetus were defeated and destroyed by her flame.

"Uncle, if you're hiding among these Ithurians, I'm saying this to you, as long as I'm alive you will never ever enter our kingdom again. Retribution will soon come to you," Sorah scoffed.

The Ithurians were lost in a riddle. They had no idea who was being referred to by Sorah. Athanax's eyes flashed red and despised Sorah and Althea. He was left with no choice but to order the retreat of the Ithurian army and return to Eres. The Ithurians then began the mass withdrawal from Fostrum. They picked up their dead and rolled their equipment's back to their airships. Some of the Ithurians cried in frustration and felt the humiliating defeat in the hands of the Arkan, while most of them were relieved knowing that they didn't have to go through that certain death crusade.

As the last Ithurian ship left Fostrum, Sorah stood firmly as she watched the Ithurian armada retreat.

"Thank you sister for sparing them," Althea said.

"They shouldn't thank me. It was their prince that they need to thank," Sorah answered.

Athanax couldn't accept the fact that he lost the Fostrum campaign and the attack at Avetus. He almost had his revenge but instead, defeat was what he obtained. He vowed that he would still have his revenge no matter what the costs.

King Ull meanwhile, arrived back at Eres with his army. As his ship hovers the sky of Enor, he turned his gaze away from the window as he tried to conceal his shock. Pain was evident from his eyes at the sight of the devastation of his beloved city of Enor burned to the ground. They received a frantic transmission instructing them to proceed to the capital where the surviving Ithurians taking refuge. Upon arriving, King Ull immediately searched for Kiran and his friend Turloch. He entered the council room and saw the exhausted Kiran, Kina and King Turloch still in shock.

"Kiran, you really are alive! What on Eres happened here!" King Ull was eager to hear his answer.

"The Fallen Arkans -- they are real and they have returned," Kiran revealed.

"We barely survived the attack, if not for the Deodarians and the two Arkans that helped us," added King Turloch.

"Arkan? What Arkan?" King Ull was bemused.

"Sarah and Narie, daughters of Altrus Sorah," Kiran blurted.

King Ull stood flabbergasted by Kiran's news. His face turned pale in disbelief at the thought that after what they did to Fostrum, the two Arkans still helped defend their people. Kiran asked for his father and inquired why the Council didn't wait for his return. King Ull informed Kiran and Kina that the king is on his way back to Eres, together with the entire army. King Ull and King Turloch recounted the event that transpired before the invasion. They told Kiran that they were against the invasion together with some of the council members and begged for the king to wait. They added that everything changed when a man suddenly appeared and blinded the Council with the belief that the

Ithurians were the rightful masters of Fostrum and that all the riches belonged to the Ithurians.

"The person poisoned the mind and judgment of the Council members as well as the people. He corrupted them with greed, which in the end led to the invasion of Fostrum. The campaign seemed even more valid and reasonable when we learned that you were killed by the Arkans, which now proves to be a lie," King Ull added.

"Then what has become of the Fostrum campaign?" the pain of his people could be heard from Kiran's voice.

"We have outnumbered and outgunned the Arkans. Their army suffered heavy but still, we couldn't break them. They are strong, relentless and fearless!" King Ull shrieked.

"What about Altrus Sorah?" Kiran wondered.

"She is the bravest and fiercest warrior of all the Arkans. She led her warriors and fought alongside them," King Ull expressed his admiration.

King Ull also revealed that the Arkans branded the Ithurian as sons of traitors, which most of them didn't understood. After hearing Ull's story, Kiran was forced to reveal to them the real truth about their ancestor's banishment from Treliseum. They were made to believe a thousand years of lies. In the end, it was truly their ancestors who have done wrong to the Arkans, and yet, the Ithurians were made to hate them. After hearing the whole truth from Kiran, Kina and the two king lowered their heads in shame for the lies that they been living for thousands of years and the lives that were lost due to the false belief.

"So, the girl speaks the truth after all," King Ull uttered.

"What girl?" Kiran queried.

"Sarah -- she stood up to your father on the day before the invasion. She told us of the coming of the Fallens and that we needed to fight them, but the people ridiculed her," King Turloch slammed the wall.

The two kings agreed that it was the man who completely deceived the Council and the people to go to war against the Arkans. When asked who the person was, the two kings weren't able to give much details about him. He just appeared, joined the Council and spoke ill of the Arkans.

Kiran's was confounded. Somehow, he managed to piece together the puzzle that the Fallens might have infiltrated their Council. He alerted Kina and the two kings, instructing them to remain vigilant and careful about whom they talk to. Suddenly, a soldier burst into the Council room and informed them that the two Arkans have returned. Kiran and the rest immediately ran down to meet them. They saw Narie holding Sarah in her arms. Due to the pain and shock of Sune's death, Sarah was still unresponsive to everyone except for Narie. The villagers and soldiers approached and stared at them as they made their way to the inner city.

"Thank you! Thank you!" a teary soldier walked alongside.

"What have we done to be thanked by you?" Narie wondered.

"We were at the village fighting the creatures! If you didn't come to our aid, we along with the villagers would have surely perished!" the soldier announced.

The villagers whom they saved came running to them and expressed their gratitude for saving them. As the villagers and soldiers thanked them, tears trickled from their eyes seeing how brave the two girls were. Kiran, Kina, King Turloch and King Ull owe the lives of their people to Sarah and Narie and acknowledged them as the Arkans who fought with them against the Fallens. Kiran and Kina met them and saw Sarah in her most pitiful state.

"What happened to both of you? Where is Sune?" Kiran blurted

Narie stared at him with sad eyes and shook her head, Sarah burst into tears upon hearing Sune's name. Narie took Sarah inside the palace to let her rest. An Ithurian scout returned and reported that the Fallens have retreated and were camping outside Enor's borders. Anticipating an attack at any time, King Ull ordered their soldiers to take position and reinforce the defense of the capital.

Narie left Sarah alone in the room. She came out and immediately held Kiran in her arm and kissed him. She was glad that Kiran was unharmed. Narie told them that Sune sacrificed his life to saved Sarah. He was mortally wounded and had died in Sarah's arms.

"The flame that destroyed the Fallens -- did it came from you?" Kiran eagerly asked.

"No. It was Sarah. I never knew she had so much power in her. My mother had once told me that being born out of love was the true power of the Arkans, but Sarah's powers were unimaginable," Narie stared in blank space.

Narie told the story of the fire of justice whose sole wielder was her grandfather, but she couldn't believe that Sarah was able to summoned it. She was likewise concerned for her mother back home after seeing the Ithurian armada on the way to Treliseum, Kiran immediately went down to his knees and begged her forgiveness.

"Narie, please forgive me for failing you. After we convinced your mother and finally attained peace, and yet this is what my father and my people repays you," Kiran's voice was filled with guilt.

"Get up, Kiran," said Narie.

"But Narie, we have no honor left to face you," Kiran couldn't look at Narie because of his shame.

Narie paused for a moment and held Kiran's head to face her.

"I don't blame you for what happened. I know that someone is trying to stop the peace. I saw that the Fallens ambushed you and surely enough this is all the work of the Fallen king," Narie spoke in a soft voice.

Everyone agreed to what Narie said. Nevertheless, they asked for her forgiveness for the weakness and greed of their people.

"Kiran, let us leave it at that. Now, you need to stay strong for your people as I for mine," Narie told Kiran while holding his hands.

Meanwhile, on the other side of Enor's border where the Fallens retreated, Bronax regrouped his army.

"Why did you order us to retreat? We almost had the city!" one creature grumbled.

"King Athanax will not be delighted after what you have done Bronax!" another creature ranted.

"Silence you fool!" Bronax yelled.

The creatures were shaken and stepped back as they heard Bronax's furious tone. He stood up and approached them.

"I just saved all of you from the fire of justice!" Bronax shouted.

"Impossible! That power can only be wielded by King Satorex and his daughter Sorah and no other!" one creature argued.

"I know what I saw and I'm very well familiar with the pain. Without a doubt in my mind, someone wielded the fire of justice that destroyed our brethren who besieged the Ithurian wall," Bronax retorted.

"Are you implying that there's a third wielder of this power?" the creature queried.

"Whoever it was, I will not risk sending the entire army for total annihilation. We will wait for the king to return and let him decide," Bronax tried to be cautious with his decision.

Bronax's critics were silenced after what he told them. Learning about the possibility of a third wielder terrifies the Fallens as they knew exactly the effect of that dreadful power. They were forced to retreat for the time being as they await for Athanax's return and have him decide when will be the right moment to strike again.

Chapter Twenty-Seven

THE PERSECUTION

At Fostrum, after the Ithurian incursion ended and retreated to their home planet, Althea asked for Sorah's permission to allow her to return back to Eres. But Sorah quickly denied her request due to the reason that she wanted her to stay and help heal the wounded and above all, she was concerned for Althea's safety.

"Your daughter may be in danger. It is Sarah's light that saved us all today and she may be in pain or hurt for her to use that power," Althea said firmly.

Sorah also learned that Narie was nowhere to be found during the battle on both Avetus and Fostrum. She ordered the warriors to search for her immediately. Althea reminded her that everything that has happened was because of their uncle's doing. He tricked the Ithurian into coming to Treliseum and waged war against them. Although Sorah once contemplated on the peace that Kiran asked, she knew however that peace between their two race will be impossible until she dealt with Athanax.

The warriors returned and reported that Narie was not in either Avetus or Fostrum during the invasion. Suddenly, Sorah's heart raced and fear crept in.

"Althea, did you happen to meet my daughter Narie in Eres?" Sorah wondered.

"Yes, I and Sarah met her when she got hurt in the forest," Althea replied.

"By any chance did you tell her the truth about me and Sarah?" Sorah added as she held Althea's arms.

"She accidentally found out when I stopped her from hurting Sarah," Althea recounted.

Sorah knew the possibilities that Narie somehow found out the truth, which explained her strange behavior and eagerness to see Althea in the prison chamber, leading her to believe that Narie traveled back to Eres to confirm if Althea was the lone Arkan that challenged her. Althea revealed to her that Athanax also had a concurrent attack on Eres. He planned to let the Arkans and the Ithurians destroy each other at Treliseum, while his main army burned Eres at the same time. Afterward, his army would move to Avetus and finish whatever was left of the Arkans and Ithurians. A warrior came back and reported that they found the lifeless body of the Ithurian king. Both Sorah and Althea stared at each other's eyes with anxiety and the thought that Athanax took the king's appearance to manipulate the Ithurians. Althea stumbled and tries to calm her heart at the thought that something bad might have really happened to Sarah and Narie. Once again, she begged Sorah to let her go back to Eres.

As Altrus of both cities, Sorah has the responsibility to stay and rebuild the defense of Avetus and Fostrum against the possibility of the Fallens attacking again. But she also knew that one way or the other, she will have to face Athanax in order to put an end to his threat of terror as well as to save her daughters from the Fallens. She then called forth Prea and the remaining elite warriors and ordered then to remain in Treliseum's defense, while she and Althea travel to Eres in order to stop their uncle. Prea didn't agree to let Sorah and Althea fight the battle alone.

"This old war was started by our mistake and I don't desire to involve all of you in this conflict. Your duties as an Arkan is to protect the kingdom," Sorah commanded her warriors.

Althea approached Sorah and hold her hand, but before they could proceed, Prea stood up.

"Our duty is to the kingdom and to the Arkans. Surely you wouldn't think that we will leave an Arkan alone in a fight," Prea answered with a grin in her face.

After Prea spoke, all the Arkan warriors stood up with their Serdeus.

"We're with you Altrus Sorah. Our Serdeus, our strength and our lives are yours to command," Prea and the warriors pledged to her.

"With all my strength and courage, for the king!" the Arkans cheered.

Sorah and Althea were teary and grateful to them. She then asked Prea to gather the warriors and those soldiers who can still fight.

"We will save Sarah and Narie. I promise you," Sorah vowed.

"Thank you Sorah. I may never deserve your forgiveness, but it's enough for me to see you reunite with Sarah," Tears slid to the side of Althea's cheek and embraced Sorah.

"I love you Althea and I forgive you. You're the only sister I have," Sorah whispered.

Prea informed Sorah that she was able to gather twenty-five thousand battle-ready warriors. Sorah decided to leave five thousand behind to guard the city and tend to the wounded. Prea rallied the warriors for them to be addressed by Sorah.

"Arkans, my brave Arkans, we will once again go into battle, but this time this battle will not be to defend our planet, nor our great cities. It is a battle to stop evil from growing, to stop evil before it consumes and destroys everything we hold dear and to save the light of our hope. With this, I ask you once again, are you with me?"

"We are with you Altrus Sorah," the Arkans shouted their support.

Sorah turned her gaze to the sky and spread her wings.

"With all my strength and courage, for the king!" Sorah roared, followed by all the Arkan warriors.

The warriors' body was enfolded with light that turned into their armored form and together they spread their wings. Sorah led her braves towards the gateway of the Fallens and onto Eres, with the hope that they would still make it in time to save Sarah and Narie.

Meanwhile at the retreating Ithurian Armada, inside the royal ship, Athanax was being violent, tossing tables and chairs, hitting the wall with his fist. He was devastated by his humiliating defeat at Avetus and Fostrum. He almost had his revenge until the light that he felt turned the tide against him. But he remained hopeful that Bronax and his main army had already burned Eres to the ground with a thought that at least, he had eliminated one target from his list.

As the defeated Ithurians approaches Ithuria, Athanax was hopping mad when he saw that the city capital still stands. Athanax scrunched up his nose and forehead, frantically searching for his army and was left with a big question in his mind. What could have stopped his mighty army from destroying the city which was defended by only a handful of Ithurian soldiers? Kiran saw his father's flagship descending. He immediately went up to greet him. As King Malkiem alighted the ship, Kiran and Kina were already there to meet him,

"What happened to the Fallens? Where are they?" was the first words that the impostor spoke of.

Kiran was puzzled when his father didn't seem to be glad that he and Kina were alive. Instead, the first thing he asked was the Fallens. Kiran and Kina quickly sensed that something was wrong with their father.

"Father, we're glad and happy for your safe return," Kiran stated.

"Yes, yes, yes. Now, where is the enemy?" the impostor harshly demanded.

Athanax learned that his army had camped outside the border of Enor. He immediately ordered one of his minion to inform Bronax of his return and to move the army to the capital.

"How was it possible that the city still stands?" Athanax asked in a voice of disbelief.

Kiran, Kina, Turloch and Ull took glances from each other and knew that the king was acting beyond his normal self. Kiran secretly instructed Kina to take Narie and Sarah and hide them while he asked

King Ull to gather information as to what happened in Treliseum. Kina hurriedly left to get Sarah and Narie out of the city before the king finds out. Once again, the impostor king demanded Kiran an explanation on how he was able to defend the city against the strength and overwhelming number of the Fallens. Kiran lied by saying that it was all because of the Ithurian bravery and their technology which gave them the advantages against the Fallens. He added that even with the overwhelming number of the enemy, they still couldn't take out the wall as it has never been breached by any foe ever. Athanax knew in his heart that Kiran was not telling the truth. He knows that their insignificant weapons and wall could not measure up against his minions. He secretly sent out spies to find out exactly how the city was defended.

Later, King Ull reported back and informed Kiran that according to the other generals, they were defeated at Fostrum. Altrus Sorah used her destructive power and threatened them of annihilation if they would not leave Treliseum. He also learned that despite the futile battle against Altrus Sorah's power, the king still insisted to attack even though he knows that he will be sending their people to their death. But the great leader of the Arkans spared their lives and forced the generals and commanders to concede defeat.

Without a doubt, Kiran confirmed that the person before him is not his father. He knew very well that his father wouldn't sacrifice the lives of his men in a hopeless battle. He sensed that there is danger around him and felt that something bad has happened to his father. Kiran secretly ordered King Turloch and King Ull to take their army out of Ithuria quietly, head for Deodara and wait for him there. Meanwhile, Kina met with Narie and told her in a shaky voice that they need to leave the city immediately. Narie looked bewildered about all the secrecy, while Sarah remained unresponsive,

"What is going on Kina?" Narie wanted to know.

"The king has returned but something is wrong with him. We sense danger if you stay here," Kina admitted.

"Why would you think he'll harm us after what my sister and I have done for your people," Narie's anger could be heard from her voice.

"Kiran and I believe that he is not our father. He may be a Fallen disguised as the king" Kina stuttered in answering,

Fear started to engulf Narie's heart. She looked at Sarah and worried for her safety.

"I'm sorry about your father," said Narie while holding Kina on her shoulder.

"We have no time to be sorrowful now. I have to get you out of here quickly!" Kina stressed.

Narie took Sarah's arm and followed Kina to escape the city. At the same time, Athanax learned from his spies that there were two Arkans that helped the Ithurian defend the city. Knowing that even in Eres the Arkan foiled his plans made his blood boil. He ordered all the soldiers in the kingdom to search and bring forth to him the two Arkans.

Kiran tried to stop the king by telling him that the Arkans helped them save the city and the people.

"You betrayed me and your people! You connived with the Arkans which led to our defeat!" Athanax shouted with eyes fiercely staring at Kiran.

Kiran knew that reasoning with the impostor is futile. He then pleaded to the generals and soldiers that the city was saved from the

Fallens because of the aid of the Arkans, but Athanax immediately ordered to arrest Kiran, which confused the generals as to who to follow. Then, King Kelon and King Gileal supported Athanax's order and thereby forcing the generals to comply.

Kina, Narie and Sarah was almost out of the city when the Fallens still disguised as Ithurians stopped them. Kina ordered to let them pass, but the soldiers ignored her and started running towards them. She told Narie to take Sarah out of the city and go to Deodara where King Turloch and King Ull will be waiting. Kina then ran towards the soldiers to stop them. Athanax was quickly informed that they found the Arkans and that they're trying to escape the city. He ordered all his spies and soldiers to capture them alive.

Kiran scuffled with the soldiers and was able to escape their grasp. Using his mechanical wings, he flew out the window and frantically searched for Narie, he found them being surrounded by a mob of soldiers that still bear rage and hate towards the Arkans after their humiliating defeat. Narie didn't want to hurt the Ithurian soldiers knowing that the Fallens have infiltrated the Council and manipulating the people. But as they tried to capture them, Narie was left with no choice but to fight back and protect Sarah. She summoned her Serdeus and fend off the soldiers while trying not to kill them.

The soldiers managed to surround and close in on them. Narie struggles to fight back while holding the impassive Sarah. As they were about to be captured, Kiran and Kina arrived just in time and pushed the soldiers back.

"Narie, Kina, take Sarah and get out of here," Kiran yelled.

"No, I won't leave you!" Narie gasped.

"I'll be right behind you! Take Sarah and fly out of here. Follow Kina," said Kiran in a reassuring tone.

Kina's mechanical wings expanded and flew upward followed by Narie holding Sarah. Athanax was watching everything unfold on top of the wall and ordered his men to aim and shoot down the fleeing Arkans. The Fallens aimed and fired their weapons which hit Narie in the shoulder and accidentally lost her hold of Sarah as both of them plummeted to the ground. Kiran quickly told Kina to catch Narie while he'll go after Sarah. Kina was able to catch Narie in time and immediately flew over the city wall, while Kiran swooped down in full speed to catch Sarah. He was able to grab a hold of Sarah but they're already too close to the ground and eventually crashed in the middle of the city market. Kiran's mechanical wings were damaged due to the impact of the crash and couldn't do anything anymore as the soldiers immediately surrounded and restrained them both.

"Kina, we need to go back for them," said Narie while looking down at Kiran.

There was no response from Kina. Narie turned to face Kina and saw tears flowing from her eyes.

"We need to go back and get them!" Narie repeated.

"We can't go back. My brother's sacrifice will be meaningless if both of you are captured," Kina sobbed.

Narie's injury prevented her from helping Kiran and Sarah. She clenched her fist and repeatedly thumped her bloodied shoulder out of frustration. She looked down at Sarah and Kiran, her eyes tight and worries for the fate that lies ahead of them. Kiran was restrained by his own soldiers while Sarah sat in the pavement still benumbed.

"I'm the prince of Ithuria. I order you to let us go," Kiran yelled, confusing the soldiers.

The impostor king arrived at the scene and told the soldiers that Kiran is a traitor to the Ithurian kingdom for brazenly committing the act of aiding the enemy. Kiran countered it by telling the soldiers and his people that the king that stood before him is not his father but a Fallen disguised as the king. The people frowned and looked at one another, puzzled by Kiran's revelation and became indecisive on whom to follow. Athanax accused Kiran of being a liar and for poisoning the mind of the people.

"You are the poison here. A lot of my people perished because of you!" Kiran's voice trembles in anger.

"Your people? They're also my people, and those cursed Arkans killed many of us for claiming the land of our ancestors!" Athanax snarled as he pointed a finger at Kiran.

"Our ancestors' land you say?! Our ancestors were mere caretakers of Fostrum," Kiran rebutted.

Athanax blinked out of his stupor upon learning that Kiran has discovered the truth. He balled up his fist and slammed it to Kiran's cheek, bringing him down unconscious. Athanax ordered the soldiers to put him in prison and he would deal with him later. He then turned his attention to Sarah whom he remembered as the girl who stood up against the Council and revealed his plan and his army. He also saw her in Althea's memory, but he still didn't know the truth about her. He approached Sarah and held her forehead to tap into her memories. Athanax's face scrunched up after seeing the truth that the girl in front of him is the lost daughter of Sorah. Athanax suddenly had a thought that his plan might still be salvaged. He intends to make the Ithurians kill Sarah through public execution and with her death in the hands of the people, it would surely enrage her mother Sorah and her rage will turn to revenge, which will lead to the destruction of the Ithurian race. Suddenly, the spies informed him that King Turloch and King Ull's army and Kiran's loyalists had moved out of the city and traveled to the south to seek the Deodarian aid. They also believed that they took the other Arkans there as well. Athanax sent words to Bronax ordering him to move the main army to attack Deodara and kill everyone and leave none alive.

Sarah was taken to the prison chamber and awaits her fate. The day ended with so much revelation and emotion. That night, Athanax devised an evil plan to hasten Sarah and Kiran's executions that will trigger the destruction of the Ithurian in the hands of Sorah once she learns about the fate of her daughter. He called forth his aide and ordered him to inform the people that a public trial will be held a day after tomorrow at first light. A day had past and the Ithurian gathered within the city courtyard. Athanax called the Ithurians to witness a public trial and execution for the traitor and enemy of the kingdom. The soldiers dragged the unresponsive Sarah and presented her to the people. They pulled her up on top of a stage. Afterwards, Kiran followed with his hand tied behind his back kneeling down.

"My people, I present to you a gift. Behold the daughter of the one who slaughtered our soldiers -- soldiers who were husbands and fathers!" Athanax sneered.

The people stared at Sarah with disbelief although some of the villagers already knew who she was.

"People of Ithuria, please, I beg of you! Don't be deceived by this impostor's words. He is not your king!" Kiran pleaded.

"Silence! You traitor! If you will deny our ancestor as the rightful lord of Fostrum, then I disown you as my son. Hear this, from this day

345

forth this person here in front of you is no longer my son," Athanax announced.

Kiran wanted to speak some more but the spies silenced him. Athanax fueled the anger of the Ithurians by accusing Sarah of committing genocide to the Ithurian people. The people's judgment was clouded by their hatred and anger towards the Arkan and towards Sarah. Athanax then sentenced her to death. The people didn't hesitate and wholeheartedly supported his decision. Athanax approached Sarah who was still unemotional and detached to reality. He grabbed her and threw her to the mob where she was stoned, spitted, kicked, punched and brutally beaten. Kiran's face scrunched up and stare with open mouth. He was screaming at his people to stop, but none of the Ithurians heeded his voice. He watched in horror as Sarah was being persecuted by the same people whom she protected and saved from the Fallens. Tears gushed from Kiran's eyes. He tilted his head down and couldn't stand seeing Sarah's ordeal anymore. He fell to his knees and prayed for a miracle to happen -- a miracle to save Sarah from this terrible fate.

Chapter Twenty-Eight

THE AWAKENING

Kiran desperately begged his people to cease hurting Sarah and calls on to the villagers that she saved before.

"To the people whom this girl saved -- please come forth and claim innocence for this Arkan," Kiran pleaded.

But the villagers were too afraid to speak up as they might be accused of sympathizing with the enemy and feared facing harsh consequences. The villagers and soldiers whom Sarah and Narie saved turned their heads away and kept their silence. It was heart-wrenching for Kiran to watch them abandoned her. He cried anger and frustration, his face was contorted in fury. Suddenly, Kiran scrunched his face and took a sharp intake of breath, he had a flashback of memories surging to his mind, and in those memories he saw his ancestors' same act of betrayal and abandonment they committed against the Arkan king. Sarah was repeatedly being beaten by the mob. Her clothes were torn and was left almost half-dead. Kiran wailed helplessly watching Sarah slowly dying in the hands of his own people.

Athanax's henchmen walked towards the battered Sarah and grabbed her by the hair. Athanax nodded his head and without remorse, the henchman forcefully pierced his sword, twisted it deeply into Sarah's chest. Kiran froze witnessing the gruesome act while Sarah stood motionless for a brief moment. As the henchman pulled out his sword, Sarah staggered back as she held her chest. She slowly tilted her head down and gawked to see blood in her palms. Sarah breathe heavily and fell to the ground. Athanax smirked while watching Sarah's tribulation and turn his attention next for Kiran's demise. He ordered his henchmen to execute Kiran by hanging. The henchmen forcefully dragged Kiran up the hanging platform. As Sarah's life was about to fade, she glanced at Kiran and saw the henchmen putting the noose around his neck. With all her remaining strength, she crawled towards the platform to reach Kiran, leaving a trail of blood on the pavement. Seeing her struggles to reach Kiran, the mob went on kicking her, spitting and throwing rocks at her.

"Die you Arkan filth!" the people shouted.

Kiran was at the platform and awaiting his death. He called on to Sarah and stared at each other's eyes.

"I'm sorry, I've failed you," Kiran murmured.

Athanax raised his hand and the henchmen grabbed the lever that will open the hanging platform upon his signal. Kiran closed his eyes and raised his head. Athanax forcefully swung his hand down and the henchmen pulled the lever, sending Kiran down to his death. Sarah watched in horror as she saw Kiran in pain and slowly dying in front of her. Paralyzed by terror, Sarah suddenly saw Sune and Althea's faces flashing in her mind. She has totally lost her sanity, she slowly stood up while her body steamed out a red aura, the soldiers were taken aback and recalled the same terror they felt during the time they faced Sorah. Sarah raised her head and glared at the Ithurians. Suddenly, a loud and terrifying scream of agony deafened the people. Sarah's screamed had

348

unleashed another pillar of flame and a powerful blast that destroyed the people near her, as well as the hanging platform where Kiran was being hung which eventually saved his life. Athanax couldn't handle Sarah's extreme power. He didn't expect that she was the origin of the light that led to his defeat in the hand of the Arkans and couldn't believe that her flame has resurrected her. Fearing that she might use the fire of justice, he cowardly fled the city to join Bronax and his main army, leaving the Ithurians at Sarah's wrath.

Kiran managed to free himself from his bind and ran towards Sarah. Blood drained from Kiran's face at the sight of Sarah being completely changed into a dark Arkan. Her wings were black and her eyes were red as blood. Sarah's transformation sent chill down his spine and paralyzed him with fear. He couldn't command his legs to move. He was in a state of shock to see Sarah as the harbinger of death. The Ithurian soldiers formed their ranks and attacked her by firing their weapons, but with just her fierce gaze, she turned all the soldiers into ashes in an instant. Kiran was horrified to see how Sarah easily destroyed the soldiers. He ordered his people to run away from her before her flame consumed them. He instructed the soldiers to lead the people out of the city and to Deodara and seek help.

The Ithurian soldiers attempted to stop Sarah by using all the arsenals they have at their disposal. Sarah's dark power however, was too strong to be stopped. King Kelon and King Gileal and the villagers were in panic as they desperately try to flee the city away from Sarah's flames. Kiran however, followed Sarah but couldn't come near her due to the extreme heat of her red flames. Sarah's light of agony once again rippled across the galaxies. The light passed through the approaching Arkan army in space which disoriented Sorah, Althea and all the warriors. Sorah felt the familiar feeling of despair and darkness. She fears for her daughters for not knowing what had become of their fate.

Sarah's light of agony again reached Avetus and damaged the chambers where the king was sleeping. Suddenly, the king's hand moved.

"Sorah, did you feel that?" asked Althea.

"Yes, a great agony -- a feeling I'm very familiar with," Sorah quavered.

"Something bad has happened to Sarah. I felt it," Althea insisted.

Sorah ordered her warriors to make haste before it is too late. Back in Eres, Athanax finally joined his main army and heads toward Deodara. He took the helm of command from Bronax. He was quite satisfied of the outcome of his salvaged plan, and in the end, he got Sarah do the annihilation of the Ithurians for him. At Deodara, Narie was restrained to fight because of her injury she obtained from their escape at the city. King Turloch and King Ull, together with King Zairel of Deodara, discussed and prepares their armies to face the Fallen once again. The city of Deodara didn't have towering walls to protect them, but it was situated on top of a high hill. The Deodarians and the Ithurians would have to fight the Fallens on open grounds.

Narie still had difficulties moving her left arm, told Kina that she would join the battle.

"You couldn't possibly fight in that condition. You better return to Treliseum. This is our fight now!" Kina blurted.

"My only sister is still out there. It worries me that I have no idea what has happened to her and Kiran. This is my battle too -- whether you accept it or not," Narie retorted.

Kina looked at Narie and smiled.

"Well, we surely are grateful that you would stand alongside with us again, yet this might be the last time that we'll be fighting together," Kina surmised.

"There's still hope," Narie uttered.

Narie and Kina shook hands and put a soft smile on their faces. A scout suddenly came inside the throne hall and informed King Zairel that the Fallens were visible in the open field. This time, they could clearly see the strength of the main army and saw their numbers ranging to a million strong. King Zairel stood up and announced to his people that he would have Narie take command of the entire Deodarian army, fulfilling the prophecy that an Arkan will lead them to their path. In the absence of Kiran, Kina also handed the command of the Ithurian army to her as well. Narie look dumbfounded for the great responsibility handed to her by the people of Eres.

"You're more suitable for this job than I am," Kina asserted.

Narie stared at the soldiers and warriors who were clearly afraid and anxious. She felt similar emotion in her heart at the reality that they were facing an enemy whose strength was far greater than theirs. She felt disheartened ad suddenly remembered her mother and Sarah and asked herself what they would do in these situation. She was lost in finding the answers, but she knew for sure that both of them would not be defeated easily and will not give up the fight as long as there is life in them. Narie believed that she needs to think and act like her mother and sister in order to raise the spirits and morale of everyone around her. She showed the people courage in the face of an impending danger.

"Ithurians and Deodarians, we may be different from one another in this age, but you were once Arkan. Today, there is no differences among us. Today, we fight as one. Today, we fight to stop

351

evil that is upon us. I know that most of you are afraid, but bear this in your hearts and minds that there is still hope for us. As we go into battle, as we fight, don't ever let go of that hope until the bitter end."

Narie's words somehow lifted the spirits and morale of the people and cheered behind her. She positioned King Ull's army and a brigade of Nephatrons to take the defense of their left flank, while Kina and her army of Zeltkovas, including a battalion of Nephatron, took the right flank. At the center was where Narie and the Deodarians were to take their stand, while King Turloch and his remaining army was in charge of both Deodarian and Ithurian artilleries as well as the defense of the city.

"Prepare for battle!" Narie shouted.

As they await the approaching Fallens, Deodarian scouts spotted the fleeing Ithurian villagers and soldiers from the capital and were approaching them from the west. They saw the Ithurians were in chaos as they desperately trying to reach the city of Deodara. Because of the panic and confusion, the fleeing Ithurians didn't notice that they were directly in the path of the Fallen army. Narie saw the people as they ran for their lives, but the creatures were much in reach to the fleeing Ithurians. Athanax saw the flustered Ithurians and ordered his men to chase and kill them all. Bronax sent his Draakabs and foot soldiers to chase and kill the escaping Ithurians. Kina, King Turloch and King Ull, on the other hand, gawked in horror as the Fallens were able to catch up with their people and were mercilessly being slaughtered. They watched helplessly from the Deodarian city and a hope for a rescue seemed impossible. Narie suddenly transformed into her armored form and summoned her Serdeus.

"Stay here and hold the line. No one comes with me. I'll try to give them some time," Narie shouted.

Kina and the two kings didn't agree with her plan and tried to stop her, but before they could, she immediately flown towards the fleeing Ithurians. She flew directly in to the Draakabs, slashing them, burning them with her flame and destroying as many she could to give the Ithurians a chance to reach the city. King Ull asked King Turloch to raise the cannons up high to give Narie close artillery support. King Turloch fires his guns and hit just about a meter away from Narie's location. Some of the villagers and soldiers managed to reach the safety of Deodara. Narie did everything she could but many of the Ithurians perished in the hands of the Fallens -- including King Gileal and King Kelon. She didn't have any other choice but to abandon most of them and return to the Deodarian line.

Athanax finally arrived at the last bastion of the resistance -- the alliance of Arkan, Deodarian and Ithurian that stood in his way.

"Children of Varkelos -- today you will die and I shall have my revenge on all of you for the betrayal your beloved ancestors committed against me and the Arkan king. You are not just the descendants of betrayers, but also of cowards!" Athanax sneered, followed by a hideous laugh.

The Deodarians and Ithurians were shameful of the truth but it didn't affect their spirits. Athanax raised his hand and gave the signal to unleash hell. The combined Deodarian and Ithurian artilleries opened fire and the battle began. The artilleries destroyed some of the creatures that dashed towards the line, but it didn't stop them from coming. Narie ordered all the Nephatrons and soldiers to open fire. A long stretch of lines blazed in muzzle fire, which served as a shield, firing all together and emptying their ammunitions.

Back in the Ithurian capital, the soldiers desperately try to neutralize Sarah, but nothing could stop her.

"Cease this futile action!" Kiran yelled.

The soldiers were confused whether to follow his order or not.

"Is it not yet clear to you who speaks the truth? The Fallen king tricked us and this is what it brought us!" Kiran retorted.

After realizing the devastation, the soldiers finally listened to Kiran and once again gave their allegiance back to him. He rallied what remained of their once proud army and ordered them to follow him to Deodara, away from Sarah. Sarah was still hovering the sky in the center of the city, burning everything she laid her eyes on. Kiran, together with his army, tries to avoid her gaze and made an escape from the burning city.

Kiran was told by his commanders that only around one hundred thousand soldiers were left to follow him. He ordered his commanders to set forth to Deodara to join King Turloch and King Ull in the fight against the Fallens. As they again embarking on another battle, most of the soldiers felt weary and thought that they already had enough of war. They just came back defeated from the Fostrum campaign and now most of their comrades who came home alive were killed by Sarah's wrath in their own city. The soldiers felt shattered, they had given up the fight and wanted to just go back to their homes.

"And who is to blame for all these miseries? Who is to blame that our great city, our homes were destroyed? And who is to blame that our race, the Ithurian, is about to be annihilated by the Fallens? Is it not our ancestors' and our own doings?" Kiran asked his demoralized soldiers.

"It is the Arkans that are to blame for our suffering," the soldiers retorted.

"It was the Arkans that saved our people from the Fallens earlier, but none of you believed me. We trespassed into their land and claimed it as our own. We were blinded by our greed and that greed led to our suffering. If the Arkans were truly to be blamed, then answer me this: why did the powerful Arkan leader spared your insignificant lives?" Kiran's voice was shaken with rage.

The soldiers began to realize the truth behind Kiran's words.

"My sister Kina and both King Turloch and King Ull are at Deodara fighting the Fallens together with the Deodarian to stop them from destroying us forever. The Arkan that you immensely despise is fighting alongside them," Kiran words pierced through the hearts of all the soldiers who now couldn't face him.

They knew that there is no time for them to feel neither shame nor guilt. It was a time for them to gather their courage, their determination and their dignity, it is a time for them to fight for Eres and their right to exist. Their morale was uplifted, they applauded Kiran and then led them to Deodara in order to join the final battle of the Ithurians against the Fallens.

At the field of Deodara, the continuous firing of the cannons didn't even slow down the never-ending enemies rushing in. By then, the situation was dire when the Ithurians ammunitions near depletion. Narie knew that they'll be fighting the Fallens face-to-face soon. She jumped in the middle of the line and summoned her Serdeus.

"Lock your shield and draw your swords!" Narie ordered the Alliance.

The soldiers dropped their projectile weapons, picked up their shields and drew their swords. She turned around and looked at the combined armies of the Deodarians and Ithurians.

"Let it be known today that the Arkan, Deodarian and Ithurian stood together and fought alongside to the very end," Narie proclaimed.

She then turned to face the rushing Fallen and shouted:

"With all my strength and courage, for the king!"

Narie flew to charge the enemy's center head on, followed by the Deodarians and Ithurians. They attacked the center, while both King Ull and Kina simultaneously engaged the enemy on each flanks. They fought as if there was no tomorrow, they faced the enemy bravely and fear was not in their hearts on that day, for they're fighting with the belief that their race need to survive and continue no matter the cost.

As both armies fight the Fallens, the line was slowly being pushed back by the overwhelming number of the Fallens. Then from the left flank, Kiran arrived in time with his army and reinforced King Ull's forces. Kiran asked King Ull about Narie's location and was told that she was fighting with the Deodarians. He immediately rushed to the center in order to be with Narie. Kiran managed to made his way to where Narie was and fortunate to be reunited with her. Tears of joy slid down from Narie's eyes upon seeing Kiran alive.

"I thought I've lost you!" Narie sobbed.

"I was almost killed, but Sarah saved me," Kiran's voice sounded apprehensive.

"Where's Sarah? Where's my sister?" Narie's heart raced as she asked him.

"I can't get to her because she changed into a dark winged Arkan and her powers were fully awakened," Kiran stuttered.

Narie's brows furrowed to what Kiran said and wanted to go and see Sarah, but she couldn't leave Kiran alone in the battle. Athanax was annoyed upon the sight of the alliance putting up a feisty resistance. He ordered his Draakabs and Diurox to attack at the same time in order to break their spirits and moral. Narie countered him with the Ithurian Zelridar and Deodarian airships, but the dragons were just too many for them to fight. Some of the dragons passed the airships ranks and descended over them and inflicted havocs to the left flank where King Ull and the Nephatrons stood. Even the Brigade of Nephatron was slowly being destroyed by the Diurox. Kina was also suffering from the right flank as she couldn't fight both the dragons from the air and the creatures on the ground at the same time.

Narie looked at Kiran. She wrapped her arms around him and kissed him. She put a grin on her face as she let go of him. Kiran knew that she's going to do something that would put her life in danger. He tried to grab Narie's hand and stop her but she quickly flew to the sky and fought the Draakabs. She kills as many she could but her injuries and the countless number of dragons coming made it too much for her to handle. Athanax was laughing at the alliance's pointless resistance. He wanted to annihilate them immediately, thus ordering another wave of his army to attack and this time it will surely finish them. Narie saw from the sky that another wave was unleashed and rushing towards all their side. Looking at the overwhelming odds against them, she knew that this would be their end, she lowered her head with her eyes closed, held her heart and whispered.

"Help us."

Without warning, a huge fire exploded in the middle of the Fallens' advancing wave, throwing the creatures in the air and burning them to death. Narie, Kiran and Athanax gasped upon seeing the wave of Fallens destroyed in an instant. A trumpet was heard across the battlefield — it was a sound that Narie was most familiar with. They turned their gaze to where the sound was coming. It was coming from the top of the hill and couldn't believe what they saw. The Arkans were in a line formation to join the battle against Athanax. Sorah and Althea then emerged from the center of the Arkan line. Althea cautioned Sorah that there were Ithurians and Deodarians in the battlefield and that she needs to be careful with her flame. Sorah ordered her warriors to destroy the Fallen and aid the battered alliance. As the Arkans flew in to charge the enemy, a trail of light shone at the rear of the line.

As they landed on the center of the battlefield, Sorah and Althea, without any difficulty, warded off the creatures. Narie met with her mother and Althea and she immediately embraced them both, while Kiran lowered his head in shame for what his people did.

"Raise your head Ithurian. You have nothing to be ashamed of. Everything was our uncle's doing and we're here to stop him," Sorah stated.

Kiran heaved a sigh of relief and nearly fell over in elation after hearing Sorah. He was very grateful for her forgiveness. Althea immediately asked for Sarah but Kiran was reluctant to tell them what happened to her. Althea insisted to tell her.

"Sarah is still in the capital, but she has changed," Kiran voice trembled.

"What do you mean she has changed?" Althea grabbed Kiran's collar and stared at him with her fearful eyes.

"She finally became an Arkan with terrifying powers. She became even darker than her mother Altrus Sorah -- full of hatred and rage," Kiran gasped.

Sorah didn't hesitate to ask Althea to go and look for Sarah, while she and Narie stays with the alliance to fight the Fallens. Althea hastily left the battlefield to search for Sarah at the Ithurian capital. Upon reaching the capital, she couldn't believe her eyes seeing the devastation. The once proud city of the Ithurian was destroyed and burned into rubbles. Fear slowly crept into her heart as she saw a frightening flame emanating at the center of the city. As she came towards the origin of the flame, she was overcome with horror, she lost her balance and fell down to her knees, seeing hundreds of thousands burned bodies of Ithurians. She looked up to the sky and saw Sarah hovering from above already in her full Arkan form. But the sight Althea's eyes laid on froze her of terror as she saw Sarah's black wings and armor with eyes blazing red like blood.

Althea called onto Sarah but she didn't respond. She moved closer to Sarah and attempted to touch her when all of a sudden, Sarah forcefully grabbed Althea by her neck and looked into her memories. Althea struggled to breathe as Sarah squeezed her neck. Althea was shocked as Sarah pulled her closer to her face and saw her blood-red eyes filled with rage up close. Sarah threw Althea like a raged doll sending her flying violently out of control and smashed into the rubbles. From Althea's memories, Sarah saw images of Sune, Sorah and Narie together with Kiran to which it made her react violently. Sarah flew up to the sky high above and saw a battle raging down the south.

"Sarah, it's me Althea!" Althea shouted.

But Sarah remained silent and ignored her. She continued gazing the battle that was happening at the south. Althea once more called on to her and attempted once again to hold her in her arms, but Sarah was intensely gazing the battle from high above. Sarah suddenly jittered after she felt a strong power emanating from the battle. The power drew Sarah in, luring her to come as if she was being challenged by it. As Althea came near her, Sarah suddenly screamed in rage and flew in an incredible speed towards the power she felt. Althea was terrified and confused as to what happened to Sarah for her to become what she is now. She followed her back to the south, to Deodara where the final battle between the Alliance and the Fallen was unfolding.

Chapter Twenty-Nine

RETRIBUTION

arah arrived at the field of Deodara. She hovered the sky and watched the battle happening below. The red aura that was steaming out of her body caught the attention of Sorah and Narie. Both felt the immense power flowing out of Sarah. Althea came behind calling out to Sarah and try holding her once again, but Sarah struck the unsuspecting Althea, throwing her back plummeting to the ground. Sorah and Narie flew to the sky and catches Althea to stop her fall. Narie's eyes were wide open in horror at the sight of Sarah's transformation into a dark Arkan.

"Who is that?" Sorah looked up to Sarah with furrowed brows.

"She is Sarah. She is your daughter," Althea gasped.

Sorah finally met her long lost daughter Sarah for the first time after the Great Arkan war thousands of years ago. Sorah was at a loss for words at the sight of Sarah as a dark Arkan who radiated pure hatred and rage. Then, in god-like speed, Sarah flew down to the ground like a red ball of meteor. A devastating explosion occurred moment after she set foot on the ground, killing many members of the Fallen and Alliance alike.

Sarah's rage and hatred went on a frenzy, annihilated everything that crossed her path. A cold sweat of anxiety trickled from Athanax's head after witnessing Sarah's presence, but it also plastered a smirk on his face seeing her savagery. Athanax thought that Sarah would be the one to carry out the revenge he long been desiring. He ordered his men to concentrate on attacking the Alliance and avoid confronting the dark Arkan. Sorah told Althea to help the Alliance and she will deal with Sarah herself. She stood directly in front of Sarah's path to prevent her from killing anymore of the Alliance. As mother and daughter came face-to-face, Sarah was fuming with rage. She balled her fist and the flame in her hand turned into a blazing red Serdeus. A haze of fear pounded Sorah's heart as she saw the sword of death for the first time. Sorah likewise, clenched her fist and the light from her hand turned into her Serdeus. Sorah stood in her guard as she prepares herself to battle her own daughter. Sarah flew straight towards Sorah and their battle began. Sorah's body was shaken and the ground she stood cracked by Sarah's sheer strength and speed as she slammed at her. She could barely keep up with Sarah's powers which evenly matched or possibly exceeded her own. Both fought using everything they had -- they fought with their flames and their skills in the Serdeus, but Sarah was unstoppable. Even with Sarah's immense power, Sorah however, was able to put up an even battle with her. Sorah never fought an opponent that matched her in every way. Even so, Sarah couldn't break through either because of Sorah's determination.

Sarah screamed in frustration at Sorah's persistence. The flames in Sarah's fists slowly expanded and the force of the flames started to build up. She was preparing to use the fire of justice to destroy Sorah. Sorah stood motionless and in horror as she realized that Sarah could wield the forbidden power. She feared for the people that were to perish if Sarah is able to use it. Sorah quickly flew towards Sarah and unleashed her flame first before Sarah could. The flame struck Sarah and viciously threw her back in the wave of the Fallens behind her. Sarah slowly stood up, but Sorah continued her attacks, pushing Sarah further away from the Alliance line and closer to the Fallen main force. Sorah tried to push her back once more, but this time Sarah was able to block her strikes and managed to smash her fist onto Sorah's head, throwing her high above the ground. Sarah quickly flew towards Sorah who was still dazed and struck her multiple times, thus sending her plummeting to the ground. Althea and Narie saw Sorah was hurt and decided to help her. Together they attacked Sarah, but Sarah was too fast and strong for the both of them and were easily thrown back. Sarah drifted to the sky and once again built her flames and prepare to use the forbidden power in order to destroy everyone below. Sorah's eyes bulged as she stared at Sarah. She realized that there was no time to stop her.

"Arkans, use your flames to shield us from her wrath!" Sorah shouted.

Sarah unleashed her terrifying fire of justice aimed at the Alliance. In the nick of time, all the Arkans stretched out their arms forward and let loose their flames to shield them from Sarah's devastation. Both flames collided and caused a massive explosion. The Arkans were weakened and their powers drained for countering Sarah's flame with their own. The Fallens near Sarah and those behind the Alliance line also took a toll, burned and destroyed by her flame.

Athanax gasped with his wide open mouth at the sight of the devastation. He ordered his forces to halt the attack and move away from Sarah. He knew that Sarah will be more than enough to destroy the Alliance. The Fallens retreated to a safe distance while the Deodarians started healing the weakened Arkans. Sorah ordered everyone to retreat back to the city. She knew that death was inevitable if Sarah would unleash another blast. Sorah stumbled as she tries to stand up. Althea and Narie came to her side and helped her.

"There is no other choice. The only way I could stop her is to destroy her," Sorah quavered.

Color drained from Althea and Narie's faces and stared wide-eyed after hearing what Sorah said.

"She is your daughter. What are you saying?" Althea shouted gruffly, while Narie was left stunned and speechless.

"I know that. How would you know the feeling I'm having right now? I've lost her and now I found her, my beloved daughter; but if we don't stop her, she will kill us all," answered Sorah as tears slid down from her eyes.

"I will talk to her – anything. Just don't kill her," Althea pleaded.

"Look into her eyes. Our words won't reach her anymore. Her heart has already consumed with hatred," Sorah asserted.

Althea and Narie couldn't hold their tears back from hearing Sorah's decision. From that point on, Sorah instructed the two to never interfere with their fight. Sorah summoned her Serdeus and started walking towards Sarah. Sarah was looking down on her as she hovers the sky. Sorah stopped and looked up to Sarah -- the two stared at each other's eyes. Tears of pain streamed from Sorah's eyes and ran down her pale cheeks. The moment Sarah saw her tears, she suddenly felt a sharp piercing pain in her heart.

"I love you Sarah," whispered Sorah as she closed her eyes.

Sorah opened her eyes and glared at Sarah. She flew towards Sarah in full speed and continues her attack. She mustered all of her strength and struck Sarah repeatedly. Sarah however, got distracted with Sorah's tears and was continuously being pushed back by her determination. Althea, Narie and everyone at the city found it difficult to breathe as they watched the battle between the two. Every time Sarah sees Sorah's tears, she was struck by an excruciating pain in her heart which simultaneously gives her flashes of lost memories in her head. Sarah tried to flee the battle but Sorah persistently chased her and was desperate to stop her. The pain she felt and the constant flashes of memories in her head drove Sarah mad, she put her hands over her head and screamed, triggering a powerful burst of energy from her body. Sorah was pushed back by the sheer force of her energy. Fear started to engulf everyone especially Sorah after seeing Sarah cry and scream in agony. As Sarah was still in a state of confusion, Sorah saw a chance to strike her down, she flew towards Sarah with her Serdeus drawn and ready to deliver the final blow. Sarah quickly recovered from her pain and confusion and saw Sorah heading towards her in full speed and ready to kill her. Sarah summoned her Serdius and likewise flew towards Sorah head on, with the intention of ending her life as well. Althea couldn't bear to watch mother and daughter killing each other. Defying Sorah's order, she spread her wings and flew directly in the middle of the fight. Sorah's eyes widened seeing Althea flying towards the middle of their path. she tries to slow her body down from the speed but she couldn't stop in time. Althea was determined to stop Sorah from killing her own daughter. She felt in her heart that she's the one who deserve to die for the sin she committed and will not allow either Sorah or Sarah to pay for it. Sorah retracted her Serdeus and struggled to slow down to avoid colliding with Althea. Sarah on the other hand, was still at full speed towards Sorah and was at the point of no return from killing her. Suddenly, the sound of sword piercing through skin and bone was heard. Althea was forcefully pushed away. Sorah's face was filled with shock as she saw Narie got stabbed at the back by Sarah. Narie extended her arms to catch Sorah in front of her.

"No, no, no, Narie! Why!" Sorah broke down.

Althea covered her mouth in shock seeing Sarah's Serdius penetrated Narie's abdomen. Narie stared at her mother's eyes and smiled while she endured the pain. Kiran's heart was shattered after seeing Narie's fate. He cried and shouted her name and wanted to go to her, but the soldiers restrained him as he tried to fly towards Narie. With her last remaining strength, Narie mustered her flame and forcefully blasted Sorah away from Sarah. Althea tried to get Narie, but was thrown back by Sarah's flame as well. Blood gushed out from Narie's wound, tears streamed down her scrunched eyes as the pain was unbearable. She turned her head around and touched Sarah's face staring at her in sadness. She closed her eyes and tears continued to flow seeing Sarah's painful memories. She saw Sarah's suffering in the hands of the Ithurians and the loss of her brother Sune. Sarah again felt a great pain in her heart looking at Narie. She pulled her Serdeus back and Narie clung onto her. She stared at Sarah with her dying eyes.

"Come back to us Sarah….my beloved sister!" were the last words Narie spoke.

Narie's arms slowly let go of Sarah, her eyes close as life extinguished from her and fell from the sky. Sarah immediately had a rush of lost memories pouring in to her mind. Narie's voice kept echoing in her head, while memories of the persecution she went through with the Ithurians, as well as the battle with the Fallens, her moments with Kiran, Althea and Sune. She then heard a faint voice slowly getting louder calling her name repeatedly. The silhouette of a woman that she always saw in her memory slowly become visible and Sarah gawked to finally see the woman's face, the face of her mother

366

and it was Sorah. Sorah and Althea watched in horror as Narie fell from the sky. They raced to catch Narie, when suddenly Sarah flew down and caught her. Both Sorah and Althea were confused as they saw Sarah doing that act. She held Narie's lifeless body and gazed at her face and slowly descended to the ground. She saw memories she had with Narie from the time they first met until the time they fought together against the Fallens. Seeing Narie's death sent pain in her heart -- the pain of losing someone she dearly loved. Tears of sadness started to stream down Sarah's eyes -- the very same tears that cleansed away the rage in her eyes. Sarah has finally awakened from her dark slumber and soon realized that Narie was gone. The feeling she felt holding Narie was the same when she lost Sune in her arms. She saw Narie's face in peace amidst the deaths and destructions that surrounded them. She held her tight -- close to her heart. She broke down and sobbed like a child. Narie's death shattered the spirits of the Alliance. Sorah fell to her knees, covering her face with her hands and moaned in despair. Althea rushed to her sister's side and gave her solace. Athanax has never been so contented to see Sorah's agony as her daughter killed her own sibling. The Alliance's spirits were shattered. They were holding on to the hope that Narie told them to never let go, but seeing her death made them feel that that same hope died with her as well. There was a moment of silence in the battlefield as the Alliance mourned for her death.

A sudden breeze gusted. Sorah raised her head and directed her sight towards Sarah who was still holding Narie. Althea held Sorah's hand as they both watched with their eyes wide open the golden light slowly coming out of Sarah's body. The gentle breeze grew stiff and became a strong wind. Everyone in the battlefield stood rooted to the ground and gaped at seeing Sarah's light. As the light became blindingly bright, fear crawled up Athanax's spine.

"No more -- I won't let someone I love to be taken away again!" shouted Sarah.

Suddenly, time stood still in the battlefield. She held Narie close to her heart and stared apprehensively into the stillness. She then saw a faint light glowing in the distance and coming towards her. As the light came near, her eyes widened and were filled with tears seeing Sune appearing as the light that was walking towards her.

"You've done great Sarah. Now it's time to let go of the past and move forward. I will always cherish the time I spent with you and will never forget it. But now, they need you -- only you have the courage and power to stop this evil," said Sune as he smiled at Sarah.

Sarah couldn't stop her tears from falling upon hearing Sune's voice for the first time. She smiled back at him and reached out her hand to touch Sune one last time. After their brief meeting, Sune turned his back and slowly walked away. Sarah watched as Sune faded away into the distance. She tilted her head down, looked at Narie and tightened her hold.

"Live!" Sarah screamed,

A powerful burst of energy was unleashed by Sarah's cry -- the sheer force of her light traveled across the battlefield and rippled throughout the entire galaxy. Everyone clung to whatever they could hold and braced themselves as the powerful blast wave swept over them. After the dust settled down, Sorah and Althea stood thunderstruck as they gazed at Sarah being enfolded in a blinding golden light -- in her golden-armored form and with her beautiful powerful wings. Because of the blast wave that passed through everyone, Sorah was healed -- her heart, her armor, her wings and her darkness were cleansed by the light of purity. Althea and all of the Arkans on the battlefield were completely healed by the light. Sorah and Althea had witnessed the full power of Sarah for the first time. They remembered their father telling them that their mother was the last Arkan to hold the power of life, but Sarah just proved that the power of life was not lost and that she was the chosen wielder of that power.

Suddenly, a miracle happened. Narie started breathing again. She slowly opened her eyes and saw Sarah shining brightly.

"I knew you'll come back Sarah!" Narie smiled.

"I'm sorry for causing you troubles. Now, I promise that we will end this together," Sarah vowed.

Sarah helped Narie stand up, which made everyone staring in disbelief after witnessing Sarah brought Narie back to life. Sorah hastily approached them and held Narie in her arms. Althea and Kiran ran towards them, overjoyed to see her alive.

"I thought I'll never see you again Narie!" Sorah whispered.

"I'm back mother and I want you to meet my beloved sister, Sarah -- your daughter," said Narie, as she pulled her mother's hand and to introduce Sarah.

It was an awkward moment for Sorah and Sarah, Sorah couldn't believe that her long lost daughter was finally in front of her.

"Sarah," Sorah uttered.

"Mother," Sarah responded.

Sorah held Sarah in her arms and cried heavily. Althea and Narie couldn't hold their tears back either seeing them finally reunited.

"My daughter, I never thought I be seeing you again," Sorah caressed Sarah's face.

"Thank you Althea for saving my daughter," Sorah's voice quavered with joy.

Then, a sound of hand clapping was heard from the battlefield. Sorah turned around and saw Athanax with a sinister laugh. He applauded Sarah for what she did.

"Well, well, well, this is something I should be grateful for a change. Not just that you brought your dear little sister back to life and healed your people, but you also healed our wounds and restored our full Arkan power," Athanax sneered.

The Alliance soon realized that Sarah's light of purity also healed the Fallens and restored their full Arkan powers. Sarah accidentally revived hundreds of thousands of Fallens back to their primordial forms. Sorah knew that her army of second-age Arkan is no match to them and that fighting them head-on would be futile. She tried to summon the fire of justice, but she had already lost that power. Both Sorah and Sarah couldn't wield the forbidden flame anymore for they were cleansed by Sarah's light of purity. Even with the combined power of Sarah, Narie, Althea and herself would not be enough to stop the magnitude of the enemy. Sarah then held her mother's hand.

"Mother, I will be with you together with Althea and Narie. Let us all fight together," Sarah gave a brave smile.

Sorah instructed Kiran and King Zairel to take their people out of the city while she and her warriors hold the Fallens back, but King Zairel and Kiran disagreed. For King Zairel and the Deodarians, Althea has shown them their purpose in life and were ready to fight and die alongside the Arkans.

370

"Our ancestors once betrayed your father the king, but this time we will correct that mistake. We will stand with you to the end," Kiran said in a proud tone.

"Then all of you will die here," Sorah stated.

"If you fall today, then what else have we got to lose?" Kiran replied.

Sorah briefly remembered Aran's words saying that he would protect her to the end. She then turns around and faced what remains of the Alliance army.

"Be brave. Stand fast in the face of death, Arkans, Ithurians and Deodarians, fight to the bitter end. Hold onto hope to the very end, as it is the last thing left for us to fight for," Sorah addressed her warriors and the Alliance for the last time.

Sorah faced the battlefield across where Athanax was and raised her Serdeus.

"With all my strength and courage -- for the king!" she shouted.

The Arkans, including the Deodarians and Ithurians shouted the same battle cry. Sorah and the Arkans were surprised to hear that they expressed their solidarity with them. Athanax told his minions that Sorah and her daughter could no longer wield the fire of justice and ordered them to leave no one alive.

"Annihilate all of them!" Athanax growled angrily.

Athanax and the Fallens have never felt so good to have once again regained their Arkan powers. They spread their wings and flew towards the Alliance with only death and destruction in their minds. Having their powers back made the Fallens even thirstier for the blood of the

Ithurians and Deodarians, but their ultimate goal is to destroy Sorah and her Arkan kin. While the Alliance immediately reformed their line, Sorah looked behind her and saw Arkans, Ithurians and Deodarians standing alongside one another. Every warrior and soldier was ready to embrace death that day, but within the ranks of the Alliance, Sarah and Narie held each other's hands and prayed for a miracle to happen as they're about to face the final moments of their lives.

Sorah, as brave as she is, flew directly to the Fallens, followed by Sarah, Althea, Narie and the Alliance. They smashed the enemy's line, killing as many they could. The second-age warriors were being overpowered by the primordial Arkans, but with the fire power support provided by the Ithurians and the healing power of the Deodarians, the Alliance managed to stand together and hold their ground. Sorah, together with Althea and her daughters, battled the overwhelming rush of Fallens attacking them. But there was not much they could do to stop it. She saw her warriors, Deodarians and Ithurians fall one by one and Althea, Sarah and Narie fighting hard with all their strength. With all the death that surrounded them, a horrid realization came to Sorah's mind -- that all of them will die on that battlefield, away from their home world Treliseum. Sorah, Althea, Sarah and Narie looked at each other and nod their heads, accepting their fate without any regrets. Together, they charged the waves of Fallen approaching them. Using their powers, they killed as many they could, but the odds against them were too high to bear. They were being surrounded by the Fallens and at the brink of being overrun.

Athanax saw that he finally had his revenge. He ordered all his remaining forces to attack and end the Alliance once and for all. As the light of hope was about to be extinguished by the Fallens, while Athanax was already celebrating his long-awaited victory and when all was thought to be lost, suddenly, a huge blinding fireball blazed down from the clouds and destroyed a quarter of the Fallen army. Athanax stood motionless in horror. The Alliance was stunned to witness the devastation of the blast. They looked up to the cloudy sky where the fireball came and saw King Satorex slowly descending from the clouds. The Fallens faltered and trembled in fear as they saw the Arkan king alive.

Breathless, Sorah and the Arkan nearly fell into happiness to once again see their king saving them from the evil that befell them.

"This is impossible! How could you still be alive? I poisoned you! You should be dead!" Fear pierced through every bone of Athanax's body.

"Brother, you're still as evil as the day I fought you. Surely enough your poison almost ended my life and our race, but to stop that from happening, we put ourselves into a deep sleep and waited for the day that a miracle would come to restore our great race and kingdom to its glory and peace. Well, that day has come -- a light of hope and purity has awakened us and cleansed us from your filth," King Satorex retorted.

"You should have died and I should have reigned our kingdom. No, MY kingdom! You've always been the obstacle in my life -- even at the brink of your death, your bloodline still hinders my plans!" Athanax ranted.

"Well, wait no longer my dear brother, for I come before you today to tell you that your threat of terror and evil ends today," King Satorex asserted.

"You will stop me? You alone couldn't possibly stop my army!" Athanax sneered.

"Alone? I am not alone. I brought your retribution with me," King Satorex countered and glared at Athanax.

Then, from the clouds descended the king's army -- the male primordial Arkans all healed with renewed powers, together with the warriors of the light the strongest warriors joining the king in battle. Sorah and the Alliance were jubilant to see that salvation has come upon them. In desperation, Athanax ordered all his Draakabs, Diurox and Fallen warriors to attack the Arkan and the Alliance. Some of the Arkan warriors fought the dragons in the sky, while King Satorex and his warriors of the light descended to join Sorah and Althea in the battle below. Bronax ordered a swarm of Draakabs carrying the dreaded Diurox to specifically target King Satorex, but before they could even come near, the flame of the Arkan king easily destroyed all of them. The king, together with his strongest warriors plowed their way towards Athanax. Some of the Fallens cowardly fled the battlefield after seeing the rage in the eyes of King Satorex who was coming towards them.

The tide has once again been turned and Athanax was clearly in desperation. Sorah together with her sister and daughters fought their way to reach the king. Athanax's heart fluttered wildly to see his brother King Satorex slowly making his way towards him and killing everything that stood in his way. Unwittingly, he took a step back as he witnessed the anger and the powerful presence of the Arkan king. With immense fear, he ordered Bronax to send their last wave of Fallen to stop the Arkan king and the Alliance. Hundreds of thousands of Fallens made a desperate charge, hoping to turn the tide in their favor. King Satorex saw the approaching multitude of enemies and knew that the hordes posed a great obstacle in reaching his brother. The Alliance already suffered so much from the previous battle and his male warriors couldn't stop them alone. It left the king with no choice but to use the forbidden flame once more. The king flew in front of the line and began building up his flames. As the hordes came near, he unleashed the fire of justice, destroying more than half of Athanax's remaining forces.

The Fallens were slowly being defeated -- their center was completely decimated by the king's flame. Athanax foresaw his inevitable defeat and retribution. As a last resort, he mustered all his strength and prepared to use his poison to end the Alliance. Sorah saw his action and remembered the power of decay he once used in the first war. Sorah rushed to her father in order to shield him from the danger. Athanax was at the rear and didn't care enough to move his army aside. He treacherously unleashed his power of decay, sacrificing his army so he could destroy his brother and the Alliance. Sorah was able to reach the king in time and shielded him with her flame, but the poison spread like wildfire exposing the Fallen army and the Alliance. Althea, Sarah and Narie were able to shield some of the Alliance, but most were exposed to the poison. The faces of the unsuspecting Fallens scrunched up in pain as Athanax poison slowly destroying them. Bronax's eyes flashed with anger and resentment towards Athanax for betraying them just so he could attain victory. Their bodies rapidly decayed and the entire Fallen army were destroyed by Athanax, their patriarch himself.

Members of the Alliance were dying too after being exposed to the poison. Prince Vasuril and some of the Deodarians bravely stood up, disregarding their safety and fully exposing themselves to the poison, gave their last strength to heal the stricken Arkans and Ithurians. It pained King Zairel seeing his son's sacrifice, but he was proud of his bravery and accepted his son's decision without hatred in his heart. The Arkans were astounded to witness the Deodarian's courage to face danger -- many of the Deodarians including Vasuril perished on their final act of heroism. As it seemed to be the end for the Alliance, Sarah unleashed her light of purity to heal and shield the Alliance from Athanax. The awakening made Sarah even more powerful than any

Arkan alive -- her light slowly pushed the poison back to Athanax, which greatly weakened him. In Athanax's struggles to hold back the light of purity, Sorah saw a chance to kill him, but her father King Satorex stopped her.

"This is a task that I must do," said King Satorex.

King Satorex extends his arms towards Athanax and mustered the fire of justice in his palm. The king was on the brink of tears to see his brother for the last time. After all the evil he had committed, in the end, they're still brothers who shared the same blood. With heavy heart, King Satorex unleashed his flame and hit Athanax directly. Athanax momentarily paused and felt the flame of his brother inside his body. His body became a torch. He screamed in pain and anger as he was slowly being devoured by the flame of justice. King Satorex and his kin, as well as the Ithurians and Deodarian, were transfixed by the horror of the final moments of the Fallen king, until he was totally consumed by the flame, reduced to ashes and swept away by the wind.

Chapter Thirty

RETURN OF THE RIGHTEOUS

As the dust of the battle settled down, a moment of calmness was felt in the field of Deodara. Sarah was still in the sky, radiating her light of purity and healing all that were injured. King Satorex looked up to Sarah, smiling -- even laughing to his confusion and disbelief for what he saw. He didn't know how to react to Sarah's powers. He even blinked his eyes several times thinking that it couldn't be real that he's seeing a wielder of the power of life, which was thought that its last keeper was the late Queen Vasilia. Sorah told the king that the wielder of the power of life is her and Aran's daughter. King Satorex looked at Sorah and gaped in surprise upon learning that she was alive and has grown to become a beautiful maiden.

In a distance, Althea put her hands on her pounding heart seeing her father once again. She felt reluctant to approach the king for she still bore the shame that she brought into their family and started the entire conflict. Narie approached Althea and took her hand. Together, they walked towards King Satorex. The king turned his gaze and happened to see Althea. His eyes opened wide, inhaled sharply and ran quickly towards her. Althea's breath was caught in her throat and stood rooted to the ground at the sight of her father rushing towards her. She thought her father would hurt her for the suffering she brought to the Arkan. But suddenly, the king held her in his arms and wept.

"My daughter! I'm so glad to see you're alive -- my daughter!" King Satorex sobbed.

Althea stared openly, uncertain about what to say and left confused as she heard those words from the king. For many years, she was stuck with the thought that her father hated her.

"My king, please forgive me for my sin," Althea whimpered.

"No my foolish child. It is I that need to seek your forgiveness. I was blinded by my self-righteousness that I didn't realize how much I've hurt you and your sister, by taking the man you both love and the son of my trusted friend. I should be the one to blame for all of this," King Satorex sniffled.

Hearing those words from her father made Althea cry so hard, prompting her to hug her father tightly, a hug that she always wanted and waited for a long time. Even the mighty king of the Arkans shed tears in that moment when he was reunited with her daughters and finally put their past behind them. Sorah held Sarah and Narie's hands and introduced them to the great Arkan king and their grandfather. King Satorex could hardly contain his joy to meet his two granddaughters. He felt as if he gained another pair of daughters. The king then embraced them both.

"I'm so sorry I wasn't there when you were growing up. I wasn't there to protect you," said King Satorex.

"Grandfather, you have already saved us – today. You were here when we needed you most. Our prayers were answered," Narie replied.

378

King Satorex then looked at Sarah.

"I would never imagine that you've inherited the power of life, whose last keeper was your grandmother. You my child have saved us all today and we are eternally indebted to you," the grateful king said.

After the king spoke, the entire Arkan people kneeled before her, including Sorah, Althea, Narie and the king himself, to express their eternal gratitude. Kiran and the Ithurians as well as the Deodarians also thanked Sarah as they kneeled together with the Arkans. King Satorex saw the Ithurians and Deodarians and asked Sorah who are those people. She revealed that they were the sons and daughters of Varkelos and the banished Arkans. As he learned about the people of Eres, the king slowly walked towards Kiran who was still on his knees with his head down. He commanded them to stand up, as Kiran stood and faced the him, King Satorex's mouth gaped open -- the shock robbed him of words to say seeing Kiran's face resembled that of Aran. He promptly looked at his daughters, bemused. Both Sorah and Althea nods their heads.

King Satorex stared fiercely through Kiran's frightened eyes. Narie walked up to Kiran's side and held his hand. The king was appalled to see Narie and Kiran's bond, for he was still vividly reminded by the sins committed by Varkelos and his people.

"What is the meaning of this Narie?" King Satorex demanded to know.

"My king -- this is the man I love," Narie bravely answered.

King Satorex's face turned red. He showed his disapproval of them being together and would never accept such relationship. Sorah and Althea asked their father to understand and grant the chance to get to know more about Kiran and his people.

"Silence!" King Satorex yelled.

His voice echoed throughout the plain, striking fear in the people.

"Grandfather, my king, please allow me to speak for these people," Sarah requested.

"And why is it that you wish to speak for them?" the king retorted.

"Because not so long ago, I once thought that I was an Ithurian like them, and it was also the Ithurians that awakened the Arkan blood that flows within me." Sarah's words intrigued the king.

The king paused for a moment. He held his chin and with a furrowed brow. In the end, he allowed Sarah to convey her message.

"My king, I was brought here in this planet ever since I can remember. I was brought up with the belief that I was just an ordinary person -- I was not allowed to meld with them in order that the truth about my past and my powers be concealed to them. My aunt Althea guided me and raised me to be strong and to be the person who is in front of you right now. The same goes for Sune, my best friend, my only brother who was always there to protect me until the end," tears filled her eyes as she remembered Sune.

"Kiran was the first Ithurian I came to know. He showed me their proud city and taught me their culture and way of life. Believing that I was an Ithurian, I easily embraced this world that they were living," Sarah then paused and took a deep breath.

"But before all of this, the Ithurians held great animosity towards the Arkans. They were made to believe the lies told by their ancestors -- the dishonored and exiled Arkan," the king suddenly remembered his friend Varkelos.

"Even though these lies were told, there were some who refused to believe but instead embraced the Arkan faith and obedience to the commandments and these people are the Deodarians. This great conflict gave birth to the thousand years of war between the two empires. But not all of the Ithurians believed in their ancestors' teachings. There were also a few of them who held their faith to the Arkans in secret and one of those is the man my sister loves and those who fought with us today," Sarah asserted.

Sarah further revealed to the king that Kiran was the one who made the first step in pursuing peace with the Arkans as attested by her mother Sorah. It was unfortunate that King Satorex learned about Athanax's deception and how easily the Ithurians were deceived. They were weak to resist their greed, leading to the battle of Fostrum. King Satorex interrupted Sarah and asked her directly the reason why she stood with the Ithurians after the persecution she suffered in their hands. Sarah frowned, puzzled as to why King Satorex knew about it. The king told Sarah that it is her light that awakened them and through the light he also felt and saw her pain, her sufferings and her unrequited love. Sarah paused and in deep thought. Narie quickly interrupted and told the king that it was his brother Athanax that plotted everything in order to kill his bloodline. But the king nevertheless insisted that the Ithurians couldn't be trusted because they are weak and easily corrupted by greed.

King Satorex made up his mind about forbidding Narie's relationship with Kiran and about the Ithurians. Sarah looked up to the sky and saw a bird flying.

"I've always dreamed of having wings," Sarah blurted out.

Everyone especially King Satorex put on a bewildered face.

"I've always wanted to have wings to fly across the sky and to be free, but knowing then that I was an Ithurian, I couldn't have that dream – it's impossible, it's unthinkable and unacceptable," her voice was shaky, barely covering the sob that was about to break out.

King Satorex wanted to know what she was trying to convey, so he listened more to her words.

"Then, Althea and Narie came. They told me that I have the blood of an Arkan that flows within me, they taught me how to become an Arkan -- how to use my powers. They helped me believe that if I could just hold on to that faith, someday I may be able to reach my dream to soar the sky with freedom," a small smile was painted on her face.

Sorah and Althea were tearful as they hear Sarah's words of wisdom. They felt so proud of her, while the king stood still and listened.

"My king, I believe that the Ithurians can someday be worthy of your forgiveness -- they were once Arkans after all. They just need to be guided to the path of the Arkan as I was when Althea and Narie guided me back to my mother, to our people and to you," Sarah stated her hope for the Ithurian.

"I too believe my daughter's words. The prince spoke of peace between the Arkans and Ithurians. He and his loyal people stayed to fight alongside with us. They didn't abandon us in the hour of our desperation, they heeded our call to fight, which their ancestors failed to do. So Father please -- can you find in your heart to forgive the Ithurian?" Sorah kneeled before the king and begged for his mercy.

The Arkans, Deodarians and Ithurians all stared at the king and waited for his judgment. The king was in deep thought about his daughters' and granddaughters' plea. King Satorex thought that Narie's love for Kiran was similar to the love that her mother had for Aran. He didn't want to commit the same mistake he made before, a mistake which led to her daughters' suffering when he took away the man they loved. King Satorex then turned to Sarah and requested her:

"My child, lend this old king your strength."

"With all my might, my king," said Sarah, kneeling before the king.

"After all the hardship, the pain, the humiliation and the suffering these Ithurian inflicted upon you, do you in your heart, still believe that they will be worthy of my forgiveness and regaining the honor of the Arkan?" King Satorex wondered.

Sarah stood up and turned her gaze to Kiran and to all the Ithurians.

"My king, I believe that the righteous deserves your mercy." Everyone looked puzzled after hearing Sarah's answer.

"True to what has been said about the Ithurians, they're weak and easily corrupted. Give it time and they might forget what we had fought here today," sweat beaded on the forehead of the Ithurians after hearing Sarah.

"The Ithurians who will remain righteous until the end of their time are those who are worthy of your mercy and earn the right of passage to reclaim their Arkan honor," Sarah exhorted.

King Satorex and all the Arkans were impressed by Sarah's wisdom. The king felt that her words reflected on her experience living with the Ithurians and knew that she had carefully thought of her judgment. Heads turned at every corner as the Ithurians mumbled with one another.

"How can we follow your ways for we don't know the Arkan's path to righteousness?" Kiran reasoned.

Sarah asked for the king's permission to allow her to offer a proposition, which the great king obliged. He was also eager to listen to her.

"My king, it is true that the Ithurians doesn't know the path of the Arkan that is why we need to teach them, we need to let an Arkan live with them to teach them the path. That Arkan must live with the Ithurian as a mortal with her Arkan powers sealed. This is to show all of you Ithurians that even without our powers you can walk that path -- only if you have the strong resolves to follow it," Sarah boldly stated.

King Satorex saw fairness in her proposition, but finds it difficult to have one Arkan living with them as a mortal. Nevertheless, the king agreed with Sarah and turned the question to Kiran and his people.

"Do you Ithurians have the strength to accept this?" King Satorex challenged Kiran and his people.

Kiran looked at Narie as she nods her head, giving Kiran her support. He then looked at his people and said:

"My people, the Arkan king is gracious enough to give us a chance to be free of our forefathers' sins. The king has given us a way to regain our honor, our Arkan honor. The path will be long and hard, some might falter and not make it, but if we persevere, we can finish it. My people, are you with me to walk the path of the Arkans?"

The Ithurians cheered and gave Kiran their firm determination. He then faced King Satorex and boldly answered:

"Great Arkan king, with strong resolves, we the Ithurians accept your bidding,"

Afterwards, King Satorex announced to all present on that day that a new path will be created for the people of Eres -- a path for them to follow and walk upon until the end of their days. The path will lead the righteous to reclaim their Arkan honor and will be granted the right of passage to Treliseum. Althea walked towards his father and kneeled.

"My king, King Zairel and his people the Deodarians, have always embraced the Arkan path from the day of their founding forefather Ihram. They chose to remain true to the path even being banished here in Eres. They are the people who live and die following the commandments -- the same commandment you and the council of the light forged thousands of years ago. So with this my king, may I ask you to grant them their honor back?" Althea pleaded.

King Satorex called forth the Deodarian king and his people.

"King Zairel, it is truly gratifying to hear that even in this far and isolated star that the Arkan path is being walked on and the commandments were truthfully being followed by your people the Deodarians. I have seen with my own eyes the bravery and courage you have shown in the battlefield, the sacrifices made by your own son for us Arkans and Ithurians to live. For your loyalty in staying true to the path of the righteous, for all the hard work and sacrifices you and your people made, I hereby restore your Arkan honor and grant you the right of passage to Treliseum," proclaimed King Satorex.

The Arkan king raised his hand towards the sky, a bean of sunlight passed through and shone upon the Deodarians. The Ithurians were amazed and bewildered as they witnessed the Deodarians being enfolded by the light and slowly, wings were coming out from their backs. They were witnessing the power of King Satorex as he restored the honor of the righteous Deodarians. Seeing her grandfather doing that act, Sarah used her power of life and brought all the Arkans,

385

Ithurians and Deodarians who perished in the battle back to life. The hard work and faithfulness of the Deodarians to the Arkan path have finally found their rewards. With the grace of the Arkan king, the Deodarians were no more, their honor has finally been reclaimed and became Arkans once more. Zairel was so happy to be reunited with his son Vasuril who was brought back to life by Sarah's light. The once proud Deodarian people rejoiced as they could once again return to their home world of Treliseum. Zairel and his people thanked the Arkan king and Sarah for the reward they imparted to them. They pledged their lives to the king for him to command. The Ithurians couldn't help but watched the Deodarians with envy after seeing their honor restored. Most felt anger in their hearts for believing a thousand years of lies, while some were disheartened at the thought that they had lived a worthless existence.

King Satorex then turned to the Arkans and posed the difficult question. He asked if there is someone in the Arkan rank who is brave enough to take the task of guiding the Ithurians. Sarah was about to come forward to take on the task when Narie pulled her hand back.

"Sarah you have already done so much for both our people and the Ithurians. Let me take this task for you. You are much needed in the kingdom and also mother needs you," said Narie.

Narie stepped forward to the king and stated her intention of taking on the task. King Satorex was already expecting either Sarah or Narie to accept it, but it was a choice they made and a choice that they have to stand by.

"Are you sure my child? This task will ask you to stay here in Eres -- your Arkan powers will be sealed. You will remain as a mortal and feel death as a mortal. But for all of this I promised you my child, that in your hour of crossing death, judgment has already passed and you shall return to us unchanged from the time you became mortal," King Satorex promised.

Narie looked at Kiran and held his hand. Together, they faced the king and she wholeheartedly accepted the task. Sorah knew that she couldn't change her daughter's decision because of the love she have for Kiran. Sorah walked towards Kiran and stared at him.

"My daughter made an important decision today. She chose to be a mortal in order to be with you. As her mother, look after my daughter, don't ever waste her sacrifice," Sorah told Kiran.

Kiran gave his word to protect Narie. Sorah held Narie in her arms -- she knew that she couldn't change her mind anymore. The hardest thing for a mother could do was to let go of her child. Sorah cried and held Narie tight.

"Mother, I have made my decision and I will try my best to lead the Ithurians back to Treliseum. Please don't be sad mother. You will have my sister Sarah and she will be there in my stead," Narie whispered to Sorah's ear.

Sarah approached Narie to share her thoughts about the task.

"Are you sure about this? It's really difficult to live as an Ithurian," said Sarah with a grin.

"If you were able to do it, then so can I," Narie replied.

Sarah told Narie that she had Althea and Sune by her side as her strength during her period of isolation and it would be different for her because she will be alone, but Narie felt confident because she will have Kiran by her side, the man she loves. Sarah held on to Kiran's promise of protecting her sister. Kiran and his people once again thanked Sarah for everything she has done for them. Even with the persecution she suffered, she still chose to save them and gave them a chance to reclaim their Arkan honor. Kiran vowed to lay his life in protecting the path. Narie will be the path for the Ithurian and Sarah will be their guiding light. Both of them will be the key in leading the Ithurian back to Treliseum.

As everything had been said, the Arkan king again raised his hand towards the direction of Treliseum and unleashed his power to close the gateway of the Fallen forever and to open a new gateway where its location was kept unknown and unreachable for the Ithurians -- only the righteous can find it and pass the gateway back to the Arkan home world. The Arkans began to ascend to the sky towards the new gateway, back to their home world and vowed never ever set foot on Eres again. King Satorex called forth Narie to stand before him, Sorah and Althea stood beside the king, while Sarah and Kiran were behind Narie. The king then sealed her Arkan powers and Narie finally became a mortal. It was a teary moment for Sorah and Althea but they understood the decision she made. Sarah however, was moved by her sister's courage and admitted that Narie's resolve was stronger than hers.

After her power was finally sealed, King Satorex embraced Narie for the last time.

"I'll be waiting for your return-- my child," King Satorex promised.

Sorah walked up to her,

"I will always be with you," said Sorah, then kissed and embraced Narie for the last time.

Althea was next.

"You've made us all proud today -- Arkans and Ithurians alike. You and Sarah are the light and the bridge that your mother and I lost. I too will wait for your return," said Althea.

King Satorex, Sorah and Althea began to rise towards the clouds to return to Treliseum. They never looked back at Narie. Tears streamed down Sorah's eyes as she flew farther away from Narie. Althea held her sister's hand, looked at each other and smiled. The Arkan king was happy and at peace seeing his daughters finally moved on from their past. Sarah was the last Arkan to step off the field. Seeing all the Arkans leave Eres made Narie feel uneasy. She held Sarah once again while her hands shiver.

"What is wrong Narie?" asked Sarah, feeling the trembles in her hand.

"I'm worried sister, I don't know if I could fulfill everyone's expectations of me," Narie quavered with her head down and tears dropping from her eyes.

Narie didn't admit to Sarah her real feelings -- that she started to feel scared as she saw her sister leaving her behind. Sarah could clearly see what Narie was going through. She held Narie's chin and raised her head.

"You were everything I had expected, not just as my sister but as a person as well. You were there by my side, you taught me about my Arkan powers and together faced countless dangers without faltering. And now you took the greatest challenge an Arkan could ever dare take, and that is choosing to be a mortal," she proudly told Narie,

Sarah's words gave Narie the strength and confidence she needed to face the task ahead of her. She held Sarah in her arms for the last time.

"Thank you sister. I won't fail you and mother. I love you so much," Narie whispered to Sarah's ear.

"I know you won't. I love you too. I promise that I will be the first one to welcome you back to our home," she answered in a soft voice.

Sarah then gave Narie's hand to Kiran and smiled at them. Sarah took a few steps back, spread her golden wings and slowly ascended to the sky. Narie, Kiran and the Ithurians waved at her to bid their final farewell. Sarah's entire body glowed in golden light as she went farther. The Ithurians saw her light as a bright star.

"I will be your light of hope to guide you back," Sarah's voice was heard throughout Eres.

The light that shone brightly in the sky signifying the end of an old story and the birth of a new tale. It is a new beginning that awaits the Ithurians and their journey back to the path of the righteous.